Dedication

In memory of my father, a loving parent, and a dedicated, lifelong, forward-thinking public servant who did more for my family and our community than anyone will ever know.

And in memory of my mother, a true life-loving caregiver and a visionary artist whose physical life ended far too young. Your memory and your art will always live on.

Special Thanks

To my wonderful wife who has supported me without end in al things I attempt. You are my rock!

And to our kids who had to bear with all my advice over the y I'm super proud of each of you and I hope you can all liv its fullest! Safely of course!

A Brief Note on Notes

There are several pages of Writer's Notes at the end of this book. The notes are broken out by chapter and discuss some of the events that led to certain themes in each chapter. I recommend reading the notes relevant to a chapter either after that chapter is read, or after the book has been read in full. The notes will bring depth and potential present-day connections to some of the themes…but they may also contain spoilers! So I don't recommend reading any chapter's Writer's Notes until after you've read that chapter. I hope you enjoy the reading!

Prologue:

Elena

Tampa, Florida
September 1, 1985

The drive through my neighborhood was surreal. Quiet. Desolate. Very few cars, and those were utility or law enforcement vehicles. There was no power. All the traffic signals were out. My father was driving, and we were only allowed into the area because of his high-level role with the city. That role gave him a pass to enter the area and assess damage to city infrastructure. He had no intention of looking at any city infrastructure. He went straight to our home.

Home is a 1950's ranch style house a block off Tampa Bay where we'd lived for over ten years now. We had some vicious storms during that time. I remember one in particular, a no-name storm in 1979 when I was about ten years old. The roads filled with water. My father made the decision to stay put and not leave for higher ground. So we were in the house, stuck watching as the water began to rise. Soon, very soon, it was too deep to leave. We sat in the dark powerless house for hours watching as water crept inch by inch, foot by foot, up the driveway. Nearly halfway to the house.

back of our house. Again, stopping about an inch below the sliding glass door leading into the main house.

My mom was a wreck. My younger brother, just two years old, and me, only ten, weren't of any help. The stress was slathered across my dad's face, red, evidence that his blood pressure was through the roof. I'm sure our anxiety wasn't helping matters. He snapped our childish suggestions away. He just paced around the inside of the house, watching through the windows and looking for any signs of water oozing in through doorways.

As fast as the water came up over that last hour, it began receding just as fast. That last push was a tidal flow that forced the bay water up into our neighborhood through the storm sewers. Storm sewers that usually drain our rainwater out. As the tide made its way out, so did most of the water in our neighborhood. Some water lingered in the roads for a bit longer, though most roads were passable within a few hours. But there were still two impassably deep spots blocking the only two roads out of the neighborhood. That was ok. They would go down in time. And we didn't have anywhere to go that would be better than where we were.

For this storm, six years later, my dad didn't hesitate. If there's one thing my dad's good at, it's not making the same mistake twice. When the potential for flooding was mentioned, he packed us up and we went to my aunt's house in the brand new, still developing, much drier inland Northdale neighborhood. We waited out the weather. A strangely long wait because of this storm's behavior, approaching the coast and then stalling for two days before looping around and heading back out toward Louisiana. It never even made landfall here.

At my aunt's house, we had power. Air conditioning. And food.

mission back to the flood zone. Sixteen now, I guess he felt I was old enough to help, so he agreed. And here we are. In our driveway.

Driving into the neighborhood I got a sense that things wouldn't be good. But I still held out hope. Now in the driveway, that hope was pretty much lost. There was a distinct line around the house. A dirt accumulation. Like the bathtub ring after a day of playing pad-less tackle football in the grass-challenged fields near the school. The bathtub ring now was more than a foot above the bottom of our front door. My childhood home had flooded.

The power was out so garage door openers weren't working. The front door was sealed with duct tape we didn't want to peel off yet. So we went around to a door at the back of the garage that accessed the laundry room. The door was swollen from water and was difficult to force open. Once we pried it open, we couldn't get it closed again. Inside the laundry room, things were out of place. But mostly just things that were piled on the floor that floated around. The washer and dryer looked fine, but there was a bathtub ring high enough that meant some of the electronic parts would have been hit with salty flood water. The hot water heater met a similar fate. My dad kicked a few things out of the way and went to the fuse box. He looked closely to make sure all the power was shut off to the house. It seemed unnecessary since he shut it off before we left, double checked that he shut it off multiple times before we drove away, and now, on our return there was no power

We stepped carefully through the garage. The cars were moved to higher ground, but water had gotten into stacks of boxes, shelves and cabinets. Some of the stacks of boxes collapsed when their weight crushed the soaked boxes beneath them. Higher boxes ended up in the water beside the lower boxes. One of the box towers collapsed but the upper boxes stayed mostly dry. The lower box of that tower must have collapsed after the water receded, upper boxes landing on damp concrete instead of in a pool of water.

My dad unlocked the door from the garage into the main house. A door I always went through. But one that now sent chills up my spine. This door was also swollen, but its thinner material made it easier to force open.

Before noticing anything else, the first thing that hit me was the horrible smell. I briefly had a fish tank as a kid. When I'd change the water and used the suction hose to clean the fish shit and food residue out of the gravel, the water in the discard bucket always had a foul smell. This smell in my home was that discard bucket smell tenfold. With an added beachy saltwater tidal pool smell.

"Help me get all the windows open." My dad said.

I did. We opened everything that still had a screen to protect us from the bugs. As I walked through the house opening windows, I felt the deep soaking wet shag carpet squish like a sponge beneath my red and white Air Jordan high tops. Although the Jordans are generally coveted, these sucked. There was a red liner in them that bled on my white socks every time I wore them. I wasn't a fan of the pink stained socks left behind, so the shoes usually sat unworn in my closet. I was glad to wear them this one last time, in the flood's muck, so I could justify throwing them out, possibly even

A lot of things had to be done immediately. Carpets had to be ripped up and taken outside. Anything cloth that got wet also had to go, which meant all our beds and sofas, and anything in water's reach in our hampers, drawers and closets, and in my case, floor. That effort alone took several exhausting days. Anything that was damaged had to be photographed and documented for insurance. And through all of this work, there was no power. No AC. It was September. And the heat was brutal.

But nothing was as brutal as seeing all my cherished things destroyed. Things I thought were high enough to be out of harm's way. My cheap particle-board stereo cabinet had floated off balance and toppled. It's turntable, dual cassette deck, and equalizer lay on the floor, dripping water when I picked them up. Plastic milk crates filled with albums had somehow been toppled into the water too. The covers melted their wet paper into the grooves making them useless. The full-size floor-standing speakers were fine. I thought enough to get them off the floor and laid them on top of the bed. Somehow the water didn't seep up high enough through the mattress to damage them. One bright note.

That bright note dimmed quickly when I focused on my desk. Every kid had some kind of cheap student desk in their room. Mine was bright white. And it was an after-thought during the mad rush to get out of the house. Who cares if my notebook paper, pencils [illegible] were on top where families took us in different directions for the summers, and newspaper clippings of my sports achievements, were all in clumps, stuck together now like paper machete. This was my history. At least the history I wanted to be able to look back on and remember. Gone.

It took more than a month to get the house back in a livable condition. Drywall, appliances, electric wiring, all had to be replaced before we could turn power back on. My aunt and cousins are wonderful people. But after more than a month, we were all ready for our two families to separate and go back to our neutral corners of the city.

Even though our house was still in disarray, by Thanksgiving the tensions had eased. The family got back together at my aunt's house for the big meal. Sitting at the table, my cousin asked me what I was thankful for. Only one thing came to mind.

"I'll be thankful if I never have to go through anything like this ever again."

Chapter One:

No Coup for You!

Venezuela, January 1992

Too hot. It's too hot for January. The heat adds to all the other odd things odd about this trip. The call in the middle of the night. The car and driver waiting on me in my driveway instead of me waiting on a ride. The weirdly high amount of traffic on the Tampa roads in the middle of the night. Being driven to Macdill Air Force Base instead of our very nice, tops in the nation, Tampa International Airport. The usual sight of military transport planes on base traded for…what? Looking out from the hanger toward the plane it looked like a common commercial jet anyone would see at any airport. So why the base and not the normal airport? But getting closer it was clear this wasn't one of your everyday Boeings seen all over the US, it was something a little different. A European made Airbus. Stark white. No company name, emblems, or military branch lettering. Just tail ID numbers. Odd.

I looked over at the Command Chief Master Seargeant, who earlier introduced himself as Jack, as he escorted me and my hastily packed go-bag to the plane.

"Better if you don't ask," he said, not even glancing my way. "It the international terminal on the other side of town, and all the hassles that involves for foreigners. We…convinced them…to make a quick detour here. There's not a lot of time. We don't want you to be late on the plane's first day on the job."

We stopped at the foot of the boarding stairs to let two airmen off the plane. Their clothes were drenched with sweat, clearly double-timing whatever they were doing in this odd January heat.

"I hope they get paid extra for that." I said just loud enough for them to hear.

"Ha." Jack leaked a partially repressed laugh. "This is the military. Their easy night shift was ruined by this. How old are you? About 20?"

"A little older than that." I realized how apparently protective I am of my age. So much stigma on the younger generation. Better if I left people guessing. Luckily, I was blessed with an appearance that could look a few years older or younger with a simple switch of hairstyle, beard or glasses.

"Well, you've probably got a good decade or so before you figure out the way the world actually works. It takes time to get past that college ideal crap that only exists in books and Disney movies."

"Hopefully sooner rather than later." I said somewhat honestly, but really trying to ease the generational bias.

Stepping into the plane, I noticed it had, well the only way to describe it is that new car smell. It smelled like cloth and carpet that hadn't been spilled or vomited on, like metal that was freshly oiled, and plastic, whatever that smell of plastic is. But over the top of all those smells, was that…ozone? I took a deep breath and looked over at Jack.

oxygen in the air which supposedly keeps people more alert and makes the brain fatigue go away for those long diplomatic trips."

"I'm sure they wouldn't want any fatigue induced decisions by their diplomats," I laughed.

"You laugh. But Venezuela is one of the largest oil producing nations, Shell, you may have heard of them, on every street corner in the US? Anyway, those diplomats are often engaged with the middle eastern oil groups and spend the flights hammering out ways to screw over the US."

I tossed my bag on the front seat. All the seats looked like first class, so I figured it didn't matter where I sat.

"Just me and the pilots on this flight?"

"Yes sir. It will be a quick one. This sucker can move with those big engines and no passengers or cargo weight. When you get to Caracas that's when the real fun begins. Can't wait for you to meet Reggie!"

"Who's Reggie?"

"In the South, Reggie would be called a colorful character. But most people just think he's about half crazy. Rumor has it he was one of those genius kids that went to college at twelve years old, but his brain snapped a few years in. He left, or fled, the country depending on who's telling the story. Ended up in Venezuela flying [illegible] forest to see Angel Falls and

The engines already humming started to get louder, made worse by the echo of the open passenger doorway.

"That's my cue to leave. Remember, everyone down there has a personal agenda, it doesn't matter if they're wearing a uniform or passed out drunk in the street. Be careful who you link up with. News travels fast and you don't want to alienate the people you need."

The door closed behind him somehow. No one inside pulled it shut. Automatic? An airman now scurrying down the already rolling stairs outside must have pushed it shut. I didn't even know he was there.

There was an immediate almost deafening silence inside once the door was closed. But there was still the tell-tale vibration letting me know the engines, the very powerful engines, were powering up. Jack wasn't kidding about the engine power. But what he forgot to mention was without the passengers and cargo there was nothing to help absorb the vibration. Just pulling onto the runway it felt like my teeth were gonna vibrate out of my head.

"Well, this should be fun."

Too hot. Clearly that's gonna be a recurring theme. It's January in Venezuela and it's about 80 degrees before dawn. The air is thick with humidity, which you would think I'd be used to from Florida's summers. But there's an oddness to it. It's hot and humid but also has some brief spurts of chilliness. In the open doorway of the Airbus, I didn't know whether to pull up my collar to the cold or strip off my outerwear down to my t-shirt. Like I said, odd.

and before I could get my head turned there was a tire screech in front of me.

"You're not going there. Get on."

"Wait…who…"

"Shut up and get on. We need to get out of here before people finish their coffee and start wondering why this big ass plane with one person on it landed here! Let's go!"

I don't think I climbed on willingly, but I also wasn't grabbed or pulled on. Like some strange force was guiding me onto this rickety, twenty-year-old dirt bike with this lanky guy who looked and smelled like he just woke up in a ditch after a binge.

My brain was telling me first and foremost just try not to die. But my body was trying to get my bag over my shoulder so I could feel better balanced riding bitch on this archaic hand-me-down motorcycle that couldn't possibly have any shock absorbers.

"I need to start packing lighter. Maybe a backpack instead of a gym bag." I thought to myself, probably trying to distract myself with mindless minutia rather than digesting what was happening around me.

The motorcycle zipped through a seemingly too small chain link gate in a fence behind one of the hanger buildings. Next thing I knew I felt the familiar bounce of a dirt road beneath us. Pitch black. I realized the hobo rider that picked me up never had his lights on. Not sure if this piece of crap even has lights. After about a five-minute ride we slowed, sliding to a stop in a small gap in some underbrush. Who knows how far we rode. It sounded and felt like we were going about fifty miles an hour. But that could have been about fifty feet on that crap-sickle of a bike.

The rider killed the engine, leapt off and grabbed me by the shoulder to encourage me to follow him. I did. Ass numb and spine me some comfort as I'm a huge Jeep guy. Loved them all my childhood growing up and recently got one of my own. The rider scraped my reluctant bag off my shoulder and threw it in the Jeep.

"I'm Reggie." He said passively and pointed me to the passenger seat. "There's some beer in a cooler in the back if you're thirsty."

I looked at the cooler in the back. Well, not so much cooler as a bunch of Styrofoam pieces of cooler duct taped together in the shape of a box. No ice inside. Just a few obviously warm beers with Spanish labels I couldn't read.

"Grab me one would ya. This dusty road shit makes my throat dry, and we've got lots to talk about."

Calling Reggie a colorful character was quite the understatement. A lot about him is exactly what you might expect from an awkward genius kid dropout. He's well spoken, with a clear command of the language, but still almost purposefully dumbs it down to essential parts, almost autistically, making his actual conversations seem a bit disjointed. But over the half-hour Jeep ride I became more familiar with his patterns and was able to follow what he was saying with less of a dumbfounded look on my face.

"They diverted you from Simon. Apparently there's some extra civil disruption tonight and the powers that be were afraid you might get caught up in it."

"Venezuela."

"No shit!" well, maybe given the flight time and diversion I could have been in a few different countries so that was probably a bit harsh. "Where in Venezuela?"

"You landed at Oscar Machado. A new airport just southeast of Caracas. It's better really. Less prying eyes there. Nobody uses it yet. There's no taxi services or anything so it's really only the rich locals with cars and private drivers. They don't look at each other. And the government's pretty hands off there. Don't bite the hands that feed you ya know. We're headed to a little private airstrip near El Raton. That's where I keep my plane. Even cheaper fees there, just throw a few important people a few free flights and those fees go away. Expenses are a wash when you work the system down here."

"How long?"

"To El Raton? Probably about two hours. Not a lot of people on the road yet. This area's poor, no cars. Mainly migrant work. As long as we don't get stuck behind some farm equipment we should be ok."

"Two hour drive and only a couple beers left?"

"Trust me…you don't want to pound beers so much we have to stop on the side of the road and take a piss. If the pterodactyl mosquitoes don't get you, well, something else might."

"Good to know."

"Dawn is coming soon. But the sun will be legit up when we get there. Less mosquito danger."

With the darkness and the droning engine noise, I wasn't sure when exactly I drifted off, but brake squeals shocked me back to alertness.

El Raton is more a name than an actual place. A few random structures, but nothing resembling an actual house or business. And no one is around. Not sure why we had to squeal the breaks on the way in.

“We gotta stop for a minute. Sorry about the brakes. Old jeep is kinda all or none when braking. Back in a sec.”

Reggie jumped out of the jeep and jogged into an open crack in the building, it may have been a door, but it was hard to tell. He was gone just a few minutes before coming back out with a five gallon can of, maybe gas? The container was red, that’s usually gas. And a soaking wet paper bag.

“Breakfast. And a little gas to make sure we can get my plane off the ground.”

“What?!”

“Breakfast? Or the gas thing?”

“Gas thing! Pretty sure five gallons, of who knows what kind of contaminated gas, isn’t gonna be enough to keep a plane up!”

“Ha. No. Definitely not.”

“Well?”

“It’s for the generator. When the plane sits for a while, the old batteries lose their charge. Gotta juice them up before we go. Once it starts it works just fine.”

[illegible] Makes sense. Breakfast?”

this time of the morning there's sure to be a skillet with some heated up and ready to eat. They threw it on some tortillas for us to make it easier to eat on the go."

Reggie handed me a dripping tortilla that may have been more grease than meat.

"What's it taste like?"

"Chicken, like everything else."

Looking at the sopping mess I couldn't believe chicken was going to be the flavor. But I was starving, and it did smell pretty good like most pan cooked meats. I could definitely smell some seasoning.

"Ok. Here goes nothing." I said, flopping one of the soggy ends of the makeshift nutria burrito into my mouth…only to almost immediately spit it right back out.

"Oh yeah. I forgot to tell you, they also like a lot of hot spicy stuff down here. That may be a little more heat than you're used to."

My entire mouth immediately began to engulf in flames. My lips went numb. I could seriously imagine my lips being blue and ready to die and fall off my face from some pepper induced anti-frostbite.

"Don't worry. You get used to it. The second bite is a lot more tolerable. Weird peppers they use down here. Super-hot up front but then the flavor hits. Kinda the opposite of the peppers in the states."

I really don't know why. But I did take a second bite. Reggie wasn't lying. The second bite wasn't as traumatic. Third was actually much better. But that was it. I forgot how small portions are down here. A few bites are all you get. I knew there was grease smeared on my face. I could feel the light sting just as my lips were starting to regain their senses. But of course there was no napkin or towel of any kind to wipe it off.

“Reggie, how fucking old is that plane?”

“Not sure. I’m like the tenth owner or something. Still flies mostly ok.”

Reggie was pouring some very dark gas from the red container into a generator near the front of what appeared to be an old DC-3. The old silver planes with about 20 seats inside that always took travelers to exciting vacation destinations back in the 1940’s. It had a lean. Actually, I couldn’t tell if it was a lean, or if it just didn’t look sturdy. Maybe a flat tire on one side? Parked in a hole? Landing gear bent or jammed upward somehow? You couldn’t really tell. It was missing a few small pieces of outer paneling showing the metal rib framing in places. Reminding me of the old dilapidated airstream trailers in the deep south countryside. But those never had to fly.

“Reggie…there’s no door on this thing.” I said as I walked around and saw the open hole where the door should be.

“Sure there is. It’s right in front of you.”

I looked left toward the wing and saw the prop engine, also missing some of its paneling, exposing the metal ribs, some wiring and piping inside. I was starting to have a bad feeling about this. I turned to look out down the dirt strip runway. I was looking straight into the rising sun. But still It seemed far too short for something this big and clunky to get airborne. The full-grown forest growing a few feet off the dirt didn’t make it any more comforting.

The dizziness may have been from the generator fumes or the panic, but I was starting to feel generally rough when I heard the generator shut off.

“We’re almost ready to go. Be back in a sec.”

Reggie disappeared toward the shed with the generator and the gas can, returning a few minutes later with five old plastic milk crates like you used to see piled up next to grocery store loading docks.

“Not sure. I’m always up here in front flying.” he replied nonchalantly but with a side eyed grin.

“And what about the whole cabin pressure thing. I mean there’s no door…”

“Nothing to worry about. We don’t fly that high around here. As long as we stay around ten thousand feet or lower there’s enough oxygen so we won’t pass out.”

“How high are those mountains we’re flying over?”

“About sixteen thousand feet.”

“And that math works out for you? I heard you were some kind of genius.”

“Don’t believe everything you hear.”

“Definitely feeling that thought” I said to myself as Reggie did some kind of mechanical Heimlich to get the engines started.

“The professor said on the call that he was going to be here to meet me.”

We started to sluggishly trod down the dirt strip.

“He’ll be there when we land. I’m sure he’ll have plenty of hugs and kisses for you. What’s it been? A month since he’s seen you?”

***

I knew Reggie was joking about the hugs and kisses. Professor Clarke was probably the most stoic person I know. I definitely had an interesting college experience and had lots of different types of professors, from the touchy feely types all the way to the can’t-even-speak-English types. Clarke was different. Stoic yes, but still somehow mesmerizingly engaging. Is charismatic stoicism a thing? Or maybe it’s just me. I’m kind of a knowledge junkie.

My college career started off away from home, trying for an Engineering and Philosophy double major. I dropped Engineering fairly early on. Hate math. But I stuck with philosophy. Unfortunately, before I finished the last two classes of that degree, my mom nearly died from a ruptured brain aneurysm. I felt it was my duty to come home to help take care of her.

The experience of caring for her changed me. The things that happened in her brain, the way she processed thoughts, her personality shifts, even what she found funny before and after, showed striking changes. I became almost obsessively focused on psychology.

For a while I just bombarded myself with psychology related magazine articles. But that was really just self-help crap for the masses. Psychology journals were more interesting but expensive for someone like me. So I made a decision to begin an actual psychology degree program at my local university soon after my mother stabilized. The psychology program was definitely fulfilling. Along the way I finished the last two philosophy classes I needed and still had a lot of elective credits I was required to take. As one elective, just because the time slot was convenient, I ended up in a class called International Terrorism.

Growing up in the United States, I, like other kids, rarely thought about terrorism. The few times we heard about it occurring it was far away, usually in the middle east, and we had forgotten about it by the next commercial break. But on a college campus the information placed in front of you is very different from what the [illegible] public may see. Radical freedom of speech is generally the [illegible] their claims about a

Middle Eastern countries that lived it. They told first hand stories that went along with the curriculum. The books for the class explained how to make the cheapest most effective bombs, where to place them, who to target and why. I couldn't believe it was allowed to be taught. But it was still fascinating.

In the hallway outside my terrorism class one day, I saw the terrorism professor talking to another professor about the situation in the Soviet Union. I later learned that the other professor was professor Clarke, a Soviet-American Relations professor and head of the International Studies degree program at the university. Until recently I had no idea international studies was a thing you could study much less get a degree in. But the knowledge junkie in me kicked in and I went to talk with professor Clarke. Everything about the program was fascinating. The teacher backgrounds, the content, all of it. And as luck would have it, I could get the degree using the elective credits I needed anyway. So I was back on the path of dual degrees.

The psychology classes came and went. They weren't boring and were able to keep my attention, but the fire just wasn't there. I found myself leaning on the international studies classes, all exciting in their own right. I quickly found myself up in the middle of the night, diving down rabbit holes reading journals and papers to follow the psychological links between the international events. Professor Clarke saw me several times a week, even when I wasn't taking one of his classes. I'd burst into his office with some revelation. He'd hear me out. Ask me questions and engage in discussion. Usually afterward handing me some article from his stash where someone had already made that revelation. I guess I should have been embarrassed. But in a world that existed before the true internet as we now know it, it was just two people talking. And he never made it embarrassing or uncomfortable.

Almost two years later, a few months before graduation, Professor Clarke called me into his office. I assumed it was to go over the course credits to make sure I could graduate, and to do the obligatory satisfaction survey. At the end of the term all the professors seemed to act a little nicer, some would even beg for

I leaned back. Okay, this must be serious. The paper had a bunch of official seals on it, but I couldn't pick out what they were just at a glance. But it was soon apparent from the writing.

> *By signing this document you agree to adhere to any and all formal clearance processes for viewing, possessing and exchanging information and materials of a confidential nature that are of importance for the security of the United States of America and its allies.*

I must have had a startled look on my face, or maybe my mouth was just gaping open, but the Professor continued talking while I was reading.

"I know you're going to sign that, so I'll get started. The fall of the Soviet Union was carefully orchestrated through a series of events to collapse their economy and embed democratic thoughts in the minds of the people there. This happened on many fronts. One of those fronts was led by my team."

I looked up from the paper, "Your team?"

"Don't get me wrong. We're not like James Bond spies or anything like that. We're just people that know how to make connections with others quickly. Instill feelings of trust. And know what to say and not say to convey certain ideas. We mainly attend meetings or conventions, and give lectures. But the lectures aren't the real job. The real job is hanging out with people after the lectures, at the local pubs, restaurants or private after-parties. That's where the real connections happen and where the grass roots changes get started."

"I need you to sign the form." He said as I realized he had stopped telling the story and I was just staring blankly at him. I forced my gaze back to the paper and finished reading. Nothing too crazy, it seemed like just a promise to keep any secrets. So I signed.

"Thank you" he said taking the form, putting it back in the folder and setting it aside on his desk. "Now where was I."

The professor went on in surprising depth about a handful of former students and colleagues he had worked with on a few different missions, for lack of a better word. When he finished, I had a million questions swimming in my head. But only one came out.

"Why me?"

"I usually don't reach out to students this early on these things. I wait and select those I think may work out and watch them for some time while they enter their lives, start new careers, you know, life. I want to make sure what I think I see in the classroom is who they actually are in their own environment. Then, for the few that still seem right for the role, I reach out." He paused for a minute, letting it sink in, that somehow I had something unique that made him abandon his recruiting routine.

"So why me? Why now?"

"Do you remember early in your psych program, during your class on psych testing, you took all the tests you were being taught to administer?"

"Yes."

"Well, after having you in one of my classes, and knowing you would have taken those tests as a psych student, I made a few subtle inquiries and got your results."

"Funny. I seem to recall there was a confidentiality form I signed about that too. Said something about the results were for my educational purposes only and would not be retained or given to

"Second," he said shushing me with a hand gesture, "your scores were highly unique. Unique enough that the psychology department was also watching you. They were mainly interested in your intelligence score. You recall that one?"

"Vaguely. They told me not to put much weight on it since I was a student in the field which would skew the results."

"In short. They lied." He said standing and pulling a hardbound book off his nearby shelf. After thumbing through some pages he handed it to me.

"What does that book say is the normal range for an IQ?

"Eighty-five to one hundred fifteen."

"Do you remember what your score was?"

"I don't know. Like one hundred thirty or something maybe."

"It was one fifty-five."

"Ok. But skewed because I was a student. So…"

"Turn the page. What does that second paragraph say?" he said while walking to his mini-fridge and grabbing two bottles of water.

I read for a minute. "It says the value of this test is that it cannot be scammed and there is no way to study to improve scoring."

"Not only was your score on that test in the top one-tenth of a percent, it was corroborated by several of the other tests you took," he continued, setting one of the bottles of water in front of me. "But wait, there's more…" he quipped mocking a popular infomercial, "and that's where your uniqueness lies."

He opened his water, and I followed his queue taking a sip of my own.

"My uniqueness?"

"Most people who score that high on intelli

friends. They're usually considered the odd one of the group, if they have any real friends at all. They usually end up being the weird loner type." He put the cap back on his bottle. "But that's not you. You scored high on the socialization tests too. That unique combination is priceless for what my team does."

"So…" I began but he again silenced me with a hand gesture.

"So in short, you're smart enough to read and digest detailed material from several sources, form opinions, and engage with others in a beneficial manner based on those opinions. In real time. You have a deep grasp of the material and can also read the room, so to speak."

"Yes, but…" again silenced.

"Which also means you're probably already about three to four layers deep trying to resolve questions about what I'm saying and asking. Or about to ask, if you haven't already sorted it out."

"You want me on your team."

"America needs you on my team."

"So what's that mean?"

"It means I put you on a list, in my head. And when a situation arises, I'll reach out to you. It could be today, next week, next year, maybe never. You commit to participate now. And I'll find you when you are needed. You'll get the situational info in route, with plenty of time for someone like you to digest it. And we'll go to work right away when you get on site, wherever that may be."

"So drop everything in my life at your beckon call. What do I get out of this so called commitment?

"Access. You get access to powerful people with whom you can develop relationships. You get an easy get-out-of-jail-free card for all the tedious things that can happen in life. And you get real time access to intelligence information, from multiple sources, on situations developing throughout the world. And a pager. So everyone will think you're cool." he ended with an unmuffled laugh.

"So you think being a pager dork is a selling point for me?"

"No. No I don't." his muffled laugh waned. "But I do think the access to real time, real world information being available upon request for a knowledge junkie is like winning the lottery."

"Upon request?"

"You picked up on that did you. The other piece of this is you will be afforded the highest level of clearance the American government has."

"Top Secret?"

"One higher…Top Secret with SCI. TS/SCI clearance not only gives you access to the information, it grants you access to the source of that information. You don't just get to read analyst reports, you can talk to people on the ground that originally provided the information. You can get it directly from the spy's mouth, so to speak," he smiled as he said it, knowing I was totally sold. "You can even walk directly into the White House without an appointment if you really wanted to. But I don't recommend it. Nothing important ever actually happens there and you'll end up stuck discussing the presidential tea cup saucers with someone bored out of your mind."

"Do I get paid for this?"

"You'll hold a real job. We'll find you something in the psych world with an understanding boss. It is a real job. You must actually work. But you'll be freed up, no questions asked when we need you. And there's some bonus pay in your normal paycheck when you get back."

I took another sip of my water, thinking for a moment about what it all means.

"Sounds too good to be true. What's the downside."

"You already determined the downside while you were quietly thinking a moment ago. But if you want me to confirm it for you, it's friends and family." He stood, walking over to a few photos on his wall and pointed to those who appeared to be a wife, children, maybe some friends. "No one can know. You'll need to establish, and maintain for eternity, a complex set of lies…well at least deceptions…so no family, friends or coworkers become security risks. They have to find comfort in a reason why you disappear for a week at a time without much notice, sometimes in the middle of the night. You have to make sure your wife doesn't think you're cheating on her, that your friends don't feel abandoned, and that your real-life coworkers don't feel like you're always dumping work on them. It's a tedious veil you have to stitch together, and remember, forever."

"That's not how I live my life. I'm an open book."

"Yep. That's pretty much how we all were. Which is why it's so hard to do. Most of us end up single, childless, friendless, just because it gets too hard."

He walked away from the photos and sat back down, reclining in his desk chair.

"So that's the decision you have to make. Information, connections with powerful people, and possibly changing the world. Or, the typical life in suburbia with a wife, two point five kids, and trips to school music concerts and soccer practice."

I sat motionless and quiet. Surely with a blank stare.

"The security clearance background takes several months to go through. You've already signed for that. You can go about your life for a while, do the graduation thing, with honors I hear, well done. And then I'll reach back out for your final decision once the clearance is granted. At that point I will need to know if you are all in or all out. There's no in-between."

Professor Clarke stood, clearly dismissing me. And I started walking toward the door.

"One other thing" he said, "Don't call me Professor Clarke anymore. Just Clarke from now on."

I nodded, turned and started the dazed walk back to my apartment.

I was jolted from the memory of that walk by the spinning of the plane that left me flung to one side of the wobbling seat, and then to the other as we slammed to a stop. To my relief I saw we reached the forest end of the dirt strip and turned around to take off in the other direction with far fewer obstacles.

"Fasten your seat belt. Just kidding there are no seat belts." Reggie quipped as he gunned the props and we gained surprising speed.

"Woo Hoo! That never gets old!" he yelled over the engines as the wheels eventually made it off the dirt.

"You should really get some seat belts!" I yelled back, feeling my hands digging into the arms of the seat.

"Wouldn't matter, those seats are held on by rusty bolts in rotten wood. If you fly out the seat would too. Then I gotta get another seat!"

Anything within a hundred yards of the end of the airstrip would have absolutely been decapitated as we flew by. But eventually there was a clear upward momentum that left my stomach a few feet below the rest of me.

"Now we're up and going. Wasn't sure for a minute there."

"Wait…what?"

"Just kidding. Takes a bit for these older planes to get up and catch the draft. We're flying a bit slow, so we've got about an hour to get south of the Orinoco River. Then about another hour to Angel Falls. I'll give you a close up, it's really spectacular to see from the air. Then we'll head to our destination deeper south into Canaima.

About three hours total. Get some rest if you can. I'll wake you up for the fun stuff."

I woke to a sense of falling, well more tipping than falling. Like the seat was about to turn over on its side. I looked through the missing door and saw treetops far too close.

"What the hell? What's going on!?" I yelled forward.

"Sorry about that. We're at Angel Falls. I told you I'd wake you for the fun stuff."

"What's happening?"

"It's pretty tight in here. Look out the door in just a sec and you'll see the bottom of the falls, well the mist really at this altitude. We're gonna do a spiral upward in this canyon until we get to the top. You'll have an awesome view. This is a perk I give my paying guests who fly with me. I think it could be bad juju if I don't do it for you too."

"What!" I yelled with no response. I could see both sides of the canyon and we were spiraling upward like some little spitfire cartoon plane. Every few seconds or so I caught a glimpse through the open door. Angel falls. This close up you could hear the roar of the water almost pulsing soft and loud over the sound of the engines as we spun. It was nauseating but still breathtaking. At the top of the falls, we came almost to a stalled stop and hovered for an elongated view. The sight was truly breathtaking. But then the bottom dropped out of the world, and it would have been nice to have that breath back!

"The spiral down part isn't as much fun. Hold tight. We're gonna get some speed from this falling and zip up over that far ridge. Might be a little tough on the stomach. And you might pass out a little. G-force greater than the old Space Mountain ride at Disney."

“A little? How do you pass out a little! What’s gonna stop me from falling out that door if I’m passed out?!”

“Nothing.”

“Just kidding. I’ll be tipping the plane so you would fall to the inside. No worries.”

“And what if you pass out?”

“Well, I guess we’re both fucked if that happens. Fingers crossed!”

Everything got blurry. Then I was limp and couldn’t control any body parts, then I came to with a massive headache, leaned, or more like hunched over to one side in my seat, toward the inside though, so there’s that.

“Did you like that?”

“No.”

“Not a roller coaster guy are you.”

“Roller coasters are fine. I’m not a plane crashing into a mountain guy.”

“Then I did good. We missed the mountain.”

***

Again I woke at the turning motion of the plane. This time it was more gradual, more familiar, like on the regular commercial flights I’ve been on. The ones without a psycho stunt pilot flying.

“Are we there yet?” I said, hearing my inner seven year old in my voice.

“Almost. We gotta do a quick lap. We’re gonna go pretty low. Don’t freak out if you see us below some trees.”

“Why are we going below the trees?” I asked, surprisingly not as freaked out as I probably should have been at the thought.

“Hang on! This part’s fun!”

The plane was flying mainly level, low, but a good bit off the tops of the trees. Hardly scary compared to the falls.

“This isn’t so bad.” I said, very prematurely.

The plane rapidly plummeted downward. Now more than a little low. If I didn’t know any better, I’d say the wheels were on the ground. I saw tree trunks, not tops, and a shed of some kind went racing past. Then we darted back up in the air just above the trees.

“What the hell was that?” I yelled.

“Monkeys.” Reggie said simply.

“Monkeys?” I yelled back, definitely needing more from Reggie on that.

“They’re smart. Learn fast. They know the tourists that land on these strips love to see them. Feed them. Even if the tourists don’t feed them, they dump their trash for the monkeys to rummage through. There’s usually about fifty monkeys in the area on and around these airstrips, especially the ones deeper into the forest like this one. You gotta do a fly by to get them off the strip, then turn around and land before they get back.”

The plane made a hard turn to get back on approach. Then the bottom dropped out again. This time I did feel the wheels hit the ground. Well hopefully it was the wheels. It didn’t feel so much like we were rolling, more bouncing and skipping side to side down the strip.

“Welcome to the jungle!” Reggie sang “The real one, not that Guns and Roses city jungle crap.”

The plane rolled up toward the shed that was partially behind the edge of the trees. A narrow dirt path led from the landing strip around to the far side of the shed. I couldn’t wait to be out of the plane, so I jumped down right after Reggie who hadn’t offered the fancy milk crate step option for my exit.

The dusty air from the landing blew past and I saw someone walking toward us on the little path.

"Only one this time Reggie? You're slacking!" I heard in the familiar voice of Professor Clarke. I mean Clarke.

"One what?" I said looking at Reggie.

"Yeah. Little fucker. Your guys eat yet? Reggie said.

"Not yet." Clarke offered, lifting his chin at me to look back toward the plane.

The landing gear on the far side had what I assumed was a monkey, or at least some monkey parts wrapped around the shaft.

"Saves us a hunt." Clarke finished, refocusing on me. "Good to see you. It's been a while."

***

"Not really a while" I said questioning Clarke with a look as much as my words, "you told me it was going to take months for the clearance to go through. I was surprised to get your call only a few weeks in. In the middle of the night no less."

"What can I say. We had an urgent matter come up. And I thought you'd be perfect for it."

"Why me?"

"Like I mentioned before, I looked into the available information on you. You have something no one else on my team has for this job. A legit backstory that fits. We didn't have time to get a fake backstory in place. So here you are."

"What backstory? What can I have possibly done in my life that makes me perfect to be in this very hot, humid, dense, monkey filled jungle?"

Clarke laughed, “Not much. But this is just our meet up spot. We need to stay well away from the prying eyes and ears.”

“So what’s the backstory?”

“If I recall correctly, and I do, you spent about 6 weeks playing competitive soccer for the US in Mexico in high school, didn’t you?”

“Yes. But what does that have to do with anything? I’m way out of shape. I hope you don’t expect me to try and play soccer down here!”

“I’m sure you’ve had more than your share of shandies these days” he said, obviously also knowing that I was playing rugby instead of soccer now, where sideline shandies are the refueling drink of choice. Beer to numb the pain of the game, and the sugar of the lemonade to give a bit of a sugar rush to go back on the pitch. “I never understood that beer and lemonade mixing thing until I got down here. I’ll be damned if it wasn’t the perfect thirst quencher.”

“Alright, here’s your lunch” Reggie said tossing a slightly mangled but still monkey looking monkey on the table. “I’m heading out. Gotta get back and pick up some fancy folks for a tour of Angel Falls at sunset.”

Reggie turned without any handshakes or goodbyes, just left on his way with high jump, grab and pull into his plane. As soon as the plane was off the ground you could hear the forest. Some birds. But mainly monkeys making their way through the brush and back out onto the dirt airstrip, sniffing around and grabbing at random things hoping they’re edible.

“We should get going. It’s a bit of a walk to the camp. Need to get there before it’s too late to have a fire to cook. Grab that will you.” Clarke said pointing at the limp monkey. “The guys are probably tired of monkey already. But you eat what’s available.”

“What’s it taste like?” I asked.

“Monkey.”

“Not Chicken?”

“Why would monkey taste like chicken?”

“I don’t know. Doesn’t everything taste like chicken? Reggie gave me that nutria stuff and it tasted like chicken. What I could taste under the ridiculously hot seasoning anyway.”

“Ha. Reggie fed you nutria? Back in El Raton?”

“Yes. Why?”

“I just find it funny that you ate swamp rat in a town named after a rat.”

The camp was just that. A bunch of makeshift tents. Some looked well used and worn, some looked like they were bought from a ten year old at a yard sale. All I knew was that I didn’t have one. My go-bag was only some changes of clothes for hot and cold weather, a few toiletries, some painkillers, a few ointments and bandages. And a sleeping bag.

“I don’t have a tent. How long will I be here?”

“Just tonight. We have a tent for you. Wouldn’t want you out exposed to the forest evils in that cheap sleeping bag I’m sure you brought.”

One of the handful of people in the camp walked over. Long pants, boots, no shirt.

“Ah you brought lunch. How nice of you.” He said taking the limp monkey and swinging it up in the air. “Monkey again, anyone hungry?”

Lots of groans emanated from around the camp. There were more people here than it originally seemed.

“That’s courtesy of Reggie” Clarke said.

“Reggie? That fucking asshole. He knew he was coming here. He could have brought us some hamburgers or something!” one man said walking past us back toward the airstrip.

“At this point I’d even eat one of those fucking rat burger things he always has” the man said, his voice fading into the jungle noise.

“How long have they been here?” I asked Clarke.

“Good question. The camp’s kinda always here. Different people rotate in and out depending on what’s going on. Sometimes they spend a few days in town and then come back. Some are always in town and never come out here. Just depends on the job.”

“So, what’s the job? You never finished about the soccer connection?”

“The US national soccer team happens to be in Venezuela this week. You have some newspaper articles about playing soccer in Mexico. I thought you would be able to say you’re with the team somehow, assistant of some kind, if anyone stops you. You speak the speak and probably know some of the players personally.”

Clarke had definitely done some research. I was a decent soccer player in school. I was on the State select team for Florida, and I was lucky enough to play for a while in Mexico City.

“Not sure that article will help much. It’s several years old now and barely mentioned anything about me in detail. Maybe a sentence or two. The rest was about why the team was there. It was in a local Florida newspaper, and I doubt there are any copies of it anywhere down here. Definitely none in Spanish. What good is that as a backstory if no one can look it up and read it?”

“You have it. Well, I have a copy of it for you that you’ll keep on you in case you need it.”

I shook my head and laughed at the forethought.

“So what’s the actual job? When we were talking in your office it sounded like I would be staying in hotels, at conference centers, giving lectures, drinking at pubs…not camping in the rainforest.”

"This is the first stop. I'll give you all the background you need while we're here tonight. Tomorrow you'll head back to a town on the outskirts of Caracas, near the stadium, where you'll meet up with someone from the team office that came on the trip. She'll give you their itinerary. You'll be speaking at unaffiliated events nearby. Talking on the impact of sports and how there's a change in the mindset from the focus on fun as a kid, to the competitive job focus of sports in college. I believe that's right up your alley, no?" Clarke smirked.

"So you read that too?" I said, referencing a heavily toned paper I wrote bashing the purposeful elimination of fun solely for the competitive advantage, win at all costs, drive sought by colleges. College scholarships drove me out of competitive sports because there was zero fun left, all struggle, all infighting and back-stabbing, nothing ever good enough. None of the things I enjoyed were left in the sport that I loved so much growing up. So I ended up starting over and playing college rugby. Competitive, but not with profitable prospects for the school or professionally. At least not in the US. Which meant there was still fun in it. And there were beer and shandies on the sidelines during practices and games to keep it that way.

Clarke just smiled and opened a water, quietly taking a sip. He clearly wasn't going to comment further on that.

"Okay. So that's the cover. What's the underlying message, you know, for the pubs?" I asked.

"Not sure there will be a lot of pubs on this one. Maybe a couple. Mainly it will be gatherings at some homes. What have you heard about the government down here? Friend? Foe?"

"Not much really. Just seems like typical third world corruption. Unstable-ish. With big oil money and maybe some middle east influence from what Jack told me earlier." That conversation at the air force base felt like days ago, but it was really just a few hours.

"We're counting on that corruption. The middle east thing isn't too big of a deal. They are kind of competitors that hate each other but pretend to play nice publicly. Iran would be fine if Venezuela were blown off the map and vice versa."

Clarke took a larger swig of water, finishing off the bottle before continuing.

"We actually like the current government and President Carlos Andres at the moment. But there have been rumblings of an uprising. He's a pretty weak liberal leader who is taking less of a hard line toward democracy and US interests. But a guy named Hugo Chavez has a lot of people riled up. He's more radical, anti-capitalism, at least the American version. He has a lot of the population wound up and blaming the sitting government for their poverty. It's completely true. But we want to get in the ear of some of those soccer fans that have some powerful friends. Get them the message that the US government believes they will be in better shape under the current Andres regime and should push back on Chavez."

"How the hell am I supposed to do that with a few conversations after a sports speech!?"

"That's where your genius comes in. Do some research when you get to town, read the room, and say whatever you need to say. They'll expect you to speak English because they know you're part of the team's tour. Easy. They may even try to thank you with some free hookers. I'd steer clear of that though. But follow your personal preference."

"What?!" my voice definitely rising and a few people otherwise engaged glanced over briefly. "So you want me to make it up on the fly? And make sure it's good enough that it changes peoples' minds about their lives, and at the same time making sure it doesn't piss anyone off and get me killed?"

"Exactly like you just summarized. Do that. Digest the information around you when you get there. Read the room. Speak your thoughts. They'll follow. If you do it well."

I was on a panel of four people. Three talks, they were talks, casual, not more formal lectures. In small assembly centers that were less than half full. Maybe twenty people at the first one. Maybe a hundred at the last. I got to vent my frustration over sports as a business, which was met with differing opinions.

The first venue was the back room of a tavern that was just big enough to hold small town hall type meetings for its neighborhood. Afterward, the evening was spent uneventfully in the front room of the tavern sipping beer, watching soccer on the TV and listening to comments about how terrible US soccer is compared to other countries, even as the US had dominated and won a game earlier that day.

The second venue wasn't much different, just a restaurant instead of a tavern. A complimentary tapas buffet may have been what drew the small group in that night. No one seemed interested in anything anyone had to say from the panel. And no one initiated talks during the follow-up meal.

The third event was different. It was a daytime event, not in the evenings like the others. It was in a small theater, no complimentary food or beverages. The crowd, if you could call a hundred people a crowd, was definitely more affluent. The manner of dress was a step up from the blue collar attire of the other events. There was a more balanced mix of men and women. But perhaps most distinguishing was that everyone spoke English. Accented. But very clearly English. Conversations at the prior venues almost invariably began in Spanish and then switched to very broken attempts at English when they realized my Spanish was pitiful. Not here. This crowd was well versed, probably in several languages. A different crowd. There were well thought out questions asked of all the panelists. And many enlightening discussions ensued on the topics. The impact of soccer, professional and international in particular, on businesses for this group was eye-opening. Branding, equipment sales, and marketing were similar to how companies like Nike and Adidas operate in America, with very familiar logos, commercials and billboards. The surprising discussion was about the impact of soccer on education.

In Venezuela, school is a luxury not a right. Less than half of kids in the country completed a single year of school. But, similar to how American scholarships can get a player to college when that player might not have the grades or money otherwise, kids that demonstrated emerging soccer skills playing in the streets were often invited or encouraged to attend schools. Through soccer skills the poorest child could befriend a wealthier family's child, who then would help them integrate into the social group and be accepted at school. Servants of the wealthier families would often bring their young kids to work in hopes that such a friendship would develop. Kids that lacked the sports skills were often shunned and treated poorly, kept at a distance like the servant class usually was. They could be tormented and abused. So it was a gamble by the servant parents. But for a large number of kids, it was successful, a way for them to climb at least one notch up the social hierarchy.

Hearing the stories and seeing some of the data provided by the speakers in the crowd was enlightening. The most effective way of getting more kids into schools was when the equipment and clothing companies began widely sponsoring teams for the schools. The companies were unabashedly trying to expand their markets by creating new, larger generations of players to buy their products. But it also created educational opportunities. Even small elementary schools would have more than one soccer team. Schools were often classified based on how many teams they had, with the best rated schools having the most teams. Schools had to start seeking players to fill teams so they could get more sponsors to get more highly rated. This made the streets a type of tryout venue. A kid playing soccer in the street in tattered clothes and no shoes one day, could be decently dressed in a classroom a week later.

Where the other events lasted well under an hour. This one went on for three hours. We panelists were just as fascinated by the crowd comments and stories as they were by ours. Not everyone was like-minded, but exchanges were respectful and thoughtfully digested. Everyone was learning something new. And the event likely could have willingly continued longer if the sponsor didn't force closing remarks.

The after-party for this one was also much different from the previous two. I was escorted to a nicer than average car, Mercedes of course, and politely assisted into the back seat. I assumed others would be joining me. But as my door closed, the car began to pull out into traffic. Just me and a non-talkative driver clearly focused on not letting the locals dent the fancy car. Understandable. Traffic in South American countries is not well regulated. There are lanes, signs, signals and laws. But in practice drivers aggressively force vehicles of all types, often in various states of disrepair, into and out of chaotic races from one signal to the next. Lane lines and laws are ignored. If they think they can get to a desired spot they do it. It's not unusual to see five cars lined up across the front of a traffic light that only has two lanes. And the honking bottleneck that occurs once the signal turns green is terrifying for most of us from the States. A few mini heart attacks later we were on a more calmly flowing highway. I decided it might be a good time to ask where the hell I was being taken.

"Excuse me. Where are we going?"

The driver looked at me for a minute. I couldn't tell if it was because he wasn't used to being spoken to or if he was mentally translating what I said.

"Gobernador, te veo para hablar." He replied.

Ok. Definitely a translation thing.

"En Ingles por favor?" I replied, glad I bothered to commit that phrase to memory.

"Governor Perez. You talk him." He eventually translated for me.

Stunned, and not sure the driver could translate any of my follow up questions to that bombshell, I eventually turned my head back toward the traffic outside my window. Clarke told me this would be grass roots work, with ordinary everyday people. But if I understood correctly, I was apparently invited to meet the Governor. Before I left the camp in Canaima, I read through some documents about the main government players for Venezuela. I never expected to meet them, I just wanted to know about them so I could recognize if I heard their names or could speak less ignorantly if I was randomly asked about them on one of my panels. Luis Perez-Rodriguez was the Governor of the Venezuelan Federal District which included the capital city of Caracas. He was personally appointed by Venezuelan President Andres several years earlier and was thought to be a close confidant of the President. But I couldn't imagine why I was being taken to see him. My first thought was dread. Like I was a nuisance cop being taken to a drug lord so the drug lord could tell me to stop being a nuisance. Maybe those sports business people didn't like my anti-sports business comments. Maybe my opinionated ranting was going to finally do me in.

I dwelled on my doom for the rest of the ride. At least until we got to the coast. The view was breathtaking! Lush tropical forests lining the glistening crystal clear water. Pockets of pristine white sand, clearly private and not accessed by the public. But almost as soon as we got to the view, the main road suddenly dipped back into the forest away from a jutting peninsula. The car slowed and I saw a small, paved side road. Maybe a driveway. We turned and drove about 100 feet into the forest before coming to a stop in front of a massive iron gate. Two guards came out of a guard house hidden amongst the lush landscaping. Both in black fatigues adorned with Venezuelan flags and both armed with assault rifles, one rifle less at rest than the other.

The guard approached the driver-side window, which had been lowered in anticipation. There was a polite exchange in Spanish that I couldn't follow. But it appeared that the guards and driver knew each other and were just going through formalities. The second guard walked around the car looking hard at me in the back seat before getting to the trunk. The trunk began to rise as the guard reached the rear of the car. After a quick glance, the guard closed the trunk and nodded to the other guard at the driver-side door. The driver side guard made some parting comments, and the two guards walked back to the guardhouse without a second look back. It seemed like a long time but was probably only a minute or so until the iron gate began to crawl open.

The driveway wound through the forested peninsula for what had to be a quarter mile. On both sides, the view through the dense green trees occasionally got a burst of bright blue ocean. The driveway snaked hard to the right and opened into exactly what you would expect a Governor's ocean front mansion to look like. The asphalt driveway crossed through two sandstone block columns into a courtyard of multicolored pavers surrounding a large fountain. Sandstone foot walls with decorative iron fencing on top surrounded the courtyard. About thirty cars were parked here. Mostly Mercedes. Mostly black. But there were a few outliers, a champagne colored Rolls Royce and two supercars with names I didn't recognize. The driver of this Mercedes didn't park. I was driven to the front carriage house entrance of the massive three story castle of a home.

Two men in white linen that resembled resort valets hustled to the car and opened the rear doors, assisting me out of one side, and my go-bag from the seat on the other side.

"Welcome to La Mirada, the summer residence of Governor Perez. My name is Carlos and that is Roberto with your bag. We will be your personal valets for your time here. If you need anything let us know. We will be nearby at all times to assist."

I wasn't sure why I was getting this dignitary type treatment, but it did make me feel less doomed. And the solid grasp of English made me much more comfortable than I'd been on the drive up. Comfortable enough to start asking some questions.

"Thank you. I'm still not sure why I was brought here. The driver wasn't able to explain. Do you know why Governor Perez would want to see me?"

"No sir. But the Governor entertains many people from all over the world. I'm sure he'll let you know when you see him."

We started walking up an ornate concrete staircase toward the main glass paned doors of the house.

"Do you know when I might…" my thought trailed off as I reached the top of the stairs. The glass doors in front gave way to a massive three story high room with three story glass walls overlooking the blue waters of the Caribbean. No tourists, no fishermen, no cargo ships, nothing to mar the view. Amazing.

"I love seeing that look on faces for the first time when they arrive here. Wait here a moment and enjoy the view. I'll be right back."

"It's a remarkable view." Said a voice behind me. I wasn't sure how long he'd been standing there. I turned a little startled. "I'm sorry for not being there to greet you earlier. My name is Luis. I want to personally welcome you to my home. Can I get you a drink?" the Governor humbly offered holding out his hand in greeting.

"I…" I stuttered, returning the handshake. "I really don't know protocol here. I apologize."

"Ha ha. No worries. This isn't a state dinner. I'm on summer break." he said smiling, guiding me with his outstretched arm toward a smaller but still grand room off the main room. "Roberto, dos cervesas por favor, con lima, y dos vasos."

"Please sit. Roberto will bring us some beers to quench our thirst. We have much to talk about."

I suppose this was an office, of sorts. There was a grand desk, but it was off to the corner of the room. It was couches and chairs near the towering glass windows in this part of the room. I sat on the couch where directed. The seat had an uninterrupted ocean view. The governor sat in a chair to my left, angled partially toward me and partially out the grand window.

"We have a mutual friend" he began, "who said I should meet with you. He tells me you've been doing good work for the cause of my people. I very much appreciate that."

"I'm just out there telling my story when people care to listen. But it's a surprise and an honor to meet you Governor Perez."

"Please, call me Luis. I don't like the formalities of my job, so I do my best to dispense with them in my home. To everyone here I am Luis."

Just then Roberto arrived with two frosted glasses of beer with fresh limes on the rim.

"Gracias Roberto." Luis said, in one motion squeezing his lime into the beer and raising his glass, "Here's to another beautiful day in the Caribbean. It's good to be alive! Salud!"

I raised my glass likewise and we both took a large first sip.

"This is good." I said gazing at the color of the beer in the glass and the perfect flow of the escaping carbonation. "Really good."

"Thank you. We make our own here on site. Small batch. One time in my life when I first started brewing my own beer, I made the mistake of making many cases worth of one recipe. But I found that a few bottles into that batch I was already wanting to make a new batch, tweak it somehow. So now I just make and tweak and make and tweak. This is my latest batch. But I have a refrigerated room full of the one or two leftover bottles of all my prior batches. You know, for beer emergencies." He said catching my gaze and swirling his glass. "I'm never bored with it and if I hate it, I don't feel bad about throwing a small batch out."

"Do you have the same problems with commercial beer here that they have in Mexico? With the workers I mean."

"Definitely not. I assume you're referring to the workers at the Corona plant that were pissing in the vats of beer being bottled to export to the US. I like to think our people here have more respect than that. No. Really, it's just a matter of taste for me. Don't get me wrong, I like my beer piss free too!" he laughed. "Let's take a walk. There are some things I'd like you to see."

***

Luis stepped lively down a spiral staircase in the corner of the office. Stopping halfway he looked back to me. "Other than the fantastic view, what you're about to see is my favorite part of the house."

He stepped the rest of the way down the staircase to where it gaped open into a room, one massive open-air room, that must be the size of the entire upper house. Directly in front of me was an indoor-outdoor infinity pool overlooking the Caribbean. A swim up bar merged into a traditional bar as the pool flowed under the ceiling above. The bar served several open but separate spaces throughout the room, divided by houseplants, trellises, and seating types. There were conversational areas with groups of couches and chairs. Other spaces were more solitary, with private loungers, hammocks and hammock chairs. And a common pool deck just outside the covered space for soaking up some sun. All were adorned with perfectly manicured local plants and trees, giving even the more indoor portion of the space a very outdoor feel. The angle and design kept this more casual lower level completely out of view from the elegant floors above. A benefit for a busy man that may be playing host to very different people at any given time. I got to see both. Hopefully that means something.

"This is a great space. Did you have this specially designed?"

“I wish I could take credit for that. But no. This was a home of a former President of Venezuela until a few years ago when I acquired it. There’s a two-story master bedroom suite above my office. The suite, the office and this space can be completely isolated from the rest of the house by closing a few larger than average doors. You can keep private spaces private and still entertain and allow guests to freely wander the rest of the home and the grounds. I like that separation.” he said, slightly waving his near empty glass at Roberto who was nearby as promised.

“What are those?” I said pointing to what looked like two glass rooms framed on the edges in sandstone like the other walls but seemingly out of place in the middle of the space.

“Originally those spaces were for exotic dancers. The dancers could perform in full view safely away from hands of guests. The former President had a bit of a naughty side. When I moved in, I had them converted to showers to rinse off from the pool or beach below.”

“Beach?” I said.

“Like I said before it’s what I like about this house. Everything is hidden from everything else.” He walked and I followed out to the edge of the outdoor pool deck where the crowns of the lush tree canopy topped out the coastal forest below.

“That staircase drops down to ground level and there’s a sandy path that runs about twenty yards through these trees to a secluded beach area just over there.” He pointed. “The entire peninsula grounds are restricted. Even the water is considered restricted space for about two miles from here in all directions. So what happens on this deck, or down by the beach is out of sight of prying eyes.”

“A perfect home for someone who enjoys his privacy.” I said.

“Yes, it is.” He said, turning around as Roberto walked up with two fresh beers for us. “Gracias Roberto.” He said handing me one of the beers, “Salud!”

We silently drank our beer, standing and looking out over the calm Caribbean waters. I knew the temperature was in the eighties, but the cool breeze blowing in off the water made the whole area very pleasant, even in the direct sunlight. I could see how time would just disappear here.

Other than the help, there appeared to be just a few people mulling about this lower space. Certainly not enough to warrant the number of cars in the courtyard. All were clearly minding their own business, making only courteous nods or greetings when engaged. But it seemed even this was too many people for Luis to speak openly about anything of importance. It had been all house tours and pleasantries so far. I wondered when the real talk would begin.

"Let's head back upstairs for a few minutes. I have some things I'd like to discuss with you more privately." He took my now empty glass and handed it with his to Roberto, who was again nearby as needed.

Entering the office again, Luis walked back to the desk. I wasn't sure if I should follow or wait by the seating area near the window where we were before.

"Two beers in. So I need a cigar. Do you smoke?"

"No. None for me. Thank you though." I answered as he prepared and lit a cigar in one of the leather backed office chairs. He waived me over to sit.

As the smoke oozed into the air around him, I realized that I could barely smell it. In fact, I didn't get the faintest whiff of smoke when I was last in the room. My lungs are especially sensitive to smoke, and I usually know if anyone near me has smoked within the last week. I smelled no warning signs earlier. And even with a lit cigar a few feet from me I still could barely smell it. He either noticed my curiosity or was used to offering an explanation for his guests.

"Fresh air next to a man smoking a cigar. I bet you've never seen that before." He puffed, watching a cloud of smoke rise and disappear. "I like things to smell crisp and fresh. I don't want my…" he swirled his cigar "bad habits to interfere with that." He pointed to the ceiling, “I had a high-end smoke removal system installed. There are small gaps in the decorative rings you see there on the ceiling that hide an exhaust system that draws the air upward away from guests through a filter and out of the house.” He shifted his gaze toward the wall beside the door where we first entered. “The house also has an enhanced oxygen system. Like they use in your Las Vegas casinos. Helps the air feel fresh and keeps your brain on point.”

“It seems that’s a popular amenity.” I said.

Luis stood and walked behind his desk, opening a drawer and retrieving a colorful envelope.

“That reminds me, I never thanked you for bringing me my plane. I apologize for the last-minute flight plan changes. Things occasionally get a bit…problematic here. The other day there was some minor civil unrest, a few folks with guns broke onto the domestic airport property.”

“Trying to shoot someone?” I asked.

“No. Not really. They shoot mainly in the air. But they create enough of a disruption that some of the news channels pick it up, then it gets hyped on news channels around the world and people start to rethink their visit to my beautiful country. With that news coverage around I felt it would be better if my new plane, and you, not land there.”

He took a few more puffs on his cigar.

“And as a bonus it pissed Reggie off.” He chuckled. “I had to smooth things over with him by giving him a case of my leftover beers. He had to haul ass to the other airport. I hear he almost missed you.”

“You gave him a case” I laughed recalling the three beers that were left when Reggie picked me up. “Sounds like he drank about nine beers on that ride to get me. I’m surprised he got there at all.”

“Once you get to know him, you’ll see that he functions better drunk than most people function sober. I guess that genius brain just processes alcohol differently.”

Luis handed me the colorful envelope, which now up close I saw was a plane ticket.

“I apologize. No private flight on this leg. You’ll need to fly with the masses. But it is first class, non-stop back to Tampa.”

He stubbed out his cigar at his desk and stood to walk me back to the front of the house.

“Geoffrey is waiting for you out front to take you to the airport.”

“Geoffrey?”

“Haha. Well, Juan. One day Juan tried to speak in a British accent. He can’t even speak English so of course we decided to razz him. Now we call him Geoffrey. Been so long I don’t know that he even notices anymore.”

“Geoffrey. Got it.” I laughed.

“Don’t be alarmed. But I’m having a truck of my men escort you. Lots of guns to dissuade any bad ideas those rebels might have.”

We got to the carriage entrance and…Geoffrey…was waiting. From somewhere beside me Carlos appeared and opened the door, laying my bag inside and walking me around to the far side of the car.

“You’ll want to sit on this side.” He said opening the door behind the driver.

“Thanks.” I said.

Roberto appeared with a to-go beer in hand and a small sandwich for the drive.

“Thank you as well.”

The car door closed, and my window rolled down as Luis walked over. He held out his hand. I shook it.

"It was nice to meet you. You are always welcome in my home if you are back in this area. When you see Clarke tell him thank you. I will certainly take care of that situation before anything comes of it."

"Will do." I said barely getting the words out as the window rolled up and the car drove off.

At the end of the driveway, just outside the guard gate, there was a military truck of some kind. A large, mounted gun in back, and six uniformed, fully armed soldiers on board. The truck spun its wheels with surprising force for its size and headed out onto the main road ahead of the Mercedes I was now in, a different Mercedes than before.

Most of the drive was uneventful, leaving ample time to finish my sandwich, which was ham, chased with the beer. I thought to myself that beer goes much better with ham than rat or monkey. And then I thought to myself that I couldn't believe I even had that thought. As I was mulling the unusual first leg of my journey things started to get dicey outside.

The main domestic airport and the international airport are near each other but not on the same property. The stretch of city between the airports is one of the more dangerous places in Caracas. There's almost always an uprising of some kind and the rebels take advantage of hypervigilant tourists traveling from the international airport to the domestic airport for their connecting flights. Building and car fires are frequent. Gunshots are heard. Chants are yelled. Rocks are thrown.

We pulled into the international airport terminal at Simon de Bolivar and into the typical crowd of confused passengers trying to get to their ticket counters.

"Glad we had that military escort to get us to the front of the line." I laughed, not expecting Juan to have any idea what I was saying "Right Juan?"

"Who's Juan." He said. "I'm Geoffrey." He handed me my now distressed go-bag. "You won't need to stop. Your ticket gets you straight to the gate. Just flash it if anyone tries to stop you."

I looked at him puzzled. A hint of a British accent and perfect English grammar from the guy that a few hours ago couldn't answer a simple question in English.

"Don't worry. You're not the first to be fooled. Have a good trip." He said, closing the trunk and making his way back into the car while I stood dazed at the curb. Driving off he waved out the window just as the loudness of the bustling airport around me stormed back into focus.

"Ugh I just want to be home."

I was back in my apartment in Florida, after several days still on the couch sleeping off the stress of the impromptu trip. I hate watching golf. But for napping a good golf match makes for soothing background noise. But then the phone rang. And rang. And rang. I ignored it, shifting my pillow to drown it out. Then the pager vibrated and bleeped loudly. That one I couldn't ignore. I rolled over to look. It read only "CHNL 30". I turned on channel 30, assuming that's what it meant. It was a news channel, Headline News Network back when it was news and not talk shows. The main story was just coming on.

"Gas prices are expected to drop in the coming weeks as the Venezuelan government was able to hold off a surprise coup attempt by political rival Hugo Chavez's Revolutionary Bolivarian Movement. Chavez's incarceration is believed to be stabilizing for the country which produces most of the oil purchased by American gas stations such as Shell. In other news…"

I shut off the TV and laughed to myself. Even my high school soccer newspaper article said more than that. I guess I'll need to get used to it. I rolled over and drifted back to sleep.

Chapter Two:
The Rise of the Multiverse

Tampa, Florida
Arlington (Crystal City), Virginia
San Antonio, Texas
1992

College life. There's a common belief about what that means. And I'm pretty sure it doesn't include this!

"Professor…professor!" I yelled ahead of me, desperately trying to get Dr. Mori's attention, "Professor!"

"Yes, what is it?" he replied, clearly irritated.

"I've been trying to get time with you to discuss that final thesis idea…" I began to elaborate but was abruptly cut off.

"You'll need to see me during office hours next week. I'm booked up until then." He replied dismissively as he quickly turned and walked away.

"But we have to commit to our thesis topic by Monday." I said awkwardly following through the crowded hallway.

"Go to the Psychology Department office and sign up for a time next week. As long as I see your name on the list, I won't hold you to the Monday deadline. I know you've been trying to meet with me. Somewhat incessantly. I appreciate the effort. But there are a lot of students, likely most of the class, that need more help than you. They haven't even figured out what they want to do yet. You clearly know exactly what you want to do, you just need help doing it. That puts you on the back burner so to speak. Please be patient."

He said, shuffling the papers and books he was carrying and stepping into the men's restroom.

Patience isn't really my biggest attribute. I'm pretty sure Dr. Mori knows that. He's had me in several of his classes as part of the Psychology program at the University of South Florida. I've spent time in his office debating several topics over the years. He was always pretty harsh grading my assignments and tests, and acted like I was asking ridiculous questions at times, but my ultimate grades in his classes seemed fair. So he was my go-to mentor type person, whether he liked it or not, and both a victim and facilitator of my drive to learn about psychology.

My drive for psychology had an unusual beginning. Around 1989, I was taking a generic Sociology 101 class required for my associates degree. In those days students were required to take a certain number of their credit hours at community colleges in an attempt to bolster funding for their waning appeal. I was enrolled at the University of Florida at the time, pursuing a Philosophy degree after some wasted effort attempting to double major with Engineering. After dropping the engineering curriculum some time was freed up. So I opted to take the Sociology class at a nearby Santa Fe Community College in Gainesville rather than during the summer in my hometown of Tampa, where most of my friends were doing it. It was an unfamiliar campus, an unfamiliar class, generally felt strange all around.

One familiar thing about the Santa Fe campus was animals. Santa Fe had its own zoo on campus. A legit zoo. Unusual for a college campus for sure, but very comforting for me. Because my hometown had two major zoos, Lowry Park and Busch Gardens. My home town zoos were massive and touristy so we would only go in the off season or during odd hours. Santa Fe's zoo was smaller, more intimate. It was created as part of their veterinarian training programs and was free to wander for any student. Though smaller, it was as nicely kept, or better kept, than the big Tampa zoos. Natural style enclosures, not just cages, and pristine paths meandered through the different collections. I found that no matter how stressed I was, I could pop out of the main buildings between classes, take a ten to fifteen minute walk through the zoo, and be miraculously relaxed on my return. It wasn't a crowded zoo by any means. But there were always a few people out there at each enclosure, observing and jotting down notes. I met several veterinary students there and we often had chats comparing animal behavior theories from veterinary medicine perspectives. I know. I'm a dork.

After one of my walks, I entered the classroom for a Sociology lecture. But there was no lecture that day. The class was just the professor discussing an upcoming assignment. A paper. On any topic we wanted. A bunch of students started throwing out topics, some jokingly, but the professor reiterated that it could truly be on anything. The object was to get the class to learn about background research and he felt it best for the topic to be anything that sparked enough interest for the writer to actually do that research.

One of my classmates, who was part of the veterinary program, was curious to find out if there had been any prior research on whether animal brains fill in gaps like human brains do on those optical illusion puzzles that seemed to be everywhere at the time. Another classmate was interested in how holograms worked.

I wasn't really sure what I was interested in. But I did always like physics. I know. I'm a dork. I was curious about the hologram idea. I'd seen one in person a few months earlier and thought it would be cool to learn how they worked. I knew I couldn't do my paper on it though since my classmate was going to do that topic. But that was my starting point at the library. Yes kids, back in the dark ages of the 1980's and 1990's there was no real internet to speak of. Research had to be done in actual libraries, with card catalogs, books, journals, or God forbid the dreaded microfiche and what not. But I digress.

The library at the University of Florida was massive and well stocked. My dual enrollment allowed me access twenty-four hours a day. Night was generally best to avoid the larger crowds. That night on my way into the library to start my search, something caught my eye almost immediately. Sitting on a coffee table in one of the informal break areas was a magazine. I think it was a Time magazine, but I don't fully recall. On the cover was a hologram of a human head.

The magazine article itself wasn't really informative. It was mainly about how holograms were hopefully going to be used for teaching medical students so they could visualize a condition or procedure in three dimensions without needing to cut open a cadaver. Apparently, cadavers are super expensive and getting harder to find with the growing trend of cremation. But this innovative new approach was going to save money for the schools and allow medical training to be decentralized from the major colleges into smaller schools, possibly even high schools. Buried in the article were a few sentences that caught my eye. The sentences referenced groundbreaking work by Karl Pribram using holography as a key to map the brain, and that it "could revolutionize the way we think about how our brain works."

I pulled all the books and articles I could find by Karl Pribram. I selected a few to actually check out and take with me, for the others I made photocopies of what seemed to be relevant information.

Back in my apartment late that night I was looking through all the articles in more detail. By pure chance, I found an article by Pribram on his own work that was in much more detail than the brief mention in the other magazine but was still written in layman's terms so I could understand it. It was an article about memory. More specifically, how he believes the brain makes and stores memories based on wave patterns similar to how a hologram is made.

I was fascinated. Though those researching the deep sciences were familiar with quantum theories already, the work hadn't really made it into the general textbooks yet, at least not in any detail. So the younger generation wasn't well educated on them. This article combined cutting edge quantum theories, still in their infancy, and the known reproducible physics of the hologram, something the general public can see even if they don't fully understand it yet. While the theoretical details of how Pribram proposed memory to work were very complicated, the general concept was much more simplistic, especially in the framework of a hologram. It was a great introduction to the topic. And a great topic to research for my Sociology paper.

All of the sudden I found myself excited about college again. But then, near the end of that term in Gainesville, I received word that my mother back in Tampa had fallen very ill and almost died. I rushed home to confirm assurances by others that she was stable. She was stable. But after spending time with her, and seeing how she was struggling, I decided to withdraw from the University of Florida and return to Tampa to help care for my mother.

Doctor's described that my mother had experienced a rupture of an aneurysm in her brain. Luckily it happened while she was at her doctor's office for an exam, so she had immediate knowledgeable treatment. Otherwise, according to the doctors, she would have certainly died.

While I was caring for her, my mother demonstrated changes in her ability to communicate, interchanging words for unrelated words in the middle of sentences, mispronouncing words, and attributing the wrong names to people she knew well. In recounting certain memories, there were some observable differences in what she described compared to what she had told us at other times before the injury. Her recollections weren't vague, they were still very detailed. But my relatives regularly contradicted her recollections, even when my mother was adamant that her recollection was accurate.

I accompanied my mother on visits to various medical specialists and listened to explanations and theories about why her word use and memory changes may be happening. The doctors were very gracious. Rather than dismissing my questions, most spent time with me to discuss things in more detail than they likely normally would have. A few even provided some specific topics I could research independently. That research ultimately led me to psychology.

As soon as my mother recovered enough to be self-sufficient, I enrolled in the psychology program at the University of South Florida with an emphasis on neuropsychology. I wanted to study how the brain worked and how injuries like my mother's led to such changes. Because I was at a new school and they required more credits taken, I decided to add an International Studies curriculum. Though interesting because of the timing of events around the world, my focus was really on psychology.

For the first term, the psychology curriculum was pretty general. Nothing overly exciting, just entry level prerequisites. Over the early months of the program, I continued to dwell on that concept of holography and memory. In my spare time I found myself reading and studying principles of quantum physics related to the article by Pribram.

Starting with my second term in the psychology program, the courses got a bit more interesting. I had my first course specific to neuropsychology. It was a difficult class with a lot of medical terminology and hard science mixed together. Out of his generosity and dedication to help the class understand, the professor left an open invitation to visit in his office. That professor was Dr. Shigeru Mori.

At my first visit to Dr. Mori's office, I brought my Pribram article and with excitement in my eyes asked for any feedback he could give.

"He's a new-age hack. His work is unfounded, and he tries to attribute that holographic theory to everything." Dr. Mori said.

I was immediately deflated. Spirit crushed. How could this concept that seemed so fresh, so cutting edge, and so well supported by the science I'd read, be so abruptly dismissed by a scholar. I wasn't sure what to do. I didn't know what else to say. So I excused myself and thanked him for his time.

Days were spent mentally processing that office visit. It was a true grieving process. Some denial. Lots of anger. A little bargaining. And a hint of depression. But I never reached the acceptance phase. I just couldn't accept that. I went back to the books and journals. And for about a year I regularly went back to Dr. Mori's office to make arguments about it. It had to be the right direction. It made too much sense.

Now here we are, near the end of my time at USF and I'm definitely doing my thesis on the quantum holographic theory of memory and brain functioning. The professor was right, I do know exactly what I want my thesis topic to be. What I don't know is what it will take in that thesis to convince him. He was the main faculty member that would be grading my work, so I really needed that feedback from him. I braved the crowded psychology department office and made my appointment. It was several days beyond the Monday thesis deadline, but despite our disagreements on the topic, I did trust that the professor would grant me the deadline extension.

"Come on in." I heard the professor respond to my knock exactly at my appointment time.

I eased the door open, expecting to find the professor alone and an empty chair for me, like the dozens of other times I'd been there.

"I have someone I'd like to introduce you to." He said as a man I didn't recognize stood from my usual chair and held out his hand, which I shook as the professor continued.

"This is Dr. Edwin Ellison. Dr Ellison is the Chief Psychologist for the Army and Director of the US Army Research Institute for Behavioral and Social Sciences in Arlington, Virgina."

We all sat as the professor continued the introduction.

"Edwin was in town for a meeting at Macdill yesterday and we happened to bump into each other. I had to let him know about this student that was nagging me about this crazy quantum holography stuff. I thought we were going to fall into some jovial student bashing. But to my surprise Edwin seemed interested to meet with you. Apparently he too has been following Pribram's work."

"It's very rare for anyone to have heard about Pribram, much less read up on him." Dr. Ellison added "None of that is being taught anywhere that I'm aware of."

"Not sure I have much to add," I said, "it was really just a convergence of disjointed situations that put Pribram's work in front of me in the first place, and a coincidence of timing that I was free enough to dig into it. It was also a good distraction during a painfully emotional time. And apparently it was motivating enough for me to annoy Dr. Mori about it for a year and a half. That was just a bonus." I smiled at my clever response to the professor's jab about student bashing.

"However you came about it, it's a unique knowledge set that not many people have." Dr. Ellison continued "When I heard about you, I wanted to run some ideas by you, after running them past Dr. Mori of course."

"I know you have been looking at this concept of Pribram's for a long time." Dr. Mori began "it seems almost redundant for you to rehash it all into a thesis paper. That seems like a waste of time. Besides, other than what you've shared with me on it, I don't think any of our other faculty have any idea what it's about. It would be impossible for them to effectively grade it. This is PhD level stuff you're looking at. Not what the faculty expects from a Bachelor's student."

"So, after a couple of lunch beers." Dr Ellison chuckled, "We had an idea."

I appreciated the backstory, but I was starting to see looming changes that could affect my life, and I didn't know what they were. The two PhD/MD doctors must have seen my anxiety peaking so they cut to the chase.

"The Institute is working on some classified research right now." Dr Ellison elaborated, "It's based on a blend of quantum theory and psychology."

"Using science to build a better soldier!" Dr Mori laughed.

"Now Shigeru, that may be one of the results." Dr Ellison winked, "but the results will likely be much more far reaching. We think we can change the way our world is understood. And I'd love for you to be a part of it." he said giving me an encouraging glance.

"I can get a special consideration approved for you," Dr Mori explained, "In lieu of the thesis, you can do independent study with Edwin's team to meet that last graduation requirement."

"It will also be a paid position, with free room and board" Dr Ellison added "and the project will likely last a few years. So you can stay on well past graduation if you like."

"What exactly is the work I'd be doing" I said, realizing it was the first time I'd spoken in some time, and I really have no idea what I was actually being asked to do.

"Unfortunately, I can't tell you that detail here and now. It's all highly classified. And ole Dr Mori over there doesn't have clearance to know about it. But if you're interested, we can start our clearance process. I heard through the grapevine you were already processed through the State Department for something recently, I believe with Dr. Clarke? What we do is much more highly classified so there are a few additional checks, a few more forms to sign and oaths to take. But I promise there will be no body cavity searches involved." He laughed.

"I don't care about the cavity searches" I quipped, "just promise me I won't have to eat rat or monkey!"

"Not unless you want to. To each his own." Dr. Ellison stood, "I need to head to the airport for my flight back to Arlington. Here's a way to contact me." He said, handing me a blank white card with a hand scrawled phone number on it and nothing else. "Just leave a message with your name and if you've decided to join us. I need to know by Friday. That's a hard deadline. That phone number will be disconnected."

"Thanks. I'll be in touch by then for sure." I said.

“I’d really love to have you on the team. I think you bring a unique element that the others don’t have. That’s good for the science. And for the team morale. Never good to have too many pure scientists in a room without a non-scientist to supervise. You know what I mean?!” He laughed. “We’ll talk soon.”

Dr. Ellison politely dismissed himself after shaking my hand. I sat back down and waited while Dr. Mori walked him to the department door. When the professor returned, he closed the door behind him. I was a bit dazed. Lots of questions but not sure where to begin.

“At least I don’t have to talk with you about the Pribram stuff anymore.” He said with a sarcastic smile, drawing my attention back to the moment.

“I don’t even know where to begin. So many questions.”

“Good news is I really can’t answer any of them.” He smiled again. “You’ll basically be excused from the remainder of your classes. We’ll process your grades and confer your degree automatically. You won’t need to do anything else. Like a get out of college free card.”

“I do have my other degree in International Studies. Two classes still have a few weeks left.”

“Don’t worry about those. If Dr Ellison knows about whatever you did with Dr. Clarke, then I’m sure he can encourage Dr. Clarke to give you the same latitude we are. I don’t know about the Clarke thing. Nobody tells me anything. I’m starting to get a little self-conscious about that.”

I laughed, breaking the numbness for a moment with a realization.

“I guess having a major college in the same city as US Central Command at Macdill ensures some crossover for recruitment from both sides.”

“Good observation.” The professor said standing up, “Can I go home now. I’m missing happy hour.”

I laughed again, looking at my wrist. No watch. So I switched my gaze to the clock on the wall. After five o'clock already.

"Thanks" I said standing and making my way to the door. "I really appreciate everything you've done over the years. Sorry for being such a pain in the ass."

"I'm glad you were. You may change the world someday because of it. Now go away and do whatever you do when you're not here."

Arlington, Virgina is really a beautiful place. But not at all what I expected. I think I expected it to be old, with narrow roads and fragile historic buildings. Two friends from high school went to the Naval Academy in Annapolis, not too far away, just on the other side of Washington DC. They always talked about how hard it was to adjust to the old buildings and narrow roads. I guess I just assumed everything around this area would be the same. I couldn't have been more wrong.

The area of Arlington I was brought to is apparently not Arlington at all. It's been known as Crystal City since the late 1970's. It's strategically located within the I-495 Beltway that encircles the Washington DC area. The Zachary Taylor Building, where I was due to meet Dr Ellison in a little over an hour, is in the heart of Crystal City about seven minutes south of the Pentagon Building. I could see the Pentagon on my flight into Reagan National Airport so I was hopeful that I wouldn't be late.

Emerging from the terminal's sliding doors I was breathing in my first hint of seasonal Virginia air when a voice approached.

"Will you need a cab ride sir?"

I shifted my focus from the cherry blossom trees still bursting with blossoms across the way and saw an elderly black man in a perfectly pressed uniform shirt standing a polite distance off to my right.

"We have the cleanest cars, cheapest rates, and will get you anywhere in under an hour."

"I do need a ride. But hopefully it's not far."

"Where to?"

"The Taylor Building, the address is…"

"Oh, I know that address. Are you sure you don't want to just walk? It's real close. You can almost see it from here. Maybe a mile or so right up this road."

"I'm due for a meeting. First time I'm meeting my new coworkers. Probably best if I don't walk in sweaty from a rigorous street hike."

The cab driver, whose shirt had the embroidered name Collins, gave a bit of an exaggerated laugh, "Well alright then. Just trying to save you some money."

He reached toward my bag with a questioning look. I slid the bag off my shoulder and handed it to him.

"Full service." I said, "I'm not used to that."

"Yes sir. Nothing but the best from Friendly Cab." He replied carefully laying the bag in the open trunk and gently closing it without a sound.

I sat on the back passenger side and closed the door behind me. It also made no sound as it closed. There was no creaking of metal door hinges or clinking of loose latches like most cabs. There was no smell in the car. No smell of body odor. No smell of cleaner or air freshener. No new car smell. Though I didn't expect the new car smell given the age of the car. The interior was immaculate. No stray dirt or leaves on the carpets. The upholstery was well nourished with no blemishes or rips.

“It’s a beautiful day to be above ground, even if you’re in a cab” Mr. Collins said making conversation as he checked mirrors and began to navigate our exit from the cab line traffic jam.

“Your name is Collins?” I said, noticing the name on the cab license on the pristine dash that said William Collins.

“Yes sir. But you can call me Collin. I hated my parents most of my childhood for that.” he laughed. “But I got over it. People tried to make a nickname CC stick. But I wasn’t havin’ none of that. Some of my people call me Double C. I guess that started at the family gatherings to tell me apart from my father who they called Big C. The name on my birth certificate is William. My mom just called me Collin or Double C all my life. So it stuck.”

Still scanning the inside of the cab, I saw a looseleaf binder in a pocket on the back of the front seat. It looked like something a student would have, or maybe a businessman’s notes for a presentation. I pulled it out to alert Collin Collins, thinking someone had left it accidentally. But then I read the cover. Above a classic headshot of an older black businessman it read, *Friendly Cab Company…Our History*. Below the headshot was a name, Ralph Collins and the dates 1896-1951.

“Is Ralph Collins a relative?” I asked.

“That’s my father. He started the company. The whole history’s in that binder. But it’s long and we only got about a five minute drive. So I’ll give you the summary.” he smiled at me in the rear-view mirror, making me think the binder was a plant so he could tell the story. He just seemed like the story telling type.

“Back in the 1940’s things weren’t like they are now. Everything was segregated. This was before Rosa Parks refused to give up her seat on the bus. Most black people were fearful, and few would brave confrontations with the white establishment.” He looked back in the mirror again, “and before you ask, yes I’m black” he laughed. “I’ve been black my whole life. Nobody in my family ever referred to us as colored, and we’re several generations deep here in America, not one of us living has ever been to Africa. So we don’t go for the trendy African American thing. We’re just black. Except I got a couple cousins pale as all get out. Not sure what they are." He laughed some more.

"Where was I. I'm getting old and sometimes lose my place." He said finally getting out from under the terminal cover area and onto the airport exit road, ironically named Entrance Road, which wasn't moving much faster.

"Oh yeah. So during segregation us black folks couldn't get anywhere easily. Buses took excessively long to get places and at certain times there weren't enough seats for all the black people. Only a few black seats were reserved at the back of the bus. You might have to wait for two or three busses to stop before a black person could get a seat even when other seats in front were empty. All that time we had to stand exposed to the weather and had to try to ignore the constant instigation of those white college boys trying to start fights. No offense."

"None taken. Just don't ever call me Caucasian American or European American. I'm with you, my family's been here more generations than I can count. I'm white and American, and you're black and American."

"True words." He said continuing, "So my father had a little money he earned and was able to get a car, an old Chrysler. He started driving our neighbors to medical appointments in his free time. Medical appointments were the most difficult. They were usually in very white parts of town where all the doctors' offices were. Because of Jim Crow laws, the blacks weren't allowed to take the white owned cabs into town, not that they would pick anyone up in the black neighborhoods to begin with. It was hard to get doctor appointments and getting a seat on the bus in time was like rolling the dice. Most doctors didn't want to see black folk to begin with. But they were required to. That is unless they found a way out of it. Being late to an appointment was all those doctors needed to justify refusing service. So the bus was never really an option. Word got around that my dad was driving people to appointments. Rumor has it that one of the doctors reported my dad to the feds. They started looking into my dad and asking why the neighbors were always giving him money and doing extra things for him in exchange for the rides. Tax man gotta get his cut you know."

He took a drink of water from a ceramic cup in a cupholder before continuing. "To steer clear of jail, or worse, my father turned the idea into a legit cab company back in 1947. When he died in 1951 the company had a few cars. All Chryslers. Off duty black fire fighters from the fire stations in the black neighborhoods would do the driving. They knew their way around town and where things were. And more than the rest of us, they had a little bit of respect in the community and people didn't harass them so much. Over time that respect rubbed off onto the cab company. Making us one of the safest options to get around at the time. Business boomed. My uncle took over the company when my father died. By neighborhood demand he expanded from medical appointments to giving rides anywhere for any reason. My uncle later transitioned the company to me when I was old enough and ready to take it on. We have about a hundred cars now and lucky for you we don't limit it to the black neighborhoods like we did back then." He laughed, glancing back and confirming I was fully engaged in the story.

"So you own the company? And you're out here doing the driving?"

"Yes sir. That's part of the deal. Never forget your roots. We provide a service and can't ever forget what that means. It's a privilege to serve. But I am getting older now. My son William Jr. is getting ready to take over the business. I hope to fully retire in the next few years. So I only get out occasionally these days. I'm a bit of a people watcher, which is why I like to do these airport runs. Lots of good people watching. And as a bonus I get some satisfaction being able to stand in the crowd and start a conversation with a person like yourself and the fact that I'm black never crosses your mind. Reminds me how far the world has come."

The Friendly Cab pulled over to a building with no distinct features. Just a typical ten-ish story office building you could find on any downtown street. There were no distinct names anywhere on the building, at least not that I could see from where we pulled up. There was just an address over the sliding door entry. The address was right. So I got out. Before I was fully upright, Collin Collins was standing beside me with my bag at the ready.

“Here you go sir. Thank you for choosing Friendly Cab.”

I pulled out my wallet to pay and then realized I had no idea what the fare was. The car didn’t seem to have one of the highly visible fare meters you see on TV shows.

“It was a great ride, and thank you for the history. How much do I owe you?

“No charge on this one. I’m heading to that little place down there on the corner for lunch anyway. This drop off was on the way. Wouldn’t seem right to charge you for that. You have a great trip. Enjoy this weather. It’s nice this time of year.” He said closing the trunk and my door simultaneously, one with each hand. “If you get a chance, I recommend you grab some lunch over there. You won’t be disappointed.”

Before I could argue and try to at least force some tip money to him, Collin Collins had slipped into the car and started off down the block. Halfway down he gave a wave before closing the window. One last courtesy from a man that I was sure always goes above and beyond.

“Good afternoon” I said to an elegantly seated woman wearing a headset at a curved reception desk, “I’m here to see Dr. Edwin Ellison. I’m a little early.”

“He’ll appreciate that. I’ve seen him give some looks to the late ones” she replied with a smile. “I’ll let him know you’re here. You can have a seat right over there” she continued, pointing to a few individual chairs I didn't even notice when I walked in, "It shouldn't be too long."

Only a few minutes later a bell dinged, and an elevator door opened. A man in a dress shirt and slacks came my way.

"Hey! I'm glad you made it! Welcome!" Dr. Ellison beamed.

"Nice to see you again. The trip went pretty smooth. Thanks for making all those arrangements."

"No problem. Let's step outside," he said, and seeing my confusion, expecting to go in not out, he continued "The team is running late, and I missed lunch today. Have you eaten?"

"No. I generally don't eat breakfast and there wasn't anything on the flight."

"Lunch is on me. We've got this great little place right up the street on the corner. You'll love it. The concierge will take care of your bag."

After finishing one of the best sandwiches I'd ever had, Dr Ellison and I made the walk back toward the Taylor Building.

"That place was great. We've got something like it in Tampa called Wright's Deli." I noted.

"Oh yes. I've been to Wright's. We try to get some of our events at Macdill catered by them when we can. Great food. Bozzelli's Deli is a lot like Wright's. Just newer. Only been around a couple years." Dr Ellison said gesturing me toward a side street, "Let's go this way. It's a little closer and keeps us out of that front lobby. It's about to get busy in there."

The side street wasn't really a street. It was more like a pedestrian street. Like Frankin Street back home in downtown Tampa. It was once a street but was since closed off with bollards so only pedestrians and bikes can use it. Franklin street ran several blocks though. This one only ran about half a block, to the back edge of the Taylor building. Making it more like a pedestrian plaza. There were nice entryways into all three buildings surrounding it, not like the back-alley delivery doors I guess I was expecting.

Dr Ellison swiped a badge on the frame of the sliding door, and it opened into a small room with a military guard in a seat next to what appeared to be a metal detector. He stood as we entered.

"Good afternoon Dr Ellison. Good to see you."

"Hello Frank. How is your son doing? He get over that ankle injury yet?"

"Almost. He's trying to be back in shape for the last game of the season. Fingers crossed!"

"Wish him well for me." Dr. Ellison offered looking back towards me following close behind, "He's with me. You'll be seeing a lot of him in the coming months, but he just got here so his credentials are still upstairs in the office. You ok if I vouch for him this time? Or do you need me to have Clarice bring down his identification?"

"Oh no. I'm good. It's been a nice day. No need to bring Clarice down." Frank laughed.

"Thanks Frank. Have a great day."

"You too sir."

Dr Ellison led me through the security arch. It sort of looked like a metal detector but something was different. A little more bulky, and the opening was a lot wider than the detectors at the airport.

"That's some new tech. You'll probably see it in airports in about ten years. It creates an infrared image that gets fed into that computer over there. It has a metal detector too of course. But it also has what we call a sniffer. It can detect chemicals related to bomb devices. The guard can watch the computer screen and see if there's an infrared cool signature shaped like a gun or knife along your belt line and compare it to where the metal detector pinged metal. That's new. Helps them to tell the difference between a sturdy belt buckle and a concealed weapon. Not sure those would be considered different if you asked my grandmother." He laughed, "the computer that runs it is something special. Not something you can get in a cow spotted box from Gateway. That computer alone costs about $40,000. Highest imaging tech, fastest chips, massive memory."

A badge swipe at the other end of the room led us through a door and into a carpeted hallway. Several doorways along the hallway appeared to lead to staircases. And we passed a few single car elevators. All with badge swipe entries. About halfway down the hall there was a bank of windows looking into what appeared to be a security room. Countless monitor screens and several watchers sitting around making notes and pushing buttons.

"Everything around here is hyper monitored. Most of what happens in this building has national security implications of some kind. If anything ever goes wrong, they want to be able to trace it back to where it began. We're gonna take this next elevator on the left."

Badge was swiped and we stepped in. It was a typical elevator inside, except that you had to swipe to be able to press a floor button. Badge was swiped again and the button for the eighth floor was pushed.

"Eight floors is a bit too much for me on the stairs. But if you're up for it, the staircase next to us can get you there. And only there. The staircases are single floor access. Helps for security tracking."

There was no ding or chime when our elevator opened this time. But as we stepped out, I heard an elevator chime off in the distance beyond two ornate wooden double doors.

"The main lobby for the floor is out through those doors. We have a few offices out there where some of the team does therapy work with some of the higher-ranking officers. Back here is all research. Everything you see or hear back here is classified. Don't even repeat a lunch order if you hear it back here." He smiled but with some serious undertones behind his eyes.

I noticed the floors in this hallway weren't carpeted like downstairs. It appeared to be covered with large marble tiles. Nothing fancy looking. But I'm sure it was very expensive. And I'm not sure what purpose it served. You would think sound absorbing carpets would be better for these areas where people are trying to think.

"We have the southern portion of the eighth floor. The hallways are shaped kind of like an H. We're on one of the longer hallways. There are two short hallways connecting between the long hallways. Bathrooms and break rooms are off those shorter hallways. The team suites line the outside of the longer hallways. Each suite has combinations of offices, cubicles, work areas, conference rooms and labs as needed. At the end down here is the administration suite where my office is."

"Welcome back. How was lunch?" a sharply dressed woman asked as we entered the administration suite.

"Wonderful as always. I would have brought you something back you know."

"I know. But I can't be eating that stuff every day. I've gotta be able to pass my PT tests. Is this him?" she pointed.

"This is him. Fresh off the plane and lunched up ready to go."

"I'll go get his credentials and bring them to your office."

"Thanks. That saves us a trip. Right this way." Dr Ellison gestured me toward an open door.

The door led into a roomy but not opulent corner office. There was the expected desk and chairs. A separate seating area with a couch, coffee table and chairs. Both near the windows. And a small conference type table and chairs on the inside with large monitor screens along both walls.

“Have a seat.” He gestured to one of the chairs at the desk as he walked around to his executive chair behind the desk.

“I just realized I have no idea where my bag is. Do I need to go back down and get it?” I asked.

“Nope. They went ahead and took that over to your apartment. It’s a couple buildings over. Nice place. You have two roommates from your team there. Not that you’ll ever see them at the actual apartment the way everyone buries themselves in work around here. We could probably save a lot of money on that by just adding a few futons in the team office suites.”

“I don’t know, there’s a lot to be said for a good night’s sleep in your own bed.” I rebutted.

“True. But it seems we have to lure them back there by stocking the fridge and shelves. The only day they go back is the day after we stock it up.” He laughed. “About that, your roommates will tell you how it works in detail. But generally speaking, you’ll have a list available for the apartment tenants to choose from. It’s mainly toiletry items, chips, snacks and drinks. A few of these guys are hooked on that Jolt Cola stuff. I recommend you steer clear of that.”

“No worries there. I tasted that once. Like syrupy sludge. And one sip gave me what I’m sure was a blood pressure spike. Not my thing.” I said.

“That’s good to hear.” He shifted in his seat, “For actual meals there’s a cafeteria on the ground floor of the apartment building. It’s buffet style but you do have to swipe your card for the items you take for tracking purposes.” He stood up looking toward the door “speaking of cards, here are yours now.”

The woman walked in with a lanyard with two plastic cards on it, a small flip wallet, and a folder and set them down on the desk in front of Dr. Ellison.

“Thank you for getting these for us.”

“Sure. It’s no problem.”

"Are you Clarice?" I asked, noticing I hadn't been introduced.

"Oh god no! Did you tell him I was Clarice?" she said looking somewhat irritated with Dr Ellison.

"No no." he laughed, "I threatened Frank with a Clarice visit to bring his ID if he didn't let us through earlier."

"This is Catherine" he said "She's a little touchy because people tend to switch her name with Clarice's since they both start with C. Catherine is wonderful. We try not to expose newcomers to Clarice on their first day. She can be a bit much."

"Catherine keeps everything going smoothly around here. She's an attorney on the side but don't let that skew what you think of her." He smiled as Catherine nodded an enough-already gesture to him.

"Dr Ellison and I have worked together for over a decade. We know where all the bodies are buried. Figuratively speaking. So others don't mess with us too much. But if they do, I can put on the attorney hat and get them off our backs. Don't take too long signing the papers. The team is waiting to meet you. Better to get to them before they're over caffeinated." Catherine recommended walking closer to the table and gesturing at the paperwork.

"Thanks Catherine." Dr Ellison said as he pulled out a fancy pen, "Let's get to it."

After about twenty minutes of reading and signing papers with words like, national security, treason, imprisonment, etc. Catherine administered the oath which I repeated and swore to uphold.

"Time to meet the team." Dr Ellison said, "Or at least the ones that are here."

We walked briskly down the marbled hall to a set of doors back near the elevator we rode up on. Without pomp and circumstance, the doors were opened, and we walked into a common area. There were couches, chairs and tables for eating. What looked like a TV mounted on the wall in one space. Against a wall in the corner was a bank of hutches with desktop computers humming. People were hunched over three of the computers. No one budged when the door was opened.

"Don't everyone jump up at once." Dr Ellison admonished.

"Oh, sorry. We were just…"

"I know. Working." Dr Ellison said, "Take a break and come meet our newest team member.

"Hi I'm Mel," an energetic twenty-something woman said jumping up from her seat and extending her hand.

"This is Mel Garrett." Dr Ellison added "she and Mr. Jeffrey Osbourne here have been working on something called astral projection, cutting edge stuff. You might have heard of it by another name, lucid dreaming, dreams that feel real, where you feel like you can control what's happening in the dream."

"Hey man. Nice to meet you. Call me Oz" he said in a monotone stoner voice while Mel bounced in place beside him as if a week's supply of caffeine was pent up in the balls of her feet.

"And this is Captain Marcello Guerra. Marcello is one of our Army graduate student researchers."

"Good afternoon sir. Nice to meet you." Marcello said more formally and stiffly than the others. "Call me Marc."

"Marc is putting the final touches on his graduate research project. He knows everything there is to know about the concept of remote viewing. He's been a lead researcher on a number of scientific projects to quantify the phenomenon where a person in one location can somehow describe the layout of a space in another location they've never seen before. You'll usually find him buried behind stacks of unreleased research papers. Turns out there's been a lot of classified research around the world being done on the topic. Our own intelligence gathering agencies find it very intriguing. Though they'll never admit to it. They still refer to it all as parapsychology or pseudoscience."

"They are for now." Marc said, "but when they see the data in my paper they're gonna stroke out."

"We'll see who freaks them out first!" Mel exclaimed as some of the energy left her feet and found her voice. "If you think about it, between us all, this tech we're working on, nothing will be able to stay secret. It will be a whole new world."

"I'm not sure a secret-less society is a great thing. And it's probably not good to make your commanding officers stroke out" Dr Ellison laughed "but there's a lot of good that can come from this. We're just missing that last key part that sews it all together."

I noticed all three immediately turned their gaze to me.

"That's where you come in." Dr Ellison emphasized pointing at me "from our conversations I think you can take all of these puzzle pieces of narratives and turn them into an actual story that makes sense. We need someone that can identify the overarching connection of it all and weave the new ideas in with accepted thinking to create a true theory. Something that can get support of our leaders."

"It won't hurt if it drives funding for more research here." Oz said "I'd much rather work on this stuff than get a real job in some college somewhere teaching Newton's apple to sex crazed hungover freshmen."

"Like you weren't a sex crazed hungover freshman!" Mel blasted.

"I'll give you the sex crazed part. But I was never hungover. I was usually enjoying some other form of altered consciousness." Oz defended, or indited himself, hard to tell.

"You'll be rooming with Oz and Marc when you're here in Crystal City." Dr Ellison continued with my orientation. "But a lot of our work takes place at other sites. So there's some travel involved, and the team often splits up for that."

"Speaking of travel, what's the plan for San Antonio?" Oz asked. "Do we need to start packing?"

"By packing he means does he have to get his laundry done so he has clean underwear!" Mel quipped.

"I think you guys can sit this one out. Your partners at JBSA are gonna be in Zurich for a conference. There's only a skeleton crew there, and the administrative commanders of course." Dr Ellison noted "but since Colonel Johnson is taking a plane that way in a couple days anyway, I figured I'd take our newbie down for a meet and greet. Show him some of what is going on at the research facility and let him have some quality time on the flight with Under-Secretary Johnson."

"Thank God. I really didn't feel like doing laundry." Oz exhaled.

"You never feel like doing laundry." Mel started to lay in, "You should be more like Marc. I think he just wears his clothes once and then throws them out. I never see dirty laundry on his floor."

"I owe that to my drill sergeant at camp. He smelled a sweaty shirt in a footlocker in front of the bunk beside me during an inspection. That soldier may still be crying to this day. Harsh." Marc described, "Any of my dirty clothes get properly hidden away in a hamper and washed as soon as possible. The PTSD is real."

"Alright, alright. Let's not scare off our newcomer with terrifying laundry stories." Dr Ellison laughed. "Colonel Shadrick Johnson is the Under-Secretary of the Army. He's in charge of all the civilian non-military personnel and services contracted with the Army. He's also technically my boss. And he's one of the reasons we have funding to do what we do."

"Excuse me, but what's JBSA?" I asked, realizing they were my first words following the barrage of conversation among the team.

"Sorry about that. We speak in letters a lot around here." Oz said.

“Joint Base San Antonio. It’s a large combined forces base run by the Air Force. It includes Fort Sam Houston where a lot of our work gets done. Some of our cutting edge research facilities are there. And a new high tech behavioral sciences research campus is being built as we speak. Won’t be done for a few years yet though.” Dr Ellison explained.

“It’s hot down there. Plan on sweating the whole time.” Mel said.

“Weather’s hot. But the food is hotter. Tex-Mex. Can’t even get butter down there without some kind of hot pepper ground up in it.” Oz complained.

“Oz has a sensitive stomach from all the…what shall we call them, mind enhancers, he’s ingested over the years?” Marc said and Oz chuckled. “You’ll be fine. Food’s great there. And a little heat helps the beer go down.”

“I’m not sure if I should be drinking my first week here.” I said cautiously, “There’s gotta be a ton I need to catch up on.”

“Well, if you’re on a flight down with the Colonel I’m pretty sure you’ll end up with a beer or two on the plane before you land.” Oz said. “He keeps that executive jet pretty well stocked. You never know who might be on the flight. He uses that thing like a flying taxi service for important people.”

“You kids are lucky,” Dr Ellison added “When I first met the Colonel about twenty years ago, he was pouring everyone tequila shots. I hate tequila. But when he offers you something you have no option but to take it. It’s like a Jedi mind trick. I hope he’s still peddling beer instead of the hard stuff these days.”

“I’m starving. Can we take him back to the apartments now to show him the cafeteria?” Mel whined.

“Mel’s been awake for at least three hours so it’s definitely time for a meal.” Oz joked as Mel gave him a solid punch in the shoulder. “Ow. Easy. That’s my mousing arm.”

“Yeah. I’m sure it’s your computer mouse skills you’re worried about” Mel jabbed.

"Tomayto, Tomahto."

"You guys gotta lay off that Jolt Cola. It's got your blood sugar all out of whack." Dr Ellison said. "Go ahead to the apartments. Get a good breakfast in the morning and be back here by nine tomorrow. We'll start going over everything."

"That reminds me" Mel said hopping over to a table and grabbing a stuffed four inch binder. "We put together some summaries of what we've done. It's all classified stuff so it has to stay here. It mainly shows how I succeeded and Oz crashed and burned."

"Hey!"

"Ok, how we succeeded and how we crashed and burned. Is that better Oz?"

"Well, I would have played up my part a bit more. But ok."

"This is gonna be fun." Marc said "Looks like I'll be playing the role of mediator tonight. We're gonna need to stop and get some more beer."

***

The four of us went down an elevator that opened into the main lobby where I first arrived. The three of them led the way as I followed closely behind. But instead of going out the main entry door the three walked to the left toward an open stairwell off the lobby.

Marc looked back seeing that I fell behind with the unanticipated change of direction.

"We're gonna take the underground. It's this way." Marc said.

"The underground? Like the subway? I thought it was just the next building over?" I said very confused as to why anyone would take the subway for a half block trip on a gorgeous day when the cherry blossom trees are in full bloom.

"The subway system here is called the Metro. The underground is…"

"Shhhh. Let's surprise him!" Mel said, shushing Marc as she hopped the rest of the way down the staircase to a landing with a sliding glass door. "This is the way, hurry now, much to see."

"No not much to see. Straight to the beer and then straight to the apartment." Marc said.

"We'll see" Mel said smiling with a smirk.

The sliding glass door opened as Mel approached. The door was tinted somewhat so it didn't offer a good visual as to where we were going until it opened. But when it opened, I was bombarded with an odd combination of lights and sounds. The lights were somewhat neon, like you might see in a bowling alley, but not as harsh. The sound was an almost echoing low rumble, like a group of people having a conversation in nearby room. The ground was, what, cobblestone maybe? Looking up I saw what appeared to be shops, like a village center lining both sides of a, yes, cobblestone…street? Floor? Hallway? There was ambient lighting near the ceiling which helped tone down the fluorescent lights near thc shops and made it appear like any main street USA at dusk. The ceiling looked very industrial, with pipes and vents. But it was all painted a matching color to help it disappear and keep your focus on the more well-lit shop entrances below. The entrances all had architecture to look like they were independent buildings along a main street. It felt old, new, American, and European all at the same time. It was actually pretty amazing.

"We're kind of at the south end, so it's a little darker down here. The main stores are just up this way." Mel said with a little gleam in her eye.

"Mel, we're not here to shop, just to the grocery to get beer." Marc reminded her.

“This is an underground mall” Mel continued, “It runs under most of this part of Crystal City. It connects to all the major buildings, the hotels and a couple residence buildings, including our apartments. The parking garage is actually above us, between the mall and the ground floor of the buildings. There’s a lot more people up on the street today because it’s so nice out. But when it’s cold or rainy this mall is packed with people going to and from work or lunch or whatever. Then there’s the people that just come here to shop.”

“There’s a grocery and a liquor store right below our apartment.” Marc added, trying to keep everyone on course.

“And there’s a bunch of boutique shops, antique shops, clothing stores, and a radio shack for Oz.” Mel said looking back while bouncing ahead of us, “and lots of food spots!”

“Definitely a lot of good food down here.” Marc said, “but we need to show him the cafeteria upstairs. We should eat there.”

“Free food is always better” Oz said.

“Fine. Losers.” Mel succumbed.

The grocery was small, but slightly larger than the other shops around it. Its main products were obviously staple foods, which it had in abundance. There weren’t a lot of brands to choose from, but there was at least one brand of most things you might need in a fridge or cabinet. The beer fridge took up a large portion of the store. Still not a lot of brands, but ample volume.

“Coors is king around here these days, now that they ship it east of the Mississippi.” Marc said grabbing a cold case “You ok with Coors?”

“Doesn’t matter to me.” I said. “I don’t see things like bread or deli meats.”

“The shops down here have some kind of agreement not to step on each other’s toes.” Oz said. “There’s only liquor in the liquor store because the beer is here. There’s no deli stuff here because there's a deli shop a couple shops up the way. Same with bread, there's a bakery next to the deli. So no bread here."

"It's a little bit of a hassle because it's not a one stop shop experience." Marc noted, "but it has that traditional neighborhood feel, you know like up in the northeast where you get your meat from a butcher and bread from a bakery."

"It's a bit more pricey than the regular stores. But the big grocery stores are across town. It's worth the extra cost so I can walk and don't have to drag my car out of the garage and fight traffic across town and back." Oz said. "Besides, most of our stuff is free upstairs, so our trips down here are just a bonus."

"They won't buy us beer though. So we make a trip down here more often than we should." Marc laughed looking over at Mel who was disinterested in the grocery talk, gazing across the hall at a beach themed clothing store. "We just need to keep sister-shops-a-lot in check, or we could get stuck down here for hours!"

"There are a couple cafés that serve beer on their patios. So Marc and I can relax while Mel tries on every pair of socks in the mall." Oz giggled, suggesting some backstory there.

"Oh shut it Oz." Mel said, then looking to Marc "are we done yet? Please tell me you're not paying with loose change again."

"Nope. Real paper money this time."

"Marc refuses to get with the times and pay with his card." Mel jabbed.

"You pay your way. I'll pay my way." Marc replied collecting his change from the cashier.

"You're like an old woman with those pockets full of spare change. Got any unwrapped candy in there?" Mel jabbed some more.

"If I had candy in my pockets I wouldn't be able to keep you out of them." Marc rebuffed.

"It would take more than candy and seventy three cents in pennies and nickels to get me into your pants!" Mel said, opening the door and heading toward the apartment stairwell, ending the battle of wits for the moment.

"Here's another quarter" Oz offered to Marc, "That might be enough."

Marc and Oz laughed as the three of us made our way to the stairwell behind Mel.

The apartment was just an apartment. Nothing really special about it other than each bedroom in the fourteen story building had its own key locked door for individual security. The plainness of it was somewhat surprising given that the lobby was so opulent it could give the Waldorf Astoria a run for the money. The massive lobby was a collection of separate gathering spaces with plush area rugs over marble floors, oversized chairs, and deep sofas filled with throw pillows. Lots of deep red colors. Everything was accented by polished brass lamps, rails, light fixtures, signage and chandeliers. Together the deep red and brass made it feel somewhat royal. I'm sure that was the intent. There was even a formal dining room with long carved wood tables that could easily sit twenty guests each. The dining room was available for residents to reserve when not rented for other parties.

The trip from the lobby up to the apartment was a tale of two worlds. The lobby was the very flashy outward persona of the building. The apartments were the behind the scenes working class persona of the building. Simple. Functional. Not flashy. Some of the apartments had a very nice view over the Potomac River, the parks along the river and the airport. This apartment overlooked the single story portion of the building along Clark Street. The single story area had a lot of operational spaces like the laundry, storage and the cafeteria. But the roof of that space had a pool and spacious pool deck entertaining area. It wasn't elegant looking from this higher view. But I could see how it could be nicely decorated for fancy events.

“The pool isn’t open yet.” Oz said walking up behind me through the open balcony door “It was supposed to open last week but we had a burst of cold weather late in the season. I think there was a sign for it opening next week.”

“That’s strange to me.” I said “Where I live in Tampa, private pools never close. Some of the public ones do, but even those only close for about a month.”

“They brought your bag up and set it in your room.” Marc said joining Oz and I on the balcony “Your key is in your bedroom door. It opens the main door to the apartment and your bedroom.”

“We won’t be offended if you wanna lock up your room since you don’t know us” Oz said, “but we really only lock ours up when we leave town.”

“I don’t really have anything valuable in there. Unless my underwear’s in jeopardy on one of Oz’s laundry days.”

“Boxers or briefs” Oz replied.

“Boxer-briefs. Only the trendiest for me these days.” I said.

“Just kidding” Oz said, “It doesn’t matter. I don’t wear underwear most days anyway.”

“Oh God. More info about Oz no one needs to know!” Marc said. “Let’s go eat before Mel polishes off the good desserts. I don’t want to be stuck with that weird pudding again.”

The cafeteria was just a cafeteria. Access was from a long hallway off the main lobby. The hallway, though decorated with paintings and intermittent decorative tables with flowers nearer to the lobby, became downright institutional by the time you got toward the cafeteria. The soft sounds of background piano music gave way to the typical clinking and clanking of cafeteria workers refilling buffets and dropping forks and plates in the bussing bins. The smell of clean floors and wood polish gave way to a potpourri scent of competing food types, some kind of fish, some grilled meat, probably hamburgers, and lots of fried things. There were a lot of people moving around the tables and buffet spaces. But the room was maybe only about half full.

"Small crowd today. Everyone must be taking advantage of the nice weather." Marc said.

"23rd Street, up off the lobby, has a bunch of restaurants and bars. People that have been couped up all winter go sit on those outside patios for dinner the first nice days of the year." Oz added.

"This place has been packed this winter. A few times we couldn't get seats and had to take food to go." Marc said. "There's Mel."

Mel was already seated. Two plates sat in front of her. A salad piled high with about everything you could put on a salad. And a plate of assorted dessert pie slices, mini cakes and cookies. She waved to let us know where she was. Marc gestured to the line to let her know we were getting food first.

There was a good assortment of food separated into different serving tables. There was the salad bar that Mel's giant salad extraction didn't even put a dent in. There was a sandwich table with several types of premade subs and sandwiches with assorted toppings that could be added. The hot table area had burgers, hot dogs, fried chicken, fried fish, and baked fish for the health conscious. There was a pan of something Italian that may have been lasagna or baked ziti. No one had cut into it yet, so it was unidentifiable, just a massive layer of baked cheese across the top. There were some basic sides like mac and cheese, French fries, mashed potatoes and a variety of vegetables. A dessert table with ample desserts despite the pile on Mel's plate. At the end there was a table with coffee and tea urns. A small table with water pitchers. And finally, a glass fronted fridge of assorted soft drinks.

After making our selections we approached a sweet older lady at a cash register. We handed her our badges in turn, and she tallied our meals.

"Here you go boys. Have a great night." She said handing back the last badge as we moved past.

On the counter was a flyer announcing a Taco Tuesday Mexican Fiesta and Wok and Roll Thursday.

"I get Taco Tuesday. But what's Wok and Roll?" I asked Oz in front of me as we made our way to the table.

"A hodge podge of Asian stuff. They always have the burgers and stuff like today. But some days each month they have themed foods. The Asian days have stir fry stuff, noodle dishes like pad thai, fried rice, lo mein, eggrolls, that kind of stuff. The roll reference in the name is for sushi. I haven't braved that yet. This cafeteria doesn't seem like the right place to eat raw fish. Mexican day is tacos, burritos and nachos. They have a BBQ day too, but that's usually during the summer months. It's good. Ribs, pork, chicken."

"This is kinda cool." I said referencing the whole free cafeteria situation as I sat down.

"It is. I hope it stays." Mel said.

"There have been rumors for years that this whole single story portion along Clark St is going to be divided off and sold for retail stores." Marc explained. "Success of the ground floor business on the other 23rd Street side has them seeing dollar signs. Not sure what that would mean for our little free setup here. We'd probably be stuck with a stipend or something."

"That won't happen anytime soon. The government has a long lease on the Taylor and Polk buildings. And this cafeteria mainly serves them. I doubt they would let it go away. You know how the Army loves its cafeterias." Oz said, smiling at Marc.

"It's better than the Navy food. You should see what they serve on those ships!" Marc rebutted.

After some light conversation, mainly about the history of the Crystal City area and seasonal differences between our hometowns, our meals were finished, and we headed back upstairs.

"We're not going back to the cafeteria for breakfast?" I asked as the three of us finished our morning routines.

"Nope. We usually get to Taylor between seven and eight. Since the boss gave us until nine today, and specifically mentioned breakfast when he dismissed us yesterday, we decided to take you out for a treat." Marc said.

"There's an awesome diner not too far away. Been around since the 1920's. And they are known for their breakfast." Oz added. "Stacks of pancakes like you wouldn't believe. Made to order with any add-ins you want. You name it…bananas, strawberries, chocolate chips. I get mine with chocolate chips and crumbled bacon. Real maple syrup and butter on top. So good!"

"Oz, how are you still alive?" Marc joked.

"No idea. But of all the things that should get me, I think my hearty breakfast habits are pretty far down the list."

"One of these days David Letterman will have a *Top Ten Things Likely to Kill Oz* list." Marc quipped.

"Well, he'd better hurry up before one of them actually gets me." Oz laughed "Now let's get going. Bob and Edith's Diner needs my patronage!"

Bob and Edith's was great. A true diner. And definitely a hearty breakfast. But now, about fifty pages into skimming the big binder summary, I could barely keep my eyes open. I could definitely see why the team favored the double caffeinated Jolt to keep them going. Just then, as I was reading, something caught my eye. A pattern in the studies they were doing. I didn't want to say anything yet. I wanted to run something past Marc first.

"Hey Marc?" I said as Marc looked up from his computer station, "For the work that you've been doing on remote viewing, how did you choose your research participants? Was it random? Did you look for certain traits? Or just took anyone that signed up?"

"A few different ways." Marc said shifting his chair toward me. "Some of the studies were random selections of enlisted soldiers, but the main ones used psychic professionals, or those who claimed to be psychic, you know palm readers at the fair, psychics, psychic hotline services. A disproportionate number of them came from the New Orleans area. They must have told each other about it in their sewing circles. Why do you ask?"

"I was reading the binder, granted I'm only a little ways into it, but I kept seeing a pattern in the way participants were chosen. They were always referred to as *healthy* males or females with *no known medical diagnoses*." I said, "Did you screen your participants like that too?"

"We did. Both of our projects required subjects to be screened by a medical doctor to be sure there weren't any underlying medical conditions that might confound the results."

"Even the random ones? Did the random soldiers get screened? And if something showed up, were they not included in the study?"

"Well, yeah. Everyone in the studies had a clean bill of health and weren't on any medications."

"Hey Oz, Mel, can you guys pop over here for a sec?" I called into the neighboring room where they had their work spread out.

"What cha need?" Mel asked, genuinely wanting to assist in some way though she had no idea why I was calling out to them.

"Were all of your research subjects healthy? No medical issues, drug use, family history of mental illness, things like that." I asked.

"Of course. They all have clean medical exams. That was protocol." Mel noted.

"And your results all mainly fell within a bell curve for success but with no predictability as to who would be successful or why?" I asked.

Both Mel and Marc nodded as Oz finally walked in.

"Tell me about Joint Base San Antonio. Why is the bulk of work being done down there?" I asked.

"Subject change much?" Mel quipped.

"Not as much as you think," I replied. "What is it about JBSA?"

"For starters it's a big base. Lots of people to choose from. Most of them are on base for a pretty long time in active duty terms, it's a stable station for them. That's good for us because they can be a part of the longer studies." Marc described.

"Anything else?" I probed.

"It's a big medical facility. So there's a lot of the expensive equipment we need. And they have a lot of good spaces where we can do the interviews and experiments." Marc finished.

"And the inpatient psychiatric facility is there. Treating a lot of psychiatric and psychological issues. So, it hides us good on paper since Dr Ellison, as head of Psychology, would be expected to have his teams going back and forth between here and there." Mel offered. "To help keep the actual research confidential and not raise red flags."

"Did you ever include any of the psychiatric inpatients in the studies?" I asked.

"Definitely not. They wouldn't meet the study criteria protocol." Marc said.

"I think you may be leaving out a key demographic." I began, trying not to sound critical of their work to date. "Let me throw an idea out for discussion. Bear with me for a minute, it's kind of hard to explain."

My concept was pretty hard to explain probably because it was only half baked in my head at the time. I started by sharing a bit of my background in psychology and how the work of Pribram got me interested, knowing they were very familiar with Pribram's work by now. That seemed like the right starting point.

"So Pribram's idea is that the brain operates like a hologram. All information from all the senses at any one point in time converges in the brain. And the resulting wave patterns from the sensory inputs interacting with each other are what the brain records as memories, some conscious, some not. And that later, when a new experience interacts closely enough with that imprinted wave pattern, the original memory is evoked. This is why a certain smell of perfume can remind you of a certain person." I made eye contact to make sure they were still with me, and they nodded to continue.

"But the big question then was why does the perfume remind you of a person instead of the ingredients of the perfume. Why an ex-girlfriend that wore rose scented perfume instead of just a memory of a rose bush. Especially if you smelled a rose bush much more recently than your ex."

"True. That's where Pribram brought quantum theory in." Oz added.

"Exactly." I confirmed. "Quantum concepts like entanglement and tunneling solved that linear time quandary. It made perceived recency a part of the equation, but made its actual importance variable. Why?"

"It removed the single universe linear model and incorporated a multiverse model instead. Using the multiverse concept, in a portion of the universes the subject may have been with the ex-girlfriend more recently than smelling the rose bush." Oz went on. "And even considering an infinite number of universes there are a portion where the girlfriend is not an ex. Or where the subject never met the girl in the first place."

"And then we take the leap to entanglement." I continued "The wave pattern creating the memory for the subject is not only impacted by what he perceives directly around him in *this* universe, but also by wave particles that are entangled with other particles in other universes."

"And that explains the phenomenon of…" I began.

"Why people may behave contrary to their own desires and judgement." Oz finished. "But this isn't really new. How does it change what we're trying to do here?"

"Bear with me. This may sound bizarre but it's the only way I can visualize it to explain it." I said, now entering more sensitive territory where I could completely embarrass myself with my ignorance.

"Have you guys seen those glass balls with the electric sparks in them that follow your fingers when you touch them? They always have them at Spencer's in the malls. And I always stop and fidget with them, moving the spark around."

"Yep. A plasma ball. Those are cool." Marc said

"Do you notice that when you touch them the bolt of electricity doesn't come straight to your finger? It kind of zigs and zags, like a bolt in the sky during a storm?" I asked, seeing the nods.

"And did you notice that there are other less dense bolts too, some that reach the surface and others that disappear." I continued seeing nods again. "And there are offshoots from the main bolt as well."

"So here's my giant leap." I said, somewhat hesitating now even though they seemed fully engaged.

"If you were to freeze it in time, for lack of a better description, and take a perfectly straight hair thin rod and stick it into that plasma ball so one end is where the bolt started in the core, and the other is where it hit the outside surface at your finger…making the centerline of the expected path…the actual zig zagging bolt doesn't ever actually touch that centerline except at two points, the beginning and the end. And probability shows that the bolt and its off shoots are more likely to be farther away from the centerline than near it."

I could see Oz's brain starting to churn through the idea, or at least where he was thinking I was going with the idea.

"Now before you get too far into thought about this let me explain some more of it." I said walking to a sitting area and dropping myself into a chair. The three others also sat.

"Using probability, and again time, for lack of a better construct. Assume that plasma ball is made up of an infinite number of surface layers nestled inside each other like those Russian nesting dolls. Each surface is a point in time. Given where the bolt was in the prior surface, you can use probability to guess where it might land on the next surface layer. A bolt moving toward your finger has a higher probability of hitting the next layer in the direction of your finger than it does in the completely opposite direction. But you don't know exactly where. Which is why true prediction is impossible in my opinion."

"Ok. So where does that take us?" Oz said, trying to stick with my thought flow and not drift too far into his own.

"Now think of the point on each layer where the bolt hits. And make that point a new core. Where a new bolt would start. It starts a new branch of universe."

"So in essence, what we need to look for isn't the rod it's the individual point on the layer." Oz said.

"Yes. And I think the rod is what you've been looking for with your perfectly structured studies and medically flawless patients. The rod would represent the invariable straight logical path between two points, call it cause and effect. I think you need to look at the variances away from the rod to find what you're looking for."

“How do we do that? Mel asked “If you take away those controls the science isn’t sound.”

“Don’t yell at me when I say this. But…” I hesitated “Is that rigid adherence to science more necessary than the end result?”

“But…” Mel started and then abruptly stopped seeing a gleam in Oz’s eyes.

“It was right there the whole time. I can’t believe we didn’t think of it.” Oz said.

“What was right there?” Marc said with Mel nodding.

“An inpatient psychiatric facility.” I said smiling “with lots of people who are known to have sensory variances that fall…off the rod…so to speak.”

“Schizophrenics!” Mel said.

“Bingo.” I said pointing to her. “My personal theory is that hallucinations, heavily present in schizophrenia and other psychiatric disorders are actually fledgling attempts of our brain to evolve. Evolving to be able to grasp more than one universe at a time. Their senses are hearing actual voices and seeing actual things, just in a different universe, so it doesn’t make sense to them in ours and to us it appears they are responding to something that isn’t there. They are more likely to be directly interacting in that variance area around the rod. Right now, with current thinking of the world, the goal is somewhat stringently to get them to stop hallucinating and get back to the narrow rod. But what if…”

Oz jumped in “What if we started with schizophrenics and tried to increase access to the hallucinations for our studies instead of trying to create hallucinations in healthy subjects. Expand the rod. That’s brilliant! And I can’t believe I didn’t personally think of it, ya know!”

Oz leapt up and went to the phone on the desk, grabbing the receiver and dialing a memorized extension.

“Dr Ellison, It’s Oz. I think we all need to be going to JBSA with you tomorrow.”

***

“Quite a crowd we’ve got today” Colonel Johnson said laughing as he walked up to our group waiting in the private hanger, “I’m gonna need to requisition a bigger plane.”

“Good morning Colonel.” Dr Ellison offered, “Colonel, this is the young man I spoke with you about yesterday. Turns out he’s already had an idea so good we needed to bring some of the gang down to San Antonio. You remember Marc and Oz. Mel couldn’t make it today. Not enough seats.”

“She didn’t get her laundry done.” Oz said under his breath to Marc as they both snickered.

“Good to see you again Marc, Oz. And nice to meet you. Dr. Ellison says a lot of great things about you.” Colonel Johnson said shaking my hand and making good eye contact that maybe lasted a smidge too long.

“Thank you sir. A pleasure to meet you.” I replied.

“This is Joe Fischer.” Colonel Johnson gestured to the man beside him, “Joe was the head of the Political Sciences Department at Oklahoma State until a few years ago. He’s been working with a law firm here in DC and doing adjunct lectures at Georgetown. He may be interested in taking over my position when I retire. I wanted to give him a tour of JBSA. Lots of crazy shit happening down there. Can’t have him going into this decision thinking it’s all rainbows and unicorns.”

“Good to know about the dark, seedy underbelly before I sign the lease.” Fischer laughed. “It’s a pleasure to meet you all.”

“We can talk more on the plane.” the Colonel said “we don’t want the beer to get warm.”

Oz looked at me, smiled and nodded toward an airman carrying a cooler onto the plane.

“We’ve got two new ones, Pete’s Wicked Ale and Lowenbrau, both won medals at the Great American Beer Festival this year.” The colonel boasted. “And something called Coors Light, not sure what that is but people keep talking about it. Not sure if the whole diet beer trend will stick around but I think altogether I brought enough beer to make the flight down with a Poly Sci professor tolerable.”

Everyone made their way onto the small-ish executive jet. Marc stayed up front nearer Colonel Johnson, likely because it would be helpful for his Army career to develop that relationship. Oz and I loaded up at the end. We didn’t want to accidentally miss-seat ourselves and generate some kind of drama.

When we got into the cabin, there were a few forward facing seats up front, but most of the seating toward the rear was bench seating on each side facing each other. The forward seats were taken by the flight staff. Dr Ellison and Marc sat across from the Colonel and Fischer on the bench seats. Others filled in around so there were only two seats left. One at the far end away from everyone important. The other immediately next to Fischer.

Oz, jumped in front of me when I hesitated at the entry, and made his way to the far seat. Leaving me the seat in the conversation group with Dr Ellison, the Colonel, Marc and Fischer.

Maybe the beer is a good idea, I thought feeling my anxiety ratchet up.

Anxiety aside, the flight was unremarkable. The conversation was utterly polite and generic. Lots of *where are you from, that sounds great, do you know so-and-so*, and other pleasantries. There were a few interesting hometown stories told by the Colonel. No national secrets or other important comments entered the dialogue. I tried all three beers. The Pete's Wicked Ale was wonderful. I needed to remember that next time we went shopping. The other two I politely choked down.

You would think a massive multi-branch military base run by the Air Force would have runways on base. Nope. Apparently the JBSA runways we were using were in an annex about twelve miles away on the other side of San Antonio city proper. I didn't know this when I elected to skip the restroom line right when we landed, thinking I was a few minutes from a much nicer restroom option. But we had a little bit of a drive in San Antonio traffic to get to the base. The Colonel referred to it as a scenic tour. All I knew was after three beers on the plane my bladder was painfully full as we sat in traffic for nearly an hour to go that twelve miles. And the tiny transport bus, though big enough to comfortably seat us all, was not large enough to have its own bathroom. My brain pre-occupied with the bladder pain, wasn't very attentive to the tour.

Apparently, I wasn't the only one in misery. When we finally got parked at the actual base, Marc and Oz eagerly strode off the bus and into the main bathrooms at the command center. I followed closely. I didn't realize then the oddity that the three youngest men went rushing for the restroom and not the three older men in their fragile prostate years.

"If we would have hit one more bump I would have popped." Oz said.

"Yep. We were waiting so long at the check in gate there I was about to ask if I could go over to visit Pat the Horse!" Marc said.

"Pat the Horse?" I asked, "Is that like gotta see a man about a horse?"

"Ha. Not normally. But this time maybe. I absolutely would have visited a nearby tree!" Oz said as we all finished washing up and headed back out toward the others.

"Pat the Horse is a local legend." Marc continued "Back in 1912 the Cavalry trained here using actual horses. Pat was a thoroughbred horse that everyone loved. Usually, after a few years of training time the horses were decommissioned, stripped of their rank and slaughtered or sold to farms for breeding. But Pat was so loved by everyone that the calvary soldiers went to Washington and demanded that he be allowed to live out his days on base with them. A reluctant Congress succumbed to public pressures and agreed. In 1953 when Pat died at the old age of 45, he was buried in a grave up near the Cunningham entrance where we came in. Fancy marble headstone with his portrait on it. And four horseshoes embedded in concrete. Rumor has it they were his last shoes, but I'm not sure if that's true."

Dr Ellison walked our way as the other men headed toward a different building.

"The Colonel and his guests are heading off for some meetings. We need to get you guys registered and then we'll have a few days to ourselves on base." Dr Ellison said motioning with his finger for us to follow him. "The airmen took our bags over to the usual base hotel. So we can grab some lunch and then head straight to the research center or the inpatient hospital, whichever you prefer."

"Not sure there's much to do at the research center until after we see what the situation is at the hospital." Oz said.

"Sounds like a plan." Dr Ellison said opening the door and letting the military base scented building air hit us as we walked in.

Buildings on military bases, just like hotels, prisons and schools, have distinct smells. This building was air conditioned, if you can call a few degrees below the ambient outside temperature air conditioned. It may have even been the same temperature as outside but just felt a tiny bit cooler without the direct penetrating Texas sunlight. Either way, I could physically feel the sweat evaporating off my skin as I walked in.

The check-in was otherwise uneventful. Dr Ellison was given keys to a generic white Ford government car with JBSA emblems on the front doors and a black inventory number on the rear bumper. It seemed like the car was overkill and we could have walked or used a golf cart or something to get around. Well, that was what I thought before we actually started driving.

I used to think Macdill AFB back in Tampa was a large base. It could be a long walk between the main destination areas of Macdill, and I wouldn't want to do even a short walk there in the warmer months. At less than 6,000 acres, Macdill is tiny compared to the over 46,000 acres of JBSA. And even the cooler months at JBSA are hot by comparison. So, a car, with AC, it is!

"Our first stop will be Medical Command, what we call MEDCOM" Dr Ellison said, clarifying the terminology for me, "We'll get everyone some specialized credentials to make access to the usually off limits areas much easier. I'll need to spend a few minutes schmoozing Dr. Belkin, the director of CDID, the Capability Development and Integration Directorate. He usually has a couple weeks to process us in. I'm sure he's pissed since he probably didn't hear about us all coming until this morning when he got my message."

"Sorry about that" Oz apologized. "We didn't know until after our talk yesterday."

"I know. No worries. But I think he was planning to get some R&R this week while everyone on his team is at that conference. Nothing like waking up to an urgent call back to the office on your vacation." Dr Ellison explained. "I'll take him out for a good dinner and a nice bottle of wine and he'll be fine. But just be aware he may be cranky when we get there."

"Will we be able to get into the labs if no one's here?" Marc asked.

"The new badge operated security system should allow us access. That's one of the reasons we need to stop at MEDCOM. Our older badges have been upgraded so we'll need to swap them out."

"And we will have access to SUPERDOC?" Oz asked Dr Ellison then looking to me "SUPERDOC is the big fast computer they use here. It can query a massive number of documents, even handwritten notes from medical charts. It can do overnight what it would take us months to look through and sort manually."

"Yep. There should be a card reader that will accept the badge and let you in." Dr Ellison affirmed.

As we entered MEDCOM, we could see that Dr. Belkin was a little more than cranky. We tried to avert our eyes as Dr Ellison bore the brunt of a flurry of foul language and arm gestures. It might have been more frightening if Dr Belkin wasn't a truly tiny man. At about five foot two and a hundred pounds soaking wet with a brick in his pocket, Dr Belkin's voice and arm gestures seemed more like a tantruming pre-teen than a grown man dressing down a fellow professional.

"You're damn right you're taking me to dinner! My Choice. And whatever I want off the menu. And as much wine as I can drink!" we heard Dr Belkin say as his rage began to acquiesce. "Pick me up at my place. 7pm sharp. Barbara will get you what you need. Now get the hell out of here before I change my mind."

Barbara indeed got us what we needed, handing each of us a number of badges on a lanyard. She'd obviously been in early getting them made for us. We thanked her profusely as we accepted them, knowing she was really the one inconvenienced by our request.

"We need to get her something to thank her," Marc said as the door closed behind us. "Chocolates, flowers, something."

"Wine or booze might be more appropriate." Oz said, "Candy might just remind her of her oompa loompa boss."

We all snickered at the visual. But we agreed we needed to pitch in and get her something nice.

***

We approached our main destination, the Brooke Army Medical Center. BAMC was on the far eastern portion of the base nestled against I-35 where it meets I-410. It's a sprawling complex of medical office buildings, support services and the main hospital with all its expansions over the years.

"I don't think any of you have ever been to this inpatient psychiatric floor." Dr Ellison said, "It's on the sixth floor of the new combined service tower they call COTO. The pediatric center is on the first floor, so don't be alarmed when you see a bunch of kids on the way in."

Upon entering the first floor lobby, the receptionist directed us to a private staff elevator bank. Dr Ellison's badge swipe got us in, and a second badge swipe allowed him to select the sixth floor.

"When the doors open we'll be in a secure staff only area behind the nurse's station. We'll have access to some space there to meet with staff and to review some charts. Under no circumstances are any of you to wander out onto the main floor without me. If we go out on the floor, we'll need a thorough pat down to make sure none of us have anything dangerous on us. And we'll need to coordinate to have a couple of the jumbos with us."

"Jumbos?" I asked.

"The big body builder orderlies." Dr Ellison said. "The people on this ward are all trained killers. And they're unstable. These aren't the kookie old ladies you find in other psych wards. If one of these patients perceives you as a threat, you could be dead by their bare hands before you can count to three. Most of the rooms are locked. But there's a lot going on and people going in and out, being transferred for tests or medical care. Just keep your eyes open."

I'm not sure what I expected, but when the doors opened there was total silence. It was so quiet you could hear the scrawl of the pen as the nurse seated at the counter was updating patient charts.

"Oh. Hello Dr Ellison. I didn't know you were going to be visiting." The nurse said, clearly familiar with him "what brings you to see us today?"

"Hello Mary. How are you doing?" Dr Ellison inquired. "Everything good with those grandkids?"

"The little ones are doing great. The oldest is going into middle school. She's still wonderful with her ole grandma, but she and her mother are not getting along. I can't tell which one is most angry these days." Mary laughed. "I just lend a listening ear and let them both vent to me. Then try to take one or the other out for a meal or dessert or something. Just to give them a breather from each other."

"Spot on for the teenage years" Dr Ellison laughed "How's your husband?"

"He's still an idiot. He started playing in some old retired man's rugby league. There isn't a part of his body that's not wrapped in some kind of brace during the matches. He looks like a robot with all those straps and brackets. Then he gets home and whines for a week about how everything hurts."

"Those retired calvary guys, always looking for new ways to push the limits." Dr Ellison acknowledged. "Could be worse, he could be staying home and fixing up the house."

"Don't you dare wish that upon me!" Mary laughed. "So what can we do for you guys."

"We have kind of an odd request. Oz, can you explain to Mary what we need?"

"Hi Mary, it's nice to meet you." Oz said, "How many patients do you have on the floor?"

"About 60 at any one time. A little more during the stressful holidays or when the weather's bad."

“How many of those have a psychotic disorder with prevalent hallucinations?”

“Prevalent hallucinations? Maybe two or three. A few others are intermittent. Most of the people in here are dealing with PTSD, depression, suicidal ideation or rage issues.”

“That jives with the statistics. I think only about two percent of those seeking mental health care get the hallucination based psychotic diagnoses.” Oz said.

“You know, there’s recent data that more than a third of healthy individuals have experienced hallucinations.” Dr Ellison offered “Not to the point that it debilitates them but it’s enough to make them talk to a professional about it.”

“We were hoping to capture those in our studies before. But I think when the hallucinations are so intermittent it’s too difficult to properly time the testing. We couldn’t get a large enough sample size for the data to matter.” Oz dismissed. “Mary, are any of those two or three patients able to follow directions when they’re actively hallucinating? Obviously, they may be very distracted, but are they able to respond to you verbally, or walk where you tell them, sit when you tell them, that kind of thing?”

“Not these three. They need to be physically moved by us. Can’t follow any directions. Totally off in their own world. Not sure they can even hear us.” Mary said.

Oz nodded, getting a dejected look on his face.

“But there was this one guy.” Mary recalled “he’s very high functioning when he’s on his meds. Has a job. Talking to him you would think he was a college professor or something. But about once a year for some reason he goes off his meds. He ends up here for a couple weeks to get the meds restabilized and then he’s discharged. He’s actively hallucinating when he comes in but still listens to our directions pretty good.”

“That’s perfect” Oz said perking up, “Could we see his chart?”

"Sure. I just need to ask a few people around here if they remember what his name was. My memory isn't that great these days."

***

"Mary was right. I think this is our guy." Oz said looking through the chart. "And better yet, I think I have a way we can find more like him using SUPERDOC."

"How's that?" I asked.

"We can query SUPERDOC to look through all the hospital records to find patients with psychotic diagnoses and compare that to the delta of the GAF scores, for when they arrived and when they were discharged. Global Assessment of Functioning scores tell how debilitated they are, what they can and cannot do reasonably normally. From things like basic hygiene all the way up to being able to follow complicated directions like you would need to hold a job. Those with a similar diagnoses and similar improvement of their GAF score range, probably have a similar presentation."

"So, we're not really looking for anyone that's hospitalized here today?" Dr Ellison asked.

"At first I thought we would be. But this makes more sense. Only down side is we would need to find them. Not being here and all." Oz said.

"And then convince them to come back here and stop taking their meds for a while." Marc added.

"And that." Oz agreed. "Once we get the numbers down a bit, we can look through the charts. Maybe there will be some patterns of admissions we can use. We can try to work with their brain's timing. We can ask to be alerted if they come into the hospital here."

“Maybe one or two at a time, over the next year we maybe get ten participants.” Marc said doing some math in his head. “I think that will work for my stuff on remote viewing. It will get me a large enough sample to compare with the other research going on. But that probably doesn’t work for you and Mel.”

“No.” Oz again agreed. “But if we piggy back on your sample we can use any successes to compare to a separate sample. For that second sample, maybe we reach out to the group Dr Ellison mentioned. The thirty percent of otherwise healthy people that have admitted to some form of hallucination to a professional but are never dysfunctional or officially diagnosed as psychotic. That’s a big group. I’m sure we would get a lot of them that have had vivid dream experiences that could be a basis for lucid dreaming. I think it could work.”

“I think the hallucinations while awake, and the lucid dreaming while asleep may be more related than you originally thought.” I offered “And I think if these studies are coordinated right, it may show that relationship not only between the two conscious states, but also between anchoring in one universe and bridging to another.”

After a year of research, Marc’s data supporting remote viewing was even stronger than we anticipated. Under different conditions, several subjects were able to produce drawings reasonably similar to items or spaces that exist elsewhere but with which the subjects were not familiar. The problem with the research was the variability of the conditions. For some it was induced by hypnosis. For others by drugs. But most troubling was that for a few it required hypnosis one time and then drugs another. Marc’s research essentially proved that remote viewing does actually happen. But without being able to clearly understand and control the mechanism behind it, it wasn't deemed sufficient to warrant further research.

Mel and Oz's research was essentially dismissed outright even though results showed that nearly half of the subjects were indeed able to demonstrate some level of control of their dreams. Though the scientific community dismissed much of their work, they teamed up to author numerous books and give lectures on lucid dreaming and related topics.

As for me, I still believe that both hallucinations and dreams are indeed evidence of evolutionary attempts to move the human race beyond clinging to a sole material universe and toward an ability to perceive and function in more than one universe at a time. The brain's attempt to merge its material and quantum properties. Maybe someday this concept will be more generally accepted and studied further. Who knows, maybe there will be a Nobel Prize in someone's future!

Chapter Three:
Serial Terror

Jacksonville, Florida
Oklahoma City, Oklahoma
1995

Bored. Deeply, deeply bored. After the team's research got into its groove, I wasn't really needed. And I never really saw Marc, Mel and Oz as they were buried in data analysis and writing. I was staying in Crystal City at the apartment and doing some odd jobs for Dr Ellison. His most recent pursuit was related to the threats of terror in the United States that had escalated significantly over the past few years. Terrorist activity overseas had been well known by the American public for decades. But no one had any concept of domestic terrorism or foreign terrorists acting on American soil. Dr Ellison was well connected in the national intelligence community, and he was convinced that the probability of a terrorist attack on American soil was imminent.

"A terrorist attack on American soil is imminent." Dr Ellison said, gesturing for me to close the door as I walked into his office to take my normal seat.

"Now that we have your support on the funding, we will get this response team built, trained and ready to deploy at a moment's notice." Dr Ellison said into his phone, waving me to sit quietly.

"No. Thank you Senator Biden. Please let President Clinton know I'll make this my top priority…." Dr Ellison confirmed, "You too. See you at the luncheon next month."

"Another goose chase?" I asked as Dr Ellison put the handset back on the receiver.

“This is a good goose. And right up your alley. Your timing is impeccable.” He said with a sneer on his face I couldn’t quite read.

“Haven’t had many good geese lately.” I responded with a little more expression of my frustration than I intended.

“I know it’s been rough for you around here the last several months. But I think this will legitimately get your interest.”

“Ok. I’m listening. What’s the scoop?”

“You know how our research has us pretty embedded with our US Intelligence teams. And I know you’ve heard me saying we’re due for some kind of terrorist activity.” He continued as I nodded, “Well that call was to confirm funding for me to set up a special program to train a new class of first responder. Someone trained in the psychology of terror and trauma response as well as HAZMAT response.”

“Like embedding a psychologist in every fire department? That doesn’t seem possible.” I said.

“Not exactly. One team, to train those first responders on basic principles so they can do it themselves.”

“That sounds more reasonable.”

“This team will have a threefold mission. First, the team would be a first responder for potential terror events. It would arrive on scene, make assessments of the terror situation and help guide other responders. Second, even first responders are subject to trauma. So the team will do what they can to help lessen the impact of trauma on those first responders from the earliest point possible during the terror event. Lastly the team will travel the Country to train first responders in setting up their own local teams for this. Behind the scenes here we’ll dig into data after events and see how we should tweak the program.”

I was intrigued now. And Dr Ellison knew it as he continued.

“We’re creating a special certificate and title for team members. Bio-Terror Trauma Intervention Specialist.” He said, somewhat proud of the name, but then adding "We went with the Bio-Terror title mainly because the bulk of funding is coming from the US Army Medical Research Institute on Infectious Disease. Funding from the senate for that USAMRIID coffer is easier to get since the public has been seeing a lot about mad cow disease and bird flu lately, not to mention all the recent movies about escaped biological weapons. But this will also include responding to chemical and nuclear weapons, especially dirty bombs. The collapse of the Soviet Union and their inability to account for much of their nuclear material suggests that a dirty bomb should probably be our main worry right now."

"Sounds great. But what's my part in all of this." I asked, genuinely curious since I was not a first responder and really wasn't well schooled in the biology and chemistry of it.

"I want you to lead the team of course."

"What?! But I don't…"

"I know you don't know the nuts and bolts of the science. But you do know people. You've proven here over the last few years that you can identify the right people and keep them motivated to accomplish tasks…even when your own heart may not be fully in it." He said, "And this is starting from scratch. Well, not entirely from scratch, it's based on the Critical Incident Stress Management model, CISM, developed by Jeffrey Mitchell. I have a lot of ideas that we can hash out over the coming weeks. Ways we can adapt that model to address terror events. Then once we settle on a direction, I'll introduce you to the key players and let you go do your thing."

I sat dazed. I surely had a blank look or a terrified look on my face. Maybe both. I couldn't tell. As always, Dr Ellison read my face and continued.

"Your top secret clearance is still in effect. What I'm about to tell you may come as a surprise, but you cannot speak of it outside of this room."

Now very intrigued, I sat up in my seat and met Dr Ellison's strong eye contact.

"I understand."

"You have something no one else around here does. A history with an individual that will be key in this endeavor."

I racked my brain trying to think of who in the world I might know that would be at all related to this.

"As part of your International Studies program at USF you had a class. A very specific class. Taught by a very specific person." Dr Ellison said, clearly dragging it out.

"This person is very well known to the US Intelligence community, and to other intelligence agencies around the world."

"Who?" I asked, legitimately dumbfounded. "Dr Clarke?"

"Oh no. Well, Dr Clarke knows about him too since he's been so involved in the ongoings in Venezuela and the Middle East." Dr Ellison corrected, "Do you recall a class you had called International Terrorism?"

"I do." I said, now some bells were starting to go off. For my International Studies degree I had to have at least one class related to each of the key regions of the world. The Middle Eastern History class wasn't appealing to me. And the only other class offered to meet the requirement was International Terrorism.

"Do you remember your professor for that class?"

"Vaguely. It's been several years now. And we had a lot of guest speakers." I replied, searching my memory, "his name was Sammy, actually Sami, with an i. I don't remember his last name. I think it was Arabic or some other middle eastern style name."

"Al-Arian. It was Sami Al-Arian." Dr Ellison added, "Dr Al-Arian came to the United States through our CIA and State Department. He is very well connected at the highest levels in the Middle Eastern government regimes as well as with several terrorist organizations. He's not a part of those organizations mind you. But he's generally respected in their community."

My eyes were wide, and my jaw surely dropped to my chest.

"Al-Arian is a true scholar and educator. He has studied his culture and its interaction with western society and wants to fix it all. He insists it's all just miscommunication and misunderstanding. A true believer. So much so that he refused to be a spy when it was offered to him. He instead insisted that that he be allowed to live here in the states to teach us about his culture, and also learn about ours so he could teach his middle eastern brethren about what western society is really like. He wants to remove the political rhetoric that's been skewing beliefs about the other on both sides. He has no secrets. If he knows it, and someone asks, he doesn't care who that someone is, he tells them, or likely teaches them, what he knows. An open book."

Thinking back, I recalled that he was very open and very direct but never belittled anyone for what they didn't know.

"He earned formal degrees in Computer Science here in the states and then became a professor at USF." Dr Ellison expanded, "He also co-founded the World and Islam Studies Enterprise, known as WISE for short. WISE is a think tank on issues where the Middle East and Western worlds collide. They discuss and problem solve religious conflicts, political conflicts, and a lot of economic conflicts. Then offer their conclusions to anyone that is interested. Much of what the State Department does in that region these days is based on information coming out of that think tank group."

"I really only have one vivid memory from that class" I said.

"Oh? What was that?" Dr Ellison encouraged.

"There was a lot of time spent discussing what you said, the various sources of differences behind the conflicts between the middle east and the west. But what I remember most was when he brought in a speaker one day, with books and articles on how to actually commit a terrorist act." I said shaking my head, "I remember thinking, I can't believe he's just teaching people how to do this."

"That's who he is as a person." Dr Ellison said.

"I mean it was in detail." I continued, "The speaker explained that the heart of the event should be fear. And that often the first event, bomb, or whatever, is not the main event. That the main event is often to lure and target the first responders that come to rescue everyone. He said deaths of first responders create an exponential amount of fear. So it impacts the general public more, but also creates a reduction in available responders. Sometimes the healthy, available responders are hesitant to respond. Which has a trickle-down effect, even on normal everyday emergency calls. They may be late or may not have a full crew to handle the everyday situations. He even taught us the best materials to use in a bomb and where to place it for best effect."

"The bomb making bit went a little too far I think. We heard about that up here in DC and that shook a few folks who were previously supporting the CIA's use of him for information." Dr Ellison went on, "Dr Clarke got reamed out over it. Clarke was supposed to be keeping an eye on that stuff. But apparently he was doing some preliminary work down in Venezuela when Al-Arian brought that speaker in."

"Come to think of it, that was just a short while before I went down to Venezuela." I recalled, starting to put some pieces together.

"US Central Command is located down at Macdill Air Force Base in Tampa." Dr Ellison said, beginning to weave another thread of information for me. "So Tampa, including USF, is an intelligence community hotbed. A place where all the US military and other intelligence agencies can mingle with the natural migration of foreign students, professors and professional speakers without raising red flags. More useful intelligence information is exchanged in Tampa than anywhere else in the country."

"More than DC?" I asked.

"Definitely more than DC." Dr Ellison reiterated, "Most of what comes through DC is solely governmental politics, things the leaders don't want to say publicly, and usually that's at the tail end of years of other work elsewhere. It's just confirmations of information in DC, but the trails are blazed and deals are made in Tampa."

"So back to the *why you* answer," Dr Ellison continued, "In a nutshell, your terrorism class taught you as much as the terrorist training camps teach their bombers. Your class gave you some solid insight into the leadership of how terrorist groups operate. And your psychology studies have taught you what to do, what to say, what not to say. All of that is what we want to drill into our first responders to keep them safe."

"Will our first responders listen?"

"That will be your role. Figure out how to get them to listen. Most of them are of the GI Joe mentality and want to rush right into dangerous situations without taking a moment to assess what's going on. We need to change that. And I think you can be that change. Of course, we'll need to bring in others for the physical safety stuff, biohazard suit trainings and differences between biological, chemical and radiation event patterns. But we have a lot of those specialists to choose from, hopefully we would have a few of them on the team full time."

"OK. I guess I get why you thought of me. What's the plan?" I asked.

"I think we will get you set up in Jacksonville for a bit." He said.

"I thought Tampa was the hotbed?"

"It is. But for this first part you'll be doing dual duty. You'll be working with some of the best folks in the business. Mayport Naval Base in Jacksonville is a maintenance and refueling station for our ballistic missile submarines. It's a good source for people with knowledge on radiation and chemical hazards."

Why Mayport? Isn't Kings Bay the main submarine base on this coast?"

"True. Kings Bay is only about forty miles away. But that's in the middle of nowhere and it's easy for unsavory types to keep eyes on everything going on there. And then there's the running joke between Mayport and Kings Bay engineers."

"Oh yeah? What's that?"

"King's Bay engineers know how to play softball and break submarines, Mayport engineers know how to actually fix them."

"And Mayport has one other benefit" he continued, "I'm good friends with the head of the psychology department at the University of North Florida there in Jacksonville. So we're gonna go ahead and get you a graduate degree while you're there."

"What? What if I don't want to…" I began.

"Easy now." He offered, "They've got a great program there. The coursework will be easy for you. Dr Brady knows a bit about what I do and knows why I send people that way on occasion. It won't be a waste of your time. And we can get you set up in a special internship that will give you access to some other folks we need to know more about in order to make this Bio-Terror team work."

"Other folks? This is already a lot to digest…" I could tell I was squirming a bit.

"Dr Brady will tell you all about that later. First things first…let's find you someplace to stay down in Jacksonville. You leave in two days."

There was obviously a big plan already in motion before I was told about any of this. And I was gradually coming to terms with how it all made sense. Or maybe I was just accepting it at face value because I was looking for a change. Regardless of the reason, I was motivated again. And it felt good to be back in Florida. I have relatives in Jacksonville that I enjoy spending time with and was looking forward to having an opportunity to catch up with them.

My new home was now an old vinyl sided one up, one down rental in Neptune Beach, a block off the water on Orange Street between First and Midway. I had the upstairs level to myself. But being mid-block there wasn't much of a view past the cramped two story homes on all sides built virtually on top of each other. The best view was actually off a small wooden deck built out toward the street over the short driveway that served as a makeshift carport for my downstairs neighbor. Looking toward the dead end of the street from the deck, you could see some of the sea grasses at this edge of the beach, some sand dunes, and some water beyond.

The view nearer to me was cluttered with cars parked erratically around the small streets and jammed into tiny single car driveways. Almost all the original homes were converted into two independent apartments, one upstairs and one downstairs with separate entrances. But each only had one parking space in the single car driveway. Some of the homes had a couple living upstairs and a couple living downstairs, four cars, which left one in the driveway, one on the tiny, sandy, weed infested patch of lawn, and two somewhere on the street. And these streets were small. Probably originally intended to be one way single lane streets that have evolved to this makeshift mess over the decades.

There was an interesting collection of neighbors here. You had some trendy metrosexual types that said they wanted the close proximity to the water, but really just wanted close proximity to the ever-changing trendy restaurants and bars that were popping up in the area. There were plenty of surfers and some anti-establishment types that truly wanted proximity to the water. But they also took advantage of being within walking, or stumbling, distance to a dive bar or some ancient food shack. And then there were a lot of random people like me. Some students and military people wanting the cheap older housing, some people trying to restart their lives after bad relationships, and in a few instances restarting after prison sentences. Despite the seeming lack of similarities, everyone got along well. Everyone knew each other by name. And I didn't hear anyone spreading rumors or talking bad about anyone else. Most importantly, everyone knew what car belonged to whom when someone was frantically trying to get to school or work and was blocked in.

"I'm doing ok. Getting adjusted." I said on a call to Dr Ellison on my second night in town.

"We tried to get you out away from the base so it will be easier to engage with both the university and the base without mixing the two and needing to answer uncomfortable questions." He said.

"It's nice. Walking distance to anything I need outside of school or work. Nice to not have roommates. I hope I won't get bored." I laughed at the irony.

"That's good to hear. We've leased the upstairs unit for two years. And we're gonna try to lease the downstairs unit too if it opens up. It could be beneficial for you to have a confidant in the area. To make sure you don't get bored." He quipped "And someone will be coming by to install a safe. We didn't have time to get that done before you got there."

"A safe?"

"Everyone needs a safe. Are you ready to start school?"

"I don't really know."

"Don't worry. You're gonna love Dr Brady. You'll get to meet the good doctor tomorrow for an office visit I set up for you. About ten in the morning. I'll call in while you're there and we can talk through some things to make sure everyone's on the same page."

"Same page? I don't even feel like I'm in the same book right now."

"That reminds me. While you're on campus you can try and get your books for your classes. We'll reimburse that. But they might be sold out already since you're a late arrival. Most of the students got there last week for tomorrow's first classes."

"Late already." I laughed.

"Your first class isn't until the day after tomorrow. So technically you're not late. We started you off light for this first term since you're also gonna be heavily involved in the Bio-Terror team setup. By the way, you'll be getting some paperwork delivered to the house. It will be in a mesh packet with a padlock on it. The key is in the kitchen drawer. Be sure to check for that on the porch. It rains there out of the blue. Best if it doesn't get too wet."

"When it rains it pours."

Getting to campus was easy. Traffic flowed well. And the campus itself was nicely designed, with clear road markings, signs and good parking. The campus is inside a nature preserve, and buildings are, at least for now, organized nicely to form grassy quads and other college style spaces without encroaching into the preserve area around it. It reminded me a lot of Santa Fe College and its zoo. Only here it would be a quick walk through the preserve to clear my head between classes.

The campus was bustling with students, but it didn't feel uncomfortably crowded. It was easy to find the right building and the third floor office I was looking for.

"Good morning. I'm here to see Dr Brady" I asked "I'm not sure if he's around. I know I'm very early."

"He's not. But I am." A small statured woman said standing up and walking over to me with a smirk on her face. "I'm Dr Brady. Dr Brenda Brady, if that clears up any confusion."

“I’m sorry. I guess I never heard your first name from Dr Ellison.” I said clearly embarrassed and surely red faced “It’s nice to meet you.”

“No worries. It happens all the time in this male driven academic world.” She said, clearly softening and smiling now. “Our psych department is about fifty-fifty men and women on staff. In case it comes up again for you.” She winked. “It’s a bit odd since the students are almost all women. You’re one of only two guys in this twenty person graduate class.”

“I apologize for not knowing as much as I should, I tried to read up on this program, but there wasn’t much available.” I said “Can you tell me more about it?”

“Of course.” She said, offering me a seat at a small round side table with a phone and some stacks of books and papers. “The short of it is, this is a Master’s program that is intensive and results in PhD level training. But unlike a traditional psychology graduate degree that’s quite broad in scope, this program is narrow. It’s based on psychological interviewing techniques, selecting, administering and analyzing psychological tests, and identifying the proper counseling techniques based on that analysis.”

“That’s the narrow scope?” I laughed. “That’s what I thought the entirety of psychology was.”

“Seems like a lot. I know.” She acknowledged “but traditional psychology graduate programs have a heavy emphasis on research and history. Maybe eighty percent of their programs are buried in that. Our program focuses on that last twenty percent, the actual implementation aspects, the *what* and *how* of it. And we have intensive internships that support it. So much so that our graduates are not required to do the typical two years of supervised work before they can get licensed. They can test for national licensure right after graduation.”

“That sounds like a great program.” I said honestly “but the intensity of it concerns me. Dr Ellison suggested the program would only last about eighteen months and that it would be…well to use his word…easy…so I could do it alongside my responsibilities for him. I assumed the pace would be slower, not faster."

"Don't worry. It's not a lot of fact memorizing like other programs. What we teach here is likely what you already know naturally. Most don't have that natural feel for it, so it's harder for them. But from what I've heard, you're definitely a natural." She said as the phone rang, "I bet that's Dr Ellison now."

Dr Brady answered the phone, fumbling to untangle the cord while speaking the initial pleasantries. Then she hit the speakerphone button and set the handset back into the cradle.

"Ok. You're on speaker." She said.

"Good morning. I hope everything's going ok on day one." Dr Ellison said.

"Good morning. Everything's smooth so far. But I'm a little worried about the intensity of this program on top of my other work."

"It seems like a lot on paper. But once you get into it, you'll see that you already know it. It's already how you think. You won't need to learn much new information. You'll just be honing the skills you already have inside that are dying to break out." He laughed.

"Speaking of," he continued, "Brenda, I got confirmation today that John will be in your area and is willing to take on that mentor role we were talking about. And I also heard back from our friends at the State and Federal Department of Justice. They will grant us the access we spoke of."

"Wow! That was fast!" Dr Brady said, "And that's gonna be a great opportunity for him."

"I feel like I just got signed up for something again." I said warily "Who is John? And what is this opportunity about?"

"John Davis. He was the founder of what became the FBI's Behavioral Analysis Unit. The people that hunt serial killers." Dr

Ellison began, “He’s supposedly in the process of retiring from the FBI this year. I’ll believe that when I see it. Anyway, he’s retiring to Florida and agreed to be your internship sponsor.”

“Really? Why would he be interested in me, in this?”

“Terrorists, at the essence, are killers. Part of what we need to do to understand terrorists is to understand the minds of other killers, specifically mass murders and serial killers. We need to be able to differentiate, or find the overlaps, if any, between that and terrorism. Right now, we only understand terrorism from a military and political standpoint.”

“I guess that makes sense. But why would he want to do this in his retirement. Isn’t retirement for golf or RVing around the country?”

“You’ll probably figure out that answer as soon as you meet him.” Dr Ellison said likely exchanging a virtual smile with Dr Brady before continuing.

“We need to better understand the mind of the person that might be drawn to a life of terror. John and I have talked a bit and think there is a bridge between your work and his work that can lead to that understanding. You’ll learn what you can from John and incorporate the relevant parts into your team training program.”

“Okay. But that seems like a lot on top of the regular class stuff.”

“I believe Brenda has agreed to let that intensive internship with John be substituted for some of your coursework. Is that right Brenda?”

“Somewhat grudgingly.” Brenda said with a smile “But I’ll get over it.”

“You’ll be starting your internship much earlier than the other students.” She continued, “as soon as John gets down here. He’ll go over everything with you and will explain how he wants to handle it. I’m sure you’ll be visiting the state prison in Starke, Union Correctional, and Lowell, those are not far from here, about thirty minutes away. But you’ll probably also go down to Coleman, the Federal prison near Wildwood. That’s a little farther. We’re gonna schedule your classroom time on Tuesday and Thursday so you can have those longer weekends for quality time at the prisons when needed. I think it will work out. You'll just need to keep straight that the normal we speak of in classes is different from the normal you'll see with John."

"You've got a couple weeks to get settled before John gets down there." Dr Ellison said, "but once he gets there you'll be going full steam with him. He's not the kind of guy to ease you into it. He's a jump straight in the deep water and see if you can swim kind of guy."

"Two whole weeks?" I said, unconvinced, "that's not like you. Are you sure he won't show up here tomorrow?"

***

It wasn't tomorrow. But three days later Davis arrived in town. And on that same day I was thrown into the deep water.

Despite his doctorate, Dr Davis did insist that I call him John. That was the extent of our introduction before I was coaxed into his generic government Ford sedan.

"I'm pretty sure I just violated every rule about getting into a car with a stranger." I said.

"Yep." He said, not adding anything further.

"Where are we headed?"

"Florida State Prison" he answered, again not adding anything further.

"What will we be doing." I probed.

"Interviewing a prisoner." He said, again with nothing further.

"Is there anything else I should know?"

“Probably. But where’s the fun in that.” He said, turning toward me and offering a smile.

“Torture and anxiety on day one. This should be fun.” I said.

The scenery out the window changed abruptly. The suburban homes and businesses of Jacksonville gave way to the more industrial buildings on the outskirts of town. Beyond the industrial buildings were farms and forests. After about twenty minutes of driving past farming communities, the prison came up on us out of nowhere. Literally nothing but the prison, in a field, with a few support buildings off site. And a tiny post office. That sums up the entire town of Raiford.

Between the country road and the prison buildings themselves was a massive parking lot worthy of any large shopping mall. The lot was only about half full and most of the vehicles seemed to be parked by what must be an employee only entrance. That left us plenty of space to park near the administration building.

“Bring your wallet and ID badges. Leave everything else here in the car. Empty your pockets. No pens or pocket knives, no pocket change, nothing metal. Your shirt’s fine. Believe it or not some idiots try to wear ties to show their authority. Nothing like giving a killer a pre-tied noose around your neck.” John warned.

“I’ve spent time working in some inpatient psych facilities, one at JBSA” I said defending myself a bit.

“That’s good. So you know some of the safety stuff. We’re gonna keep it easy on your first day. No one too randomly violent.” He smiled, “but you’ll meet some doozies later on.”

A well-paced walk later and we were in the lobby waiting to speak with the warden. I just followed. And stood silently waiting for instructions that would hopefully come. My IDs were checked, but not rigorously. It was clear that the warden knew and trusted John.

Unlike many movies, visitors, lawyers and others don’t walk through the area where the inmates are housed. There are visitation areas set up specifically for family members, with lots of security. A bank of separate partitions with plexiglass windows on the prisoner side. The visitors are in a room together with their own partitions and a separate entrance.

For the attorneys and other professionals there are different meeting rooms. In a high security prison like this one, the rooms have clear unbreakable windows to the hallway, with a guard posted outside. Inside the room, a table resembles a picnic table. Except that the table is metal, about twice as wide as a regular picnic table to keep safer distance, and with metal loops for securing the prisoner's arm and leg restraints. There are four round barstool-like seats, also metal, welded to the table frame or bolted to the ground so the chairs can't be picked up and used as a weapon. Attorneys often ask for guards to stay outside of the room so they can speak confidentially with their clients. But for situations like ours, where we're just conducting an interview and there's no confidentiality needed, there's no reason for the guards not to stay inside the room. Or so I thought.

"Here you go. He's ready for you." The warden said as we walked up to the room. "Let the guard know when you're done and he'll radio me to come pick you up."

"Thanks." John said, "we'll probably be about an hour."

"No worries. Take as long as you need. He doesn't have anywhere to be." The warden said as he walked away.

I couldn't see into the room from where I was standing. And John hadn't given me any heads up about who we would be talking to or what we were asking about.

"He's all yours. I'll be right outside here if you need me." John said.

"Just me? You're not coming inside too?" I asked quietly but with concern, feeling my body start to shake.

"You'll be fine. This is a good one for you to cut your teeth on."

"What do I ask him about? There's no notes or list of questions or anything."

"Just sit with him and talk. Ask whatever comes to your mind." He said with a smile as he stepped aside so I could see who I would be talking to.

I swallowed hard. Probably visibly hard. And turned my head looking into the room for the first time to see who was waiting for me. It was Danny Rolling.

A flood of emotions ran through me on seeing Danny Rolling. Five years earlier, in 1990, Danny Rolling killed five students in Gainesville. Four from the University of Florida and one from Santa Fe Community College. I was living in Gainesville attending both of those schools at the time. And, to add to it, his campsite during his murder spree was in the woods right behind the apartment complex where I lived. I was one of tens of thousands of students living in fear for weeks, staying home, going in groups if we had to go out of the apartment. I even stopped jogging after hearing of the first murder because my route took me through some isolated areas of the campus. I shuddered when I later heard about his campsite location. One of the preferred jogging paths I took from my apartment was a shortcut on a nature trail through the woods which would have passed near Rolling's campsite.

Rolling appeared oblivious to my rush of emotions. Either that or he simply didn't care. I was still standing, frozen in the doorway when John spoke.

"Go in there and ask some questions. Find out what you want to know."

I slowly walked in and sat across the table in front of Rolling who looked in my direction for the first time. I struggled but maintained eye contact. He didn't speak. He just sat. Emotionless.

"Do you know who I am or why I'm here today?" I finally forced out.

"No. They just told me someone was here to see me." Rolling said flatly. "Are you a reporter or something? That's pretty much the only ones coming to see me these days."

His voice was soft-spoken. His words came out slow but not slurred, as if he were patiently explaining something to a child. There was no inflection in his voice, every word was at about the same pace, tone and volume. This matched his facial expressions. Flat. Drooped but not sad.

"I'm not a reporter. I'm a psychology student. I'm trying to learn more about emotions and thought patterns of people that not only think about killing someone but actually do it."

Rolling sat quietly and didn't offer any thoughts.

"I'm sure you've talked to countless psychologists, investigators, doctors, and who knows who else." I said, trying to acknowledge his indifference to my presence. "So I apologize for anything I ask that's repetitive."

Rolling shrugged slightly but didn't offer any thoughts.

"I'll get right to it." I said, "Which one was your favorite?"

"Favorite what?" he asked, the tiniest bit less flat.

"Killing. Which was your favorite?"

"No one's ever asked me that before. I don't really know." He responded thoughtfully, looking off to the ceiling clearly reliving some series of memories.

I sat quietly for several minutes and allowed Rolling to scroll through his crimes in his head. Eventually he spoke.

"The second one, I think. The first one in Gainesville." He said, clarifying that he had also killed three people at a scene in Louisiana.

"If I recall correctly, you killed two that first time in Gainesville. Roommates." I said, "What was it about those that made them your favorite?"

"I guess because it was clean. It all went to plan. No surprises to deal with. It was the art of it." He said, "It wasn't the rapes. Everyone makes such a big deal about that. That was just to blow off steam."

I didn't know all the details of the murders. But I knew a few things from what I read in some court records republished in local newspapers. The first two murders were two roommates, eighteen-year-old Sonja Larson, and seventeen-year-old Christina Powell. On August 24, 1990, Rolling broke into their apartment. Christina was asleep on the downstairs couch and Sonja was asleep upstairs in her bedroom. He stood over Christina on the couch briefly but decided to go upstairs. Upstairs, he taped Sonja's mouth shut and then stabbed her with a Ka-Bar knife until she died. Then he went downstairs and taped Christina's mouth and then her wrists behind her back. He cut her clothes off. Raped her. And then stabbed her in the back several times until she was dead. According to the court documents, he then went back upstairs, raped Sonja's corpse and when done, posed both bodies in sexually provocative positions before taking a shower and leaving the apartment.

"What does clean mean to you," I asked, not sure if he was referring to the shower, if he was just describing the ease of the actions, or something else.

"It was just really quiet. Easy. Nothing got broken. They were right where I needed them to be."

"And what did you mean when you said you liked the art of it?"

"The art was me. I liked the posing of them. Like there was nothing wrong. They were just being themselves. When I walked out it was like I lived there and was just leaving for work or something."

"Did you pose any of the others?"

"I posed them all."

"I thought you only posed the women?"

"Yeah. All the girls. The others were just in the way, so I left them."

"If I remember what I read at the time, including the scene in Louisiana, two of the four apartments had men there. The Louisiana scene also had an eight year old male child." I said leading up to my next question. "So, your favorite was the one with two girls and no others to get in the way. Is that right?"

"I guess. I never really thought of it that way."

"The women you posed in your favorite, you posed in what you suggest were natural positions for them. Did you pose the other women in natural positions as well?"

Rolling sat quietly thinking for a few minutes. I waited until he eventually spoke.

"No. One was not natural."

"Which one was that?"

"The third one. Second in Gainesville."

"Why was that one different?

"It was messy. I guess I was frustrated. When I was done, I cut her stomach open."

Rolling was noted in court documents to have sliced her from pubic bone to breast bone.

"I don't know. I just did it and then left."

"Was that all?" I said, recalling there was much more to that scene in the newspapers.

"I got back to camp and couldn't find my wallet. So I went back." He said, "It didn't feel right when I went back in. It wasn't the right scene. So I cut off her head and put it on the shelf. I guess I was trying to scare people when they came to find her. People needed to feel something when they walked in there."

Court documents noted that Rolling posed her headless corpse upright on the bed and placed the head on the shelf looking toward the corpse.

"Did you feel better about the scene when you left?" I asked.

"I guess." He said. "The last one was just off. Everything was wrong. Nothing felt right."

I was encouraged because it was the first time he offered information without being asked a specific question. So I continued.

"What happened with the last one?"

"A guy was there. He was in the way. By the time I got him out of the way she was already yelling and being loud at me. She locked the door and I had to break through. It wasn't how it was supposed to happen."

"How was it supposed to happen?"

"Her roommate shouldn't have been a guy. It should have been a girl. Then everything would have been quiet and right."

"Were you frustrated? Did you do anything different like you did when you went back on the other one?"

"Not really. I guess I felt let down. I just put her in position and left."

"You were arrested about two weeks after the last one. Did you know they were looking for you? I never heard of any new victims. You killed five people over the course of four days or so. What stopped a fourth scene in Gainesville?"

"I was around. Walking. Or in camp. I kinda felt let down. Wasn't really looking for anything."

"I read that a lot of professionals were saying all the girls you killed looked like your mom." I said, watching as he dismissed that notion with a frustrated eye gesture. "But I don't know if I believe that."

Rolling re-engaged eye contact with me.

"And you want to know the real reason why." He said.

"Do you know?" I asked.

We sat in silence for a few more minutes. I could tell he was thinking about it. But I couldn't tell if he was going to be honest or not. He had nothing to lose since he pled guilty last year and was already sentenced to death. Eventually he made a sincere comment.

"It's hard to explain. You know when you wake up in the morning, and you go to the bathroom and brush your teeth. You don't really think about it. It's just habit for that combination of things, waking, then bathroom, then teeth, all that." He explained, "but for some reason you do realize it if you wake up and go straight to brushing your teeth without the bathroom first. It doesn't bother you really. But you notice it. You're not on autopilot anymore. Just because you didn't have that bladder sensation when you woke, it changed how you focused."

"So were the killing days or non-killing days the habit days?" I asked.

"The regular days were habit. Routine. The killing days were the ones where there was some change. Something that made me get focused on that specific kill. I couldn't shake it. Like the bladder sensation you can't get rid of until you actually go to the bathroom."

"Before you ask, I don't know." He continued, "I've tried. Believe me, I've tried to figure out what it was about those days that got me out of the daily habit. I just woke up and was focused and thinking of it."

"You mentioned in your bathroom example that if you woke with the normal bathroom sensation the day kept going like habit. And that if you didn't have the sensation, that was what breaks the habit cycle." I summarized before continuing with a connection forming in my head.

"So, tell me…on those days…do you remember having realistic dreams where it felt like you were controlling what was happening in your dream?"

"Edwin was right about you." John said as we were walking back to the car, using Dr Ellison's first name which I wasn't used to hearing. "He told me you have great instincts."

"Why's that?" I asked.

"When we first got to the cell and you saw Rolling. I thought you were going to punch me in the face. But you didn't."

"You could have had me interview anyone. But you knew I was in Gainesville when that happened. And you put me in there by myself. You set that whole thing up to test me. Frankly I should have punched you!"

"Maybe. But you didn't. And besides that, even though you didn't have a script or any details of what we were looking for, you went in there and got a completely indifferent man to confide in you. You came up with questions he'd never heard before and that he actually cared to answer. He even thanked you for it when you left for Christ's sake."

I was still a little too disturbed to accept the complement.

"And you knew when to shut up. You didn't need to fill the silence. You gave him time to think so he could give genuinely well thought out answers. None of my BAU recruits have ever been able to do that without years of un-teaching. They want to fill the silence. Even me. I didn't get good information like you got today until I had years of practice. You're the real deal!"

I sat quietly and digested that.

"What do you know now that you didn't know when you woke up this morning?" he asked.

"That John Davis, hunter of serial killers, has an evil streak and his own brand of torture!" I answered with a forced grin.

"Yes. But besides that. What do you know about Danny Rolling?"

"The main thing that caught my attention was related to the posing of the first scene in Gainesville." I said.

"What about the posing?"

"When he talked about it, he described that he posed them like they were being themselves and everything was normal like he was just leaving for work." I recounted, "But the poses were described in the court documents as sexually provocative."

"What's that mean?" John probed.

"I think it means that was his ideal. Women solely as sexual objects with no other purpose. Fully under his control. And his taking a shower at that scene suggests a level of comfort with it. He didn't have that with the other scenes."

"What was different about the other scenes?" John continued to probe.

"I didn't ask him details about it, but the first scene in Shreveport was a family. A grandfather, his twenty-something daughter and her eight year old child. The grandfather and child were collateral damage. The daughter was posed, the males were not."

"And the last scene in Gainesville, the woman had a male roommate." I continued "That clearly bothered Rolling. He said she shouldn't have had a male roommate. She was posed. But the male was left where he was killed."

"But the thing I don't understand is the second scene in Gainesville. That was a single female victim. No males involved. But he went beyond the killing and mutilated her post mortem, slicing her stomach before he left, and then cutting off her head when he returned. The posing wasn't sexually provocative in that one. The head on the shelf. The body sitting upright. I think he meant it when he said it was to frighten whoever found the scene."

"Exactly." John said. "That second Gainesville scene was the problem. What are your thoughts on that?"

"It's so out of synch with the other three scenes, my first thought was that it wasn't him. Maybe a copycat. The other scene had hit the news and maybe someone was using that as cover. But he confessed to it in detail. The direction of the stomach cut. Going back for his wallet and all. A lot of detail. And it was laid out too cleanly for psychotic rage to have been the driver."

"So what's your theory?" John probed a little more strongly.

I sat thinking. Hesitantly thinking. If that's a thing. I kept going back to my time at JBSA. Thinking about the multiverse and my idea that lucid dreams and hallucinations were a bridge that connected sights, sounds, smells and emotions of two or more separate universes that might play out most dramatically in only one. And that for observers in that one universe, what they see wouldn't make sense without knowing what was happening in the other universes. But that is way too inconsistent with the current norm of psychology and criminology. No way I could mention that. But maybe I could start the conversation.

"Since that scene had only one victim, maybe there was some left over adrenaline. Efforts to curb the adrenaline could have led to the stomach cut before he left. Then maybe the stress of breaking his desired pattern exacerbated that from everyday adrenaline to extreme adrenaline related hallucination. When he came back maybe he wasn't able to deal with the hallucinations and acted out more violently by decapitating her and changing the pose."

"He never reported any hallucinations. In fact, he consistently denied them." John said.

"In the world he lives in, within his mind, would he have identified it as hallucination? Or would he have just thought it was real? If I remember correctly, he had a violent, abusive father that would be violently abusive to his mother and the kids over otherwise insignificant things like breathing too loud. Who knows what all he may have witnessed and experienced. I know he downplayed it, but he did acknowledge that all the female victims resembled his mother."

"And…" John prompted.

"His mother kept trying to leave. Kept trying to report the abuse. But the father was a Shreveport police officer and a Korean war veteran. So the official reports were never followed up on. I have to assume the violence of the abuse in the days following those reports had to escalate. Father's revenge for her tattling."

"So…" John again prompted.

This was going to be a leap. But I decided to just say it.

"So maybe Rolling saw his mother as the problem. Abuse was everyday stuff for his whole life. He never knew anything less. But the increased abuse after the mother took actions to stop it, either pushing back at home, or voicing it to authorities, may have led him to blame his mother. The escalation of abuse was his issue, not the everyday abuse itself. And in his mind, she caused that escalation."

"And now…" John prompted.

"And now, maybe he's trying to shut his mother up and make her behave how he thinks she should behave." I said hesitantly, because I hate the thought of it. "Quietly sexually subservient. The tape over the mouths and the pre and post mortem rapes. But something about the second victim or likely the scene itself was more related to memories of the tattle tale escalated abuse. So he took that one a step or two further."

"Now you're thinking like a serial killer." John said smiling. "I had a different take. But your direction shows promise too. Thank you for…eventually…sharing that."

"You studied Philosophy right?" John said.

"Yes."

"Beware that, when fighting monsters, you yourself do not become a monster...for when you gaze long into the abyss…the abyss gazes also into you. That's Nietzsche not me." John offered, "This work is very difficult. What you're doing for Edwin, and what we're doing here is very similar. We're trying to get into the minds of people who, to us, do unspeakable things. In conflict with our own beliefs that we feel should be universal. That can be very hard to sort out. You start to view our world through a different filter. And if you're not careful, if you don't somehow ground yourself, you can end up destroying yourself. You won't necessarily become a killer, but you can easily lose sight of the good in the world. It can change who you are and change the positive relationships in your life. So don't do that okay."

As the weeks of my first term of graduate school went by, I began to see what Dr Ellison meant about classes being easy and coming to me naturally. So, the school part was going pretty smoothly. I found I was always looking forward to meeting up with John when he would swing through town. He was still planning to officially retire from the FBI but was doing double duty, giving lectures and consulting, which brought him to Florida more often than you would think. Whenever he was in the area, we would always make a trip to the Florida State Prison at Raiford. He had me interview a number of serial killers and mass murderers. Always by myself. It was much harder for the ones I didn't know much about. Which was most of them. He never told me in advance who we would be seeing so I couldn't look it up. Other than Rolling, the only one I knew about personally was Bobby Joe Long.

Bobby Joe Long killed at least ten women in my hometown Tampa Bay area when I was in middle and high school. As teenagers, we weren't really paying much attention to it. We were in our own world. But after he was captured in late 1984, some of the details came out and got our teenaged attention.

Long was captured in November 1984 a few days after he let his last victim go free. Her name was Lisa McVey. She was a seventeen-year-old high school student that was working nights at a donut shop in the area. Long abducted her when she was riding her bike home from work one night and held her hostage in his home for over twenty-six hours. But she was smart. She assumed she was going to be killed. So even though she was kept blindfolded, she tried to touch everything she could, leaving fingerprints to try to help the police catch her would be killer. It's still unclear as to why he eventually let her go.

The fact that he let her go was intriguing. It meant there was a lot of witness testimony about him. But his childhood history was more intriguing. It came out in the media that he suffered from Klinefelter Syndrome, a genetic disorder where he had an extra X chromosome. The disorder led to him developing female traits, including breast tissue, for which he was ridiculed by his classmates. As an adolescent he had breast reduction surgery. When this oddity hit the news, it was quickly passed around my school. So more of us teens started paying attention.

Long was linked to ten murders and was initially convicted for nine of them. However, one of the convictions was overturned and a higher court ordered his acquittal on that charge. Ultimately, his convictions for the eight murders, kidnappings, attempted kidnappings, and sexual batteries, led to twenty-six life sentences without parole and two life sentences with possibility of parole. Only one led to a sentence of death.

My encounter with Long in early 1995 was about ten years after his death sentencing. But there was still constant legal wrangling going on. Because of that wrangling, and his general personality, my interview of Long went very differently than my interview of Rolling. Long was confrontational, belligerent, and avoided any direct answers to questions. At one point he said "You're just like my wife and I divorced that bitch." Long had married his high school girlfriend in 1974 when he was twenty-one years old. They had two children before she divorced him in 1980, three years before he moved to the Tampa area and began his crime spree.

Frustrated with the Long encounter, I refocused my efforts away from the serial killer research and more toward getting the Bio-Terror team set up. After several discussions with Dr Ellison, he agreed to take a short cut and simply get one of the special Chemical-Biological-Radiation-Nuclear (CBRN) teams assigned to me. Unfortunately, those teams were in high demand, and we couldn't get a whole team assigned as we had hoped. But it led us down a promising path.

One of the CBRN teams had two members that had been injured and were not going to be able to return to their team due to the extreme physical rigor of the daily CBRN job. The team leader was looking to find them a new role. He felt a team like mine would be a good landing spot. Still in the same CBRN world, but less vigorous, mainly teaching and talking. We gladly accepted and welcomed them to my team.

Bob and Kevin were a good fit personality-wise. Both were in their early thirties, each with a decade or more of experience with the military CBRN teams. Before they joined the service, both actually went to Seminary and had degrees related to pastoral counseling, which made a good crossover for the trauma counseling aspect of my team. They weren't in your face about religion. I'm sure they've seen quite a bit of the religious conflict that can arise out in the world. So their religious underpinnings were low key. Just a backbone of how they made choices and treated people. They didn't drink though, which took some getting used to after living with Marc and Oz for so long. Bob and Kevin didn't seem to mind being in bars, or around others that were drinking, so it really ended up being a non-issue. When Dr Ellison eventually leased the unit below mine, Bob and Kevin moved in. My unit and the attached deck were where the beer was, but their unit below always had the late night snacks. Synergy.

In early April 1995, we were a team of three. Well three and a half. Angelo wasn't permanently assigned to my team. He was one of the nuclear engineers at Mayport, who did repairs on the nuclear power systems, ballistic missiles of various types, and weapons systems in general, literally the MacGyver of deadly stuff. We were granted access to him on an as needed basis.

We were working on two others. Keith and Alex. They were on bomb squads that worked with the US Border Patrol's HAZMAT team. Kevin knew them from his early training days and suggested we reach out. And it was a great suggestion. They had a decade of experience in bomb detection and what they jokingly called calculated disassembly, or what Kevin called blowing things up just because they can. Kevin constantly joked about what they must have been like as kids, sticking firecrackers into everything to see what it would do.

So, by mid-April we were a team of three and three halves. And we were about to get our first call.

The phone rang. Forever. I eventually picked up.

"You got your go bag ready? A car will be at your door in about ten minutes."

"What?" I said still trying to process how I answered the phone in my sleep. It was about 10:15am on Wednesday morning. My alarm is set for 11:00. Wednesday is my day off from classes and I didn't have any meetings at the Mayport base until late in the afternoon. Bob and Kevin were likely at the gym pretending they weren't both rehabbing injuries. This was my precious sleep time.

"Get your team together and get to the hanger at Mayport. A plane will be there to pick you all up in less than an hour."

"What's going on?" I asked as the fog cleared and I finally recognized Dr Ellison's voice.

"There's been a bombing at the Federal building in Oklahoma City." He said, "You've got your first official mission."

The Oklahoma City (OKC) bombing was a horrible event all around. An unthinkable tragedy for the victims and their loved ones. A striking blow to American society's sense of safety. And an awakening to think that terrorism could happen here at the hands of US citizens. And for my team, it was an utter failure in terms of our performance.

We landed at Tinker Air Force Base in OKC and set up our temporary headquarters at the Tinker Air Logistics Complex (ALC). On the flight over we only had a couple rudimentary satellite images of the scene, and those were from bad angles. Not much to get our bearings. The Tinker ALC Command Chief Master Sergeant, Chief Kelly, became our primary source of current information.

Chief Kelly quickly got us set up with what we needed, acquired a helicopter and a pilot, and personally accompanied us to the site of the bombing about eight miles away. On the helicopter flight into town, Chief Kelly was on the ball, keeping constant contact with people on scene, occasionally updating us when he felt it was relevant. But his level of energy seemed almost nervous in nature. Unusual for someone of his rank, even for an event in his local area.

The helicopter had to drop us off about three blocks out, the safest clear space to land that wouldn't blast the crime scene with rotor wash. We barely touched down and Chief Kelly was out the door, running toward the scene and didn't look back.

"You may lose him in the crowd." The pilot said over the headset, "Go straight up this street, 5th Street, about three blocks and you'll see the lights. Don't bother with the local police. Find someone in a military uniform like mine and tell them you're with Chief Kelly. They'll get you situated."

"I thought he was supposed to take us there." I said, wondering why he would just run off.

"He's a little distracted." The pilot explained, "His wife works in that building. And their son is in the daycare on the second floor."

We were late. The time getting to the airport, the flight over, and the prep at Tinker before we got on the helicopter meant we were getting to the scene over four hours after the incident. For four hours, workers had been struggling to find their coworkers. For four hours employees, families and friends had been worrying about loved ones. For four hours, first responders had been finding and removing the bodies, and body parts, of innocent men, women…and children.

Four hours after the explosion there was still dust in the air. Random pieces of paper, some looking like they may have been important documents, were blown up and down the streets for several blocks by the early afternoon winds. From the ground it looked like fully half the building had collapsed, rubble piled over two stories high and spilling across the street. The surrounding buildings and parking lot within the blast radius had massive amounts of damage as well, making it difficult to get around.

There were paths partially cleared by first responders going back and forth between debris piles, moving the six hundred or more injured to medical tents. Intermittently responders moved lifeless bodies, and body parts, to a large makeshift morgue. There would ultimately be one hundred sixty eight innocent people killed that day. That number was likely higher as there was at least one leg found that could not be matched to a body. Nineteen children died. Fifteen of the children were in the America's Kids child development center on the second floor.

After finding someone in a military uniform that would help us, we were taken to the medical tent where we could see Chief Kelly standing, weeping in the center of several firefighters. As we got closer, we saw he was holding the lifeless body of a small, one year old child.

"Is that his child?" I said stopping one of the firefighters as he left the group and walked past us.

"No. But they were in the same class." The firefighter said, "we haven't found his son or his wife yet. There's a lot to go through. But I don't think we're gonna find any other survivors."

"How in the hell was he able to hold it together waiting on us back at the base?!" I asked looking at Bob and Kevin.

They didn't answer. Just shaking their heads the slightest bit. We turned and looked out toward the rubble swarming with people carrying five gallon buckets. The people looked like ants moving in different directions before taking their perches and passing the buckets back and forth. Full buckets going down the pile, empty buckets coming back up. Little attention was paid to the contents until the buckets got to the bottom.

At the bottom was a makeshift sorting station. The first group of sorters were mainly looking for human remains, fragments of clothing, wallets, purses, IDs, anything to help confirm who may have been, or may still be, in the building. The items were placed in piles on a taped grid on the ground labeled to try and maintain information about where they were found. Looking back and forth from the sorting piles to the building, it was hard to imagine how you could possibly tell where anything came from. It was a massive pile of rubble in front. Behind the rubble the building appeared almost like a doll house. You could see into all the floors. You could see offices. Cubicles. Conference tables. Desks. Some of the spaces looked untouched except for the layer of dust kicked up from the collapse.

I imagined that's what made the scene the most horrific. Seconds before the explosion, countless people were sitting or standing a few feet away from a coworker, many mid-conversation at the early morning hour, and then without warning that coworker simply dropped out of view and disappeared as a cloud of dust and rubble curtained down from above. Sucking winds pulled paper and small items off desks, and larger winds pulled nearby people off their ledge and into the enlarging pile. Life was normal one second. The next…

"What's the plan here." Bob asked solemnly.

"I have no idea." I said.

One of the goals of the team was to get into the mix early and try to pull aside and help first responders that were witnessing such terrible things. But those responders had been going nonstop for hours at this point. It was a little late for that.

"I guess we focus on the debrief." I offered looking for their thoughts. "Bob, can you get with the incident commander to see what types of shifts they're running. Most importantly, find out when those very first responders will be taking a break. Let him know we want to huddle up that first group briefly. If he gives you pushback let me know. We'll find someone to give him a call and tell him to let us do our thing."

"What about me?" Kevin asked.

"We need to get a hold of the news teams. The cameramen and anyone trying to broadcast live or get pictures out." I explained, "these images will likely be traumatizing for many of those watching from afar. I need you to speak to the news teams and anyone else with a camera and try to impress upon them the impact the footage may have if not carefully screened. The FBI is here investigating already. They will want all of the footage and may have some arrangement in place. You may be able to piggyback off that to slow its release. And maybe ask the FBI to use their influence to move any live on-the-scene reporters back a few blocks."

"What will you be doing?" Kevin asked, not rudely, just wanting to keep track.

"I think this scene is set up like NTSB does plane crashes. But I think the FBI is taking it over, using their bombing investigation tactics they've used in embassies around the world. This is a massive scale though compared to those smaller embassy bombings. So I guess my first stop is getting with the FBI to try and understand how this process of theirs will move forward."

"At some point we'll need to get a list of anyone who pulled human remains out. First responders, the surviving office workers, or bystanders that were helping." Kevin said.

"I'll get that started." Bob said, "A lot of that info will come from my talks with the incident commander."

"As soon as I'm done talking to the news folks I'll head to the medical tent and start talking to the wounded survivors." Kevin added.

"There are probably hundreds of injured survivors. And who knows how many uninjured bystanders. We won't be able to get to everyone. So we have to try to be selective somehow. Let's plan to meet up in two hours at the incident command tent. If something urgent comes up before then that you think we all need to know, you can ping the walkie-talkies." I said, then offering somewhat tentatively, "And let me know if you hear anything about Chief Kelly's wife and son."

The incident commander provided some basic information but directed me to the FBI Agent in Charge (AIC) for much of what I needed to know. The AIC was in the morgue tent getting an update on casualties when I finally caught up with him.

"Special Agent James?" I asked.

"Yes. Are you the one that's looking for me?"

"Yes sir. I'm with a special terrorism trauma response team set up through the Army Special Operations Psychological Operations Unit." I explained for introduction.

"Psy Ops? I thought you guys just dropped pamphlets and mega sized American condoms on our enemies." He said somewhat dismissively.

"I can't speak to any of that." I responded, "My team is new. Mainly geared for CBRN terrorism event response. But we were asked to participate here due to the nature of the mass casualties in a public space. These types of events produce higher levels of trauma for responders, federal workers and others in the area. The goal is to intervene wherever we can to limit potential causes of PTSD. So they don't re-experience such high levels of trauma re-emergence later in life. Those later in life PTSD elements often lead to dysfunctions, alcoholism, drug use, violent outbursts, and other things that can be debilitating to our responders and workforce."

I'm not sure how much of that he heard since he was walking around the bodies, taking notes, and asking questions of medical staff. But eventually he did turn and acknowledge me.

"That's noble." He said, "But I'm not sure how I can help with that. We're trying to identify bodies, sort through many tons of evidence, and catch the guy who did this. I don't have a lot of time at the moment."

"Yes sir. I understand. All I really need is a general breakdown of your process here so my team and I can determine where it might be best for us to do our job without getting into anyone's way. We want to stay out of the way as much as we possibly can."

Special Agent James called out to a nearby agent. They spoke out of earshot, but it appeared Agent James was asking him to give us the information we needed.

"Special Agent Kline here will answer any questions you have. He can give you about fifteen minutes. But I recommend you get back in touch with the Incident Commander from the local fire department. They provide the vast majority of first responders, and he'll have most of the info you'll need on them."

"Thank you, sir. I've already got someone from my team talking with him." I said as Special Agent James walked away.

Special Agent Kline indeed gave me what I needed to know. I just wish I had known it several hours earlier. I was still mentally digesting the FBI process information as I caught up with Bob and the Incident Commander. Bob was just finishing up and gave me a quick head shake and glance suggesting I not approach and wait for him to disengage from that conversation.

"I think I got everything set up that we need from him," Bob said, "He's agreed to ask the responders to huddle with us as they leave their shifts. He can't guarantee that they will. He said they've never done that before. Their debriefings are always days later and focus on process details, never touchy-feely crap. His words not mine."

"When's the first shift change?" I asked.

"That's part of the problem. Several fire crews have already left the area. Mainly those from the neighboring areas. They were at the end of their shift when the explosion happened and needed to get back. They're on tight rotations to keep their shifts minimally staffed to deal with their everyday emergency response stuff. Some individuals from those crews stayed as off duty volunteers."

"So when's the best time?" I asked.

"They run twelve hour shifts here. So probably not for a few hours yet. Around 8pm or so." Bob answered, "But there's another issue."

"What's that?"

"There are hundreds of them. And only three of us." Bob said. "No way we can get to them all individually. Not even as small groups. They're exhausted and emotionally spent. They'll get irritated and leave if they have to wait too long."

"I guess we do the best we can." I said, feeling like a terrible leader. "Ask around if there are any particular responders having a hard time and we can try to see if they'll stay and talk to us more one on one. For the others I guess we just need to do some massive groups. Encourage them to speak to each other wherever they may get a chance. Sooner rather than later. And give them the topics and prompts. What made you the most afraid, angry, sad or upset? What was the worst thing you saw? Was there any smell that bothered you? Were there any sounds? You know, the basic things to get them talking about the stuff that matters instead of the other BS. They're stuck with self-therapy at least in this early stage. We should make appointments to visit each of the responding fire stations and meet with each shift over the next few weeks. We can follow up with some small group stuff at that time."

"That was pretty useless." Kevin said walking up to us, "They refused to delay anything. Ratings. Freedom of speech. You name it. The FBI was able to get them to move the perimeter back a couple blocks in each direction. But I think that was only because the agent mentioned the site hadn't been cleared of possible airborne toxins."

"When in doubt, scare them out." Bob said.

"Whatever works." I said, feeling frustration mounting. "Let's see if we can get an area set up for later. We probably need three spaces for about fifty. And something for us to stand and speak from. Old school soap boxes if necessary. But maybe there's some benches or raised fountains or flower beds we could stand on. It's probably too much to ask that we find a portable public address system. But we might be able to commandeer a bullhorn."

That was all pretty much unnecessary. We only had about forty show up at shift change. Mostly the younger guys who were too afraid to defy their captain's suggestion for them to attend. They grudgingly stood in smaller ten to fifteen person groups. And they pretty much refused to talk. So Bob, Kevin and I did the only thing we could do. We talked about our own answers to the prompts and hoped they heard something that could help. But if they did, there was no evidence of it. They weren't listening. Clearly disregarding us. And burst away as soon as we dismissed them. Bob, Kevin and I stood together watching them practically run away from us.

"We've got a lot of work to do if this is ever gonna work."

Back in Jacksonville several weeks later, Bob, Kevin and I sat on the wooden deck watching the breeze blow the sea oats in front of the dunes and the weak waves softly roll in the distance. It was time for our own process debrief. For my part I just tried to keep us focused on the fact that we didn't have a process yet. So, technically, we didn't actually fail. It was a learning experience. And boy did we learn a lot.

First, we can't get to the scene fast enough to be beneficial. We have to get ahead of that somehow. If we aren't able to predict where terrorism might occur, we can't target our training locations, at least not specifically, and we don't have the resources to train and place teams everywhere. After much brainstorming, we agreed that we should focus on a single fire station in each key area. And train them, certify them, and have them do presentations once a year to their colleagues. Ten percent formal training, ninety percent word of mouth.

Then we had to decide where those key areas were. New York? Los Angeles? Too large. Times Square? Rodeo Drive? Probably. But we eventually agreed that our highest percentage targets were likely theme parks, professional sports stadiums and airports. We would focus on fire stations that had those types of facilities within their jurisdiction.

Finally, we tried to put together the event scene timeline for interventions and what was reasonable to expect at each interval. Simple single sentence comments that can be made by an incident commander or other leaders while going to, or arriving at, a site. And a required, scheduled debriefing thirty minutes before the end of each shift when onsite.

We spent about six months putting the curriculum together, trying to work around my school schedule as much as we could. Our first stop was the Reedy Creek Fire Department. Reedy Creek is the development area that encompasses the theme parks and vacant land better known as Disney World in Orlando. We used recent unreleased FBI images of the OKC bombing as part of the presentation and discussed behind the scenes stories of the first responders there, those that had granted us permission to do so. Unlike our first audience at the OKC bombing scene, this group of firefighters and support staff were very attentive. I don't know if their attention was due to the recency of the images and not-yet-available-to-the-public backstory we were providing, whether they drew parallels to our other information on PTSD in military situations, or if they also harbored fears of possible terrorist events during their watch. Whatever the reason, they absorbed the information and quickly set up their own training framework. They set up quarterly drills, one in each park, each with a different type of scenario. A traditional bombing. A chemical attack. A bioweapon attack. And a radioactive dirty bomb. They invited us back for each one and asked us to critique their performance. This ultimately became the basic format we used to certify each local agency.

During my last school year, we shifted my class schedule to free Thursdays and Fridays so we could make the longer trips without interfering. This allowed us to cover most target areas in the United States. All responded with similar attentiveness and motivation shown by the Reedy Creek group.

After getting around the Country and doing the initial trainings onsite at each location, we set up a traveling certification-recertification process. For this process we set up a classroom learning style setting, centrally located in a particular state or target area, and invited first responders to travel to attend. We expected a very low turnout due to travel cost and time. But the events began to fill up quickly. We did about fifteen event weeks per year like that through 1999 when it was believed that more than half of the first responders in the target areas had received the training. The new training program was a huge success. We were personally being requested to do lectures in colleges, police and fire academies all over the United States. The requests were so frequent that we had to assign other primary teachers to teach at our more typical weekly training sessions so we could do those other lectures. But as luck would have it, it would all come full circle for me later in 1999.

Chapter Four:
Kurds, Serbs and Slavs...Oh My!

Adana, Turkey
Skopje, FYROM (North Macedonia)
Ferizaj, Kosovo
1999

"You want me to do what?!" I asked.

"It's no different than your trip to Tinker AFB in Oklahoma." Dr Ellison said, "It's just a little farther. And for the first part of it you'll be on a boat."

"Um…A boat?"

"A big boat. The Kennedy. It's an aircraft carrier." Dr Ellison said. "As luck would have it, the Kennedy's in Mayport right now. They're supposed to leave on Thursday the 16th. Hurricane Floyd may delay that depending on which direction it turns. So there's plenty of time to get you and your team a spot onboard."

"That's only like four days away. Can't we just fly there like normal people?" I complained.

"Trust me. You don't want to fly there. Haven't you been watching the news?"

"Yes. But I know the media's skewed." I quipped. "Saddam's shooting up or invading everywhere around his border and pissing off Iran and Kuwait. Yugoslavia's either in the midst of a civil war, breaking apart, or on the verge of a treaty. It changes every day. I pretty much stopped listening to those stories. Is there something new? Or more likely is there something not on the news I should know about?"

"That's the gist of it. But Saddam just offered rewards for anyone that takes down one of our aircraft in the Northern No Fly Zone." He explained, "That changes things. That No Fly Zone is protecting the Kurds in that area from genocide. It's also a nice little buffer area between Iraq and Iran. We know Iran has battlefield nukes they've threatened to use if Saddam attacks the Kurds. Saddam may have some nukes too, depending on who you believe. Both have chemical and rudimentary biological weapons. The area could literally blow up or otherwise become a bio-chemical hot zone. And that would be bad for other US interests I can't really discuss with you."

"I don't understand. Who are we training? The Kurds?" I asked.

"You'll be training the coalition forces from several countries at our forward bases in that area. Camp Able Sentry in FYROM, Camp Bondsteel in Kosovo, and Incirlik Air Base in Turkey. Incirlik houses one of our only stashes of tactical nuclear warheads in the region. That will be your first stop. But they're all considered high probability targets for a lot of folks right now. With the civil disruptions and numerous opposing factions, the Balkans are full of operatives from Russia, China, and others who would love to take advantage of an opportunity to hit an American base with a dirty bomb."

"OK. But what the hell is FYROM?" I asked.

"Abbreviation. Former Yugoslav Republic of Macedonia. No one wants to say that mouthful. It's a semi-autonomous region but not its own independent country. There's a civil war between the Macedonians, Serbs and the Yugoslavs. The US role there is mainly just to allow safe passage through the region for peacekeepers and trade. That's just the US part. But as part of NATO, US forces participate actively in combat operations. The goal is to support the Kosovo region in becoming a free and independent nation. Unfortunately, the Yugoslavs and Serbians don't want that. So there are NATO combat operations happening every day."

"Anything specific I need to know?"

“They’ll brief you and your team in more detail on the ship. While at sea, they’ll get your team qualified on a number of firearms. I expect you will get firearms issued to you while you’re active in the region. That’s a new thing. We didn’t originally contemplate your team going into active conflict zones.”

“We certainly did not.” I said, somewhat exasperated. “Adding enemy combatants to the list…”

“I know. It’s a lot. But you guys can handle it. You won’t be alone. You’ll be with a lot of professional soldiers that are very good at what they do.”

“I hope you’re right.” I said. “At least we’ve got four days to prepare before we leave.”

***

“What?!” I yelled into the phone about six hours later.

“The hurricane’s track changed and Floyd’s coming closer to the Jacksonville coast. So the Kennedy needs to sail sooner rather than later to get far enough out to sea to be safe during the storm. They’re leaving on the 13th now.” Dr Ellison said.

“That’s tomorrow!”

“I know. Sorry about that…again.” He said. “Just be at Mayport with your team and ready to board by 5am. Pack light. They’ll be issuing you clothing and other gear you’ll need. I recommend a backpack at most.”

“How long will we be gone?” I asked.

“All the stops, training time, plus travel time, probably a few weeks.”

“I’ll get back with Bob and Kevin and let them know the new timeline. If I don’t show up at Mayport in the morning it means they probably beat me to death for putting them through another last-minute rush." I said, only partially joking.

"They'll be fine. They're still technically military guys. And in CBRN, last minute is what they do. Unless they've gone totally soft lounging by the beach and traveling around the hotel conference scene." He offered "They'll be familiar with all the military procedures. You'll be the fish out of water on this one. Just stick with them."

Stick with them I did. When we got to Mayport the base was slammed with sailors processing in due to the last minute change of departure date. When we finally got through the gate we were redirected back to our normal hangar area rather than straight to the Kennedy boarding area. Waiting for us were bags of uniforms and gear. The uniforms were the standard tri-color desert combat uniforms, known as DCUs. They were a light tan base with some beige camo splotches and a few narrow brown splotches mixed in. Thick. And looked heavy. And hot.

"I swear Dr Ellison said they'd be getting our gear to us once we were on the ship." I said to Bob and Kevin, who were essentially ignoring me, both having learned to just go with the flow.

"He probably wanted us to have the desert color Army uniforms rather than the blue navy ones they keep on the ship." Bob explained, "These still need to be built. See the ziplock bag stuffed in the pocket? That's the patches that need to be sewn on. Ours say Army since we're still official, but yours will say Contractor and you should have square patches with a triangle that say US. Those will go on your sleeves and above your contractor plate. They'll sew your name on a nameplate with their machine on the ship and then they'll sew all the patches to the uniforms. We'll have time to show you everything about the tactical gear when we get on the ship. But right now, we need to hurry to get the basic uniform and boots on so we can get to the Kennedy before they leave us."

"It looks like there's a lot in here. This is a massive bag." I said starting to rummage through.

"You should have three full uniforms. Nine pairs of socks, underwear and t-shirts. A tactical vest. A coat. A soft hat. And combat helmet. Boots. And some basic toiletries" Bob said, almost reading off as he was sorting his own gear. "Hurry up and get changed. We'll leave our street clothes here with Angelo. He'll keep them safe until we get back."

"Welcome to military life." Kevin added with a smile.

The gear was indeed heavy. Carrying it from the hangar, and holding it while snail pacing forward in line for check in, was brutal. And with the September heat on top of it, I was realizing just how badly out of shape I was.

"When we get to the Officers Brow, what you would probably call a gangway, I'll be going first." Bob said beginning to explain the complex procedure for ship entry, "Kevin will be behind you. At the top of the brow, when we reach the quarterdeck, just do what I do. I'll salute the deck officer and request permission to board. You'll do the same. But since you have no individual papers and a blank uniform with no insignias, they may stop you. You're specifically identified on my orders. I'm to escort you. I'll do my best to impress upon them your role before you step up. Hopefully it will go smoothly since they are trying to board everyone as quickly as possible due to the storm."

"And Kevin," Bob snickered, "It's 5:30 in the morning. So you don't have to salute the aft flag."

"One time! One time I was half asleep and saluted the flag by habit in the dark and I'll never hear the end of it." Kevin rebutted.

"You only salute the aft flag, also called the national ensign, during daylight hours" Bob explained, "And since daylight can be different in different parts of the world, it's defined onboard as 0800, 8:00am, to sundown local time."

Bob stepped up to the quarterdeck and very smartly saluted the deck officer while requesting permission to come aboard. After Bob was granted permission to board, he stopped and spoke what seemed to be only a few words to the deck officer while showing his paperwork. It took moments but felt like anxious years to me as I was realizing I had no idea how to properly salute someone. My heart was pounding when my turn to step up came.

"Request permission to come aboard sir." I said giving my best, but likely laughable, salute.

"Permission granted. Welcome aboard sir. Please stay with your escorting officer until told otherwise by command staff." The deck officer said pointing to Bob.

"Yes sir." I said as I walked past to where Bob was waiting a few steps into the quarterdeck.

"Easy peasy." Bob said. "Turns out he was an enlisted guy I've known for years. Must have done something bad to get deck officer duty today."

"Enlisted? And you still have to salute him? I thought the enlisted had to salute officers first?" I asked, still not understanding the protocol.

"In that role he's considered an extension of the Commanding Officer and as such everyone salutes him." Bob explained. "Just inside this passage I'll find us an RLO, that's the Reserve Liaison Officer. The RLO will take us to our assigned berth to stow our gear and then give us a quick tour of the key spaces, showers and toilets, the mess, laundry, etc. The RLO may likely go over emergency procedures in more detail since we're going out in a storm. They don't usually do that. It's usually just deferred to the ship-wide announcements when we embark."

"I'm totally lost on the protocol. I have no idea what the emblems and stripes mean, or who outranks whom." I said, worried a bit as always, “Is that going to be a problem? Am I gonna end up in the brig if I don’t salute someone?”

“If you end up in the brig it won’t be for that.” Bob snickered, “Actually, once we get settled in the berth, our first stop is going to be the laundry. We need to get to them asap this morning before the regular laundry duties start piling up. They’ll be the ones sewing on your patches. That Contractor patch will be your get out of saluting free card. Contractors aren’t expected to know that stuff. Just be respectful of everyone and you’ll be fine.”

Once onboard, the three of us were escorted to our berth area by the RLO. The RLO was respectful and conscientious in explaining the parts of the ship we passed through. A lot of time was spent explaining how the stairs work, well, really more ladders than stairs. There are specific up ladders and down ladders. And that I would be placing my life in jeopardy if I tried to go up a down ladder. Apparently those familiar with the ship don’t climb down the ladder, they slide down as fast as they can, often with reckless abandon for anything below.

A few ladders later we reached our berthing deck. And a confusing maze of narrow passages after that we were at our quarters, and I got my first glimpse of my assigned berth.

We had our own space, meant for four, so we had more space than the enlisted sailors. Not that you could tell. The space was about nine feet wide, wall to wall, with two bunk berths on each side and about a three foot wide center aisle between the bunks. At the end of the center aisle was a set of lockers of various shapes and sizes. None large enough to hold a two-liter soda bottle. Small. Clearly intended for locking up small valuables and storing toiletries. Our bags were designed to stow under the bottom row of bunks. The mattresses were maybe two inches thick. When laying on the mattress I rolled on my side and my other side almost touched the bottom of the top berth. Not a good time to have broad shoulders like mine. Even laying flat on my back there wasn't much room between me and cracking my head on the metal above. The top bunks were a bit better. There was a higher ceiling there, but the criss-crossing pipes and wire bundles were still at head cracking height.

"Top bunks must be for the claustrophobic." I said jokingly.

"Space is precious." Kevin said "There's about three thousand crew and officers on board now. That's just to run the ship. But once the airwings start arriving that will go up to over five thousand people. With the pilots, aircraft mechanics and flight crews."

"Do the officers live like this too?" I asked.

"These are officer quarters." Kevin laughed. "For the lower ranking officers at least. The more senior officers have it pretty cush. They have a space this size for only two of them to share. Depending on how senior they are they might have a room like this to themselves with their own small sink."

"We got lucky with this one." Bob added, "Late add-ons like us usually get split up and mixed at all ends of the ship in the enlisted berths."

"Yep. That's a logistic nightmare." Kevin said. "Gotta plan meet ups and there's no way to get a hold of anyone without going through a bunch of different intermediaries. Huge pain in the ass."

"Look in that locker. There should be a canvas bag. That's your laundry bag. Put all your uniform shirts and jackets in there." Bob directed.

I stuffed the bag as asked. From somewhere Bob pulled out a sharpie marker and wrote a series of letters and numbers on the bag that made no sense to me.

"What secret code is that?" I asked.

"Essentially it's coordinates to your berth and your ship ID number." Bob explained. "The first string of numbers is your berth location. The first number is the deck. The second is the frame. The frame is a line that runs across the width of the ship kind of like a roof trellis. The third number is the compartment, you can think of like the room. They are numbered from the centerline of the ship with even numbers increasing toward port, and odd numbers increasing toward starboard. The last letter in that list describes what type of space it is. In this case the L is for Living Quarters. The five characters under that are just your last initial and last four of your social."

"We'll get that laundry bag dropped off asap. With any luck, since they shouldn't be too busy yet, they may even deliver the finished uniforms back to your berth. Save you a long trip trying to carry that bag through the ladder-wells." Kevin said, hopeful for me.

"Breakfast is only served from 0600 to 0800. So let's get to going toward the laundry so we can get back to the mess and eat before they close up." Bob said.

"What do I wear if my uniform shirt is in the bag?" I asked.

"Just wear your t-shirt. If anyone asks, we'll explain. We won't be in the more formal captain's mess so it should be fine." Bob noted.

"Okay." I said hefting the bag up over my shoulder. "Here goes nothing."

Things went smoothly at the laundry. They even said they'd deliver everything back to the berth in a couple of hours. Impressive. So off we headed to the mess.

"Don't get too excited." Kevin said "It's gonna smell great when we get there. But don't let that fool you. The food's pretty bland at best."

"At least we know it will be fresh on the first day." Bob clarified.

"Ha! True! You gotta be careful when you've been out to sea for a while." Kevin warned "Almost rotten fruits and vegetables, and moldy foods get put out in the mess. Gotta double check it all. Best to eat the packaged stuff like energy bars those days."

"Now, now. They usually try to trim off the moldy rotten parts before putting it out." Bob consoled, seeing the nauseated look on my face. "It's just when certain groups are on mess duty that standards are…less precisely adhered to."

"15,000 meals a day on a finite food supply. If you're hungry enough, you'll eat whatever's left." Kevin concluded.

"They replenish supplies at ports of call. So the day after port is the best food you'll have on the ship!" Bob said while Kevin affirmatively nodded along.

Kevin was right about the smell. We turned a corner near the mess and it smelled like you were standing in grandma's kitchen while she was frying up bacon and baking pies. The smell seemed to diminish when we actually entered the mess. I'm not sure if it's actually a thing…but it seemed like the noise was so loud it became hard to smell the food. There was the hum and vibration of the ship in general. But on top of that was the hum, rattle and clank of the mess cooks, servers and patrons trying to prepare, consume and clean up meals in mere moments. It was like a beehive. The tables were full but there was little actual conversation happening. Perhaps the regulars know better than to try to fight the noise for conversation's sake. Or perhaps they knew they wouldn't be sitting long enough to have a conversation. It seemed there was a constant up and down at the tables. Amidst it all, possibly the majority, were people just popping in, grabbing food and taking it back to their berth or workstation. There was a massive sense of urgency here. I felt a little of that at check-in, but nothing like this.

“The hot mess is about to close so everyone’s trying to grab what they can. At closing time, the cooks and servers pretty much leave the area and lock themselves in back cleaning and getting ready to prep for the next meal. At that point you’re stuck with whatever’s left out here.” Bob said, pointing to a half empty rack of assorted nutrition bars and some large metal pans with whole apples, bananas and oranges.

“It doesn’t look that bad. That’s more than I had in my apartment in college.” I laughed, also just realizing where the term *hot mess* came from.

“You say that now. We can survive on anything for our week long voyage. But these guys are deployed for six to nine months at a time. Nutrition bars and half rotten fruit get old quick.” Kevin said, as he piled his plate with sausage and pancakes.

“And you think it’s bad now. It’s twice as crowded when the airwing gets onboard. At that point everything gets scheduled around which hot meal you really want to eat, because it’s likely you’ll miss two of the three on most days.” Bob said, not painting a very pleasant picture of shipboard life.

“I feel guilty now.” I said as I put pancakes and sausage patties on my plate. Bob grabbed my arm as I reached for the spoon to scoop some eggs from the pan.

“Easy on those.” He said, “Good rule of thumb is to see what’s almost gone and get that. Not too many people eat eggs onboard. At sea they’re almost always reconstituted powdered eggs. Not sure what they are today. But the pan’s almost full and it’s been out here for a while.”

“I get them sometimes. When I crave hot sauce and need something to put it on.” Kevin added.

“Some people don’t digest them well. And if you think the berth spaces are uncomfortably small, wait until you see the toilets” Bob said.

“And there’s often lines for those too. You can’t just rush to a toilet in an emergency and expect to find one available.” Kevin said.

My sarcasm dripped. “Sounds wonderful. I can see why we wouldn’t want to just fly over.”

I needed to step up my game and start moving much faster. I first noticed this in the mess when I was a few bites into my food while Bob and Kevin were almost finished. Now, moving through the passageways and ladder-wells, everyone was moving fast. Bob encouraged me to keep up and trained me to step aside when someone was moving faster and needed to pass me. Only a couple hours onboard and I could tell life here was just a series of rushing and waiting. Rush to get to the mess, wait in line to get food, rush to eat, rush to the toilets, wait in line for a toilet, and so on. The Kennedy was a twenty four hour a day, seven days a week sprint. The work for the ship’s crew was constant, around the clock. As soon as one thing was fixed there were two new things to repair. But amongst the hustle and bustle there were some occasional signs of normalcy.

While Bob went somewhere to do some sort of official something, Kevin gave me a full tour of the accessible parts of the ship. Many of the areas were closed since most sailors were at their various stations preparing for departure. But there was a pretty good-sized gym for weightlifting, spin-cycling, treadmills and aerobics. Kevin explained that the room, like a lot of others, had large outer doors that could be opened, allowing views to whatever was outside, but most importantly to allow air to better circulate. It was still morning, and the September heat seemed to already be creeping its way into the ship. It wasn’t air conditioned at normal times by any means. But even the passages deep inside the ship seemed to be a little warmer than they should be.

“You get used to the heat.” Kevin said, noticing me repeatedly wiping sweat from my brow. “And once fully underway, as long as the waters are reasonably calm, they open all those doors and hatches, so it gets a little cooler and less stuffy feeling.”

We slowed our pace as we approached a larger open area. Larger does not mean large by any means. Compared to the other ridiculously tight spaces it was large. Maybe the size of a school classroom. There were a few couches and a few tables big enough for board gaming or cards. There was a TV up in the corner broadcasting CNN’s tracking of Hurricane Floyd. And a smaller TV next to it broadcasting ship information. There were several groups of people chatting that appeared to be friends or old coworkers catching up after being separated at different landside stations. A few had paper coffee cups with them.

“This is one of the lounges. There’s a room across the hall where you can check out board games, cards, poker chips, even coloring books and crayons.” he said. “Right down the passage is a coffee shop. Nothing fancy, just a walk up. But they can make specialty coffees, like cappuccino, espresso, caramel macchiato, all that crazy stuff. They use fancy beans and grinds, not the bulk Navy coffee they serve in the big urns at the mess. But you gotta pay for it. So they’re pretty much just an occasional treat for most people.”

“That storm’s getting close.” I said looking at the track on the CNN feed, “It looks like it’s coming right up the coast into us. How long until we leave?”

“We left about an hour ago.” Kevin said. “It’s a slow move at first. Pretty unnoticeable unless you’ve got a related job to do. We’re just passengers, so inside all closed up in here you won’t feel it. But don’t worry, with this storm heading our way you’ll feel it soon enough. Once we get out off the coast it will probably be a rough ride for the first day. We’re still pretty close to shore. You could probably swim back to the beach from here if you had too.”

“It feels odd not knowing where we are. Not having windows to see out.” I said.

“Yep. Several of the lounges have windows even though this one doesn’t. And a lot of the larger rec spaces, like the weight gym we saw before, all open up to the world outside. The smart people eventually figured out that natural light is necessary to stop five thousand people cramped up together for nine months from killing each other.”

“How long did it take them to figure that out?” I laughed.

“Longer than you would think.” He said. “But now, when the hangar deck and cargo elevators aren’t being used, they do outdoor events, aerobics, stretching and other field games on them. Get people fresh air and sunshine. One of the most popular days is the swim day. Ship stops and they lower the aft elevator to nearly water level so people can get on and off to swim. Some of the higher testosterone guys even jump off from parts of the ship way up near the flight deck. But someone hit the water wrong one time and got injured so I think they’ve banned that.”

“Those elevators get used for all kinds of things when not moving cargo or planes.” Kevin continued. “It’s where they do pistol and rifle re-certifications, shoot toward targets at the edge of the platform. Bullets go safely out to sea and lead dust is dissipated by the wind way better than any indoor gun range you’ve been to.”

“I didn’t think about needing a gun range on board. Is that where we’ll be going to do the training Bob mentioned?”

“Nope. There’s a special place near the armory where we’ll do all of that. That will be one on one instruction. I hope we get some fun toys to take with us.” Kevin said a little too excitedly. “But that won’t happen until we’re a couple days out to sea.”

A couple days came and went. But we weren't heading out to sea. We were heading back toward the Florida coast. Into the hurricane. With thirty-foot waves.

"I thought the whole reason we were leaving early was to not be in the storm!" I pronounced to Bob through my now constant nausea. "What's going on?"

"A ship nearby is in distress. We're about a hundred-fifty miles away from them, and when they radioed the Coast Guard, they were about three hundred-fifty miles off the coast. We're the only ship that is stable enough in these seas and is close enough to get a helicopter out to help." Bob explained. "Law of the sea. Closest vessel must respond."

"A helicopter? In a hurricane?" I asked incredulously.

"Yep. HS-11, the Dragonslayers, that's the name of the helicopter squadron that's with us. They do a lot of sea rescues. Most aren't in the full force of the hurricane like this. But they'll get it done. I just hope the guys on the life raft can hang on in these waves until they get there."

"How long have they been out there?"

"They radioed the Coast Guard at about 7:40 this morning. Their tug was taking on water and going down. They cut the lines to the seven-hundred-foot barge they were towing but it didn't help."

"A tug was out at sea? I thought they worked in harbors?"

"This isn't one of those small harbor tugs. This is one of the big ones that moves barges up and down the coast."

"I didn't know they did that. But now that you mention it, I remember seeing them moving past when I was at the beach. I just never thought about it."

"Coast Guard said this one is a hundred-fifty-foot ocean tug with an eight-man crew. Life rafts on ocean tugs are more like small boats with covered cabins. But any life raft in thirty-foot waves and this wind can easily get flipped and dumped."

"It's been two hours since they radioed the Coast Guard." Bob continued, "The helos only have a range of about a hundred miles. So the ship's gotta get about a hundred miles closer for them to have a legit shot. Fingers crossed we get there in time."

I just nodded solemnly, not believing there was any hope of rescuing them.

Bob had been issued a hand-held communication radio for our upcoming expedition. He set it on the main command channel so we could listen to the rescue efforts as we sat in one of the inner lounge areas. A few sailors that weren't on duty eased their way near us to listen in. It was about 10:30 and we were approaching the helo launch zone. Things were starting to get very busy.

Command was estimating the waves to be between thirty and fifty feet, splashing over the flight deck at times. For safety during such storms, the helos are stored inside on the hanger deck. The Captain was maneuvering the Kennedy into a position where they could safely use the aircraft elevator to get the helos up to the flight deck without a wave flooding the hangar or the high winds blowing a crewman overboard.

Eventually they got the first of the helos to the flight deck. But now the winds were the problem. Sustained hurricane force winds gusting well over a hundred miles per hour. It would be easy for the wind to blow a helo into the command tower. Or for a wave to rock the ship sending the command tower into a helo hovering above the deck.

The helo was ordered to initiate a rare rapid vertical ascent when the ship hit the peak of the cresting wave. Hopefully the subsequent downward motion of the ship and the upward motion of the helo would reduce the chances of collision with the tower.

It did. And the first rescue helicopter, designated helo one, was up and away just as the elevator with helo two reached the flight deck. Almost immediately helo two was up and away as well. It was about 11:00. The tug's crew had been in the water for over three hours. Three hours drifting away from where they radioed their last abandoned ship location.

"Well, the helos got off. Each has a five man crew, two to fly, one to work the helo-side rescue equipment, and two rescue divers. Ten total." Bob described for the nearby listeners who may not have heard clearly. "Winds are bad. The helos will be at the far end of their range. They'll need to work fast. Assuming they find anything when they get there."

"Won't they have radios and emergency locators in the life raft?" I asked.

"They should. If they kept their maintenance up. All it takes is a dead battery that wasn't changed as scheduled." Bob answered. "But the biggest issue is getting gear and getting to the raft. Imagine trying to pack a suitcase while jumping on a trampoline. And then add hurricane force winds and water to the mix with a massive dose of fear. Who knows what they were able to load and what will work. Hopefully they all got into life vests."

About an hour into the rescue operation the radio squawked, and an excited pilot reported they picked up an emergency beacon signal. It was faint, but triangulating the signal and the original location they had a good idea where to start their search. This was great news since the helos wouldn't have a lot of time on target to aimlessly search.

Helo one reached the source location of the beacon, about twenty-three miles from where the tug sank. There was no raft. But there were three crewmen in lifejackets bobbing over and under the massive waves struggling to hold onto a short stick or pole of some kind. Helo one immediately got one of their rescue divers in the water and began the rescue efforts. Helo two stayed a safe distance away. There was no sign of the raft or any others in life jackets.

The rescue itself was fast. The rescue diver was only in the water for eleven minutes. Once the three crew members onboard were brought up in the basket to helo one, both helos had to return to the Kennedy to refuel. After four hours fighting the churning waves, the three crewmen were too exhausted to try and speak over the loudness of the wind and helo engines roaring their way back to the Kennedy. But once back on the Kennedy, the rescued crewmen, still exhausted but slowly recovering, told the story of what happened after their last radio transmission to the Coast Guard.

There was a life raft. Five of the tug crew were onboard the raft and these three were helping to load the last of the emergency items to the raft when the two ropes holding the raft broke free. The three left onboard the sinking tug leapt into the water to try and swim to the raft, but the waves and winds were too strong. They could only watch as the raft quickly drifted away from them. When they realized they couldn't reach the raft, they all grabbed onto a broomstick floating nearby to try to stay together. One of the three had the portable emergency beacon, about the size of a large flashlight, and held it firmly for four hours until the rescue. They explained, hoped really, that those on the raft also had a beacon, but they weren't sure. No other beacon signals were heard.

Both helos launched again after refueling. The Kennedy was much closer now, so the helos reached the target area with more time to search. Still no beacon. But eventually helo two found the barge the tug had been towing. It was still afloat, but no crew were onboard. Using the location of the barge, the helo recalculated and expanded their search area while Floyd's winds and waves increasingly bore down on them.

After an hour of grid searching, helo two miraculously found the raft and rescued the five remaining tug crew members from the sloshing waters. An hour later, both helos and all the tug crew were safely aboard the Kennedy.

The five tug crew members on the raft were adrift for eight hours in the waves of the approaching hurricane. But for one of them the rescue wasn't over. The violent motion of the raft as it was fighting the waves threw everyone inside around the cabin. One of the crew ended up with a traumatic back injury, needing urgent medical care that couldn't be performed on the Kennedy. Once again, one of the Dragonslayer helos fired up its rotors and launched, this time as a medical transport to get the crewman to a hospital in Jacksonville for emergency surgery.

The Kennedy continued back to Mayport and ended up being there for the brunt of Floyd as it passed just off the coast.

“Well, that was a fun boat ride.” I said sarcastically to Bob. “We left in a rush and ended up right back where we started.”

Bob just shrugged his shoulders.

“Welcome to military life.” Kevin said with a grin, for the second time.

Hurricane Floyd passed by the Jacksonville coast on September 16th. Except for those that were rescued from the tug, no one left the ship while we were in Mayport. A minor replenishment and resupply of fuel and water took a few hours, then on the 17th we were on our way in earnest to the Mediterranean.

It took about five days to cross the Atlantic. Five uneventful days. I was able to experience the tedium of shipboard life. But it still wasn’t a true sailor’s experience since I didn’t have a job to do. There were some meet and greets with officers from the helo squadron and airwings that were now aboard to break the monotony. But what killed most of the time was the special weapons training we had planned.

“We’re gonna do some rapid training and qualification for you on a few of our handguns and long guns.” Armie said.

Armie is the ship’s armory’s chief officer. His name is actually Arnold. He told us it morphed from Arnold to Arnie, to Armie, with an m, over the years to match his role in the armory.

“We’ll start with handguns. Have you ever shot a gun before?” Armie asked.

"Yes sir. I own a Glock 19. Been to the range with it several times." I confidently responded.

"Well, that would have been excellent and saved us some trouble since we issue Glock 19s these days. But they're newer and we don't have as many. So of course we're completely out of them at the moment. All we have now are the Sig P226, a 9mm that's been a staple as long as I can remember, and two of our other newer arrivals, the Baretta M9 9mm, and the Heckler and Koch MK23. The MK23 is a forty five caliber. A bit heavier, harder to shoot on target and holds fewer rounds in the mag, but it's pretty powerful if you hit something. Range is a little short too though, only effective to about eighty feet compared to the hundred-sixty of the Baretta. Both are threaded for silencers if you need them."

"I don't know why we would need silencers" I said, looking over at Bob who was smiling.

"I was told to give you our best and not to ask too many questions." Armie said. "In my experience you never know what you need until you need it."

"I couldn't agree more!" Bob said as Armie nodded recognition.

"Are you familiar with dot sights?" Armie asked looking back to me.

"No. What's that?"

"It's kind of like a scope on a rifle, except it doesn't magnify anything it just has a bright red dot. You look through it and put that dot on your target. When you pull the trigger, the bullet should hit whatever the dot was on."

"So, it's like a laser that puts a dot on the target?" I asked.

"Nope. The dot is on a lens attached to the gun. Nothing shines out on the actual targets. Someone finally smarted up and realized that in smoky combat environments a laser traces a nice line right back to the shooter, painting an easy target on you for your enemy."

"I've set up these three Baretta M9's with dots for you. Bob and Kevin will only take a few minutes to qualify on them. I'll run them through first. Then I'll spend more time going into detail with you. We'll go through loading, unloading, clearing jams, how to aim, and a bunch of things not to do, all the safety stuff. Then we'll shoot for a while with and without the silencer to get you comfortable."

"Tomorrow, we'll get you situated on an M16A4 Carbine rifle. That will be easy for you even though your hands will probably be tired and sore from all the shooting today."

Two days back-to-back of shooting was a lot. Thousands of rounds, mostly through the pistol, and my hands, forearms and shoulders were done for. I was dreading day three. That is until Armie told me what we would be doing.

I didn't know exactly where we were on the ship, but I assumed we wcrc somewhere on the quarterdeck since there was a substantially higher number of officers moving around. Until then, most of my time was spent below deck with more of the enlisted ranks, only occasionally seeing an officer.

"This is the HS-11 Dragonslayers Ready Room. Where the squadron meets for briefings." Armie said.

"And sometimes to watch football on the big screens" A passer-by added with a chuckle.

Armie laughed, "It's set up a bit like a movie theater with some huddle tables up front below the screens, so I'm sure it makes a great seat for game day."

"They're finishing up a briefing now. But someone should be out to get us shortly." Armie added.

"Out to get us?" I asked with a scrunching brow of initial worry "What did we do?"

The door opened and a number of people filed out of the room in various directions. The last one stopped at Armie.

"Cool. You're already here. I was afraid I was gonna need to come down and drag you out of the armory." He said turning to me and offering his hand "I'm Todd Lacoste."

"Good morning, sir." I replied, shaking hands but not really knowing how to broach that introduction.

"Don't bother with that sir stuff on me, call me Todd, or Trig" he said.

"Trig?" I asked.

"Short for trigger. Long story. Come on in and meet the team."

We walked to a group of very tired but still smiling men looking at a map near the front of the room. Trig got the attention of one of them.

"This is Lieutenant Commander Karl Northington" Trig said.

"You must be the one we're hearing about." Northington said, looking at me. "Gonna make us water guys fly through the desert."

"Oh." I said realizing they would be our ride to the air base. "Yes. I guess that's me. Well technically my boss. I'm sorry he put you guys in that position. I'm not sure why he didn't just fly us straight there."

"Probably because he didn't want you to get shot down. If they're not in a fighter jet, those air force guys can't seem to keep their planes in the air." Northington said while the group laughed at some private joke. "You're much safer with us. Even your Army guys at USAMRI know that."

"It's a pleasure to meet you all." I said "I was amazed listening to the feed of the rescue the other day."

“Trig’s the brave one.” Northington said, “that idiot jumped in the water. All I did was try to keep the helo blades above the wave tops.”

“He’s being modest” Trig said, “I don’t think any other pilot could have pulled that off in those conditions. It takes massive skill and experience to keep the helo steady enough to do a rescue on a good day.”

“Enough ass kissing already.” Northington said with a grin showing he loved the praise. He turned to me and said “I want you to meet these guys. These are Lieutenants Rivers and Towers. They’re gonna take you up in helo two with Trig in about an hour. We figured it would be good to get you acquainted with the process, beginning to end. And Trig’s gonna teach you how to operate the air cannon.”

“Air cannon?” I asked, looking at Trig.

“We had to refit the helos with the big guns for the desert trip. We took them off yesterday for the rescue.” Trig said, adding “they aren’t really cannons. Though the 50 BMG feels like it sometimes. We have a new externally mounted 7.62 mini-gun. That’s the most dangerous gun in the skies right now. But we won’t be shooting that one today.”

“He’s excited because he doesn’t get to play with the guns as much as he would like since most of what we do is water rescue stuff.” Northington said. “But we got live fire practice authorization just because of your presence. So you can operate the weapons in case Trig falls asleep during the mission.”

“I’m never gonna live that down.” Trig said turning to me, “I was exhausted and fell asleep on the ride back to the Kennedy after my hurricane swim yesterday.”

“Shad on my helo didn’t fall asleep. He was in the water a whole eleven minutes.” Northington poked.

"That was like six hours earlier. Of course he wasn't tired yet." Trig argued, as someone I assumed to be Shad gave an overhead thumbs up as he walked out of the room.

"We got about a thousand rounds of 50 BMG ammo for the M2." Northington said, "make sure Trig doesn't hog it all and lets you pop some of it off."

"I'll be good. I promise." Trig said.

"You better get going to make any last minute bathroom trips and grab a snack if you need to." Lt. Rivers said, "meet Trig and me in the hangar in fifteen minutes for a pre-flight rundown and we'll get you set up with a flight suit. We go wheels up in an hour."

The view was mesmerizing. View may not be the right word since it was more than just the visual. It was the sight, the sound and the feel of it. I was standing just off the aircraft elevator inside the hangar looking out past helo two, sitting on the elevator awaiting its lift to the flight deck. The sea was dark blue with occasional greenish swirls at the caps. The sky was crystal blue with just a few fluffy clouds. I guess we were far enough away from Floyd now. At the place where all the clouds and bad weather were funneled away back into the storm, leaving a beautiful scene behind for us.

Heading east toward the Mediterranean this time of year, the sun was well to the starboard side of the ship, so the flight deck shaded the port side elevators. It was like looking out through an open door in summer. Visually anyway. The other senses felt something different. For starters, it was cold as hell. The strong breeze blowing lengthwise down the outside of the ship gave a definite chill. I always wondered why the flight crews wore such heavy suits and coats on the flight deck. Now I know, it's at least in part because of the constant cool winds.

I could feel the ship starting to reduce its speed for the helo launch. Or more accurately, I could feel the strength of the breeze diminish quite a bit as Trig escorted me to a safe space on the aircraft elevator for the trip up to the flight deck.

"It's gonna get bright and more windy when we get to the flight deck." Trig said "But these are calm seas and pleasant skies. Nothing like we saw with Floyd."

I felt it. Almost immediately as my head crested the deck. If I weren't wearing the full gear, helmet and glasses I would have had to turn away from the wind. But in the polarized glasses, the crisp colors of everything around were amazing. We reached the top, now level with the flight deck, and I took in the view for a few minutes while some crew members rotated out the rotor blades and locked them into place. I was surprised that I hadn't even noticed the blades were all folded back before.

"We're gonna lift off straight from the elevator surface. We don't need to be rolled out to the flightline." Trig said "so be ready to climb onboard. You'll take the middle seat I'll be on your right by the open door."

"The door doesn't close?" I said nervously.

"Nope. Did I forget to mention that?" Trig smiled "the M2 gun mount crosses through the doorway. You're still sitting inside to shoot. But the gun itself is mostly outside."

"There's this metal plate between you and the bad guys. But you gotta be careful, sometimes when we're moving, the wind will catch the plate and try to spin you off target. So you gotta hold the gun really tight. It's a lot easier to hit a target when we're hovering. So that will be lesson one. We're up. Hop in."

I maneuvered my way around the gun mounted in the doorway and took my assigned seat. I buckled myself in. And looked for anything else I could use to secure me. As I got myself situated, I heard static in my headset with some voices.

“All loaded and secure.”

“Vertical in five, four, three, two…”

And then we were up. That initial lift felt a lot like one of the brief drops in a high rise elevator, or a drop on a roller coaster. A movement the body is clearly not intending to feel and doesn’t know how to react to at first. But then it all gets figured out.

“We’re gonna be about a mile off the starboard side of the Kennedy. You’ll be able to see the other ships we met up with taking position to Kennedy’s port side.” I heard through my helmet in a tinny voice that I eventually realized was coming from the pilot.

“I didn’t know we met up with other ships. I guess being down inside the ship you don’t see that.”

“We travel as a group. Who’s with us depends on what we’re doing. We’re traveling light this round. We have a destroyer, and a couple frigates with us.”

While I was listening in my headset I was watching Trig rummage around a few stacks of what looked like large sleeping bags.

“We’re coming up on the training site. Prepare to deploy target one.”

“Ready to deploy on your mark.” Trig replied.

“Deploy in three, two, one, mark.”

“Target one dropped. Auto deploy in three, two, one…”

I couldn’t see anything below us from my middle seat. But Trig explained what was happening.

“These are self-inflatable practice targets. Kind of like those blow up rafts they keep on boats in Florida. They have an altitude sensor that inflates them just before they hit the water. Once down on the water they’re about a ten-foot-wide circular target.”

"How do you know if you hit it?" I asked.

Trig laughed "oh, you'll know."

The pilot circled the target with just enough tilt so I could see it from my seat but not so much that I was worried about falling out. I guess I was starting to get my bearings. It helped to see the Kennedy pass by in the distant background.

"So here's what we do." Trig explained as he latched himself to a very sturdy looking cable inside, "This cable is attached to this belt around my waist with the straps that crisscross my groin. It's like sitting in a baby swing. Nice and secure. You can twist but won't fall forward or out. There's one on the floor under your seat. Go ahead and put it on. Best to do it kinda like a jock strap, and then buckle it tight in the front."

I fumbled a little bit, but familiar with jock straps from the ancient cup securing baseball days I was able to get it on fairly quickly.

"Good. Now connect this cable latch to the big metal loop in the back." He said handing me the end of a second security cable. It felt too long. "Don't worry. I'll cinch it up tight when you sit over here. For now, just slide over to the seat nearest me so you can see what I'm doing as I explain it to you."

He was loading a long chain of connected ammo from a large metal box in a very complicated looking process. He must have again seen worry on my face.

"Don't worry. I do all the reloading of the ammo belts. It's a machine gun. If you aren't used to it, you'll be surprised how fast the ammo disappears." He said winking.

"This is your sight." He said pointing to a six inch metal circle with a tell-tale cross of horizontal and vertical metal bars. "Put that cross right on what you want to hit. Then pull this trigger lever."

The near end of the gun had two vertical handle grips. In front of the grips was a trigger lever, one on each side. I watched Trig fire. The gun didn't kick back and forth much. There seemed to be some kind of shock absorbing design on the handle which stayed mostly in place.

“Most of these guns have a plate on the back that you press with your thumbs to fire. But I fought long and hard to get the handle trigger lever upgrade. When it actually got approved, the boss started calling me Trigger.” He said smiling as he went back into teaching mode.

“Count one one-thousand, two one-thousand. And then let go of the trigger.” He said “Very short bursts or this thing will heat up and jam. That could be a problem. So we want to avoid that.”

The target wasn’t in sight at the moment. He was just shooting into open water to show me the mechanics of it.

“We’re gonna come around on the target now and hover. I’m going to take a few shots and watch where the rounds hit the water. Then I’ll adjust my shots over the target in small bursts until I hit it.”

Trig did just that. The target came into view bobbing on the wave crests. He sent a short burst, and I could see a line of splashes in the water approaching the target. Then a second burst was dead on. Puffs of white smoke, or maybe powder shot out of the holes the large rounds put into the rubber. It didn’t fully deflate or sink. I guess they were designed with compartments of some kind.

“OK. Now it’s your turn.” Trig said sliding out of the seat and reaching back to release some slack on his harness. “I’ve got you by the back of your harness. Slide over into this seat and once you’re in place I’ll pull it snug for you.”

It was a little scary at first. Getting that first foot off the ground to move. But in the end, it wasn’t as scary as I thought it would be. The floor was sturdy and not shifting around. And there seemed like there were plenty of sturdy things to grab onto if I lost my balance. I made it to the seat without incident and felt the harness pull tight as promised. He edged up behind me and with his right hand moved my right hand, now in a thick glove, onto the right handle.

"Keep your fingers around the handle for now. Don't touch the trigger lever."

He then eased around my left side to confirm my gloved left hand grip in the correct location.

"OK. Now pick a hand and lift your pointer finger off the handle. Just one hand. You choose which. And place it on the front of the lever. When I say go, you'll squeeze that lever back toward you. It's like a regular gun trigger just bigger."

I moved my right pointer finger to the trigger lever.

"Ready! Go!"

I squeezed back the lever, but it didn't immediately fire.

"What am I doing wrong? I asked.

"Nothing. That was just to show you how hard it is. Now use both pointer fingers and squeeze hard when I say go. Ready! Go!"

The trigger moved and I felt the gun recoil as the rounds fed through.

"OK. Stop now." Trig said.

"Sorry. Forgot the two second rule."

"That was about twice as long as you want to fire. We're gonna be coming around on the target now. Get ready. Remember, one short burst to look for the splash and then a second to try for the target."

"Target in sight. Ready. Go!"

I pulled the triggers, focused on my counting time more than my aim. Where Trig's first rounds made an almost straight line toward the target, mine seemed to hit randomly in an ill-formed circular blob. My follow up target rounds all missed well off the mark.

"Not great at this." I said

"It takes practice. I guarantee you'll figure it out before we leave."

It took about four more tries before I got a single hit on the target. No powdery smoke cloud. I guess that's saved for the more accurate hit clusters. But on my fifth try it all went right. There was a reasonable pre-targeting line of splashes, not perfectly straight like Trig's but pretty good for me. Then, to my surprise, my target burst had multiple hits and clouds of powder smoke rose up to the sound of cheers in my headset.

"Alright. Now for the real fun." Trig said with a massive grin.

The real fun meant two more twists. The first was firing from the moving helo as it went past the target. That was much harder. I only made one hit in five tries. It was hard to dial back the desire to just hold down the trigger as long as it took to find the target. Something I would need to unlearn for sure.

The other twist was even better. A different type of target was used. This target dropped down to the water and inflated like the others. But it had some other setting. Trig was at the gun to demonstrate. He handed me a remote with two big buttons, one red, one green.

"When I say go, push that green button. Hopefully we won't need to push red but if I yell push red, then push the red. You ready?"

I acknowledged and pushed green when he said go. The inflatable target started rising off the waves up into the air. Once up it started to blow with the wind and shifted around a bit. But this target was more like a globe than the flatter surface targets. The helo swooped around to keep the helo between the Kennedy and the target, so all the shots went away from the ship.

Trig began firing. It took several bursts of rounds, maybe even ten bursts, before he hit the target in the air. The target burst into a powdery smokey cloud and the pieces fell back to the waves below.

“That’s a special practice target for shooting at other helos or airborne enemies.” Trig said. “The surface targets and these airborne targets are crazy expensive. We never get to use them. We usually have to use old buoys for the surface targets, and we don’t have any airborne targets. Somehow we got special permission since you’re here.”

“You’re welcome.” I said “But I’m not gonna try that one.”

“We only had the one air target. I figured I’d use it for demonstration.” He winked. “But you don’t have to tell the bosses that.”

“Secret’s safe with me.” I said.

“We’re essentially out of ammo. Let’s lock everything up and watch the festivities for a bit.” He said.

“Festivities?”

As if he had cued it up, the helo rotated so the door was facing the Kennedy. And between us and the Kennedy two jets roared past.

“It’s time for shift change.” Trig explained. “Kennedy keeps at least two jets up in the air around the clock keeping an eye on things out at the edge of weapons range. We get to watch the next group take off, and then we’ll watch these guys land. Then we’ll head back to the flight deck.”

The take-off and landing maneuvers were cool to watch, but I’d actually seen that before on a Navy family tiger cruise when I was in college. I had been on deck for that demonstration. Way closer than this distant aerial view. But it was still cool to be watching from the helicopter.

Our landing was smooth and uneventful. This time, instead of taking the elevator back down to the hangar, they towed it to a parking station and lashed it down on the flight deck. Apparently, they were going to give it a quick wash and let it sun dry before bringing it back inside.

We walked across the flight deck and down a staircase to a door just at the base of the command tower. Inside Bob and Kevin were waiting.

"This is where we part ways for now. It was a pleasure." Trig said.

"Definitely! Thanks for everything!" I said shaking his hand.

"Well? What'd ya think?" Bob said.

"It was fun. I could almost hear the Stones *Paint it Black* in my head flying in the gunner seat." I said humming the tune with a grin. They both laughed.

"We hit the mouth of the Mediterranean tomorrow in the early morning. Then we slow down. It will take us about most of the day to get to our departure point in the eastern Med. Not sure where the Kennedy intends to do a pit stop. Hopefully it will be at or after the point when we need to depart. If they do the replenishment earlier, then it may be a good bit later into the evening when we depart. They like to replenish in the Med because the food is excellent compared to the other side of Suez. Spanish, Italian, Greek, Moroccan. All good stuff. Fingers crossed on the timing. I think we all prefer not to make our trip in the dark."

"So much for crossing fingers" I said stepping up beside Bob and Kevin who were on one of the outer staircase landings watching the organized chaos of a replenishment at sea.

"No one ever throws you the pitch you're expecting when you work for Uncle Sam." Kevin said "It's always some weird curve ball that has you swinging in the dirt."

"Did we hit some magical Mercator line where we now have to speak in baseball metaphors?" I asked, suppressing a laugh, "If so I'm just gonna go back to bed until we cross the one that lets us speak pirate."

"Argggh! I hope there's rum in them thar containers" Kevin played along in a pirate voice, pointing with a pretend hook hand at the crates coming toward the ship.

I looked up, now trying to focus on what was actually happening. A funny looking ship was beside us. It looked something like a bastard child of a battleship and a cargo freighter. There were cables and tubes of different sizes lashed between the two ships. A few cables looked like they were keeping the two ships from separating. Two others looked like massive hoses hanging like swag on a presidential podium. Other cables looked like some sort of complicated pully system. Two crates were easing their way across the pulley lines in the direction Kevin had pointed with his pretend hook.

Just as I was getting zoned out watching the slow swaying crates, a roar reached out from above and behind us as one of the Dragonslayer helos lifted off the flight deck.

"Wow." I said "I didn't realize how loud those were when we were out in the ocean the other day."

"You had your headset on. And we're at a dead slow pace right now. So the wind and ship engines are quiet. You can hear the water splash below when the helos move away." Bob said. "One helo from each ship is going back and forth airlifting some of the supplies. It speeds things up compared to just the cables."

"Costs a pretty penny too" Kevin added. "That fuel ain't cheap."

"Speaking of fuel," Bob continued, pointing, "those large tubes over there, they're for fresh water and fuel. They're swagged like that to keep some slack in case one or both ships shift in the waves. If the tubes got yanked out while pumping it would be one hell of a mess to clean up."

The two helos crossed back over the respective decks and an eerie quiet fell over us. You could hear people yelling commands to each other. Commands you wouldn't hear outside of a headset when the engines are revving on the flight deck. In the quiet, you could hear the smaller engines of the forklifts and their squeaking wheels as they sped up, turned and slowed. You could hear the slow push of the clear Mediterranean water between the ships, and the low intensity churning of the other water being forced through jets in the hull to keep the ship in place. These were all very different sounds. I don't know if it was the sounds themselves, the absence of the massively loud engines, or the sight of blue sky and clear water, but it definitely had an effect on my mood. Both energetic and oddly relaxing at the same time. I felt myself opening my eyes wider and breathing a little deeper to take it all in.

"Not sure why they're using an old Oiler ship to do the replenishment." Bob said, somewhat to himself, but then to me "There's a much newer class of replenishment ship, a fast combat support ship. The carrier wouldn't need to slow down to a crawl like this. They must be trying to time their Suez crossing and don't want to get there too soon. They don't want to be a sitting duck out there waiting their turn."

Just then, Lt. Commander Northington came down the staircase and stopped when he saw us at our observation point.

"I forget you guys don't have anything to do around here. I was getting ready to tell you to get off your asses and get back to work." He smiled. "I hardly ever get to yell at anyone anymore."

"We're happy to pitch in if you have something you'd like us to do." Bob said. "We're just trying to stay out of the way, and trying to make sure our guest here gets to see some of the sights and sounds of Navy life."

"The controlled chaos of all this is quite mesmerizing." I said trying to defend Bob. "These are the little daily things about Navy life that people like me never get to experience."

"Be careful what you wish for. You never know what you might experience out here." Northington said. "Enjoy the scenery. But plan to meet me in the Dragonslayers Ready Room at 1500 hrs. We'll go over the details of tonight's little trip. Gonna be a dark one. With a lights out portion over hostile terrain. Timing for the ship's Suez passage isn't the best timing for us."

As Northington walked away, I looked at Bob. Bob just smiled back.

"Good thing they're issuing us guns." Kevin said, joining Bob's smile.

Good thing I wouldn't be needing to sleep anytime soon. My imagination ran to all the bad places and my anxiety quickly skyrocketed.

In the ready room, a somber mood smothered the playful mood of yesterday. The mission parameters clearly changed from an easy peasy quick drop to something much more dangerous. We stood off in the corner, watching the crew and the commander go over the situation on a map.

From what I could tell, the original plan was to make the trip from the Kennedy to Incirlik, drop us off and refuel at Incirlik, then fly back to meet the Kennedy before it entered the Suez. A reasonably safe route over the Mediterranean that could be done on a full tank of fuel. Doing it at night was probably a bit more difficult but that small added difficulty probably made it more interesting for the crew. Now the plans had changed. The trip to Incirlik was still the same. But their trip back was now nearly three times as long, taking them over active war zones, and would require air refueling on two occasions. At night. Before ultimately meeting back up with the Kennedy when it entered the Red Sea beyond the Suez.

Trying to listen in, and to decipher all the jargon and slang terminology, it appeared that they were switching helos, and we would now be going on helo two. Something about their pilot ratings being better for the new situation. And Trig, who was a rescue swimmer during Floyd and the guy who showed me the ropes on the M2, is the higher rated AWSO, which I found out from Bob later meant Aviation Warfare Systems Officer. The helo two crew has also had more training on the new weapon systems for combat operations, primarily the externally mounted mini-gun, while helo one was still primarily focused on sea rescues. Helo two also has a different interior seating configuration than helo one. Something about that was beneficial for the extra weapons ammunition and emergency supplies they would be required to carry for the longer flight back. At least helo two would be familiar to me from my M2 cannon practice day. Hearing all of the complexities coming into play, and the danger level quickly rising, I couldn't help but think…nothing I do is worth this risk. We should have just flown over in the first place. What the hell am I doing here!

It was cold on the flight deck. Even wearing a full flight suit, jacket, thick gloves, and boots. Cold. It may have been partly my fear causing some shivering and not the actual temperature. But it was indeed cold. I took my glasses off to try and get better air and regain some normalcy for a moment. Then immediately put them back on. The sky was dark above and the deck itself was dimly lit with a myriad of colored lights to guide the jets on takeoff and landing. The lights were crisp balls with the glasses on. But without them the light was a mass of mixed plaid stripes and shadows. It was so disorienting that had I not gotten my glasses back in place so quickly I likely would have fallen over off balance.

The three of us eventually got to helo two perched out on the edge of the flight deck. The pilot checked us in and made note of what we were bringing on board, who had weapons and where they were stowed if not holstered on our person.

"The three of you will be sitting in those three seats there. Bob and Kevin, you guys on the outside seats, and you in the middle." he said looking at me.

It made me feel like they thought I was a petulant child that needed to sit between my parents so they could keep me under control. But in this particular situation I had absolutely no problem not having a window seat. The doors were closed for this flight to improve fuel economy. The M2 was still on its mount but retracted into a vertical position and pulled back inside the door. It took up space. The M2 along with the extra ammo and emergency supply boxes took up a lot of space. The four of us in back, Bob, Kevin, Trig and I had no room to stretch out our legs. Sitting like this for almost two hours was going to be a brutal trip. At least Trig would have room to sprawl on the even longer return leg of the flight.

No time was wasted. Once we were in and seated, the doors were closed behind us and we were waved into the air by the deck crew. I barely felt the lift this time. I just saw the lights of the carrier and the strike group peel away into distance before everything outside the window glass went black.

Both Bob and Kevin leaned their heads away and seemed to drift off to sleep. The light inside was extremely dim, really just the glow from the night lit gauges up front. With the dim light and the hum of the rotors I too quickly drifted off to sleep.

"MAYDAY! MAYDAY! This is HS-11 Helo Two. Incirlik, do you copy?! MAYDAY! MAYDAY!" I heard through a com link to my helmet that must have just been opened.

Everyone around me was scurrying and shuffling in their seats doing some sort of habitual things for whatever situation we were in.

"Roger Helo Two this is Incirlik, what is your position and situation."

"This is Helo Two. We're approximately thirty clicks southwest of the intended landing zone at Incirlik. We have unspecified mechanical problems and need to go UHL" the pilot replied.

"Roger Helo Two, understand you are intending unanticipated hard landing. We are scrambling Trident helos now. ETA approximately twenty minutes to your location. Do you have locator beacons on?"

"This is Helo Two. Locator beacons are on and appear to be functioning. Please confirm." The pilot said unusually calmly.

"This is Incirlik. We have a weak beacon signal identified to our southwest. Assume that's you. Tridents will have better signal reception when they are up in the air. Confirm your landing terrain and any known combatants."

"Incirlik this is Helo Two. Looks like farmland below. Open spaces for set down. No identified combatants. Mechanical issues were not related to enemy strike."

"Helo Two do you have any medical issues the Tridents should prepare for?"

"This is Helo Two. No medical issues. We have six total persons on board. Five military. One civilian."

"Roger that. Dual Tridents on the way. Be prepared for evac on arrival."

“Roger Incirlik. Contact break for landing. Will reconnect when on the ground. Helo Two out.”

“Make sure all your belts are strapped tight and your gear is secured. This won’t be gentle.” The pilot said to us over the helmet com system.

Bob touched my arm to get my attention. He could see that I was frozen in fear.

“This seems scary, but it happens all the time. For these guys it’s like getting a flat tire on the interstate. They just need to focus to get the car over to the side of the road and then we wait for AAA.” Bob said with a gentle calmness.

“Keep your feet on the ground and hold your back and head against the back of the seat. The impact will be like the old bumper cars when you were a kid. As long as you’re in the right position and expecting the bump you’ll be fine.”

Just then the pilot came on.

“Landing in ten, nine, eight, seven, six…” the pilot counted down after the engine was shut off and the rotors slowed in growing silence. “Five, four, three, two, brace for impact…now!”

The impact was jarring. Even though I was properly positioned, I felt like I was thrown back and forth, and side to side into Bob and Kevin who were also moving within their tightened seatbelts. I felt the helo seem to tip slightly, almost lifting back off the ground on one side, and then sliding forward and toward the lower side before coming to an uneven, still rest.

“Incirlik this is Helo Two. We are on the ground. Engines off with no apparent electrical or fire concerns. Landing gear is damaged. Terrain is flat. Room for both Tridents nearby. Exact position is…” The pilot said, rattling off a series of longitude and latitude numbers that meant nothing to me.

“Helo Two this is Incirlik. Tridents are in the air and will contact shortly with further instructions. Until then, if safe, remain in helo until their arrival. The location you provided is not generally hostile, but the locals may get a little rowdy about a helo in their prize crops."

"Roger Incirlik. Helo Two will stay put. Small arms available as last resort if hostilities require it. But stowed for now. No injuries beyond minor bumps and bruises reported. Will wait for Tridents for next communication. Helo Two out."

"Everyone is ok back there, right?" the pilot asked.

"All good" Trig replied looking at each of us for a confirming nod as he said it.

"You ok? He said looking at me, "no accidents?"

"I only shit myself in my head if that's what you mean." I replied.

"Go ahead and undo all your harness buckles and make sure your stowed gear is ready to go." Trig directed all three of us, "Once the Tridents get here the six of us will get on one of their helos. It will be a tight fit. But the other helo will need to stay here for crowd control until a decision is made about our helo."

"A decision?" I asked.

"There isn't really AAA for these things." Bob said smiling. "Someone way higher up than us will be deciding if a recovery team will be mobilized to lift it onto a flatbed and get it to Incirlik for repair. Or if they will strip it of the important stuff and destroy it in place."

"I'm hoping for the former." Kevin said.

"We'll never hear the end of it if we blow it up." Trig said. "But this part of Turkey is fairly America friendly, at least compared to others in the region. So hopefully it will be safe in place for a few days until the crane can get here. Fingers crossed."

"Fingers crossed didn't do us any good last time." I said under my breath, but I could see Bob and Kevin both thought the same thing.

The Tridents helos arrived quickly. It seemed like only a few minutes. But my adrenaline tainted internal clock was probably way off the mark.

“Somebody call for a cab.” One of the Tridents crew said when they opened the door for us. “Right this way. The meter’s ticking.”

One of the Tridents helos was on the ground with rotors still turning though not at full speed. The other helo was still in the air doing circles I assumed to monitor activity in the area. Trig helped us off the stranded helo. I felt my legs almost buckle under me.

“Careful.” He said, “You were sitting still in a cramped position for two hours, then given a nice ground jolt. Your balance is probably gonna be a bit messed up. You need some help with your gear bag?”

“Thanks. No. I’ll be ok. I just need to get my sea legs, air legs, whatever, back under me.” I said giving myself a good stretch and shaking out all my limbs. It must be instinctual because I obviously had no training for it, but Bob and Kevin were doing the exact same thing. We slung our bags over our shoulders and started to make our way over to our waiting ride.

“You’re gonna need to bend down to get under the rotors.” Bob said, “Sorry you didn’t get to practice that before. Just watch what Kevin does.”

The three of us got in. And Trig. And both Dragonslayer pilots. Tight fit.

“I’m staying here on the ground with the disabled helo.” The Trident crewman said, “Our other helo will land to keep me company after you guys head out.”

“Thanks!” I said. “We owe you.”

“Oh, don’t worry. Your buddies know they’ll be buying all of our beer for the foreseeable future.” He said as he closed the door and gave it a couple hard whacks with his hand like he was sending someone off on horseback. He half crawled, half walked out of rotor range and a few seconds later we were up in the air and off.

Other than being squashed like a sardine, in the middle seat with piles of gear bags on top of me, the helo ride into Incirlik was uneventful. There wasn't much to see at night other than the generic glow of lights in the nearby city of Adana to the northwest. Lights throughout the country of Turkey tend to go out for several hours overnight to try and conserve energy. But there were enough lights still powered on so you could see where the main city was. Like just about everywhere, Adana is a growing city and is beginning to encroach on the northwest edge of Incirlik Air Base which only a decade ago seemed out in the middle of nowhere. Or so I was told over the headset by the Tridents helo co-pilot turned tour guide.

The helo set down very gently compared to the ground thrashing on our last landing. Unanticipated Hard Landing, UHL for short, had to have been someone's joke that just caught on and now has become the official term. But after talking with the Dragonslayers and Tridents, it apparently happens more often than you would think. That didn't stop the razzing the Tridents gave the Dragonslayers every chance they got. Much of it was quite amusing and the Dragonslayers took it in good humor. I guess a crash, we'll just go ahead and call it a crash…a crash doesn't mean as much when everyone walks away and there's no insurance claim, points on your license or money out of your pocket. Well except for the cost of the rescue beer.

"Sorry the accommodations aren't better" one of the base guides offered as we approached what looked like original WWII barracks. "We had a pretty bad earthquake here last year. It did a lot of damage to our main hotel. It's still closed. Hard to get the materials and labor brought in due to the conflicts in the region."

"I heard about that" Bob offered "Weren't a lot of people killed?"

"The estimate is about 145 dead and 1,500 injured. But everyone thinks that number is too low. Lots still technically missing. Pretty much all of Europe offered help with search and rescue. But the Turkish government declined. They wanted to do it with their own local resources which were totally inadequate. They wouldn't even let us help with the search and we're practically locals. But eventually they let us help with the displaced families. We gave up all our undamaged off-base housing to help house the families. They were cramming two and three families into one of our little two bedroom housing units. Most are still there. Our military guys living off base are now crammed into spaces on base. Which is another reason why this old dormitory is all we have for you guys. These are the only twenty or so rooms we have for visitors. Doesn't matter if you're a general or a civilian, this is it."

"No worries at all." Bob said "We've definitely had worse. And I love how you guys are helping out the locals. I've been in a lot of situations where that didn't happen."

"We try. There was another smaller quake last month near Istanbul. Far enough from us that there was no damage here. But we are still activated as an air relief hub. Lots of air traffic and ground crews working extra-long hours. Then coming back to super-cramped quarters." The guide said, "It's getting old. The guys that have been here long term are getting frustrated. They think the Turkish government is taking advantage of us."

"I could see how that would be frustrating." Bob said.

"Sometimes our guys forget that the Turkish government was kind enough to let us store nukes in their country. A little cramped space for a while is a tiny tradeoff for us putting that geo-political nuke target on their back."

"Speaking of nukes," our guide said. "That brings us around full circle…you guys have a tour of one of our WS3 vaults at 0500hrs. Your ride will be here at 0430hrs."

I felt like that was really early, but one look at Bob's lack of concern suggested it was status quo.

"You can either grab some food now or grab some when you wake up. The Sultan Inn Café is a pretty decent cafeteria right across the road here. It gets crowded starting about 0300. So if you think you can handle it, it may be best to grab something before sleep tonight and then push through until lunch after your tour. But that's up to you guys. The base Commander's gonna be with you tomorrow so you'll get a good lunch."

"We appreciate the recommendation" Bob said shaking the guide's hand, "And the history. I look forward to seeing this place in the daylight."

"Well, don't get too excited. It looks like everything else around here. Hot and dusty. But we appreciate you guys coming to teach our teams some new tricks. Like I said, everyone's getting a little edgy with everything going on and the cramped space. Fingers crossed it isn't an accident waiting to happen."

We took advantage of our guide's suggestion and visited the Sultan Inn before sleeping. We were still pretty awake from our helo mishap. At about 0130hrs, 1:30am, business was booming. Scary to think what it would have been like closer to 4am when it was actually described as crowded.

The food was fabulous. They had your American staples of course, but also a large mix of local options. I gravitated toward two of the dishes in particular, one was a fried soft-boiled egg, the other was something akin to an American chipped beef on toast, but made with spicy mutton. I spent my summers growing up in western Kentucky where mutton is common. As a kid I was surprised to find out mutton is fairly unheard of anywhere else in the states. But as I got older and began traveling, I found mutton on the menu in almost every country I visited. This Turkish version was definitely one of my favorites. Spiced with who knows what exotic spice blends, then partially dried and sliced paper thin like deli meat and piled high on the local toasted bread with a heavy cream sauce. It really hit home for the weird hour of our meal. The fried egg was fun too. Almost like a scotch egg, but without the sausage. It was an interesting combination of textures with crispy fried breading, the soft hardness of the boiled egg white, and the liquid runny yolk. After almost spraying yolk all over Kevin, I learned to poke a hole in them before biting down.

To be respectful of everyone's time, we ate fast. Not as fast as on the Kennedy. But definitely less than thirty minutes. Back in our dorm room I could feel the strong belly-full pull of sleep. I vaguely remembered taking off my boots, when Bob woke me up two hours later to start our next day's activities.

"You need to change into something less wrinkled." Bob said "the Commander will be with us. Which means we need to look a bit more formal. Though I assume he will be somewhat understanding given the night we had."

"I'm not sure I'll be awake enough to say my own name." I said searching through my bag for a shirt that was somewhat less wrinkled, "two hours of sleep is not my happy place."

"You'll get used to it" Kevin said, already up, fully dressed, bed made and ready to go. "If not, we'll just drag you around like that dead Weekend at Bernie's guy."

"That actually works for me." I said sitting down and making a third attempt to tie my boot strings. "Nothing on my body wants to cooperate anyway."

Despite the exhaustion, I somehow made it upright and was reasonably conscious at the roadside with Bob and Kevin when our ride showed up in an HMMV, known to most in America as the Hummer H1 or the Hum-Vee. I was surprised to see such a big truck. I guess I thought we'd be in a golf cart type of thing.

"Good morning gentlemen. I'm Lance Corporal Jones. I'll be driving you over to the vault entrance on the other side of the runway." Jones said looking us up and down "I'm glad you wore the desert camo DCUs. You can toss those camo jackets I brought into the back. You won't need 'em."

"Jackets?" I said looking at Bob.

"People don't always know what to wear out here." Jones continued "You need to blend in. There are enemies watching from the perimeters like hawks. They see folks that are dressed different, they start taking pictures and making assumptions that are rarely good for anyone."

"So no dress whites," I said with a laugh remembering the lines from the movie A Few Good Men I saw a few years back.

"Yes sir. But we don't have a fence-line like Gitmo in Cuba" Jones said, smiling and clearly getting my reference. "We have a big berm. But as the city is creeping closer there are some building rooftops that could make good perches for snipers."

"Don't worry" Bob said quietly "Turkey's friendly. Most people around here appreciate these guys. Chances of a sniper incident would be very low."

"How many sniper incidents have you had?" Kevin asked, either not hearing Bob or trying to feed into Jones' scare tactics.

"Three so far this year that we know of. Those are the ones where we found a bullet hole in a truck or saw some sand puff up. They're generally not good snipers. So they may have taken fifty shots we just didn't notice. But they could get lucky. I don't want that on my watch. So keep your heads inside the windows."

"You don't have to tell me twice." I said, shifting my way a little further toward the middle of the back seats.

It was a short drive. But we did make a stop at the end of the runway before crossing to let two Turkish fighter jets takeoff. They were fast and loud. And some of the worst exhaust you've ever seen pouring out of the backs of the engines.

"That's part of the Northern Watch fighter group heading to the northern no fly zone in Iraq." Jones explained "they use dirty fuel in those planes. I don't know how they stay in the air, but somehow they do."

About two minutes later we came to the munitions bunker field. It looked like driving onto a camp site. Dozens of small cinderblock sheds each with a single heavy overhead garage style door and a forklift-wide paved path to the access road we were on. One had two HMMVs parked in front of an open door. We pulled behind them, exited our vehicle, and walked into the shelter of the building a little more quickly than we may have needed to.

I'd been in a few munitions bunker fields in the states. They all looked similar to this one. The cinderblock shed was basically an above ground entrance that sloped down into a much larger thickly walled storage space. The spaces were designed to withstand enemy attacks from outside and accidents from inside. A lucky shot on one bunker, or one of the ordinance crewman making an error, might blow up some stored ordinance inside the bunker, but the thick walls would stop any collateral damage to other bunkers. That's what I was expecting to see as we walked in. But that wasn't it at all.

This bunker was indeed part storage room. But it was also a gateway to a tunnel, or more accurately a system of tunnels. There were several roofless golf cart types of vehicles parked inside. A group of people in desert camo were standing around one individual with his back to us who I assumed to be the Commander. Jones got his attention and introduced us.

"Commander. The gentlemen are here as you requested." Jones said offering our names as the Commander approached and shook our hands.

"Welcome to the Incirlik underworld." the Commander said. "Glad to see you made it over without getting hit by any of our enemy's rooftop spitballs."

"Yes sir." Bob said. "It's a pleasure to be here."

"I bet. I heard you almost didn't make it in last night." The Commander said, "I saw a couple of my Tridents stumbling back to their beds on my way out."

"That was definitely an experience." I said. "Glad it happened where it did though. Your teams were amazing. I hardly had time to do my civilian freakout before they had us safe and secure."

"We do our best." The Commander said somewhat dismissively, "Pretty sure you would have been ok though. That area is farm land. We have a good relationship with the farmers. We go out and buy their produce and meats. Our four thousand or so folks working and eating around the clock on base keep those farmers pretty well paid."

"What do you say we quit yapping and start the tour?" the Commander said as a question, but which everyone clearly took as an order, scurrying to their various carts. "You three ride with me. I'm driving. The only place I'm allowed to do that anymore is down here. So buckle up."

The entry tunnel sloped deep and was about twice as wide as the cart. The main tunnels were slightly wider with most offshoots being a bit more narrow. For perspective, each tunnel looked like it could hold one of those airport luggage carts pulling those luggage containers behind it. One cart. In one direction. I assumed there wasn't normally a lot of traffic down here. But during an event I'm sure it was some kind of traffic control chaos.

"Most of the bunkers back there are typical bunkers. But a few of them are access points to this tunnel system." The Commander described, "In case you're turned around, these tunnels go back and forth under the runway to a few of the hangars. We call those special hangars WS3 vaults. The actual name is Weapons Storage and Security System. They're more secure and hardened than any other munitions vaults. They can survive a nuclear blast overhead."

We came out of the tunnel and the tires screeched on the painted floor in a large room with a powerful lift in the center and a very heavy looking door in the ceiling above the lift.

“That door” The Commander said pointing up, “goes right up under one of our planes, or helos, or whatever we have up there. Our weapons can be stored below in this room and raised up to the aircraft and installed in a matter of a few minutes, instead of the fifteen to twenty minutes it takes with the normal ordinance loading process. We have about fifty hangers that are hardened. The hangers look normal from the outside. But inside they have cement encased lead walls and ceilings that are several feet thick. And the hanger doors are heavily reinforced with lead. Either that or the ground crew guys are a bunch of pussies that can’t open a door by themselves. I’ll take their word for it that it’s the heavy lead.”

“This particular vault is empty.” He continued “I figured we’d start here and do any Q&A so we don’t have to spend as much time getting our testicles irradiated in the hot vaults. So, what questions do you have?”

I probably had a million questions. Or at least ten. But I was, what, scared to ask them? I mean it’s what I was here for, and the Commander wasn’t being at all rude or off-putting. But for some reason I didn’t want to voice anything. I think that’s something all high level military leaders have in their voice. Or maybe it was just that this guy reminded me of a General whose daughter I dated in high school. I think the only thing I ever said to him the fifty times I was with him was yes sir. My ex-girlfriend called it command presence. Luckily, she broke up with me.

“I have one question” I said digging deep for the confidence to actually ask it, “These are hardened for a direct nuclear hit. But it seems it wouldn’t matter how protected these buildings are if the runway gets destroyed in the blast. I guess I could see how the helos could get up. But how would the planes take off?”

I wasn’t sure how that question was received. I noticed a bit of a glare that probably would have been worse if any of his airmen were in earshot. But I think I hit a nerve he wasn’t expecting.

“That’s a good question. You’re a smart guy.” He said easing up on the glare. “Not to give away all our defense plans, but we should have enough early warning in most cases to get these planes up and away from the blast zone well before the blast. The helos wait a little longer. They can't get far enough away from the blast fast enough. We'd keep them on the ground until after the blast like you said."

"We're not so worried about those attacks by known international actors. We have good intel on them and can track their incoming bogeys." He explained, "What we worry about is someone randomly lobbing a dirty bomb out of a Cessna or launching one onto our property with some toy rocket launcher from a nearby rooftop. Then, like you said, we'd need to do some extra work to get the planes up. We do have CBRN crews that train in that demo clean-up. Hardened equipment to clear the runway. Some of those guys will be in the group you're talking to later today. You'll have some CBRN guys, and some of the airmen crews that load the nukes on the planes, along with our first responder fire and medical response crews. You ready to head over to see the real thing?"

"Yes sir" I responded habitually, feeling the suppressed laughs in Bob and Kevin's glances.

"This empty vault is for larger bomber loading or to load several of our tactical jet fighters. We're gonna head back under the runway to the other side where the hot vaults are. You're gonna get a demonstration, beginning to end, on how the B61 tactical nukes are transferred and mounted. For safety purposes we're gonna use dummy B61 bomb casings. But all the other B61's in the space are hot so don't wander around kicking tires when we get there."

We crossed back through the tunnel system and headed in a different direction, I think northeast maybe, hard to tell underground. When we stopped, we were in room with cinder block walls, another cart and two other airmen waiting for us. The room was filled with thick metal floor to ceiling shelving and looked like a library for mechanical parts. Nothing ominous like a bomb, but it looked like you could make a bomb from these parts if you were so inclined.

“Good afternoon gentlemen,” the airman said. “The Commander has asked that we give you a demonstration of our process for transporting and mounting our B61s.”

“I’m gonna step away while you guys watch the demonstration.” The Commander said “The airman will bring you back to me after you’re done. We’ll grab a quick early lunch before you get your class started.”

“Gentlemen, if you’ll follow me, I’ll give a little history before we get started.” The airman said as the Commander disappeared from the area, “If you’re not aware, the B61 is a smaller, strategic, tactical nuclear weapon designed to be delivered by aircraft that can fly supersonic. These aren’t the fat man and little-boy style bombs of the past. We have two mods of B61’s on site, Mod 4’s and Mod 11’s. Mod 4’s are designed to be less powerful and more precise at about 45 kilotons. Those would be used to hit certain targets near sensitive areas you don’t want to contaminate. But even though considered a low yield bomb by today’s standards, the 45 kiloton output is three times more than the 15 kilotons of the bomb dropped on Hiroshima. The Mod 4 packs a punch. But most of what we have on site these days are the new Mod 11’s. They hit with about 300 kilotons. The Mod 11 is a bunker buster version of an older B61 known as the Mod 7. The Mod 11 and the Mod 4 look almost exactly alike. The difference is more the internal structure, the technical components and the type of metal the casing is made from. Both are gravity bombs, meaning they aren’t propelled. They only go as fast as the plane and gravity take them.”

“How do bunker busters work?” I asked.

“Good question.” The airman said walking us over to a maintenance poster on the wall, where he began pointing as he continued, “What makes a bomb a bunker buster is really just three things, super heavy weight, a structure that can withstand that initial impact, and a delayed fuse system.”

“The heavy weight comes from the use of depleted Uranium. U-238. Uranium is the second heaviest metal on earth. The 238 isotope is the most abundant naturally occurring on earth. It’s also readily available because it's a byproduct of the process to make Uranium fuel used in power plants and for explosive components of nuclear weapons. The casing of the Mod 11 is made of depleted Uranium. So it is super heavy and super strong. The older B61's weigh about 700 pounds. The Mod 11 weighs in over 1200 pounds."

"Isn't that dangerous? I thought all the radioactive stuff was safely tucked away inside the cone?" I asked now worried about exposure.

"You're right. Depleted Uranium is technically radioactive. But it's only dangerous if ingested or inhaled. It also has a half-life of over four billion years. It's fine to handle it in solid form. So it's used as part of a composite material on the outer casing, making the bomb super hard, heavy and slick to help it slide into the ground."

"The front end is made of an engineered material with support structures underneath that allow it to penetrate without crushing on impact." He continued walking to a different area of the poster. "You know, like that egg drop activity they do in school where you gotta build something that stops the egg from splattering."

"Yep. I did that. I didn't win. Probably why I'm here." I said laughing.

"Most people think the fuse is on the front tip." He said "that's true for your conventional bombs. But the Mod 11 fuse is in the rear. In simple terms, the sensor fuse at the front tip lets the rear fuse know it hit the ground so the rear fuse can start its countdown. Like pulling the pin on the grenade, there's still a few seconds until it detonates. Except on these bombs it's not much of a countdown, just a fraction of a second delay to allow it to get underground before exploding."

"It's designed to spin like a football in flight, and flaps in the tail can be adjusted to help guide it for precise targeting using pre-programmed GPS coordinates. The spin helps it go deeper. When it hits the target, it goes down about twenty feet into the ground before detonating. That explosion underground creates a damaging shock wave that can destroy bunkers that are much deeper, up to a hundred feet below ground even if encased in rock or cement."

"If you'll have a seat right in this cart here, we'll head over to a hot vault. I'll show you the bombs and how they're stored, then we'll do a demo with a dummy bomb for you."

"Sounds great." I said as Bob eyed me knowing it made me anxious as hell.

We rode a short distance in the cart and came to what I thought was a wall at first, but what was actually a large sliding lead door. One of the airmen entered a code on a panel and the door slid open for us. Dim lights illuminated a tunnel beyond. We came to a T intersection of the tunnel and made a turn to the left. About fifty yards later we were at another lead door. The airman again entered a code, and the door opened into a large storage space, about the size of the previous room we were in. But this one had numerous racks along the walls with cradles holding what I assumed were the bombs. They looked like the long narrow fuel tanks on fighter jet wings. About ten feet long and a little wider than one foot along the shaft.

"There are fifteen bombs stored in this room. You can see the special racks connect like loose legos, with holes in the front of the bars for our forklift. We have several rooms like this to store what we call the extras. The bombs not yet assigned to a plane based on current mission parameters. When they get assigned to a plane, we use the forklift to place them on the trailer and the cart will pull the trailer through the tunnel to the vault below the hanger where that plane is stored. Keeping them immediately under their plane does three things. First, it keeps the nukes in a safe controlled space with limited access. Second, it creates a safeguard, so no one accidentally takes off with a nuke. And third, the immediate proximity means we can get them on the lift, up to the hanger level, and mounted to the plane in just a couple minutes. Saving precious time to get them loaded and airborne. We can have ten planes loaded and in the air in less than ten minutes."

"How about the helos?" I asked.

"The helos are a bit more tricky." He explained, "the Mod 11's don't do any good on the helos because they don't fly high enough to get the good gravitational drive on the bomb to get it into the ground. We mount the older Mod 4's to the helos. Would you like to stay and play with these, or would you like to head over to the hangar?"

"Hanger." Bob, Kevin and I all said in synch. None of us having any desire to play with a nuclear bomb.

We went back into the tunnel. I could see it was a straight shot to the hangar in the distance as we passed the T where we turned before. It made sense to me that the straight portion of the T was for the route the bombs take from the storage room to the hanger. Somewhere deep in my mind I was glad someone thought that through when designing it. We went through another sliding lead door as we entered the hangar vault.

This vault was bustling with activity. Several people in different colored uniforms and matching uniform colored hard hats moving about. The lift was obvious in the room, looking almost like a giant size four post bedframe made of metal with pullies and handles. Two B61 Mod 11 bombs were in their cradles against the wall with two other cradles in front of them. The two other cradles had the dummy bombs, brightly painted so no one could mistake them for the real ones. The floor had lines painted on it running directly from the bomb cradles to the lift. A stay-clear area was painted in yellow on each side of the lines.

"We'll do the first demo with you down here so you can see this part of it. Then we'll move you up top for the second demo so you can see that side of things."

The airman walked to a nearby shelf and brought us yellow helmets and sets of headphones. He put on a red set.

"Stay here in the cart. It will keep you out of harm's way." He said. "You'll see that red light start to flash when we begin. During a real event the light will flash and there will be an audible siren all across the base. But we found out early on that using the siren for drills freaked out the neighbors too much. So we do it quiet now."

The airman said several code words and strings of abbreviations into a hand-held walkie talkie. Five seconds went by. Ten. Fifteen. The crews were just moving around like they were when we first arrived, tending to their daily tasks. Then the red light started spinning.

One person ran to the forklift type machine and started toward the cradles while two others ran to the lift, one powering it on and one testing the controls. It was mere seconds until the nearest dummy bomb cradle was sitting on the lift. The lead ceiling door began to slide open, and you could see the tips of the wings of two fighter jets on either side. The lift quickly obstructed the view through the ceiling door as it reached its apex. About ten seconds later the lift began lowering without the cradle and the ceiling door began to close. Only a moment later you could hear the jet engine power up in low gear and then the sound disappeared into the distance.

“That’s all there is to see down here. Not that exciting is it.” The airman said.

“The speed and precision of that is amazing!” I said.

“He’s kind of a dork like that.” Bob said to the airman who responded with a laugh.

“OK. Now for the fun part up top. Follow me up these stairs over here.” The airman said walking to the far corner of the room.

“I was hoping to ride the lift.” Kevin only partially joked.

“Too dangerous.” The airman said “You’ve got live jet engines only a few feet away up top. Lots of safety training before you’re certified to get that close.”

The door opened into the upper hanger level revealing an F-15 Strike Eagle with its engines powered on, idling in place ready to leap.

“Stand over here against this wall. You’ll get a good view and be out of the way.”

We were along the wall, with the F-15 angled across the space in front of us just beyond the lift door. To our right was the wide-open hanger door and the bright light of the sun flooding across the runaway and taxiway.

I was just taking in the view when the red light spun again. I felt the floor beneath me begin to vibrate as the lift door opened. Fifteen seconds later the lift was fully at the apex and an odd looking low rise cart rolled up pulling the cradled dummy bomb off the lift. Two airmen removed the top of the cradle safety mechanism leaving the bomb laying loosely in the cradle ready for pickup. The cart had a hydraulic jack lift with a curved attachment on top that perfectly fit the curve of the bomb shaft. The bomb was lifted out of the cradle and driven under the F-15 where one airman opened a panel on the bomb to secure a cord harness linking it to the plane, and a second airman secured the bomb to the brackets on the plane. The lift driver made micro adjustments to get the heavy bomb in place so it could be securely fastened. It happened fast. Thirty seconds after the lift door opened, the F-15 was making its way out through the hanger door. In two minutes, as promised, the F-15 was airborne.

"Now. Who's hungry?" The airman asked.

Lunch with the Commander was uneventful. The roles were somewhat shifted as the Commander was asking most of the questions of me, about what I was teaching and why it was important at this busy airbase in the middle of the Balkans. I must say I felt more comfortable answering his questions than I did asking him questions earlier.

It was a short walk from lunch to the training room. Since the weather was somewhat mild for the season, Bob, Kevin and I decided to take the stroll rather than the HMMV ride we were offered. About half way down the road we all stopped. We heard a roaring pulsation coming in the air behind us. Turning, we looked up squinting into the cloudless sky. It was a massive Chinook. The dual rotor helicopter the army uses for heavy lifts. And it was carrying our disabled Dragonslayer Helo Two over our heads toward the tarmac.

We veered off our training room route and headed one block over toward the edge of the tarmac to watch. The Chinook slowly lowered, inches at a time, until Helo Two's landing gear, or what was left of it, was on the ground and there was a small amount of slack in the cables. A team of airmen loosened several industrial strength buckles on the straps securing the disabled helo. The Chinook used the slack to shift slightly off to the side of Helo Two and disconnected the cable from their winch. The cable chains fell to the ground with a deep jingle like someone throwing spare change on a table, only bigger and heavier sounding. The Chinook didn't land as I'd expected. After dropping its cargo, it simply rose up and slowly drifted back off into the sky.

"At least they didn't need to blow it up on that farm." Bob said.

"Too bad for the kids. It would have made a heck of a jungle gym for them to climb on." Kevin added.

"Please tell me it's just planes from now on. No more helos." I said.

Bob just smiled and led us back toward the training room.

The next leg of the trip was indeed by plane, albeit a rough, bouncing cargo plane. We were on our way to Camp Able Sentry in the Former Yugoslav Republic of Macedonia. I could see why they started calling it FYROM. That was a ridiculous official name given by NATO trying to be politically correct and recognizing both political entities in the region, Yugoslavia and Macedonia, who were both still claiming some form of rights over the area.

We spent the first part of the bouncy flight working through the feedback of the training session back at Incirlik. The thing that struck us all strongly was that, for a group of people that were so knowledgeable in the safety elements of nuclear weapons, they seemed very attentive to our higher level discussions. They never made light of our words. And they fully engaged in the role play activities. Their feedback was very heartfelt and constructive. Much of which we already planned to incorporate into our next training at Camp Bondsteel in Kosovo. But Able Sentry was first. We weren't doing a formal training at Able Sentry, but two of their key frontline people were going to ride with us to Bondsteel for the training there.

We were in jump seats in the cargo plane so our first glance of Skopje, FYROM was when we walked out the Cargo door and stepped onto the tarmac. It turns out we weren't at Able Sentry. Apparently, many flights came into the area through a local airport with a designated area for US military planes, cargo and vehicles.

We weren't on the tarmac more than a couple minutes when a series of military cargo trucks pulled up to start unloading. Behind them was a single HMMV that pulled around to us.

"Right this way sirs. I'm here to get you to the transfer station north of town." a uniformed soldier behind the wheel said without exiting the enclosed vehicle.

"The pleasantries change the closer you get to the front lines." Bob said. "No need to expose yourself to a sniper unnecessarily."

I nodded to Bob as we all got into the HMMV. The driver didn't hesitate and immediately drove away from the airport and away from the outskirts of the city.

"There are several groups from several nations in this area." The driver said, "The US has several different spaces including a headquarters building. But I've been asked to save some time and get you guys straight to the forward deployment site. There's a

Trident helo waiting to take you and a couple of our Sentry folks into Bondsteel."

"So no plane?" I asked the soldier, glaring at Bob who was trying not to grin beside me.

"No plane sir. Bondsteel is a tent base. Only helos and trucks in and out. And believe me, you don't want to be in a truck driving up there. None of the local factions know what's going on so everyone's shooting at everyone else along those roads."

The HMMV pulled off the main road onto a gravel covered goat trail. Chain link fences along both sides were struggling to keep the forest out. Forest wasn't something I thought of around here, and not something I'd seen yet. We emerged from between the trees out into a large meadow segregated by makeshift portable buildings, tents and landing slabs. Some helos sat on the slabs, while others sat in various spaces in the dirt or grassy areas. Beyond the meadow was a series of craggy, painful looking mountains. The harsh, mostly barren mountains like you would see in National Geographic with an old wrinkled man leading a donkey loaded with blankets and saddle bags full of strange breads and vegetables.

"You're lucky. Your Tridents guys got a slab. Gonna be much less dusty for your lift off." The soldier said pulling around to the tent nearest the slab with what I assume was the Tridents helo. "Bring your gear and follow me to this tent. We'll let you meet the pilots and their team. They may be ready to head out. If you need a restroom break the tent is right over there. I recommend you go before you leave."

"This is the nicer base?" I said to Bob looking around at the thick dust, dirt and grime layered on almost every surface.

"It's not a country club." Bob said a little bitterly, "but it's welcome respite for soldiers who've spent the last month sleeping in the mud with one eye open while ducking bullets and bombs around the clock."

The soldier was right. The Tridents team was ready to go, and they too recommended we take a restroom trip before we left. They pointed us to an otherwise non-descript portable building. It wasn't a hole in the ground latrine like I was expecting. They had some sort of water tank and septic system that allowed for simple flushing toilets, sinks and at least lukewarm showers based on the temperature of the sink water. A quick stop and we made our way back to the Tridents tent.

"If you have sidearms in your gear bags I recommend you unpack them and holster them for carry. You'll also want to keep your rifles in safe mode by your side during the flight. Combat helmets and goggles or glasses, whatever you have, keep them on."

"It almost sounds like he intends to push us out into the middle of the fray." I said quietly to Bob.

"These guys talk. And they're very superstitious. I'm sure the grapevine told them we went down with the Dragonslayer helo. They likely think we're bad luck." Bob answered.

"Great. This should be fun." I said.

The trip from Skopje to Camp Bondsteel in Kosovo was very quick. I'm not sure if the pilots were recklessly speeding, but I do think they dipped us into some canyon weaving that wasn't really necessary. I'm sure it was for the civilian's benefit.

The bulk of the trip in aside, the actual approach to Bondsteel was enlightening. Maybe because it was daylight and we could actually see it. What would have been a runway on a traditional airbase was a series of about fifty helicopter landing pads on one side with some mechanical station hangers in a row alongside. Behind the hangers was a perfectly laid out grid of large portable barrack buildings. They were better than a tent. Almost like massive rudimentary cabins. My best guess was about eighteen clusters of four perfectly aligned temporary buildings. These were obviously laid out by the Army Corp of Engineers solely for efficiency. Other buildings were scattered around the perimeter. Only a few tents. So I'm not sure what the other airman meant by calling it a tent base. This looked a lot nicer than where we left from earlier.

As we came in for a landing on their designated pad, I couldn't help but hear the theme from the old TV show MASH in my head. Only helicopters here and lots of them had the red medical cross on them. I recalled Bob talking with me on the Kennedy about our upcoming trip and saying that Bondsteel was a big medical facility for the area. I guess I just realized what that meant.

Of the fifty or so landing pads, the majority of them were empty. The two on either side of us were occupied by other Trident marked helos. Our helo powered down and they didn't open our doors until the rotors came to a complete stop.

"OK gentlemen. You can stow away your weapons. We made it here in one piece." The copilot said loud enough for a snickering crowd gathering nearby to hear, "safe and sound."

There were no carts or HMMVs to pick us up since the helo pads were close walking distance to the nearby buildings in general. And the Tridents buildings were even closer to their landing pads and clearly marked with their three-pronged trident symbol. They had more than one building. And as I looked back it seemed like the Tridents and the NATO medical teams made up about half of the spaces in the helo pad line.

"Good afternoon. I'm Commander Gowers" a man said walking toward us with his hand extended, "welcome to my base."

We shook hands and introduced ourselves. Commander Gowers seemed to spend good time actually engaging in the interaction, making eye contact, and exerting a sense of welcome through his attention and active listening. It was nothing like the other polite yet somewhat dismissive commanders we had come across on the trip. He was older. And had features I could only guess were of Eskimo or Inuit lineage. Those features may have been what softened his appearance compared to the chiseled features of the other commanders. Regardless, it felt like a legit welcome this time.

We walked up the steps and entered one of the Trident marked buildings. The front of the building held everything essential for operations. A small reception type office space, a hallway leading to a ready room, a communications room and several other office spaces that collectively took up about half the building. The rest of the building was what could only be described as officers' quarters. Larger multi-room spaces with their own bathrooms, sitting areas, kitchenettes, bedrooms and closets.

"We're glad you're here." The Commander said, "I'm not sure if you heard about our scare a few weeks back."

"No, I didn't" I said, thinking back to my discussion with Dr Ellison about two weeks ago now. I wondered if he had heard and that was why he sent us over here so quickly. "What happened."

"Technically nothing." The Commander said, "But some combinations of things transpired that put fear into everyone."

I waited silently for him to continue.

"We're mainly a medical facility here. We see all sorts of trauma injuries. But a few weeks ago, we got rash of admits with illnesses that looked like straight up radiation poising. No one knew why. The Geiger counters set off low grade chirps when we ran them over the patients. We thought someone might have set off a dirty bomb somewhere. But we couldn't pin it down."

I listened intently as this was really our prime directive.

"But after a few weeks of digging into it and investigating we got it figured out. Turns out some of the allied NATO forces were using depleted uranium coated bomb shells and bullets to help penetrate the Russian made tanks and infantry vehicles used by the opposition in the area. Those bullet impacts and bomb explosions created smoke and dust laced with the depleted uranium that floated around a bit. A lot of close infantry fighting was going on along the main thoroughfare near the bomb sites, so a lot got inhaled."

"That can't be good." I said.

"Nope. It's essentially heavy metal poisoning but exacerbated with a little radiation on the side." He shook his head, "we basically treated them for the heavy metal poisoning, and they started showing signs of recovery. But they'll probably still set off a slight blip on the Geiger counter even after they're back at full strength. That radiation won't go away. Half-life on depleted uranium is like a billion years."

"Over four billion" I offered, "do you have protocol in place for those troops? Something to help them avoid inhalation like that?"

"We don't command those troops. So there's not much we can do but make recommendations up the leadership chain. Most of our guys that go in the field always have combat helmets with respirators or surgical masks. So, I guess they were able to avoid it by sheer luck of the general medical protocol."

The commander signed a few papers for a soldier that approached and then we stepped out the back of the building into the maze of the dirt path grid.

"I would take you guys and buy you a drink at one of our bars. But thanks to old General Schwarzkopf's General Order #1, we can only sell and drink non-alcoholic drinks. We'll head over to one of our restaurants and grab a bite to eat instead. Food here's pretty good. Not as good as down in Incirlik though. So don't get your hopes too high."

"Good thing no one can get drunk. They'd get lost in this maze." I said.

"The Army Corp engineers had good intentions. Everything the same size and shape made it a quick and easy build. And these SEAs, Southeast Asian huts, are the most simple design they had on hand, using the least materials and the least labor. We try to make it tolerable with fun signs and emblems on the building sides.

Once you've been here a bit you get a feel for it and can walk it in your sleep."

"I heard you say this is a medical facility…I saw all the medical helicopters. But where is the hospital?" I asked.

"The hospital is broken into a few parts. The initial assessment and emergency area is in that larger building there by the landing pads." The Commander said pointing off to the rooftop visible above the nearest SEA hut. "There's surgical suites and all the support labs in there. But the lower levels of care happen in the SEA huts surrounding the main hospital. The medical team's barracks are in the SEA huts just surrounding those medical buildings. Then everyone else is scattered around beyond that."

We walked up the steps of a SEA hut behind the Commander. It looked like the thirty other buildings around us. But beside the door was a small sign that read *South Town Eats established 1999*.

"South Town?" I said reading the freshly painted sign as we walked in.

"We have two separate spaces now within this roughly thousand acre base. There's what you see around you here, and then all that vacant space just to the north of the building complex you saw when you flew in. We just recently signed the contracts for the engineering and construction of a new state of the art hospital up closer to those northern helipads in the middle of that vacant land. It should be open by 2001. That will be known as North Town. It will have its own supporting SEA huts for services and housing. What you see today will be the South Town. North and South will evolve into something akin to twin cities. The guys here are staking their claim as Southees already so the Southees will have always existed longer than the Northees. It's all about bragging rights." the Commander laughed.

"Speaking of bragging rights," the Commander continued "I heard our Tridents were giving you guys a little grief about your UHL with the Dragonslayers back in Turkey."

"Just a little. Definitely got the feeling they were worried we were bad juju." Kevin said.

"Well, probably best if you don't mention it around here, but I did get the initial report on that Dragonslayer helo." the Commander said looking for some confirmation of the confidential nature of what he was about to say. We nodded as he continued "There was no pilot or maintenance error noted. That helo took a beating during the hurricane. They spent nearly thirteen hours in the air in those hurricane force winds doing the various rescues and medical flights. Apparently salt water was forced much deeper into the engine casing than normal. Even the extra maintenance steps they did couldn't reach it all, and they couldn't see it to know what was wrong. But inside one of the casings there was a slight crack due to age. Most of our older helos have them. Salt water got inside from the force of the wind and other coincidental factors. That salt water started to corrode some of the electronic circuitry that controls the rotor powertrain. The helo started to show slow loss of power. Luckily slow, so it gave the pilot time to get it on the ground before the powertrain fully failed."

"Wow." I said "that was a closer call than I thought."

"Your pilot knew just what to do. Even those low speed hard landings more often than not end up in rollovers, fires and other types of damage and injuries. It's usually due to the rotor inertia, they keep spinning if they aren't shut down at exactly the right time. They grab into the ground and all hell breaks loose. Getting that shut down timing right is like threading a needle in the dark. Too soon and you hit the ground too hard due to gravity. Too late and you flip over. He did good to get you guys down with just a bruised ego. That was pretty impressive."

I was taking a deep sigh of relief I didn't know I needed, when a soldier rushed into the restaurant, came to the table and spoke quietly to the Commander's ear.

"Gentlemen I apologize, but we're gonna need to postpone our meal. Something's come up that needs all of our attention."

***

I felt my anxiety go up with those words and I knew my face was red from the blood pressure spike. We all stood to leave, waiting to follow the Commander, but he stopped us just outside the restaurant door.

"There's an old smuggling route that runs along the boundary between the Kosovo region and Serbia to the north. With the conflict down in Iraq and Afghanistan, refugees have been using it to move north through Turkey and Kosovo to get to Hungary of all places. But now with the combat flare up and the NATO presence the last couple years in this region, there have been refugees coming from all directions across Yugoslavia, Serbia and Macedonia pretty much meeting at that junction point in northern Kosovo. Convoys of humanitarian aid that go through there started to stop and provide aid. So now there's a makeshift refugee city full of people trying to get aid or asylum. I was just informed that a convoy of logistical supplies for the NATO combat forces that was mingled with an aid convoy just got hit by a small scale missile strike and that they're getting larger than expected Geiger readings. I want you three to ride out with our Tridents that carry our medical response team to the scene. Whatever direction you can give to help I will make sure they know to follow it. We don't need another round of physically or mentally sick troops."

Where my face was surely bright red a moment ago. I felt the blood drop out and felt the pale pallor sweating of an old school pass out. Bob grabbed me, seeing my unsteadiness.

"The Corporal will double-time you back to your quarters so you can gather your gear. Don't forget your firearms. I'll meet you back at the Tridents Ready Room." The Commander said heading off double-time in a different direction toward the hospital area.

"Focus on my steps. We're gonna go fast." Bob said making sure we had good eye contact to help stop my shrinking tunnel vision and get me back into the moment.

We started at a walk until I got my gait back, then picked up to a faster walk, a slow jog and then a fairly good pace jog as we got to our quarters to gather our gear.

"Good job." Bob said, "Kevin would have passed out on me."

"One time! One time I passed out and he never lets me hear the end of it!" Kevin responded.

We still had our flight suits on from the trip over, so we only needed to gather our combat helmets, goggles, weapons and related combat supplies. Combat supplies I never thought we would actually be using but which we have now donned three times in the last week. Gear bags in backpack mode and weapons safe, we jogged back to the Tridents Ready Room to join a meeting already in progress. The Tridents commander was speaking to a smaller than expected group of eight people in flight suits.

"We only have three of our Trident helos available." He said.

"Three helos…shouldn't there be like fifteen people here? Five each per helo?" I quietly asked Bob who didn't answer, clearly trying to pay attention to the briefing.

"The maintenance teams are mounting the M2s and loading the ammo stacks. Our three helos will be providing support for rescue efforts. We will stay in the area to help provide overhead cover with at least one helo while the other two will be on the ground to assist with crowd control and rescue loading for the handful of medical helos that will be making the trips back and forth. I see our guests have arrived." He said looking over at the three of us, "We're really glad you're here. We have all of our pilots and co-pilots. But a bunch of our other team members are still in the medical ward recovering from the incident a few weeks back. They can't be activated for this. I hear they let you shoot the M2 before. Guess what, one of you will get to sit in the gunner seat. You decide which one. The other two will assist with ground duties when we get there. Any words of advice before we head out?"

I stepped forward and spoke firmly from some yet unknown place of confidence, "Everyone, in the air or on the ground, must have goggles and respirator masks on at all times. Make sure any cuts or scratches are covered. Do not touch your bare eyes, nose or mouth with your arms, hands, or fingers until you get back and get decontaminated. Assume everything you touch, including people, plants and objects, will have radioactive dust on it. Someone make sure the people on the medical helos do the same."

I stepped back and saw Bob looking at me in wide eyed amazement.

"All good points." the base Commander said stepping in behind me.

"I see some of you don't have all that gear on you." The Tridents Commander added, "Get it before you leave. I expect our helos off the ground in three minutes or less. We can discuss anything else once we get on site. Word is multiple casualties. We will use top speed as practical for terrain. ETA to scene is fifteen minutes. Head out."

The team rushed past, and the Trident commander stepped to us.

"I need one of you to join helo two, and two of you on helo three. Three of our guys will be on helo one, four total on helo two with one of you, and four total on helo three with your other two. The two of you on helo three will be alone in back, one will need to be in the gunner seat. How will you be splitting up?"

"I'll go with helo two" Kevin said.

"I'll be gunner on helo three and he'll be my support." Bob said pointing at me.

"Sounds good. Head to helo three and be ready to get off the ground in about three minutes. I'll pilot helo three. I need to radio the medical helo ready room to give them your instructions and make sure they get the right gear. When I get to helo three we'll be taking off immediately. So be strapped in and ready to go."

"Yes sir" Bob, Kevin and I responded as we headed toward the helipad.

“Thank god you didn’t force me to be gunner” I said to Bob.

“You had all the fun back on the Kennedy. Now it’s my turn.” He replied with a seriously sly smile.

As we approached the scene at high speed, even from a couple miles away you could see no fewer than eight large smoke plumes spread within about a quarter of a mile along the roadway. Several types of burning vehicles, a few overturned laid near the sources of the smoke. Smaller vehicles and people moved back and forth along the stretch of road to a makeshift triage site about a quarter mile away. There were several stopped cargo trucks on the other side of the attack that couldn’t get past the wrecked vehicles. And about a dozen cargo and support trucks at the triage site leaving an odd gap of space along the road itself.

Some of the intact vehicles in front and at the rear looked like combat vehicles, a few had red crosses on white background signifying they were medical or humanitarian vehicles. Nearly all of the destroyed or damaged vehicles had the red crosses or the NATO humanitarian aid logos on them. It was almost like they were specifically targeting the peaceful portion of the group and not the military teams with them.

“This was definitely targeted. Definitely state terrorism. Don’t know if it’s the Slavs or Serbians. My guess is the former.” Bob said as our helo set down in a nearby vacant space. “They hit the volunteer humanitarians, not the military guys. They think it will deter further volunteers for the humanitarian effort. Trying to thwart the hope the refugees have for aid, so they go back to their oh-so-benevolent dictator. Keep your eyes open. They may not be done. And hitting us would likely be a big prize for them. Especially if they can get a helo in the mix.”

Helo two was on the ground a short distance in front of us. To our side, on the other edge of the roadway, was what appeared to be the makeshift command vehicle with several people gathered around, and continuous commands being given judging by the soldiers running in all directions after being spoken to.

As we were making our way to the apparent command vehicle two fighter jets roared past overhead. About two miles to our west in the path of the jets we heard explosions and saw new plumes of smoke trickle upward as the fighters broke off to the north.

"I have a feeling those were our terrorists being blown up by some AMG-65 Maverick missiles off those F-16s." Bob said.

The command vehicle's motor was running and there were several people on radios inside with a semi-circle of people standing around it. We saw Helo One begin to head to the west to evaluate the impact of the airstrike. Bob, Kevin and I got to the command car and stood just outside the circle of people. A voice from inside was relaying information.

"Trident One reports all four vehicles fully disabled and no visible body movements. One vehicle had an unspecified vehicle mounted multi rocket system. A second vehicle may have had same but too damaged to confirm. Tracks lead over the terrain from our scene to the missile impact area suggesting a close attack from a short sight distance then they immediately bugged out."

"Hit and run. Definitely state terrorism. And at that close range they knew what they were aiming at." Bob said.

Two medical helos landed nearby, upwind from us. Wounded near the command group were moved toward the nearest helo. The other helo team, with goggles and masks, moved toward wrecked vehicles and the handful of people tending to the more seriously wounded that couldn't be moved.

"Captain Guerra, air control is asking if we need another pass. What say you?" said a voice from inside.

"No need. Tell them to stay ready status. We have some early warning helos now to help." Said a familiar voice.

"No way! Marc Guerra?!" I exclaimed as the apparent head honcho turned around.

"Yes. Who's asking" he said turning toward me.

"It's me." I said as he looked at me puzzled.

"Me who?" He said "all I can see is a sliver of your neck."

He leaned over and took a look at my name plate.

"Holy shit! What the hell are you doing out here!?" he exclaimed back.

"I'm not entirely sure. My team is at Bondsteel for a training on WMD response. And we got the report of the Geiger reading after this, so they sent us out to…I don't know…watch, assist, stay out of the way, something like that." I said shaking his hand.

"What are you doing here?" I asked.

"I'm leading a logistics group now. And working with a separate team that creates simulated tech, like heads up displays for training, and eventually for use in combat helmets. We're using Northern Watch sorties to test some of the new helmet tech gear. We came out of southern Germany and joined this convoy a little ways back. Just my luck I'm the most senior guy here so I get to be incident commander. Yay me."

I suddenly remembered why I was here.

"That Geiger reading means those rockets likely had depleted uranium tips. You should have all your people get goggles on and masks or respirators over their mouth and nose. The radioactive particles are also heavy metals, both will cause sickness or death if inhaled or ingested. Make sure people aren't touching their bare eyes, mouths and noses." I said somewhat desperately, "Especially anyone near the impact site or smoky areas."

“May be too late to worry about that. It’s probably been a good thirty minutes already. Everyone’s probably already exposed.” Marc said.

“Maybe. But that doesn’t mean they need to continue getting exposed.” I said.

Marc called someone over from his team and they ran off to a cargo truck.

“We’ve got some medical supplies we’ll pass out. We’ll do what we can. Unfortunately, most of the medical supplies we need are in those burnt up NATO aid cargo trucks back there.”

“There’s a pinch point right behind those damaged trucks. Our other cargo trucks can’t get by. And we can’t leave until they can be with us. Pretty sure the terrorists knew that. So keep your eye out for anything weird around the perimeter. I wouldn’t put it past them to have a second team lying in wait for a sundown attack to try and finish us off. Your helos are a big help there. Glad you guys are around to hang out with us in harm’s way.”

“Too bad our helos aren’t Chinooks. They’d get those burnt trucks up and out of the way in no time.” I said.

“Good idea.” Marc said, turning back to the radio operator in the command vehicle. “See if you can get a hold of a Chinook in the area.”

“Yes sir.” Came the response.

The medical helicopters were very efficient. The constant stream of landings and lift offs had all of the injured on their way to the base hospital within about thirty minutes. Thankfully there were no fatalities. Surprising given the shape some of the vehicles were in. One in particular was blown nearly in half, the cab split between the front seats and rear seats.

"This one only had a driver." Marc said pointing to the split cab as he walked Bob, Kevin and I down the road to do a final damage assessment, "Somehow he ended up with only a few cuts from the jagged torn metal when it flipped. The rocket probably hit the ground underneath. Most of the blast apparently went downward and the upward force lifted the truck. Gravity and the contact with the ground probably caused the actual split. Weight distribution with the heavy engine in front and heavy cargo in back leaves a lighter weaker point in the cab area."

"This next one didn't fare as well. Rocket probably hit directly to the cargo area. Blast sent all the shrapnel forward into the cab. Two were in here. Both injured pretty bad but should hopefully survive." Marc said studying the skeletal remains of the burned out truck. "This one and the next two are the ones we think we need to move to get the other trucks around. All the other disabled vehicles ended up off the road."

The next two were on their sides. It looked like the rockets again hit the ground underneath them and the upward force flipped them. But these were really big trucks. Almost the size of semi-trailer trucks. The cab on the nearest one had ripped from the trailer connection and flipped, leaving the upright trailer connections and leveling legs bent up and dug down deep into the road surface. The farther one was almost the opposite, with the cab upright and the trailer on its side.

"We hoped we could maybe use that cab to pull these out of the way. Those hauler cabs are super powerful. Unfortunately, the drive shaft was broken in the blast." Marc said shaking his head. "So now it's just in the way too."

"What's the plan from here." Bob asked.

"Well, looks like we're gonna do a few things. Most of the vehicles can hold four to six people, a few can hold more. None of them were more than half full. So, we're gonna get all the aid workers loaded up into a few of the working trucks up front and send them on to Bondsteel until we can re-group. The rest of us will stay back. Not sure if we'll be lucky enough to get a Chinook. So we may need to wait for a super-duty tow truck to move these. That may not get here until late tomorrow. We could use a bulldozer if one's nearby, but I don't think there's one in the area at the moment. In the meantime, we'll start unloading these trailers and truck beds to see if we can get them light enough to push or pull with one of our larger intact vehicles."

Marc took Bob and Kevin up on their offer to stay and help with the unloading. But they all suggested that I head back to Bondsteel on one of the helos to prepare for the arrival of the aid workers. Two of the Tridents helos would be rotating, with one refueling back at Bondsteel while the other flew security patrol over Marc and his team. The third helo would stay on ready status at Bondsteel in case there were any new attacks or hostile flare ups.

With Bob and Kevin staying on site to assist Marc, it meant that I had to man the gunner seat on the flight back. Maybe it's the psychological difference between flying over water and flying over land. Or maybe it was the difference between the significantly slower, nearly hovering training speed when I was last in the gunner seat. But sitting in that open doorway flying over land at full combat speed was absolutely terrifying. I could feel the numbness in my fingers as they gripped. I was fully strapped in and wouldn't fall out. But I couldn't seem to stop my hands and fingers from clinching the gun handles for the whole ride back.

Landing at Bondsteel was a relief. It was like that feeling when you finally get the boat back to the dock after a long day on the water. Tired. Wind-blown. Balance a little off. But each ramped up several notches compared to the boat version. I fumbled trying to get my gear bag out of the helo and stumbled for my first few steps toward the Tridents tent.

"Sir, please come this way." The co-pilot said reaching an arm out and directing me toward the hospital area in a different direction. "We're gonna need to go through the decon tent before we go into the clean spaces."

Of course we do. But it didn't even cross my mind. Even though training on this is my sole role out here, I totally didn't think of that. This is something to add to my training sessions. Making the decon so habitual that it happens automatically even if the responder is otherwise distracted.

The decon tent was set up on the far side of the hospital where the medical helo patients could be brought through on their way into the emergency triage rooms. The tent was almost the same as the ones used by the firefighters back in Oklahoma City, except this one was OD Green, not bright red, and had three separate sections. There were three lanes going through the tent. A non-ambulatory lane with a roller system in the middle with two ambulatory lanes on either side. The ambulatory lanes were set up so there was one for women, one for men.

The first section of the tent was a disrobing area. You had to remove all clothing and any jewelry or other items. The second section was a combination of three showers. The first shower was an initial water rinse. The second was a cleansing with a chemical solution to help neutralize and break down toxic chemicals and biologics. The last was another basic water rinse to get all the solution off. The third section of the tent was the drying and re-robing area. Drying was done with paper towels, and you dressed in a paper robe, much like a hospital robe, before exiting.

The uniforms and gear we were wearing would be decontaminated through a different process and eventually returned to us. The aid workers, many of whom were in street clothes or light adventure travel outfits, were given basic badge-less uniforms from the sewing shop. I found out later that many of these uniforms are old uniforms, recycled by soldiers when they get newer ones. They usually send those old uniforms to the earthquake areas. But they still had a large enough stash on site to be able to provide them for this group. For some of the aid workers that lost all their belongings in the attack it was a different story. The street clothes they were wearing likely can't hold up to the decon process like the military uniforms, so they would need to re-equip themselves in the local stores before heading back out onto the road. Just another way terrorist attacks can have a trickle-down effect, causing stress, strain, and delays that themselves can result in their own traumas. As I thought about it, I would need to add these post-incident issues to my teaching material also. It would seem this trip is teaching me more than I'm actually teaching others.

Our training sessions were scheduled for the next day. For much of the night I was worried I would be teaching alone and realized how dependent I'd become on Bob and Kevin for these sessions. But Bob and Kevin returned late that night. Not only was I relieved that they would be available for the training, but they also let me know that they were able to get the debris off the road with one of Marc's intact trucks and the help of a kind farmer with a large, surprisingly powerful tractor. The convoy would roll on.

With all three of us together in the room, the day's training sessions were excellent. Although everyone was tired and yawning from the late night and long hours, nobody took it personally. Coffee was flowing. And having the recent real-world example the day before led to excellent proactive discussions that everyone was interested in.

Exhausted after the sessions, all three of us slept through a late afternoon helo ride back to Skopje. We landed just in time. And we were ecstatic to see that our flight into Germany would be on a small passenger jet. No more uncomfortable jump seats in dark bouncy cargo cabins. It would be windows, AC, and padded reclining seats all the way back to the states.

Chapter Five:
There was Supposed to be an Earth Shattering Kaboom!

Tampa, Florida
November 2001
January 2002

"I told you after you sent me out on the Kennedy in a hurricane that I wasn't going to do any more boats or helicopters." I tried to scowl with my voice over the phone.

"It's been like two years. You're still hung up on that?" Dr Ellison said.

"Being on a boat in a major hurricane and almost crashing dead in a helicopter a few days later…those are things that take more than a couple years to get past!" I said, feeling my voice get louder. "You're the highest-ranking psychologist in the United States Army so I know you know that."

"I'm just messing with you. You won't need to get on a boat or a helicopter for this one." He said, "Once you hear about it you would probably be begging me to participate."

"What would this task be?" I asked, only the slightest bit intrigued.

"Are you sitting down?" he asked.

"No. I'm jogging in the NY marathon. Of course I'm sitting down. It's happy hour. I'm enjoying a beverage at my local waterfront watering hole." I said, dripping my sarcasm as best I could. "Since you forced me to carry this new cell phone, you're stuck talking to me at all my local haunts while I'm trying to live my life to the fullest in this post 9/11 world."

"Well, this one is classified top secret. I'll need you step away to a private area and call me back." Dr Ellison said hanging up without waiting for confirmation.

I paid my tab and made my way back to my Jeep. The top and doors were off a lot these days now that the rainy season was coming to an end. Today was no exception. If I needed privacy I'd need to find somewhere deserted to park. At this time of day, most people were crowded at the south and west facing beaches for sunset views. The north side of the causeway would be my best bet. But it's usually filled with the true shore fisherman at this time of day. Luckily, I was able to find a spot along the north side, a pull-off leading to a nice private space between two sections of tall mangroves. I shut off the engine, took a few breaths of the fresh air and dialed my phone.

"What took you so long?" he asked, skipping the typical cordial greetings.

"Had to pay my bill at the bar and get the Jeep to a private spot. Jeep season. No doors or windows to conceal our conversation."

"Ahhh. Thank you. I thought you would just walk to a vacant part of the bar."

"When was the last time you were at a waterfront bar at sunset?" I asked, "There are no vacant parts."

"True. I'm definitely spending too much of my life not at beach bars." He said laughing under his breath. "I'm sure your curiosity is peaked. So I'll get right to it. The FBI and other intelligence sources have identified and confirmed a credible WMD threat against the United States."

"Seems to be the flavor of the day." I said shifting in my seat to get my feet propped up on the open trail door's top crossbar. "Haven't we had about a hundred of those in the last few months since September 11th? What makes this one different?"

"What makes this one different is that nine intelligence agencies came up with collective information that all leads to the same conclusion."

"What conclusion?"

"There's a cargo freighter heading to the US with a nuclear bomb aboard. The intention is to detonate the bomb in port to do as much damage as possible to people and commerce."

"That's serious." I brought my legs back and sat upright in the Jeep now. "I can be packed in an hour. Where do you need me to go?"

"Nowhere."

"I don't understand."

"The threat is specific to Port Tampa. This one they're bringing straight to you."

***

"The local FBI Tampa Field Office director is going to meet with the Tampa mayor, at the mayor's office downtown at 7am. I've made arrangement for you to be in the room. The national FBI director, the Coast Guard's Captain of the Port, and a couple guys from the Department of Defense will be on a conference call with everyone at 7:30." Dr Ellison explained.

"When's the freighter expected to get here?" I asked.

"That's the rub. We don't know the exact ship. It's been narrowed down to the three most probable. The first of them is scheduled to arrive in Port about thirty-six hours from now. Which means it will be just off the coast in the shipping channel a few hours before daylight that morning. And under your famous Skyway bridge shortly after that."

"So, what's the plan?"

"The plan's still being formulated. But essentially the Coast Guard is going to do some of the old two-trains-traveling-at-different-speeds math and identify where and when to best approach the freighter with a Coast Guard cutter. They want to approach as far as possible away from populated shorelines in case the terrorists get antsy and set it off when they see us coming. After your meeting with the mayor, I want you to head over to the Coast Guard station in St Pete and give them whatever tips you can. Then head back over to the Tampa Port Authority offices and work with their first responders. That is if the whole plan doesn't change based on your conference call in the morning."

"Are you there?" Dr Ellison asked after a long silence.

"Yes. Just thinking about this. My dad works downtown. Same building as the mayor. Just a few blocks away from the port."

"Like I said. This is top secret. You can't tell your father about it unless the mayor and others on your conference call feel it's necessary to dial him in."

"I can't even ask him to call in sick to work. Even his house would be in the deadly blast radius of a low power nuke. Unless it's just a dirty bomb?"

"Not a dirty bomb." Dr Ellison said.

"Great." I said, soft sarcasm masking my painful dilemma.

"I know this is hard. But if word of this were to get out it could put thousands of lives in danger, maybe a lot more. Even if nothing ever came of it there would be deaths, injuries and disruption from the public's frantic behavior. This absolutely must stay confidential."

"Fine."

"One other thing." Dr Ellison said almost hesitantly. "You know from all our work researching terrorist behaviors that there is likely a cell of terrorists, or at least a lookout, somewhere in Tampa. They'll be looking for any changes in the routine. If they see something that makes them jittery, they could contact their buddies on the ship and just run it aground onshore wherever they are and set off the bomb. This must stay quict. We need to sneak up on them."

"I get it. My dad works in that building so I'll just make sure it seems like I'm going to visit him."

"No offense," Dr Ellison laughed, "but I don't think you're on anyone's radar. I was talking more about what happens in your meeting tomorrow. I know you're acquainted with the mayor. So that will help. Our guys will tell them not to flood the port with law enforcement and rescue teams. But he may still be tempted to. I'll need for you to try to appeal to him offline after the call. To get him comfortable with what we're going to be doing so he doesn't inadvertently do something to cause a nuclear bomb to be detonated along the Florida coastline."

"I can try to do that. And no offence taken. I'm perfectly happy and hope to forever stay under the radar. I have no desire to be a newspaper headline hero!"

"Just so you're aware, several of the intelligence reports suggest this is linked to Al-Qaeda. That means there's more at stake than newspaper recognition if that terrorist cell identifies you and sees you as a threat."

"Excellent news." I said "I didn't want to sleep tonight anyway."

"Speaking of sleep, you should go home and try to get some. You've got a very long day or two coming up."

Sleep didn't come. Not good sleep anyway. I kept running over the scenarios in my head. Dealing with the opposing burdens of telling my father versus not telling my father. We lost my mother to cancer two years ago. The thought of losing my father so soon after was almost paralyzing. In the end I decided not to tell him. I figured, why add the stress to his life. He would worry about his friends in the area. And the pain would spiral for him. Possibly for nothing, if my team does our job right. At worst he would live blissfully unaware until the moment of detonation. Dying in a momentary flash has some appeal. Especially after watching my mom lose a long deteriorating battle with cancer. Ironically, that horrible justification actually cleared my head enough to let me drift off to sleep for a few short hours.

What sleep I ultimately got wasn't enough. No way was I going to be energized for the next twenty-four hours of straight-up stress. My eyes were sleep crusted shut as I stood under the shower. My mind was anxious, knowing I needed to get moving and get my body and brain in gear. But neither were cooperating. To this point in my life, I never thought I truly needed coffee. But right now, I need coffee.

I set a 4:30am wake up alarm assuming I probably wouldn't get to sleep anyway. At least that would give me an hour to get somewhat conscious at the house, and an hour to drive into downtown to fight for a parking spot near city hall. I hoped to be sitting on the couch outside the mayor's office by 6:30am to catch the mayor for a quick chat before the others arrived. By 5:30am I was out the door juggling my keys and a massive twenty-four-ounce coffee that was extra heavy on the sugar and creamer.

Joining the already racing traffic flow, I made it to the mayor's office by 6:15. To my surprise, his assistant Sally was already behind her desk. She looked up and waved me over.

"Everyone else is inside already. He wants you to go right in."

"Thanks Sally. Nice to see you again." I said, really confused. "This meeting was scheduled for 7am right?"

"Sure was. But when he doesn't sleep, no one sleeps. You're lucky he doesn't have your phone number." Sally laughed opening the door and announcing me to the group.

As I walked in, everyone was around a large table by the floor-length window. They were focused on something that looked like a map. I saw someone in uniform I assume was the Coast Guard's Captain of the Port, here in person, not on the call as expected. Another man in a suit that screamed FBI agent was likely the local Tampa office director. The mayor looked up and walked toward me. Our mayor always greets everyone with a friendly handshake and kind words. After our brief exchange of pleasantries, and my apology for being late, even though I was quite early, we both walked back toward the table. A large man seated at the table was facing away from me but was somehow familiar. He stood and turned as I approached.

"I guess I don't need to introduce you to your dad." The mayor said laughing.

The mayor made the other introductions. Both as I suspected. And the discussion dove back into the map on the table. It was a map of critical infrastructure for the city. Power plants. Water plants. Distribution lines. Other key facilities. That's why my dad was there. I forget that with his nearly thirty years as director of the water department, he's familiar with all the utility infrastructure in the city. To me, he's just my dad. But to the city, he's an unsung hero and would absolutely need to be a part of this. I smiled proudly and looked back down at the map.

Two areas on the map had the most hand drawn circles, exclamation points, underlines and other magic marker dot punctuations people make when they talk while writing. One was the Port Tampa fuel storage facility near the wharf with the transfer cranes and all its associated piping. The other was smack-dab under the Skyway Bridge. The mayor spoke, summarizing to catch me up.

"These are our most vulnerable areas even for a conventional explosive. Our research after 9/11 suggests that a fertilizer bomb half the size of what was used in Oklahoma City could bring down the bridge, or if near the wharf at the port could cause a chain reaction of the fuel storage tanks that would destroy much of the port frontage. I don't need to tell you guys what a massive impact either of those would have on our local, state and national economy."

"Everything else aside, a hundred percent of our regional oil and fuel come through the port, including the jet fuel for all the airports." I said, knowing this part well enough to be confident speaking out. "Damage to the port will essentially shut down all commerce that requires gasoline. Semi-trucks, cargo jets, and diesel trains. Last estimate I heard was significant damage to the port, or loss of access in the case of a Skyway bridge collapse, would have more than a trillion dollar economic impact."

"That's our assessment as well," the mayor said. "So how do we make that not happen."

The mayor looked up but no one opted to speak.

"Come on now. Someone has to have an idea." He prodded, like he always does.

"Well…" I started, "assuming the intelligence information is correct, and the weapon is intended to be detonated aboard the ship, then the best plan of action is to stop the ship before it gets to the Skyway."

"That's the plan we've discussed on our end." The Coast Guard Port Captain confirmed. "We're working on that now."

"It's a delicate balance." The Tampa FBI office director added "we don't want to go all out moving our resources around and spook them. They could detonate anywhere along the Florida coast if they fear they can't hit the ultimate target. All they need to do is get the ship close enough to the coastline."

"So Mr. Mayor, all you really need to do is wait to hear more from the Coast Guard's engagement." I said as the Captain nodded. "That's the easy one."

"What do you mean by easy one" the mayor asked.

"My understanding is that most of the intelligence sources were in agreement about the detonation on ship." I started, wondering if I was overstepping. I looked to the FBI guy who didn't stop me. "But some of them suggested the weapon may be a dirty bomb. A dirty bomb could be intended for somewhere locally in the city, or we could just be the entry point for an ultimate detonation anywhere in the country."

"Even if we stopped and completely searched every vessel, we might still miss a smaller dirty bomb." the Captain explained taking my lead. "Those can be pretty well shielded in simple lead lined containers that our portable equipment isn't strong enough to pick up."

"And…" I added, "stopping every vessel and doing a complete search is extremely time consuming and could have its own substantial economic impact."

"We've got plans over the next few years to harden the security of the port." The mayor said, showing a good understanding of the problem, "but right now if a dirty bomb gets off that ship there's nothing to stop it from getting out of the port and into the city. The port is pretty much open access except for the secure area around the fuel tanks. And like you said, we can't stop and search every truck that leaves the port. That's over two thousand trucks a day. That delay would send crippling waves through the region's economy, even if we had enough manpower to do it. Which we don't."

"At that point we may be better off having our departments initiate our emergency management plans." My dad said, speaking for the first time. "Our plans identify our key assets and the people on our teams are trained in the processes we need to protect them."

"And that's less overtly visible than calling in National Guard or Reserve troops to fill the streets." The Tampa FBI office director said, "so we could get that started right away. Maybe get ahead of the curve on this."

"I can't believe I'm going to say this…" The mayor concluded as the phone rang to start the actual conference call, "but I'm hoping it's a bigger nuke."

The conference call was, for lack of a better word, useless. It seemed more like political grandstanding between the federal agencies on the call than actual cooperative discussion and planning with us locals. What did come out of it was twofold. First, there was no new intel overnight that suggested any changes in our course of action. And second, those of us at the local level were pretty much on our own. After some post-call debriefing, I approached the Coast Guard Captain of the Port.

"I apologize. I was way off my game when I got in here this morning. And I didn't catch your name." I said.

“Officially I’m Captain Thomas Brendan” he said cordially, “but most people call me Captain Tom. You’re Dave’s son, right?”

“Yep. That’s me. Well, one of his sons.” I said.

“When the two of you were next to each other at the table the resemblance was striking.” He said.

“It’s funny. My dad and his brother both have two sons. In both families, one of us looks strikingly like our father, the other completely different. I guess you can tell which one I am.” I laughed.

“I heard through the grapevine that I’m supposed to take you back to the St Pete station so you can brief our guys on some do’s and don’ts.”

“I heard that too.” I confirmed. “My team has been doing a lot of trainings for first responders related to terrorism response and responder trauma from WMD related events. We’ve worked with most of the local fire stations, Macdill AFB, the larger airports. I’m not sure how we missed you guys.”

“That’s okay. Everyone forgets about us until the news needs a sexy drug confiscation headline.” Captain Tom said. “And we’re generally good with that. No need to stay in the headlines. We just do our thing behind the scenes.”

“I heard that!” I said. “Give me a minute to talk with my dad and I’ll meet you in the lobby.”

My dad was still sitting at the table with the mayor talking about various security issues for places on the map. They both looked up as I approached.

“I need to head over to the Coast Guard station in St Pete before their cutter heads out.” I said. “Then I’m supposed to head back this way to the Port Authority office to work with their security team.”

“Good luck with that.” The mayor said as my dad chuckled, “I think the only security there is a few inbred guys with hand whittled billy-clubs. And they’re pissed off because their contract is about to be canceled in favor of an actual national security company. 9/11 was a wake-up call. You may have better luck with the oil and fuel security teams. They’re corporate and seem to have their shit together. But they only watch those fenced areas and spaces related to fuel storage and transfers.”

“If you hit a wall, try going directly to Kinder Morgan.” The mayor added, “They have the most fuel facilities in the port. Citgo, Marathon and Amalie Oil are there too. But Kinder’s the largest.”

“We didn’t talk about it as part of the port earlier,” my dad added, “but Tampa Electric’s Bayside Power Plant is just across the east channel from the port.”

“I can’t imagine they would go that route when the Ybor Channel brings them right up beside all the major fuel facilities and downtown.” the mayor said, “If the big nuke gets in, it will get everything. But we definitely need to keep that in mind if God forbid the dirty bomb theory comes to fruition.”

Seeing that the mayor and my dad were deep in the zone, I began to back away to leave.

"By the way," the mayor called out before I got to the door, "Who do you work for?"

"That's a good question." I said smiling, "There's a guy named Edwin Ellison that leads the US Army Medical Research Institute's psychology branch. He calls the shots and tells me where to go. But I'm usually part of various Joint Task Forces with a bunch of other agencies and take specific directions from whoever's in charge of the Task Force during each event. When I'm not on a Task Force, I'm usually just leading my team and doing classroom trainings and lectures about trauma intervention."

"Well don't get too attached to those guys. I could really use someone like you to help with all these post 9/11 security changes we're cramming through." The mayor said.

"I'd be honored to help in any way I can." I said humbly, wondering if that was an official job offer, "But right now I need to get on the road for St Pete. Traffic is building up as we speak."

I turned back toward the door and began to open it.

"Be safe kid. I love you." My dad said.

I turned, surprised, having rarely heard that in private, much less a public setting like this.

"I will. I love you too."

In a bit of a daze, I heard the office door clunk closed behind me as I silently walked past Sally's desk and down the hallway toward the lobby.

The drive between Tampa and St Pete across any of the major bridges is miserable in every direction during rush hour. And that's where we were. Rush hour. Worse, we were at the part of rush hour where most people on the road are late and driving in super idiot mode trying not to get fired.

St Petersburg is only one of the cities in Pinellas County, a county that has about twenty different municipalities. But St Pete sprawls somewhat awkwardly along the eastern edge of the county and then across the southern portion of the peninsula to the Gulf. The Coast Guard station is very far south, near Albert Whitted airfield, a small private plane airport on the waterfront adjacent to downtown St Pete. In rush hour this meant navigating downtown Tampa, the drive across the bridge to St Pete, then fighting traffic trying to navigate the oscillating one-way streets of St Pete's downtown area. It took a full hour. But I made it to the far eastern end of 8th Avenue South just in time.

"What took you so long?" Captain Tom asked.

"I don't have a fancy government issued car. I have a Jeep slow-mobile." I said. "But I made it. Idiot drivers notwithstanding."

"Glad you did." Captain Tom said "The cutter's getting ready to head out, probably less than an hour. I'll take you onboard, so you see what we're working with. But it will be bustling. You won't be able to corral anyone onboard to talk at this stage."

"That's fine. We'll just do what we can." I said.

"Once these guys get on the water, we can sit down with some of the other team leaders inside. You can give your full spiel to them, and they can share it down their chain."

"How many do you have here?" I asked, somewhat surprised, thinking most of the group would go out with the cutter.

"Ships or people?" he asked.

"Well…both. I realize I really don't know much about this place even though I grew up right across the bay."

"People-wise we have about 850 active and about 1200 reserves. About half the actives and a small fraction of the reserves are out on the water at any given time. So for your info session you'll probably have about thirty to fifty team leaders."

"That's a lot more than I expected. That's a good turnout." I said. "How many ships?"

"As far as ships, not that many. We normally have four or five, all in different classes." He said as we stepped through the back door of the building toward the wharf area. "Everything from barges with cranes, smaller fast patrol boats, a midsize cutter…and this one."

"Wow! That's big!" I said looking at something more akin to a Navy Destroyer than what I thought a Coast Guard ship would look like."

"It's a Hamilton Class. 378 feet long with a 43 foot beam. The largest we have." He said. "Also the most heavily armed. One of its original purposes was to act as a coastline defender to protect us from incursions. Its design came out of the cold war era and the Cuban Missile Crisis when everyone thought there would be attacks on our coast from nuclear armed warships and submarines. There's a new class coming online in a few years so these will be phased out. But it sure comes in handy for what we need to do today."

"It looks well armed." I said seeing a few mounted guns as we walked toward the gangway.

"Very. The big one you see up front is a Malera Mark 75 Autocannon. It can send big shells a long way. About 120 per minute. There are also two MK 38 25mm Autocannons. They can fire up to 200 rounds per minute with a range of over a mile. And we have a standard Phalanx CIWS. It fires 4,500 rounds per minute. That's 75 rounds per second if you're into math. But its range is shorter, only about a quarter mile. It's really a defensive weapon. There's a standard complement of six 50BMG machine guns mounted around the ship as well. What you don't see is its two MK36 torpedo launchers and our countermeasure system."

"And of course it carries an MH65 Dolphin helicopter." He said as we reached the landing pad at the rear of the ship. "The 65C variety with a couple guns mounted just in case they need 'em. They're controlled from inside, not the older hang-out-the-door type."

"The ship can stay out on the water for up to 45 days, which will give it plenty of time to harass all three of those incoming cargo ships."

"With a nuke on board I'm not sure harassing is a good thing." I said.

"We'll see. If they heave-to when asked and cooperate with our searches there shouldn't be an issue. But if they refuse to comply, we'll likely get a directive from the President to sink it in place as quickly as possible. We can do that from over a mile away. Still inside the blast radius. But with three cannons putting over 500 shells a minute, and a couple of torpedoes, on them, it will probably sink quickly, or at least they may be too disoriented or too damaged to set off the nuke. Especially since it's an unarmored cargo ship. Like the old days on the farm putting bb's through a soda can."

I smiled at that image thinking back to my days on my grandfather's farm shooting all sorts of guns at cans and water filled 2-liter soda bottle targets.

"Let's go ahead and get back inside. Best to stay out of these guys' way." Captain Tom said as two sailors were maneuvering a very large crate on a dolly with lots of dangerous looking warning labels.

The compressed version of the training presentation for the Coast Guard team leaders took about ninety minutes. There were lots of great, relevant questions. But it was otherwise uneventful. No one other than a few of the senior ship's crew were made aware of the situation due to the confidential nature of what was going on. But given the attention paid to the presentation, you would think they all knew a nuke was bearing down on them.

It was shortly after lunch time, and I was packed up to head back across the bay to Port Tampa. Things on my end were going well ahead of schedule. So I decided to take the opportunity to stop and grab a quick crab cake from a good little seafood market on the St Pete side of the Gandy bridge. I ordered the crabcake and some fried fish to go thinking I could eat them one handed in the Jeep during my drive. I got most of it in my mouth. But it turns out crab cakes aren't the easiest thing to eat while driving. I should have got the sandwich version instead. Looking down I saw I ended up wearing quite a bit of crab bits on my shirt, which I'm sure were going to smell great later tonight since I didn't think to bring a change of clothes.

The smell and seafood grease shirt stains were good to help me fit in during my very brief meeting with the Port Security. But the Billy-Bobs, as I'd affectionately named them in my mind, were less receptive than expected, even considering the mayor's warning. They were cleaned up for work in matching uniforms. Black Army surplus pants, black polo shirts and black baseball caps. Black expandable batons and walkie-talkies on their belts. Like three redneck ninjas. Talking with them for about ten minutes I understood why they were unreceptive. These were the kind of guys that spent their weekends in full blotto mode drinking warm Busch porch beers before ramp jumping their pieced together cars Evel Knievel style over their friends laying in a row beneath, beer cans raised toasting the undercarriage as it dripped and coughed over them. Nukes didn't scare these guys because before they dropped out of elementary school, they learned they'd be perfectly safe if they just crawled under a desk.

The Kinder Morgan team was the exact opposite. Extremely professional, knowledgeable and polite. If I didn't know better, I would think they were part of the President's Secret Service team. They brought me inside their building where they had already gathered teams from the nearby Citgo, Marathon and Amalie facilities.

In somewhat of a twist, for most of the meeting, these guys trained me on their operations. The area didn't look new, most of the buildings and tanks looked older and well used, some predominantly rusted. But there was high tech everywhere. There were remote cameras, audio sensor devices, air quality sensor devices, and a few other things they wouldn't tell me about, spread all around their facilities. They had teams whose sole job was to carefully watch everyone that got on or off a ship, and everyone that came and left work each day. They weren't hyper-paranoid. But they also weren't afraid to immediately investigate and address any anomalies. They have file records on every incident investigated, from someone wearing the wrong shirt to work, to a large drunk foreign guy stumbling off a ship making threats toward a country he wasn't even in. This was a well-run show.

Their companies even have an onboarding requirement to complete a training class on stress and trauma. The ranking leader explained that the trauma class had been around for about a decade now. It started after a surge in absenteeism, DUI arrests and positive drug tests following an explosion at a fuel refinery and storage facility that killed dozens of workers. They looked at the data and noticed it was the survivors on shift that day that were having the bulk of the problems, skewing the data even though they were a small fraction of the company's overall staffing. They called in a psychologist and required everyone in the company to go through a session. The majority of survivors on duty that fateful day met enough symptoms to be diagnosed with PTSD.

The company was even being proactive and getting their facilities linked up with counseling services following September 11th. The media has no idea how much damage it did with multi-channel twenty-four hour coverage of the devastation. Then, striving for ratings against their competitors, they exacerbated the country's trauma by producing constant back-stories about the victims. In the end, a farmer tilling a field in Kansas that morning, who didn't know anyone that died, would end up feeling like he had a personal connection to victims after watching those broadcasts. Leaving him to experience a form of trauma over a loss he never actually had. Kinder Morgan recognized that news-related trauma, and knew that the best intervention is early intervention, before the trauma symptoms start to appear.

Kinder Morgan was already doing what I was going around the country teaching. I was getting programs set up so first responders can huddle up and run through some brief individual and group tasks to help stop that trauma from emerging at a self-destructive level months or years later. Data has proven that doing small group debriefings immediately after finishing a shift during a mass casualty event, significantly reduces the prevalence rate of PTSD later in life. The debriefings are simple and can be led by anyone using simple prompts like *what was the most disturbing sight you saw*, *what was the most disturbing smell*, *what made you the most angry or upset during your shift*, and so on. Data has even shown that those who attend and listen at the debriefings, even if they don't speak, still have a significantly reduced prevalence of PTSD in later years.

I applauded the Kinder Morgan team on their work and left my contact information. Now it was time to head back downtown to debrief with the mayor about my own traumatic experience with the redneck ninjas.

The mayor cleared his schedule for the day but was still in his office when I arrived at about 5:30 in the evening. The mayor's door was propped open, a tell-tale sign that Sally had gone home for the day. I stopped in the doorway and knocked, surprised to see he was alone. I expected him to have a crowd around ready to receive urgent directions. But he was calmly sitting at his desk.

"Hey there. Come on in. How'd it go?" he asked with his always genuinely interested demeanor.

"It went well with the Coast Guard. The cutter got off in plenty of time." I answered, "Man that thing is an absolute warship. Paint it navy ship grey and it would pass for a destroyer. I don't think they'll have any trouble stopping the cargo ship."

"And at the port?"

"I met the redneck ninjas. They were everything you warned me about." I said laughing to myself, "But then I met with Kinder. Thanks for that tip. They have it together. Solid operation. And they coordinated already with Citgo, Marathon and Amalie. So that went smoothly."

"That's good news." He said, reclining back a bit in his chair and sipping a glass of iced tea.

"I gotta say, you're very relaxed for a mayor under threat of nuclear siege."

"Did you see the movie Men in Black that came out a few years ago?" he asked.

"I did. That was a great movie."

"There's a quote in there by Tommy Lee Jones' character. I forget his name in the movie."

"Agent K."

"That's it." He said, "at one point in the movie Agent K says this thing that was so good I memorized it. He says, 'There's always an Arquillian Battle Cruiser, or a Corillian Death Ray, or an intergalactic plague that is about to wipe out all life on this miserable little planet, and the only way these people can get on with their happy lives is that they do not know about it!'"

“That’s a great line.” I said, “And something I’ve recently begun to appreciate even more.”

“Thing is, when you get into leadership positions in government, be it local, state, or federal, there’s always a crisis. Something is always about to destroy this thing, that thing, or everything someone thinks is good. And they feel it’s your job to fix it, and they want it fixed yesterday.”

“And some days multiple crises.” I suggested.

“Probably most days.” He laughed, swirled his glass and took another sip of tea before continuing.

“Your dad and me, we go way back. I’m not sure if you know this, you were a little kid then, but I was mayor when your dad was first hired here in the 70’s. Seems like every day there was someone threatening to poison our water supply or trying to convince the media that they already poisoned the supply. Then there were the self-proclaimed experts that claimed our facilities were vulnerable, or even some that claimed we were purposefully poisoning them. Every day a crisis.” He took another sip.

“Your dad’s always been calm, cool and collected, never over-reacting. He created programs, and processes, and data, to make it easy to address all of those crises. I’m truly thankful to him for that.”

I sat quietly contemplating what was said. Thinking about some of the differences between this work-dad and the home-dad I knew as I was growing up.

“He’s been here a long time. And I get a sense that he’s planning to retire soon. He hasn’t said anything officially. But I think what happened with your mom really took the wind out of his sails.” He said.

“I’ve seen that too.” I offered, “Not so much in a bad way at home. He’s just not willing to push his point of view as hard anymore. He seems calmer and gets along better with people in his friend circle. But I could see how that could be a problem at work where he needs to fight for funding dollars or battle with state or federal regulators over something.”

“The people will never know all he’s done for them.” He continued, “but I’m gonna do something to make sure he gets remembered. I haven’t told him about this yet, so I need you to promise not to spill the beans.”

“I promise.” I said, making the cross my heart gesture.

“I’m working on a resolution with the City Council to name our historic water treatment plant after your dad. It’s on the historic registry. So it can never be torn down. His name will be associated with it forever.”

I sat speechless. I thought he was going to give my dad a plaque or something.

“And that’s not all.” He said, “We’re gonna use our Art in Public Places program to have one of your mom’s sculptures enlarged real big and turned into a water fountain to put out in front of the plant. Everyone that drives down that street to go to the golf course will see your mom’s art and your dad’s name.”

“That’s amazing.” It was all I could say. My voice dissolved. And I felt tears welling up. I’m not sure if it was the gesture, or the stress of the day, but I was paralyzed. After a moment of silence, I tried to speak.

“I really appreciate everything you’ve done for him. And I know he appreciates you.”

“He may not appreciate me today.” He smiled and laughed “I made him pack a bag to go stay at the Emergency Operations Center. Bad food and uncomfortable cots.”

“Speaking of that,” I said, finding a way to distract myself out of the emotional moment, “I haven’t received specific direction on where I should be tonight. Do you prefer that I be at the Tampa Emergency Operations Center, or over at the Coast Guard station.”

“It would be beneficial for me to have you over in St Pete. I’d love to have a direct line of communication I can trust to sort through the situational details tonight. I’ll have some hard decisions to make.”

“No problem. I’ll reach out to Captain Tom and confirm. He showed me a building there called the Maritime Defense Technology Hub. He said it’s hardened and functions like their war-room.”

“He’s already got you calling him Captain Tom.” The mayor laughed. “I knew you would be the right one for the job.”

“What job is that?” I asked, hearing a second reference to a job from him today.

“After this particular crisis passes, assuming we’re not all a smoldering radioactive mess, I need someone I trust, with a strong knowledge base about this terrorism stuff. I need someone like you. To be a consultant. To work with me to get our policies, procedures, and facilities right to keep our citizens better protected. To do what your dad did for me every day.”

I sat in my assigned space at the Coast Guard Hub for several hours occupying myself with mindless tasks. I answered the occasional question that came my way. But I otherwise sat dazed. A few people approached to ask if I was alright. I guess they thought I was freaked out about the nuke situation. But I was really just trying to process everything that happened earlier in the day. My dad publicly told me he loved me. The mayor spilled the beans about my dad retiring, and about the tributes he was doing for my dad and mom. And then offering me a job. That's a lot to handle even if there's no nuclear bomb bearing down on you.

In the end there was no bomb. About 3:00am the cutter made contact with the first cargo ship about a hundred miles off the coast of Naples. Well away from any early detonation danger. The ship heaved-to immediately, or as immediately as a ship that size can. The crew was confused but fully compliant. All containers were opened and inspected. All areas of the ship were inspected. Nothing was found. Well, nothing radioactive anyway. They found some small arms without documentation, probably heading to an off-market dealer. And the crew had some personal stashes of drugs for use on the tediously boring voyage. A shipping container of counterfeit items was found with everything from fake designer watches to fake video game consoles. That was surely bound for the streets of New York where every street vendor has a bargain. But containers like that are usually caught by the port authority anyway due to some kind of document glitch.

I reported the first cutter engagement findings back to the mayor, gave my contact info to Captain Tom, and made my way back home. Over the next twenty-four hours the cutter engaged the two other suspect cargo ships with essentially the same results. A confused crew. And some minor illegal goods. Nothing radioactive. No bombs.

After a debriefing call with Dr Ellison a couple days later, I decided to go off the grid for some much needed rest and relaxation. Hopefully sleep would come. But sleep was more and more troubling these days. I was having trouble shutting off my brain and would just lay there thinking about all the ways my sense of safety was totally an illusion. After about a week of restless relaxation, I made a decision. If I ever wanted to actually sleep again, I needed to play a bigger role in how the safety nets around me and my hometown are set up. It was time to reach back out to the mayor.

It took a few calls between Dr Ellison and the mayor, but it was eventually determined that it would be best if I eased back on my training presentations and allowed my team to carry out most of that work. Doing so would afford me time to help with the mayor's revamping of the city's anti-terrorism plan. They both loved their idea. To me it felt like I just got stuck working two jobs.

The two job thing wasn't that bad. I had a few weeks to get my feet under me in my new role with the mayor before the holiday season hit. With everyone in and out of the office at different times, and a few key people taking much of the month of December off, all work essentially came to a dead stop shortly after we started.

When we returned to the office the first week of January, the mayor organized a weekend retreat. He felt it would help to get us all back on the same page after the holiday break. It was a great idea. Except it wasn't a retreat. He just asked us to show up at the large conference room outside his office on the morning of Saturday, January 5th.

As his gift to us, he didn't schedule it *first thing* Saturday morning. He scheduled it to run from 11:00am to 6:00pm and would have lunch catered in. Ten people, including the mayor, were going to meet to digest everything anyone's seen, read or heard about terrorism and spit out a framework of where we intend to go with the city's policies. When we were done, the mayor promised to take us for happy hour at the exclusive member-only Tampa Club on top of the Bank of America Center building, the tallest building in Tampa, and a short one block walk from City Hall. Unfortunately, he only committed to buying the first round of drinks. Likely this meant I would only be having one drink. I've heard prices are very hefty there. The only other time I'd been to the club, the host member I was with paid. We never even saw a menu or prices. But I heard through the grapevine that the bill for four of us came to around $1000, and that was without any fancy bottles of wine.

I arrived at the 3rd floor conference room, on the mayor's floor of City Hall, at 10:00am. Definitely learned my lesson about the mayor's time expectations. I was neither the first, nor last person to arrive, and felt good about that. Once everyone arrived and sat down around the table, the mayor walked over from his office and joined us. He quickly spoke to start the meeting.

"We are gathered here today to celebrate…well, to celebrate me taking you guys out and buying you a drink when we're done." He said as everyone nodded and laughed, "I know why you're all really here."

I was surprised a bit at the attendees. I expected some of the folks to be from relevant local state and federal agencies, some of the Joint Terrorism Task force people from the area. But the only ones in the room were the mayor's senior city staff, the fire chief, the police chief, and one city councilman. And me, wherever I fell in this hierarchy. I was also the youngest person in the room by about twenty years. My dad wasn't here, he was away preparing to testify for Congress on some water quality issue for the American Water Works Association. So I was on my own.

For the first hour of the meeting, the group went down rabbit hole after rabbit hole on the minutia of their own programs and how someone farting in the wrong direction could bring everything tumbling down. A cacophony of fear extremism. I sat quietly and didn't offer any comments. Occasionally, I caught the mayor's glance and saw he was over the unproductive rabbit hole discussions too. But he was sitting quietly just listening.

Miraculously, mere seconds before I was going to boil over, lunch arrived. Sandwich platters and assorted cupcakes from the legendary Wright's Sandwich Shop. The official talk stopped immediately, and everyone switched into social pleasantries while jockeying for their favorite sandwich and the best cupcake. That was a lot of needless navigating since every sandwich and cupcake on those platters would be phenomenal. I let all the rabbits access the feast ahead of me, choosing instead to make my way over to the mayor and councilman who were also standing back behind the rush.

"That was awful." The mayor said quietly looking at me, "Can you fix that."

"If he can't, no one can." The councilman said. This particular councilman was a very down to earth person and insisted that everyone call him by his first name. And he and the mayor had been each other's right-hand man for decades.

"I'll do my best. Mr Mayor, can you do a lead off introduction for me when we reconvene after lunch?" I said, the three of us slowly moving toward the vacated, but only half depleted food platters.

"I can do that for you." The councilman said.

"You'd think they were starving kids from Africa the way they elbowed their way to the food." The mayor laughed, piling a plate high for himself. "He can intro you. He'll keep it short and sweet. I may get too verbose and inadvertently send them down another rabbit hole. God forbid!"

"Get as much as you want. Anything left I'm sending over to Sally. She's got those teenage boys to feed." The mayor said, not realizing the kindness of the gesture, just knowing fed people were happy people.

It was pretty quiet for about fifteen minutes while everyone ate. A few people went back for seconds on the cupcakes. They really are remarkable. The rum cake cupcakes are my favorite. There's probably enough rum drizzled on them to set off a breathalyzer, so I fended off my desire for a second one.

"Now that everyone has a full belly," the mayor said, "before we get back to work, feel free to grab yourself some authentic Cuban coffee our distinguished councilman brought over for us from Ybor City. It's fresh and hot on the table over there. You probably missed it when you b-lined for the food. We need everyone awake this afternoon. No food comas allowed."

The group compliantly lined up while the councilman oversaw the proper crafting of the coffee. I learned long ago that Cuban coffee is artfully crafted and never just poured. Not being a big coffee lover at this point in my life, I stayed at the table rehearsing in my head how to properly engage this elder group of city leaders. As everyone sat back down at the table with their coffees, the councilman made his way toward me and sat a fresh, perfect mini cup in front of me.

“You may need this.” He said, smiling as he began my quick introduction to the group before taking his own seat.

“Thank you,” I said, standing up and walking around to the front of the room as I spoke. “I’m not sure how it happened, but over the last decade I managed to become more acquainted with terrorist actors and their threats than I ever thought I would be.”

The group chuckled a bit at that. It was probably hard for them to hear such a young guy speak of experience in terms of a decade. Even though domestic terror isn’t really a new thing, it was largely ignored until very recently. So, despite their age, they had only a superficial understanding of the concept. I took a few minutes to speak about a handful of situations I was directly involved with to get them acquainted with some concepts and context. Partly to give them my resume, older folks always want to know why a younger person is giving them advice. But also to send an early point home.

“None of those situations were preventable. Not one of them.” I stood quietly for a moment to let that sink in.

“When you try to protect and defend against every possible means of terrorism, you end up going down endless, diverse, tangential rabbit holes. Like what happened this morning. Nothing productive or actionable can come from that. But it’s still important to have that conversation so everyone sees how diverse the threat actually is.”

Several of the morning's prolific speakers shifted uncomfortably at the table. The councilman and mayor both smiled quietly as I continued.

"Combating terrorism isn't about precision. It's about probabilities. Probabilities that will change depending on location, circumstances, and resources. For example, here in our area we have the largest phosphate mines in the country. You could probably go through any waste stack at Mosaic and find enough raw bomb fuel for an Oklahoma City size explosion. And with as much agriculture as we have in our rural areas, you may not even need to go to the Mosaic stacks. You could just run by a series of farm supply stores and buy a reasonable amount from each. You could end up with a legitimately dangerous fertilizer bomb without anyone taking the slightest bit of notice."

"Compare the ease of that to the difficulty of other weapons of mass destruction." I continued, "Dangerous biologic agents are generally difficult to transport or maintain. Similar to proper nuclear bombs, both have components that are highly regulated or that can be identified with reasonable diagnostic tools. The net to catch those is so far-reaching that even cancer patients that have been through radiation therapy often set them off. The chances of an actual nuclear bomb here are substantially lower than the chances of someone renting a U-Haul truck, filling it with fertilizer, and detonating it in front of city hall. So where do we want to focus our resources?"

"On what we can actually prevent." One of the department directors said confidently.

"OK. Anyone else have a guess?" I asked.

“I agree with him. We should put our money toward the few things that are most likely to be preventable.” The comment came from one of those deepest down the rabbit hole this morning.

“I’m gonna let you guys off the hook and agree, that is indeed one of the areas we should focus on.” I said. “But we should only spend about thirty percent of our terrorist allotted budget on that. Where should the other seventy percent go to get the biggest bang for the buck?”

“You can’t be saying we need to spend money on those low probability situations…” a few of them said over each other, shifting in their seats. The mayor and councilman smiled quietly again. I think they liked seeing some of these top leaders squirm.

“As fun as it is to watch you guys squirm” I said laughing lightly, “I’m gonna let you off the hook again.”

“About a third of your money should be spent hardening the city against those highest probability types of attacks. Just like you said.” I continued, “In addition to that, about a third of the money should be spent on recovery planning. Things like setting up funds for reconstruction grants or healthcare payment assistance for sickened or injured citizens and responders. A fraction of that can be used to pay for programs like mine that teach ways to decrease emergence of PTSD in our first responders after such incidents.”

“That program is worth every penny!” the fire chief said.

“You only say that because we did yours for free. Hometown privilege.” I quipped with a laugh.

“True. Free is always good.” The chief responded, “but seriously, that’s a great program. It’s so simple. We use it every shift. And even without any mass casualty event here, we’re still seeing a dramatic decrease in mental health issues across the board. I can't thank you enough for that."

"That's great to hear. I'm glad you were able to get it implemented and fully accepted by your teams." I replied. "Some agencies have had trouble getting buy-in from the tough-guys. Funny thing is, even when they sit grouchily off to the side, just being present in the room for it still has benefits. And like you said, it's so easy. I'm kinda sad it wasn't implemented much sooner. It could have saved a lot of suicides. Saved a lot of families from destructive alcoholism."

"I don't think anything will ever get the guys to stop drinking." He quipped.

"Probably not." I replied, "but they'll be happier drunks."

"So what's the third thing?" the mayor asked.

"Before moving on to number three, just to finish up on this one, we've seen a lot of good coordination for this with basic social services and emergency management services whose frameworks are already set up in every jurisdiction. Which makes this second part of the expenditure the easy button."

"The last thirty-ish percent should be spent making the city less attractive to terrorists." I said looking back at confused stares from around the room.

"Hold on now," the mayor said, seeming nervous about where this was headed, "I don't want to go ghetto up my town!"

"No, no." I said laughing and walking to a map on the wall, "nothing like that. I promise. This one's a little harder to swallow and there's often public pushback because they don't understand. The third thing is about creating redundancy."

“Redundancy?” the mayor said.

“Yep. Redundancy.” I explained, “Since my dad’s not here I’ll use our water system as an analogy. But the same basically holds true for the power grid.”

“My dad was very ahead of the curve on this and has been preaching it from the rooftops to people all over the world. It’s all about multiples. He sought out and developed multiple sources of water for the city. Some comes from the river. Some comes from the wellfield. Some is purchased from another regional source, Tampa Bay Water. And some will come from the new desalinization plant. Improvements in reclaimed water distribution take a great deal of the burden off the potable water system, which also helps. If a terrorist gets lucky and is able to actually poison any one of those sources, these others can still provide for our needs. A successful terrorist attack ends up being a light body blow instead of a knockout punch.”

I could see the lights going on in everyone’s head. Now they were thinking in the right framework to create an actionable plan.

“What are some other ways we could be redundant?” I asked.

“We could work with TECO to make sure the electric grid has loops so if a tree falls on one line, people can get power from a different source. That would help us every day, and during hurricanes.” The councilman offered.

“Exactly the idea. These things aren’t specific to terrorism. These are things that will help in a number of situations.” I added.

“One thing we’ve looked at is redesigning the I-275 and I-4 interchange. It’s a bottleneck. We could plan some improvements to our other roads that parallel the interstates. To be able to bypass an issue on the highway without destroying the traffic flow on our regular city streets." The Public Works director added just as someone else spoke up.

"When it comes to the port, like we saw recently, we may have an opportunity to develop that East channel. So if the Ybor channel is damaged, the East is still usable. We can make some recommendations for key things like fuel supplies to use both channels. Some fuel is better than no fuel. And the East channel accesses different road networks, which would help if a terrorist hit the single main entrance to the Port we have now."

"Exactly!" I said emphatically. "These are the exact things that we should talk through this afternoon as part of setting up a framework for the city's anti-terror plan and policies."

Everyone was so highly engaged they didn't realize they worked right through the break-time, and it was already almost 5:00. Just then the fire chief's phone rang, followed almost immediately by the mayor's phone and the police chief's phone. They all turned pale white as they listened. And the rest of us weren't far behind.

"That was Captain Tom." The mayor said, "The Coast Guard has a helicopter in pursuit of a rogue Cessna that was stolen from the St Pete-Clearwater airport. It's heading toward Macdill."

"Is Macdill scrambling fighters?" someone asked.

"Macdill doesn't have fighters on site these days. Only the big refuelers. Two of those are full and in ready position at the end of the runway. If the Cessna hits them, it could impact our military operations."

"No fighters?"

"No. Macdill is dependent on Tyndall in the panhandle for fighter coverage. Tyndall scrambled two fighters. They'll be here in about four minutes. The Cessna can be at Macdill in as little as two minutes."

"The jet fighters can't do much to a Cessna over the city. The Coast Guard's helo is better. Does it have time to intercept?"

"Not before the Cessna gets to Macdill."

"Will Macdill shoot it down from the ground? They have to have some kind of surface to air defense."

"The military won't shoot down a civilian aircraft in US airspace without an order from the President. I don't think that will happen. At least not in the next two minutes. It could hurt civilians in the neighborhood wherever it crashes. The president would likely rather keep the citizens safe and take their chances with the plane crashing on base. At least those at the base know the risk they signed up for."

"They patched me into the helo feed on my portable radio." the fire chief said. "We've alerted stations around the base. Rapid response full hazmat protocol."

The fire chief sat the radio on the table and turned the volume up. The feed was scratchy and hard to hear at times. And there was a lot of pilot jargon no one understood. Well almost no one. One of the directors apparently has a pilot license no one knew about. He explained what he was hearing.

"The Coast Guard helo has the Cessna in sight but can't get to it before it reaches the base. The Cessna pilot isn't responding to radio calls from the helo or the air traffic controllers at St Pete or Macdill."

"The Cessna decreased altitude. Flying very low over the base." He said two minutes later. "He apparently overflew the refueling tankers on the runway, a few hangers and just passed in front of the control tower. He was below the top of the tower. So he's dangerously low."

We all sat with bated breath. Waiting.

"Macdill tower says the Cessna has increased altitude and appears to be circling back toward St Pete. It's no longer over the base."

Everyone breathed a sigh of relief.

"The Coast Guard helo has intercepted. Cessna pilot is not responding to radio calls or hand signals from the helo."

"Coast Guard reports the Cessna has changed direction and increased altitude." The director looked up, as the blood left his face. "he's now headed toward downtown Tampa."

The fire chief was on his phone getting all stations in the downtown area ready to respond.

"The Cessna is not diverting. It appears to be intending to crash somewhere downtown. The flightpath puts it in line with…"

"Coast Guard reports Cessna has crashed into the Bank of America Center building. About half way up."

"Oh my God." The mayor said. "Thank God it's Saturday and hopefully that building isn't full. Do we have a visual? Any damage reports coming in?"

"Coast Guard reports limited apparent damage to the building. But the Cessna appears to be hanging with the nose stuck inside the building. No fire is reported at this time. The rear of the plane has apparently crumpled and is hanging vertically downward."

"Do we have anyone on scene yet?" The mayor asked "We need to get the people off the sidewalks and stop the traffic flow through there."

"That's underway." The police chief reported, "we have a marked unit blocking traffic in that direction. Other officers and building security are getting gawkers out of the area. An evacuation order has been issued for the building. That flow of evacuating pedestrian traffic is being diverted back to the east toward Franklin Street pedestrian mall until we can confirm it's safe for people to move in the area to access cars in the nearby parking garages."

"No bomb? No chemical weapon or anything?" The mayor asked.

"It doesn't appear so." The fire chief said.

"We've been getting a flood of 911 calls." The police chief said.

"It may be good to get an official statement out to the media quickly. To avoid a panic." I suggested to the mayor.

"I sent a message to our press liaison. Our video setup for those press conferences is in this building. But I don't want people coming downtown right now. Especially not this close."

"We just got a direct call transferred to us from St Pete." The police chief said "The individual claims to be a flight instructor. And that it was a 15 year old student that stole the Cessna while he was doing pre-flight checks for a lesson."

"That's good news. That will be easier to explain to calm the public quickly." The mayor said.

"The instructor said there was no cargo or bags that could have held explosives."

"Thank God."

"FAA and NTSB have been notified. Due to the precarious nature of the plane hanging off the building, they've authorized us to coordinate removal of the wreckage. NTSB gave us a number to call locally that can do that."

"Good thing. I wouldn't know who the hell to call for that." The mayor said, "I need to step out for the first of what will be many phone interviews with the local news. I'm sure you all have places to be. No need for us to hang around here. We'll pick up where we left off sometime next week."

"Don't think you're getting out of buying us drinks just because there's a plane hanging out of the building you were buying drinks at!" one of the director's said.

"Raincheck. I promise." The mayor said solemnly walking out of the room back down to his office.

My Jeep was parked about a block in the other direction and traffic was at a gridlock even though it was a Saturday. So I took the police chief up on an offer to walk to the crash site and get a visual assessment. It would be good to observe people's behaviors firsthand for my work. But I also wanted to gawk. It's not every day that you see an airplane hanging out of the side of a skyscraper.

It was quite a sight. And a crowd was gathering. Primarily people that evacuated the building and now had nowhere to go.

The police chief and I met up with the fire chief just inside the cordoned off area at a makeshift incident command center. The fire chief confirmed that there were no casualties inside from the wreckage. And that the pilot was indeed deceased. The building is forty-one stories. The Cessna wreckage is at the twenty-eighth floor. Even though there were no direct casualties, apparently there were several injuries during the evacuation. A lot of bumps and bruises. A few sprains. But mainly out of shape people craving oxygen or water after walking down so many flights of stairs. Definitely more exercise than those desk sitters usually get. Several ambulances, EMTs and firefighters were courteously tending to everyone's needs.

In addition to the physical wounds. There were several people acting hysterically, as if the plane landed in their lap. Some acting dramatic solely for attention, hoping to get on the news. And still others that looked dazed and numb, wandering, not reacting to directions. The latter were likely the most in jeopardy of PTSD. I pulled a few aside as I saw them. And tried to do what I could. But the evacuating group had been dispersed in all directions and couldn't be corralled for an effective intervention. I took note. It may be beneficial to get something set up for large buildings to add to their evacuation plans. My team would need to sit down over the coming months to try and figure out how something like that would work. But right now, it was time to try and find my jeep amongst the crowd and head home.

Chapter Six:
All Gassed Up and Ready to Go!

Memphis, Tennessee
January 2003
San Antonio, Texas
Tyler, Texas
April 2003

"I promise you, this time it's not a rush." Dr Ellison said hearing the clear statement of my silence.

"This guy, William Joseph Krar. His name came up during the Oklahoma City bombing investigation in 1995. Back then there was some tangential evidence that he was involved in bomb plots against government buildings. When we confirmed he wasn't involved in the OKC bombing we put him on the back burner. We needed our full resources to investigate OKC back then. Once the OKC investigation started to wind down, we put some resources back onto tracking this Krar guy."

"William Joseph Krar. Sounds like a serial killer name." I said wondering in the back of my mind how this casual assignment was going to blow up into urgency like the last two that weren't rushed.

"Exactly why we need you." Dr Ellison said.

"Why exactly do you need me again?" I asked, dreading what the answer would be.

"This Krar guy is very anti-government. No one that's talked to him has been able to get any good information out of him." He said, "But I remember what John Davis said about your interview of Danny Rolling."

“What about it?”

“That you somehow got him to trust you in just a few minutes, and he gave heartfelt answers to you when all he’d given to others before that was rhetoric.”

“And you think I can do the same with this Krar guy?”

“Hopefully. Yes.” He said, “We believe Krar is a domestic terrorist waiting to strike. But we haven’t been able to catch him yet. At least not with anything that would stick.”

“When we did our background research in 1995 related to OKC, Krar was on the list because of an incident way back in the mid 1980’s when he formed a company called International Development Corporation, IDC for short. He described it as a building supply company. During the 80’s he was making frequent trips to Central America for personal business. Supposedly the trips were not related to the company. But at the same time, we found out IDC was selling weapons without a license. Krar’s father was a gunsmith. So Krar had access to connections to get guns, and the tools and skills to make illegal modifications to them. But before anyone could get enough evidence gathered for legal charges, IDC shut down and Krar disappeared for a few years.”

“Krar was believed to be involved with several white supremacist hate groups and anti-government groups. So we think he used those connections to live off the grid.” he continued, “At least until 1989 when his name popped up in association with Jane Brucas. Jane and her family were known members of a prominent white supremacist group at the time. It turns out that Brucas was Krar’s common law wife. His name resurfaced occasionally in the 90’s as a person of interest in incidents related to the Brucas family. It was all small-time stuff, and nothing ever stuck to him.”

“Then out of the blue in 2001, local law enforcement was investigating a fire at a warehouse in Goffstown, New Hampshire. They found a large stash of guns and ammunition. And the warehouse was registered to none other than…”

“Let me guess, our notorious Mr. Krar.”

"Correct."

"So did he finally get arrested?"

"Nope."

"Why the hell not?"

"Turns out Krar's lawyer convinced the investigators that the guns and ammo were a legitimate part of his business. Apparently, legal modification of guns was part of his newest legit business. And in this case, all the guns and ammo had proper legal documentation. So there was nothing to arrest him for."

"Ok. So then what?" I asked.

"Well, even though he wasn't arrested, that incident gave the FBI enough information to keep track of him. He was watched pretty closely. But then the September 11th terror attacks occurred a few months later. The FBI's resources again shifted. All hands were investigating the terror attacks with little attention paid to those, who at the time, were considered minor domestic persons of interest. So he again was able to disappear off the grid."

"I remember in the aftermath of September 11th, everyone was being over vigilant, keeping a watchful eye for anything odd happening in their neighborhoods, at their local stores, schools and bars." I said, "People were listening and reporting anything and everything. How was he able to stay off the grid?"

"Exactly because of that." He answered, "The number of reports sent to law enforcement was a hundred times higher than it was before September 11th. The FBI and local agencies didn't have nearly enough resources to investigate them all. So most got ignored. Nearly all of the domestic reports were ignored because resources were so focused on international state sponsored terrorists."

"I can see that happening." I said, "I remember the mood back then. Anyone that looked the least bit middle-eastern got second and third looks from passers-by. Guilty in the public eye until they could prove otherwise."

“But then we got lucky.” He said, “In January 2002 a package was delivered to the wrong address. The good samaritan immediately turned it over to the police. The package was full of fake birth certificates and matching fake IDs for the United Nations and Department of Defense. Turns out that package even had a note, from Krar to the intended recipient, Edward Hounslow.”

> *Hope this package gets to you O.K. We would hate to have this fall into the wrong hands.*

“Irony at its best” I said, chuckling at the sheer ridiculousness of it.

“Krar was still off the grid, so we didn’t catch up with him. But it gave us this new guy Hounslow who we hadn’t looked into before. Ready for some more irony?”

“Always.”

“Hounslow actually worked for the government. He had a job with the Monmouth County Department of Human Services.”

“Anti-government government workers. What’s weird about that?” I laughed.

“Hounslow was small time. Part of a subversive local paramilitary group called the New Jersey Militia. After Hounslow talked with the FBI it was clear that Krar was funding his off-grid life through these forgery activities and small scale gun modifications for these groups.”

“So did Krar get arrested?” I asked.

“Well…” he said, pausing and trying to find the right words, “There were complications.”

“Complications?” I asked.

“An arrest warrant was issued but couldn’t be served.” He said with frustration I could feel. “His exact whereabouts weren’t known. And even though the feds had ultimate jurisdiction, there were some jurisdictional issues with the warrant between New

York, where the package ended up, and New Jersey, where it was addressed to go. Political BS."

"So that was last year. Where is he now?" I asked wondering where all this was leading.

"Memphis." He answered.

"Memphis?"

"Yep. He was pulled over for a routine traffic violation. The trooper found marijuana, fake IDs, a shit-ton of knives, a stun gun, handcuffs, a smoke grenade, and two handguns in the car. Easy to get an arrest warrant."

"So he was finally arrested?"

"Yep. He's in custody as we speak." Dr Ellison said "But that's not all. There were also three military-grade nerve gas antidote injectors, a syringe, and over forty large bottles of an unknown injectable solution. There was some white powder as well. It didn't test positive for typical drugs like cocaine or heroin when they checked it with the field kit."

"Anthrax?" I asked, remembering the attacks shortly after September 11th when seventeen people in the US were sickened when they received letters laced with anthrax.

"That's what we think right now. And it would make sense with his M.O. of using the mail for his deliveries. The powder and the injection bottles have been sent to the FBI lab. But since he's in custody they have it on low priority. It could be a few months before we get the results."

"And now I get to go to Memphis."

"You get to go to Memphis." He confirmed, "Your team isn't needed for this one. They can stay back and handle the trainings while you're gone. It should just be a three day trip. Day up. A day talking with the arresting officer and interviewing Krar. Then a day back. You have a plane ticket waiting for you. You leave tomorrow at 3pm."

"You said this wasn't a rush!" I said loudly, venting some strong emotion.

"I lied."

***

Depending on who you ask, the weather in Memphis in late January is either wonderful or awful. Skies are typically clear unless a cold front is moving through. And daytime high temperatures are in the low to mid 40's. Nights are a little more uncomfortable with low temperatures dipping down to the lower 30's.

Of course today wasn't typical. As I stepped through the automatic sliding doors toward the rental car shuttles, the wind was whipping rain from an approaching cold front across the drive lanes and onto the edge of the sidewalk. The overhang protected most of the sidewalk area closer to the building walls where scores of people were huddled to stay dry. But there was no way to stay dry once the shuttle arrived and started loading. Everyone had about a ten foot rain drenched tromp to the shuttle door. The younger passengers walked quickly or jogged the last few steps to leap into the shuttle doorway. The older folks went super slow hoping to avoid a vacation ending slip and fall injury. The mix of the two was somewhat comical to watch.

The rain was cold and felt like icy slushy sleet at times. It wasn't cold enough to truly snow. At least not yet. Which meant I got to experience the wet, cold, cloudy, windy, generally awful weather the locals complain about. Snow from a massive fast-moving snowstorm that came through the prior week was still in the process of melting. That made it extra sloppy. And it made the locals extra irritable.

By the time I was sitting in the rental car, I was a warped blend of wet. Soaked to the bone from the knees down and the shoulders up though only slightly wet in the midsection. But cold all over. I was dressed appropriately though that didn't stop the wet and cold. That's what pisses the locals off the most. No matter how appropriately they dress, on these days they always end up wet and cold.

I took my time in the rental, letting the engine warm up, but more importantly getting the heater working and the windows defrosted. There was no rush today. Nothing officially planned for me. So I made my own plan. To do something I hadn't done since childhood. I was heading for a special dinner.

There's an intersection in Memphis that is the only place I know of with a Krystal and a White Castle across the street from each other. As a child on our family road trips, we would stop and get a dozen burgers from each and argue about which was better.

"Sir. Is that a Krystal bag on your seat?" the drive thru teller at White Castle asked, laughing and turning her massive back to the window "Hey boss…are we allowed to serve people with Krystal bags in their car?"

"Only if our White Castle bag is bigger." I heard the boss reply laughing.

"Sounds fair." I said, "how about I add a second bag with a couple orders of waffle fries from you guys. Two bags are definitely better than one."

Her whole body rolled as she laughed "That will work."

Anyone that's ever ordered Krystal or White Castle at the drive thru knows that it is virtually impossible to get all the way home without breaking into the bag for at least a waffle fry if not one of the bite sized burgers. But it's been a long time since I've been in this city. With the sloppy weather, and not being familiar with these roads and all the new things being constructed here, I made the grown-up choice to put off my starved inhalation of the food.

Luckily it was only about a ten minute drive back toward the airport and the nearby hotel holding my reservation.

The generic Budget-Holiday-Quality-Hotel-Inn-Place was just that. Generic. It wasn't dirty and the people were polite enough. But I did get a couple of double-takes from giggling staff when they saw my bags of burgers took up as much room as my lone carry-on bag of clothes and necessities.

"One guy with twenty-four burgers in a hotel room. What's weird about that." I thought to myself. At least I wasn't rolling in a footlocker full of sex toys.

With everything pre-paid, the check-in went smoothly. The only bad part was having to go back out in the now very cold sleet to put a parking pass in the car. But it was fine. I had a calm relaxing night planned. A warm shower, eating my burgers and watching some free hotel HBO movies. The jail was only about ten minutes away from the hotel so I wouldn't even need to get up too early in the morning. I usually wake up on time automatically. But I set the alarm clock on the nightstand anyway. I liked that hotels were starting to have digital alarm clocks in the rooms instead of relying on wake-up calls. The last thing I want to hear when I first wake up is the voice of a front desk staffer.

"Hey. I just wanted to check in with you before you head out." Came that voice through the phone, grinding on my nerves as I lay still half asleep.

"Who is this? What time is it?" I asked wiping my eyes and trying to focus on the clock, flashing 12:00.

"It's Edwin. Who do you think it is?" Dr Ellison said.

"What time is it?" I asked, rummaging around looking for my watch.

"It's 7:30. Aren't you up yet? Your appointment is at 9am."

"I'm up now. Good thing you called. There must have been a power outage from the storm overnight. The alarm clock is just flashing." I yawned, "And I must have slept harder than usual after my two bags of burgers."

"Two bags of burgers?"

"Long story. I was up later than usual, ate later than usual, and spent the evening more bone chillingly cold than usual. It all caught up to me." I explained, "Anything new?"

"Nothing new. I just wanted to say…" he began but hesitated "be careful today. Krar is involved in a lot of stuff with a lot of bad people. And I'm pretty sure he can get word to any of them if he wants to. You don't need a car bomb or an anthrax letter in your life."

"No. I certainly do not." I said, realizing that up until now, this is the first person I would be interviewing that could actually retaliate. "Thanks for that though. In case I wasn't nervous enough already."

"You'll be fine." He said "I'm not sure what you used to connect with Rolling. But with this guy, I don't recommend giving him too much of your personal history. Anything he gets he could use to track you down."

"I'll try to be vague. Hopefully he'll like me right off the bat because of my blond hair and blue eyes." I nervously laughed.

"Probably. But you'd better get moving so you're not late."

I wasn't late. When I'm in control of my arrival time I'm usually annoyingly early. Sitting in parking lots waiting for places to open or for the people I'm meeting to arrive. But after a few times being early and getting bullied into helping people set up for events, I've been a little bit better about my timing. In this case the arresting deputy was meeting me at the jail. And I didn't want to sit in the jail waiting area, so I was happily sitting in the nice warm rental car. Assuming there would be some screening and ID confirming time needed, I made my way toward the entrance about fifteen minutes early.

The detention facility in Memphis is pretty unique for a city of this size. Most growing cities quickly move their jails out into the surrounding county to try and alleviate the stigma a jail can have on their downtown persona. Apparently Memphis is trying to do that but hasn't quite succeeded. What they now have is a multistory main-street type of building frontage with a hodge podge of additions sprawling down the block. Many years ago, the employee parking lot gave way to a new delivery and logistics addition. There was still an employee parking lot. But it had been cut nearly in half. When you have twice the number of employees there at shift change, it means most of the arriving shift's employees had to park in the common public lots for the nearby courthouse. Not a far walk on a nice day. But during bad weather like today, I could see how it would set them in a bad mood. From the looks on their faces they were still irritated as they watched me easily escape the cold drizzling rain on my very short walk in from the street-side visitor parking space just a few feet from the door.

"Sir, please move to your right and go through the security line. Thank you." A uniformed deputy said in a detached perfunctory manner.

"Please empty all items out of your pockets and place them in this bin. Then step through the metal detector." Another uniformed deputy said as I approached the security line.

"Will my glasses or belt set it off?" I asked knowing they have set off the machines in the past.

"No sir. You can leave your belt and glasses on." The deputy replied matter-of-factly.

I stepped through the detector toward a deputy on the other side and heard the telltale buzz.

"Sir, please step over to the side for a security check." The deputy directed.

"Sir, please hold your arms out to the side," another deputy said while running a metal detector wand around my body. Another telltale buzz as it crossed my belt buckle.

"Sir, please untuck and lift up your shirt." The deputy said running the buzzing wand over my belt buckle again. "Do you have any weapons on you today sir?"

"No sir." I said, trying not to let my frustration show. "It's my belt buckle. I can take my belt off."

"That won't be necessary. Collect your belongings from the bin and head to the reception counter just to your left."

"Thank you." I said to the bin deputy that completely ignored me.

I walked to the reception desk back on the other side of the room and patiently waited my turn behind the three people in front of me. A clock over the receptionist's head read 8:55. Twenty minutes later it was my turn to speak to the receptionist.

I gave my information to the receptionist and again patiently waited while she checked her computer system.

"Sir, I don't see that you have an appointment." The receptionist said picking up the phone before I could speak. Again, I patiently waited until she was finished.

"Our meeting rooms were full this morning, so your meeting was moved next door to the clerk of court's building. Go right out the door you came in and go to your left. It's the first door you'll come to at the tall building on the corner. Next person in line please." She said, politely dismissing me before I could ask any questions.

The annex was close, on the same block, but it was drizzly and cold, and I was irritated because it was already 9:20. The guy who's always early is already twenty minutes late. I stepped through the first door on the left as directed and heard the droning voice of a deputy.

"Sir, please move to the right and go through the security line."

"I just went through this next door. They said my meeting was moved over here." I pleaded.

"If you want to get into this building you need to go through security."

I grudgingly stepped into the security line with my pocket items in hand. I began taking off my belt.

"Sir, leave your belt on." A deputy directed.

"My belt set it off next door just a few minutes ago."

"Sir, put your belt back on or we will escort you out of the building."

My irritation clearly showed as I grudgingly put my belt back on. The deputy paid no attention to my frustration and offered no customer service effort to explain or resolve it.

"Please empty your pockets and put all belongings in the bin then walk through the metal detector."

I dumped the items in my hands into the bin and stepped through the metal detector.

Buzz.

"Sir please step to the side for a security check."

I stepped to the side and held my arms out. The wand buzzed over my belt buckle. The deputy asked me to untuck and lift my shirt. I did.

"Do you have any weapons on you today?"

"No sir."

"Please grab your belongings from the bin and step over to the reception area."

I did. At this reception area I was asked to take a number. There were more people ahead of me. But this line was moving faster. About fifteen minutes later I was at the reception desk.

"Sir, I see you had an appointment scheduled from 9:00-9:30. It's 9:45 now. You'll need to reschedule."

"Reschedule?" I said, trying to bite my tongue but not doing a very good job "I've been here going through all your repetitive security checks since 8:45. You are the ones who moved my appointment location and didn't tell me."

“I’m sorry for the inconvenience sir. But the deputy you were to meet with left. He thought you were a no show. And our spaces are booked solid so we can’t even work you in. You’ll need to reschedule.”

“I’m here to help you on a difficult case. No skin off my back if you aren’t willing to fix this.” I said, “I have an appointment this afternoon to interview someone you have in custody, William Joseph Krar. Can you confirm that appointment and location for me.”

“Yes sir. That appointment is at 2pm in the main jail building next door. You have an interview room reserved for an hour.”

“One hour? We requested three hours.”

“We weren’t able to accommodate your request. I recommend you arrive an hour early to get processed through security so you don’t miss your appointment.”

Everything about that statement pissed me off. Other than the burgers, pretty much everything about this trip has pissed me off. I stormed off through the door out into the rain and began the walk back to my car parked so close to the door at the other building.

“Good afternoon. I’m Greg Williston, the arresting Trooper. Sorry about the confusion from this morning.” Williston said, probably seeing the still simmering irritation under my polite mask. “There’s been a whirlwind of issues going on here. They had a flood, and then a fire that damaged part of the offices and storage property so they're using a lot of the spaces here for temporary storage. No excuses though. I left them my number to give you. We could have coordinated to do our discussion over coffee somewhere in town."

"I appreciate your trying to help." I said, shaking Williston's outreached hand. "They never gave me your number. I would have gladly bought us some coffee and breakfast. I missed my breakfast. Overslept. The hotel alarm clock blinked out. I guess there was a power outage during the storm last night."

"Luckily, I was off last night in anticipation of our meeting today. The call response log showed it was quite busy. The most accidents we've had in any single day in several years. Sleet and rain in the mountains with patchy ice. The tow truck companies made a fortune."

"I bet" I said, switching to the topic at hand. "It looks like I only have an hour with Krar. Anything I should know?"

"Only that you won't need an hour. He hasn't talked to anyone." Williston said, turning and gesturing with a very thin file folder toward a small two-person consulting room. "Let's have a seat and I'll show you what we have so far."

Williston showed me the photos and documents related to the arrest. There was nothing unusual. Except I didn't see anything related to the white powder.

"I heard through the grapevine that among all the other lovely stuff you found there was some white powder. I don't see that here in these reports and photos. Was that inaccurate information?"

Williston stood and shut the door.

"With the recency of the Anthrax letters and the related public hysteria, we were…asked…by the Justice Department to exclude that information and delay its release under the scope of National

Security laws. They want to confirm what the powder is before we put it out publicly."

"Is there anything you can tell me about it?"

"Not much. Field tests couldn't confirm what it was. Which means it wasn't cocaine, heroin, meth, crushed pills or other common drugs we find. The field tests are good about identifying those."

"How much was there?"

"A good bit. A fairly large bulk pharmacy-type bottle. The kind used by compounding pharmacies."

"I see there were three military-grade atropine injectors. The kind used as an antidote to nerve gas in our frontline troops. Given there were only three, I assume they were just for him and his close associates. What are Tennessee's rules about possession of those?"

"It's tricky." Williston explained "Atropine is considered a life-saving drug. And it has a lot of legitimate uses. Tennessee is a pretty hands-off state in that regard. A lot of folks here are doomsday preppers, so they stockpile all sorts of things like that. Current law is it's illegal to sell or transfer it to another person without a prescription. But it's legal to possess it. But like you noted, the interesting thing is the number, three."

"That was my thought too. Why three. Was anyone else in the car with him?" I asked.

"Nope. Not when we stopped him."

Just then there was a knock on the door and the door opened. Williston stood as a person with an FBI badge entered the room.

"Good to see you again Trooper Williston" the man said reaching out to shake hands and then looking toward me, "I'm Special Agent Leaderman with the FBI. I'm the one that reached out to

Edwin. Probably the reason you're getting to enjoy our fabulous weather today."

"Nice to meet you." I said shaking hands.

Williston and I sat back down and Special Agent Leaderman dropped a new folder on the desk.

"This is the detailed info we have. Including some of our surveillance we had on Mr. Krar." Leaderman said opening the folder to a specific section and continuing, "After the errant mailing situation last August we were able to get a warrant for surveillance. Some old fashioned legwork traced mail back to an address in Tyler, Texas. It helped that the address in question was a mailbox at one of those mailbox stores in the strip malls. Surveillance showed three people using the mailbox, coming and going in two different vehicles. One was a white pickup truck with a New Hampshire license plate we believe belonged to Krar and Brucas. The other was a black Cadillac with a Texas plate. We ran the plate and it identified the third person as Debra Brookens. The address on the Cadillac's vehicle registration was the same address as the rented mailbox Krar and Brucas were using."

"Very convenient." I said. "But who is Brookens? How does she play into this."

"She is somehow involved with Krar and Brucas. But we're not sure about how." Leaderman said, shaking his head. "She's much younger. About twenty one years old. Brucas is in her fifties. And Krar's in his sixties. But surveillance shows that she seems to live at the same address as Krar and Brucas."

"Is she a kid of one of them? Or another relative?" I asked.

"We haven't been able to confirm any of that. It doesn't seem so. There are rumors that they are in some sort of a three-way relationship. But most people don't believe that."

"In November the owner of the mailbox place alerted us that Brookens put in a change of address form requesting mail in her name be forward to a new address in New Hampshire."

"Back home?" I asked.

"Maybe. In late October, we were able to get a warrant for a two-month mail cover."

"What's a mail cover?" Williston and I both asked simultaneously.

"With a mail cover warrant we can't stop or open the mail, but we get to see and photograph the envelopes and boxes before they go in or out of their rental mailbox. In November there were letters and boxes going back and forth with Krar's company and Bushmaster Firearms. Those are pretty normal, so we didn't pay much attention to them. But a few other things of interest popped up. First, there were some priority mail letters exchanged with a business called Kaisers House in Connecticut. Kaisers House is a military surplus store that isn't in the firearms trade and wouldn't be a typical client of Krar's company. Second was a letter to Brucas from a nearby storage facility in Noonday, Texas, on the rural outskirts of Tyler. There was also a photo envelope sent to Brookens' new address. We're not sure how important Brookens is. She doesn't seem to be doing much. But we're aggressively working on getting warrants for the storage facility and to speak with the owner of Kaisers House."

"It sounds like you've got a lot of information." I said flipping through the last few pages of the folder. "It doesn't sound like I'm gonna be able to get you much more. I hear Krar won't talk to anybody."

“He definitely wouldn’t talk to us. But if you can make it clear that you’re not officially affiliated with law enforcement and make a connection with some of your rural family stories, he may engage in what he believes is meaningless banter. That could give us some insight even if we don’t get more details.”

“Ok. I’ll give it a shot.” I said, nervously recalling Dr Ellison’s warning about the danger of sharing too much information with Krar.

The interview space for Krar and I wasn’t much larger than the small room I was in with Williston and Leaderman. It could hold four people at most. In this case me, Krar and a guard. Krar was not handcuffed or restrained in any way. He sat quietly across the metal bolted down table from me, making only neutral eye-contact, probably wondering what this was about. I introduced myself as an educator, working to understand motivations behind killers. A white lie at most but true enough that he shouldn’t be able to pick up on any cues in my behavior.

“To be honest I’m not really sure why I’m here.” I said as he quickly redirected his gaze and focused on me. “From what I can see in your file, you’re not a killer, at least not that anyone knows about. The only thing I can think of is someone wanted me to try and learn about the gun business. I’m a gun enthusiast. Do some simple mods myself. At one point I thought I would try and become a gunsmith. But I couldn’t find anyone to teach me.”

"I guess I just got lucky having one in the family." Krar said with his first words to me.

I waited a moment for more, but he didn't elaborate.

I stood and stepped over by the guard standing near the door.

"Would you mind stepping outside. Mr. Krar promises to behave himself." I said as the guard reluctantly stepped outside and I closed the door behind him.

"I feel better without law enforcement here looking over my shoulder." I said sitting back down across from Krar.

"I just want to make it clear. I'm not a cop. Not law enforcement of any kind. I'm not particularly fond of them these days." I said hoping my frustration from the morning came across on my face. "I'm not taking notes. No paper. No pens. No recording devices. No cameras in the room."

"So why are you here." Krar said seeming a bit off balance, maybe even truly confused.

"Like I said, I'm not real sure. But I am personally interested in the gunsmith stuff. So I'd like to ask you about that."

He sat quietly. No response in his demeanor. Which was better than the irritated response I was expecting.

"Like I was saying before, I'm interested in guns. How they work. How to fix them. How to improve them without ruining them. But I've never been able to find anyone willing to teach me." I started, knowing this might be a long monologue without a response. "Hell, almost my entire family lives in small rural towns or on farms. I grew up with guns all around me. But they were all just buy-and-shoot types. I have this one in my collection that was passed down to me. An old Sears and Roebuck side by side double barrel shotgun. Family legend is my great grandfather killed someone in an old west style gunfight with it back in the early 1900's. It's in decent shape. Triggers and hammers seem to work. But there's no shells that fit it. I can't figure out what gauge it is. When I took it to a shop the guy told me the shells would need to be custom made. I told him that it looked like it was somewhere between a 410 and 28 gauge shell but the 410 was too small and the 28 gauge too big. So I asked if there was some kind of adapter. He said no and strongly recommended that I never try to fire a modern shell through it."

"Not unless you want those barrels to split apart like an old Yosemite Sam cartoon." Krar said.

"Why is that" I asked, already knowing the answer but hoping he would engage more.

"Older guns, especially cheap ones from catalogues like that, used cheaper, thinner, low-strength metals." Krar explained, seeming to dive into teacher mode, or maybe just trying to prove he knows more than me. "They were meant for the poor working class or farmers. Back then the poor people couldn't afford the fancy pre-made shells in a box from the sporting goods stores. They made their own shells. Reusing casings and usually skimping on gunpowder due to the cost. Using just enough to get some pellets out and into whatever pest or animal they were trying to get rid of or eat. Usually that was small game like birds and rabbits, sometimes rats."

"Wow. That makes total sense." I said, feeding into his ego, hoping it would open him up more. "So if it absolutely has to be custom made, how do I find somebody that can do that? I just want to fire it a few times. To feel what my great grandfather felt when he pulled the triggers. Everyone I ask doesn't even call me back. I guess the order is too small for them to bother."

“You could try to make ‘em yourself.” He said hesitantly. “But you’d need to buy all the parts and equipment. It would be a pretty big cost for just a few shells. And if you don’t know what you’re doing you’d probably end up with a shell exploding in the breach, destroying the gun and scarring up your face if not killing you.”

“So how can I get someone to do it? I’ve literally called every gunsmith in the phone book for four surrounding counties. Never got a call back.” I said, trying to seem like I was legitimately pleading for help. “I went to several shops and the ones with a gunsmith on site just flat out said no. And they wouldn’t recommend anyone else that might do it. I’m stuck.”

“Going to the stores for something like that is your first mistake.” Krar said after a moment of contemplation. “These days those guys are only trained in the modern guns. Likely they’re specifically trained to work only on certain brands, Smith and Wesson, or those stupid fucking import Glocks. They couldn’t fix an antique gun if their life depended on it. And they’re all insured these days. Probably aren’t even allowed to try or they’d lose their insurance.”

“So where does that leave me?” I asked dejectedly.

“You need a craftsman.” He said matter-of-factly.

“A craftsman?” I asked.

“Some old guy that’s worked on guns his whole life but never had that formal modern training.”

“Where do I find someone like that.”

“Two options really.” He said, now in full lecture mode. “You seem too normal, so the first option of reaching out to the black market is probably out of the question. The second option will take you some time and could still put you in some dangerous scenarios.”

"What's the second option?"

"You'd probably need to find a historian. An informal historian, not some university jackass. A blue collar civil war buff that may have some similar guns in his own hand-me-down collection. Strike up a conversation and see if he'll give you any names. You're probably best to look for the oldest guy drinking whiskey alone at a bar after a civil war re-enactment. Buy him a whiskey and tell him what you told me."

"And hope he doesn't shoot me on the spot." I said subduing a laugh.

"I wouldn't have shot you over this conversation." He added surprisingly. "The guy may not tell you what you want to know then and there. But keep showing up. After passing some subtle tests he may have for you, he may give you a name. If you're genuine, it will show. And those guys are always looking for others to join their cause."

Just then, as if on cue, the guard entered.

"Time's up. We need to free up the room."

I thanked Krar for the discussion and we parted ways. As I was walking with jail staff to exit the building, Special Agent Leaderman approached me.

"Great job! You got a lot out of him."

"What do you mean? I haven't even told you about our conversation yet." I said, though a bad feeling was rising up in my stomach. "What did you do!"

"We put a bug under the table. The metal makes a great sound conductor. We heard it all. Have it recorded if you'd like to listen."

“What the fuck!” I said pushing him against the hallway wall “I told him there were no recording devices. You could get me killed!”

“Yeah. You probably shouldn’t have said that.”

“Fuck you! You shouldn’t have recorded us without telling me.”

“It doesn’t matter. None of it is admissible. It can’t be part of discovery in the case. So no one will ever hear it. Relax.”

“I’m not going to relax.” I said walking away from him and toward the door to the parking lot. “I came here in good faith at your request to try and assist. And since I’ve been here the two lead agencies have treated me like shit. I’m done. Good luck with your investigation.”

The door slammed against the outer wall opening farther than it’s supposed to as I pushed through full force. It’s a good thing my cell phone wasn’t charged. If it was, Dr Ellison would be getting a verbally violent earful. A different part of me wanted to go find an old man at a bar and have a whiskey. Or maybe just go have a whiskey. Frustrated with the day, I decided to get my things from the hotel and see if I could get an early flight back home.

“He what?!”

“Krar was released on bail” Dr Ellison said.

“Why would a judge let him out?!”

"Nothing conclusive to hold him on. The guns, knives, stun gun, smoke grenade and ammunition were legal, and his lawyer claimed they were part of his business. They don't hold anyone for that small amount of marijuana. And there are no results on the testing of the white powder, syringe and bottles of liquid, so he can't be held on that either. And the three atropine injectors are legal there."

"So where is he now?"

"Well, that's the problem." Dr Ellison said. "Since he was arrested while traveling, he was allowed to return to his home in Texas while awaiting trial. He's apparently in transit there now but isn't due to check in with the local sheriff's office for another twenty-four hours."

"Twenty-four hours. That gives him plenty of time to come knocking on my door on his way home." I noted.

"I had a talk with Special Agent Leaderman. He swears no one other than the three of us are aware of that recording. And he reiterated that you never gave your name or hinted at where you lived. So Krar wouldn't be able to find you that fast, if at all."

"I hope you're right." I said. "Thank you for the heads up in any case. At least I can be on the lookout now."

"I wasn't just calling to give you a head's up." He said with some hesitation. "I need you to go to Texas."

"I'm not gonna put myself in that guy's crosshairs!" I said firmly "You'll need to find somebody else."

"Relax. You won't be anywhere near him." Dr Ellison assured. "I just need you to go to San Antonio. The FBI's Joint Terrorism Task Force office there is gonna take the lead on any engagements. It should be the Dallas office. They'll participate but don't have enough available resources at the moment to take the lead. The operations team for US Customs and Border Protection is also going to assist. I think you know a couple of guys on that team."

"Keith and Alex. The explosives detonation guys." I answered. "Kevin knows them better than me. I've only met with them in person a few times and maybe had about ten other calls with them since the Oklahoma City bombing."

"Maybe you should take Kevin with you." Dr Ellison suggested. "Could speed things up. The Texas team is waiting on warrants to search the warehouse in Noonday and Krar's home just northwest of Tyler. But there's a rush to be ready to move quickly. Needless to say, we don't know Krar's plans. It's possible he could do something sooner than anticipated since he was caught in Tennessee."

"Did the test results ever come back on the powder and the liquid from his car?"

"We should have the results by the time you land in Texas tomorrow." Dr Ellison said.

"Of course. Tomorrow. I guess I should be happy you didn't say later today."

"I can probably get you guys on a plane today if you prefer." he said.

"No thanks. Kevin's gonna be mad enough. He likes to be home here at the beach during spring break. I don't think inland Texas has the same appeal for him."

San Antonio was already blazing hot on April 1st. But at least we got to fly a standard commercial flight to San Antonio International Airport. The drive from there to the nearby FBI complex was only a few minutes, even with the always present San Antonio traffic. So we didn't melt sitting in traffic like the last time I was here.

FBI complex may be an exaggeration, at least from what you can see above ground. Three building structures. A very nice modernized four story office building, a large enclosed two story parking garage area, and what looks like a typical large maintenance type of building. We were above ground in a standard conference room for this preliminary meeting.

"Thank you" I said to the friendly assistant as she walked us to the room and opened the card locked door for us.

There were several people in the room already. Kevin immediately recognized Keith and Alex and walked towards them for a reunion. It had been several years since we saw them in person. I don't know if I would have recognized them. They were clean cut last time I saw them. Today they have longer mussed hair and scruffy beards. They walked toward me.

"Good to see you again" Keith said reaching out his hand.

"I don't think I would have recognized you guys. What's with the hair and beards?" I asked, shaking their hands.

"We're doing a little undercover work these days infiltrating the cartel operations on the US side of the border." Alex explained.

"They have quite the operation." Keith added. "They're running guns, drugs, and people, like you would expect. But the other day we saw two Komodo dragons and a shipment of very poisonous snakes from Asia and Australia."

"Poisonous snakes? Don't we have those here?" I asked.

"Can't get these here legally unless they've had their poison glands removed." Alex said. "Apparently, they milk the poison of these foreign snakes. Since the US doesn't have them, the hospitals don't stock emergency tests or antidotes like they have for rattlesnakes, cotton mouths and the other snakes found here. So the cartels use this foreign snake venom for assassinations."

"Or sell it to other nefarious entities for assassinations." Keith added. "It's a lucrative part of their business, even if they lose the occasional snake handler."

Just then the door opened again, and three FBI agents entered the room. The hair on my neck immediately stood up. One of them was Special Agent Leaderman.

"So we meet again." Leaderman said approaching me to shake hands. "I hope there are no hard feelings about Memphis."

"Why are you here? Aren't you the Memphis district?" I said, avoiding the question and grudgingly shaking his hand.

"For the Joint Task Forces they bring in whoever has some history on a case." Leaderman said "like me and you, and…"

"This is Kevin." I said "He's an invaluable CBRN guy from my team."

"Nice to meet you." Kevin said, then looking at me. "Sounds like there's some Memphis backstory I haven't heard about yet."

"Nothing worth repeating." I said as the Special Agent in Charge directed us to our seats to begin the meeting.

"Good morning everyone. I'm Special Agent Avery Lysander. I'm from the Dallas FBI office assigned to the Tyler area. I'll be coordinating this effort. But I am by no means the smartest person in this room. Every one of you is here because you have some background or interaction related to the situation. I've read the reports. But what we need is boots on the ground input, the subtle information that maybe didn't make it into a formal report. Those subtleties are massively important and could save lives. For that reason, I don't want questions directed specifically or solely to me. All questions and suggestions should go to this group as a whole. We want to keep everyone on the same page. To do that, everyone needs to know what each of you knows. So, we're going to be issuing each of you a dedicated cellular phone. A Blackberry. These are encrypted so we will be able to communicate freely and securely with each other. And only with each other. These devices are to be used to share information, photos and documents related to the case. We have set up a VPN. For those of you not familiar with this technology, that's a virtual private network. Information sent between and among this group will be encrypted and will only go through our VPN servers and connections we control. The names and numbers for each phone are already programmed in the phone's address book. You will be able to call, text and email each other securely."

Kevin looked at me with a grin, knowing my aversion to the new cell phone fad. Now I would be stuck, at least temporarily, with two of them. I refused to meet his gaze.

"It's ok. I always forget to keep mine charged." I said quietly to Kevin.

"It's important that you keep your phone charged. I won't accept any excuses if we can't get a hold of you." Lysander said sternly to the room, not just to me, as Kevin snickered.

"There will be at least a dozen agencies represented in this group." Lysander continued. "Not all are here today. All are sworn to confidentiality in regard to information we exchange. Any of it could end up being important at trial and senders will likely be required to testify if so. Be aware of that. Write as clearly as possible. Also, although we are all on the same team, I realize that there is often politics between certain agencies. Be sure the tone of your writing does not suggest any of those political stances. The writing needs to be neutral. Regardless of the politics, do not withhold information from this group. Are there any questions?"

"What's the plan?" Someone on the other side of the room asked.

"We received the test results on the white powder and the bottles of liquid in Krar's car when he was arrested in Memphis. Powder was sodium cyanide and the liquid in the bottles was hydrochloric acid. As you may be aware, the combination of sodium cyanide and acid is what's used to make a cyanide gas bomb. Right now we're still waiting on the necessary warrants. We will provide detailed information as soon as we receive those warrants and determine their limits." Lysander answered. "Generally speaking, the law enforcement component of our group will conduct raids on two known addresses. One is a storage facility in Noonday with three storage units linked to Krar and Brucas. The other is the Krar home. It's a rural semi-secluded residence about five miles away."

"How secluded is semi-secluded?" Someone else asked.

"There's an enclave of about ten small manufactured homes on one acre lots running in a line north-south off a narrow, poorly maintained access road. Krar's house is about halfway up. The land is flat in that area. Pine trees are of moderate density between the street and the homes. The rear of the lots are fenced off from a pasture. So, it's open clear sight from the rear. And trees from the front. Density of the trees is much higher across the street from the homes all the way to Dean Road. Only one road in and one road out."

"And the storage facility?" yet a different person asked.

"The storage facility is situated pretty well for our purposes." Lysander explained, pointing to a different map. "It's just south of the intersection of Saline Creek Road and 155 South. No residential properties around it. Only a few businesses at the hard intersection. We can get those evacuated quickly in case we find chemicals or explosives. Which we expect to find."

"As I understand it, the role for Kevin and myself was to meet with the local emergency management team and first responders to give them a rapid-fire refresher on terror-trauma." I said. "Will we be able to do that if the key first responders from those agencies are busy preparing for the raids?"

"Good question" Lysander began, "We thought we would have more time. But now that we're in a time crunch, we decided your roles will change somewhat. Tyler's a small town. So we think Kevin will still go directly to meet with the local fire crew and the city leadership. But you'll come with me. We want you close by. You're the only person that got Krar to speak about anything. We need you to see what we see and hear what we hear so you can give us instant direction on how to engage him."

"We had one brief conversation on one unrelated topic." I argued "I don't think I should be considered an expert on him in any way, shape or form."

“Well, the higher ups disagree. They seem to believe you’re the Krar whisperer. So they want you nearby in case we need to talk him off the proverbial ledge. Especially since that ledge may include remote detonation of a weapon of mass destruction.”

“Ok everyone. That’s what we have for now.” Lysander said, closing the briefing, “be ready for go time any moment from here forward. Uniforms and equipment ready.”

I started to raise my hand.

“We’ll be issuing you and Kevin our FBI Consultant jackets. So don’t run off just yet.” Lysander said.

The group was mingling now. Some were making introductions. Some reconnecting with old acquaintances. Kevin and I stayed in our seats at the table. Off to our left Agent Leaderman approached Agent Lysander. Leaderman began speaking, probably purposefully just loud enough for us to overhear.

“Avery, do you really think he should be going out into the field with us? He’s not trained. He’ll just be a hazard.”

“We’ve got quite a few folks on the team with our FBI training. His training is different. And he’s the only one that’s gotten through to Krar so far. So yes. I think he is a mandatory asset for our field team. So much so that I’m assigning him to my own truck.” Lysander replied. “You on the other hand are not as immediately relevant. You will be offsite in case we have any questions for our after-action reports.”

I could feel Leaderman deflating and I didn’t know whether to smile or cry. Leaderman was a brown-nosing dickhead that needed this come-to-Jesus moment for sure. But it also means that I’m assigned to the front lines for a confrontation with a terrorist that has access to all sorts of deadly things a bullet proof vest won't stop. I turned to Kevin.

"This is not what I signed up for."

"Nope." He replied with a smile, "It's even better!"

A few hours later, after a pep-talk from Lysander, he dropped me at the gear department. I was getting issued much more than the jacket mentioned in the meeting. Which was good. The jacket was the typical lightweight style you see on all the TV shows except instead of just saying FBI on the back, sleeves and front pocket, it said FBI-JTTF to identify me as part of the Joint Terrorism Task Force. There was a matching baseball cap style hat with the same FBI-JTTF insignia. I was happy to also be issued a bullet-proof vest. But most crucial, and what really brought the fear to the forefront, was the half face respirator and integrated goggles that were handed to me. I was given a quick lesson in how to put them on and operate them in case of potential exposure to gases that may contain deadly chemical or biological compounds. The mask and goggles would help with some of the potential inhaled toxins. But so many chemical and biological weapons could also be absorbed through the skin. That meant anything short of a full hazmat suit couldn't guarantee protection.

"Unfortunately, full hazmat suits aren't a realistic option for our operations." The technician who was providing the gear said, possibly seeing the look on my face and reading my mind. "But based on how I was briefed, the intent is for you to remain in the vehicle. That should provide added protection. We have special air filters installed on our vehicles."

"That doesn't work if anyone opens a door or window, gets in or out." I countered, "And in many cases exposure to the biologicals isn't known for some time. One of the other agents that is unknowingly exposed gets back in the car and we're all exposed. No air filter to stop that."

"True." the technician conceded, "but we'll also have a portable Reeves decon tent set up. So everyone will get hosed off."

The technician was just following directions, so I decided not to argue with him about all the ways he was wrong about being safe and giving him a lecture about how biological weapons actually work. Gear in hand I went back to the makeshift ready-room beside the fleet vehicle portion of the enclosed parking building and set everything down in my temporary assigned space.

A window from the ready room allowed sight into the vehicle staging area just outside the closed door. As stereotypes wouldn't have it any other way, four black Chevy Suburbans with blackout window tinting sat in a row getting tire pressures checked and other under hood checks completed. I counted twelve assigned spaces in the ready-room area so I figured that would be about three per vehicle for the five-hour drive to Tyler. As I was watching the maintenance team ready the vehicles, Kevin walked in through the door behind me.

"No gear?" I asked noticing his arms were empty.

"Apparently not. I've been promised that if shit hits the fan, I'll be given one of the hazmat suits at the fire station where I'm doing the training."

"Feels odd." I said.

“What does?” Kevin asked.

“I’m the psychology guy getting sent into a CBRNE situation, and you’re the CBRNE guy getting sent to the classroom to teach. Seems like it should be the other way around.”

“Maybe.” Kevin said. “But there will be a boat-load of CBRNE guys there. You may be the only psychology guy. And besides, I’d rather be five miles away at the fire station with a full hazmat suit than standing at that guy’s front door with that half-ass respirator they’re giving you guys.”

“Gee thanks for that.” I said, “I thought about giving the bio weapon lecture when he handed it to me. But I guess I’m stuck just crossing my fingers on this one.”

“At least you get to ride comfortably in the big fancy Suburban. They gave me the option of some tiny two-door speck of a car, or a government-white Ford Taurus. Guess who will be driving a lovely government-white Ford Taurus by myself for five fricking hours...this guy!” Kevin said pointing at himself sarcastically with both thumbs.

“I’m kinda surprised we’re driving from here. I would think we would fly.” I said.

“Since it’s a rural location, it’s probably faster to drive from here.” Kevin explained. “Otherwise, we would need time to drive to San Antonio Airport, deal with San Antonio airport issues, get to Dallas, deal with Dallas airport issues, then Dallas traffic to the Dallas FBI office, then drive through Dallas traffic to get to Tyler. Probably breaks even time wise. And driving from here has fewer moving parts, less chance to get fucked up.”

“I guess that’s true.” I conceded.

“And who knows, if the timing works out with the warrant, you guys may get to fly high speed all the way in those Suburbans with the FBI lights flashing, just like in all those TV shows!” Kevin joked.

The convoy was going fast. But no lights were on. In Austin the convoy split up with two of the Suburbans breaking off to take a more direct route to Noonday where the storage facility was located. The two other Subrubans, including the one I was riding in, stayed on I-35 to Waco and then took a combination of state and county roads for a more direct route to Krar’s residence. I hadn’t seen Kevin in the white Taurus since we got out of San Antonio. He’s a bit of a lead-foot. So he was probably already at the local Tyler fire station or trying to explain his situation to a state trooper on the side of the road somewhere.

As luck would have it, the search warrants did come through just as we were about thirty minutes from our destinations. Lysander, who was sitting in the backseat with me in the lead residence-destined Suburban, set up a group call between all the vehicles to go over the plan. I liked the plan. I was to stay in the car.

The residence-team was going to move in and search the residence first. That way they could have Krar, and hopefully Brucas, both in control to stop any potential remote detonations at the residence or the storage facility. Once Krar and Brucas were in control, the Agents would question them on the record about any potential booby traps either at the house or at the storage facility. If all went well, Krar or Brucas would answer the door, and both would come out peacefully, knowing nothing incriminating was likely to be found in the house. They wouldn't be told about the storage facility warrant until after they were secured outside of the home. Everyone seemed unusually accepting of that. But I was still worried. Terrorists always had a portion of their plan that would harm first responders. In this remote area, I wasn't convinced that Krar didn't have agreements with like-minded neighbors to remote-destruct his house during the search. But maybe I was just overthinking it.

I expected some sort of sneak attack through the woods since so much was mentioned about the trees previously. But that's not what happened. The approach came straight up the shitty narrow road. An FBI unit from Dallas was first to arrive in an armored vehicle. It plowed up the road much faster than the road could handle. Chips and patches of sparse, elderly asphalt were ripped up in its wake and tossed amongst the gravel toward the Suburbans following just far enough behind not to be pummeled by the road shrapnel. The armored vehicle made a skid slide into the mostly dirt, gravel driveway shared with the house to the south. It slid to a stop between the two homes, likely to provide a protective barrier in case Krar and Brucas didn't come out peacefully.

The Suburbans came screeching up immediately behind but took their places on the road in front of the house at an angle to be protected by the defensive cover of open doors if needed. Two agents from the armored vehicle approached the front door with full body armor, full face respirators, and large blast shields. One agent knocked loudly on the door and announced their presence and purpose. Other agents took up places behind the Suburbans, guns drawn and ready to engage.

For terrifying seconds, I sat waiting for what might come next. I was in the driver side rear seat of the Suburban farthest from the entrance of the home. Happily remembering the maintenance techs saying the Suburbans had bullet resistant windows and bulletproof doors. I still slid lower in my seat.

The front door opened slowly just as a second series of knocks ended. It was Krar. Though the agents at the door were mic'd, it was difficult to hear what was being said as people were often talking at the same time. Krar seemed somewhat confused and was asking questions, barefoot in his t-shirt and sweatpants. Brucas came up behind him in sandals, a t-shirt and worn hand-cut sweat-shorts. Neither acted aggressively. After a moment, both complied with directions to step out of the house.

Krar was in his sixties but looked much older. He was sickly thin and somewhat hunched over as if he'd spent a lifetime leaning over a workshop table doing work on small intricate mechanical items. His hair was now fully shades of gray with no original hair color still present. He wore thick metal framed glasses. His time worn skin was pale with deep trenching wrinkles connecting his cheeks and jowls. His knuckles were covered in dark hair, though the rest of his arms only had lighter patches. In general, he looked exactly like he did when I saw him in Memphis. Only much more tired.

Lysander stepped out and joined two other agents talking to Krar. Krar appeared to confirm that there were no booby-traps since Lysander turned, made a comment, and a few other agents entered the house. Lysander handed Krar a copy of the warrant. Krar didn't seem to read it.

After about an hour of waiting quietly, hiding myself from view in the Suburban, Lysander came back and spoke to me through the partially open door.

"Krar and Brucas denied any dangerous materials here other than guns. And said the storage facility wasn't rigged so I had our other team enter the storage units. Two of the units contain boxes and bags of surplus military junk. Krar said they go through it to look for things they might be able to use or sell and throw the rest out. Which is frightening since it doesn't look like they've ever thrown anything out. But that activity occurred daily according to the storge facility owner."

"The third unit was a doozy." Lysander continued. "First look suggests about a hundred assembled briefcase and pipe bombs, a ton of illegally modified machine guns, and about half a million rounds of ammunition."

"Was that all?" I asked, somewhat sarcastically.

"Nope. There was also quite a bit of what appears to be pure sodium cyanide, hydrochloric acid, nitric acid, and acetic acid. All components of cyanide gas bombs. All nicely labeled for us. And to top it off there were a few pre-assembled cyanide gas bombs with hand written instructions on how to use them. Initial estimate suggests the stockpile is sufficient to make enough cyanide gas to kill over 30,000 people."

"Wow! That's a lot of people!" I said, "Any idea of what the target was?"

"Nothing overtly identifying a target was found so far. There wasn't a map on the wall with a big red circle around a building like you see in the movies." Lysander laughed. "But I'm sure a more detailed read of the documents we found here and at the storage facility will give us more info. Hell, it's possible he was just selling off the gas bombs one at a time to his various clients. That would fit the small time M.O. he's had in the past. But it's much harder to keep and conceal that volume of chemicals safely. He likely knows that. Which suggests he may have been planning to either carry out a big attack himself, or supply someone else that was planning a big attack."

"I assume he's being arrested based on what was found?"

"Yep. The arrest warrant was pre-signed based on results of the search. We just gave the local sheriff the go ahead to bring the paddy wagon over." Lysander said "The locals will detain them until their transfer to a secure federal facility to await trial."

"No bail this time?"

"I can't imagine any judge that would grant bail on this now." Lysander confirmed. "That said, with no standoff or hostage situation, your work here is probably done. I'll have an agent drive you back into Tyler where you can meet up with Kevin at the fire station and head home. Or stay if you want…and enjoy the absolutely nothing exciting Tyler has to offer visitors."

We both laughed at that.

"I'll be happy to get as far away from here as I can as fast as I can." I replied. "To the extent possible, since I had no real part in this, I would prefer if my name could stay out of any official paperwork. I don't want this guy or any of his underworld affiliates hunting me down thinking I had something to do with spoiling their plans."

Lysander laughed, "Don't worry. It would look bad for the FBI if we needed to use your services. I'm sure everyone will be happy to keep you off the books."

I was a little let down. I half expected that closing movie scene where the head cop says goodbye and slaps the roof a couple times to usher the car off into the sunset. But Lysander just quietly spoke to one of the other agents who calmly walked over to the Suburban and got into the driver's seat. He started up the vehicle and slowly maneuvered around the crowd that was building along the narrow road. When we got back to the main road there were easily a dozen law enforcement vehicles with flashing lights. We ignored the local officers as they stared into the impenetrable window tint trying to see who we were. Even they eventually ignored us as we gradually sped up and headed east toward town…away from the sunset.

Chapter Seven:
Rock You Like Hurricane

New Orleans, Louisiana
August-September 2005

“I can’t believe it!” Dr Ellison said with more than a hint of sarcasm “You. Calling me. Asking to get on a boat or a helicopter. Either hell has frozen over or I need to play the lottery! Maybe both!”

“I know.” I said sounding defeated in that realization, “I talked with Bob and Kevin. We saw photos and videos of Katrina’s impact on the news. We’ve done tons of work with responders in South Florida, so they don’t need us. But we haven’t been to Louisiana yet. We all think we can help with the responders and maybe even the rescue efforts. We just don’t have a way to get there through our normal channels.”

“Well, your Coast Guard ships out of St. Pete have been gone already for some time. They’ve been making rescues at sea in the Gulf or are already at, or heading to, New Orleans. All the Coast Guard helicopters were repositioned up near the panhandle for quick response once the storm passed. They’ve been operational doing non-stop rescues since early Monday afternoon, about eight hours after landfall when the winds dropped to tropical storm strength and they could fly. But…” Dr Ellison said taking a moment as I could hear computer keys typing in the background. “The Coast Guard has a C-130 cargo transport scheduled to leave from St. Pete-Clearwater Airport around midnight tonight. I think I can get the three of you a jump seat."

"That gives us a few hours to pack and get some supplies together." I said "Thank you."

"You know, you used to yell at me for sending you places on more notice than this." Dr Ellison said.

"I know. Maybe I'm maturing in my old age." I said.

"Old age." he laughed, "What are you? About 35 now?"

"Yes. But it's a hard 35 with all those short notice trips you sent me on." I rebutted.

"This one will be the hardest thing you've dealt with." He said more solemnly.

"Harder than Oklahoma City." I asked.

"Much harder. No power. No food. No water. Lots of dead and missing people. All that makes even the most helpful civilian survivors unstable. Like a time bomb. The Coast Guard has been doing hurricane rescue work for a long time. But even they have breaking points. This is the closest thing to a true WMD type of event you've come across. Natural causes, but the results will be the same."

I sat quietly holding my phone thinking about that. I knew it would be big. But had just realized how big. And how relevant to my work.

"According to the flight documents, you'll be landing at the Coast Guard Air Training Center in Mobile, Alabama." Dr Ellison added "It's functioning as the staging area for all the Coast Guard rescue helicopters, about forty of them. I'll get you guys assigned to their commander directly so he can use you wherever he needs you. Do what you can with the rescue teams when they return to the ATC. Those guys, especially the rescue swimmers, will have seen the worst of it. From what I hear, the flood waters are not expected to recede for days, maybe weeks in some areas. They'll need those rescue swimmers to push through. You know the long-term toll that can take. So help them however you can."

"We will. That's our plan." I said.

"But once the NorthCom guys get there we're going to get you reassigned to one of their teams." Dr Ellison said, referring to the United Stated Northern Command, or USNORTHCOM, a branch of the Department of Defense responsible for safety and security of North America. One of their units, NORAD, is familiar to the public for their radar tracking, mostly of Santa Claus on Christmas Eve, but really to protect the US from inbound missiles and enemy aircraft. What most people don't know is that NorthCom also responds to assist with things like wildfires, floods and hurricanes.

"Why the switch?" I asked "The NorthCom teams are fairly well trained in this stuff. We did that years ago."

"Most of them are. But FEMA has asked for all hands on deck. NorthCom's sending a unit that's never been involved in anything like this before. I want to embed you with them so you can train them on the fly."

"What unit? And what will they be doing that's so out of their realm?"

"Some 82nd Airborne guys. The 505th Parachute Infantry Regiment out of Fort Bragg in North Carolina." Dr Ellison said. "The regiment is not new. And past team members have done rescue and recovery work. But due to a bunch of promotions and reorganizations recently, the current team from top to bottom has zero experience in this specific type of event response. They've only seen it on paper, if that. You'll need to support the unit leader, so he makes the right decisions."

"I don't have any authority on…" I started.

"I know, you have no legal authority." he said, "But you do know the Incident Command Structure system. You saw first-hand how the rescue teams functioned in OKC and when you were on the Kennedy. And you've personally been through direct hit hurricanes and the aftermath. You have what they need. When one of their guys asks where the refrigerator is, you'll remind him that there's no power. You'll remind them of the dangers of contaminated flood water when they try to deploy without their waders. And you'll be there to help them psychologically deal with the starving, scared, traumatized survivors you find. You have priceless pieces of experience they simply don't have yet. They need to see you at work, learn from watching you, and then they can teach others."

"It sounds an awful lot like you planned for me to be there, even before I called."

"Who? Me?" he said with a sarcastic snicker. "I was giving you another hour to call me, then I was calling you to make sure you don't miss that flight."

Bob and Kevin were ready to go in about twenty minutes. Me not so much. I was missing some of my gear altogether. And I didn't have any food supplies. My area lost power from a tropical storm direct hit about a month earlier. I hadn't replaced any of my non-perishables yet.

"We can stop on the way to Clearwater and pick up some things to top off our kits." Bob said, "you'll probably need to get your new gear here. There won't be any supplies for miles once we get to Mobile. Maybe the Coast Guard has some extras they can part with before we leave."

"And if not, we'll just wrap you in duct tape." Kevin said "You can even pick your favorite color these days."

"For decades now you guys have been trained to get up and go at a moment's notice. Me, I'm more civilian at heart. I like to plan my trips and shop accordingly." I replied. "And Purple. If you get me duct tape, make it purple. Not mauve, or lilac, or any of that crap. Purple."

"There's a Sam's Club near the Coast Guard station." Bob said, refocusing us once again on the task at hand. "We can get more nutrition bars and maybe some mega sized bottles of medicines like ibuprofen and Tylenol. We should get antibiotic ointment, gauze and hand sanitizer too. If they have camping stuff we may need some of that, and some water purification tablets. And of course, duct tape."

"Et tu, Bob" I said.

"Duct tape is a great tool in a pinch." Bob defended himself "When medical supplies aren't available, duct tape can stop bleeding, cover a wound, support a sprain, can hold together pieces of wood for a brace or a crutch. For this trip it can be a quick fix to patch a leak."

"Glad you got on board with my whole duct tape thing." I said "I believe I was the one who informed you the only tools you need are duct tape and WD-40."

"Maybe." Bob said "But good luck making a respirator out of them."

The three of us had two carts full of items at Sam's Club, including a few large travel backpacks to stuff it all in. The backpacks were the most expensive part. But we knew they would definitely come in handy. As we were approaching the checkout line, we saw an open over-head door at the side of the store with a forklift moving pallets of water to a large rental box truck parked just outside. Several men in Coast Guard uniforms were standing by supervising the loading. Bob left us in line and walked over to them.

"Excuse me," Bob asked "Are you guys with the C-130 that's flying out tonight?"

"We are. Who might you be?" the ranking member asked walking with Bob off to the side.

The two talked for a few minutes and then shook hands before Bob walked back our way.

"They're on the C-130 with us later. They came and bought pallets of water on their unit credit card. I told them I'd pay for another pallet for them to take." Bob said.

"I'll pay for a pallet." I said.

“Me too.” Kevin added.

“I’ll let them know to take three more, on us.” Bob said heading back over to their group.

“They said thank you.” Bob conveyed on his return. “And for their part they said they’ll make it a nice smooth flight for you.”

We were welcomed with open arms when we got to the Coast Guard station an hour later with a few bags of McDonald’s cheeseburgers and fries to share. Food always makes a good first impression, or in this case, second impression. Most of the people in this group had been through a recent storm or two, lost power, eating only the bland, non-perishable rations they set aside, while desperately waiting for nearby fast-food restaurants to re-open. The McDonald’s burgers were a reminder of that feeling. It put everyone in the right frame of mind for the last hour of packing up the plane before takeoff.

Surprisingly, other than the pilots and crew, we were the only ones on this flight. I guess most of the locals went down toward Miami to deal with the Florida impacts Katrina had last week before it popped out into the Gulf. Whatever the reason, the massive C-130 cargo plane seemed a little empty. With our three, there was a total of thirteen pallets of water, between 25,000 and 30,000 bottles. A couple pallets of what looked to be emergency food rations, like the old MREs, Meals Ready to Eat, seen in the old army movies. Possibly that old. I heard they don’t really expire. There were also two RIBs. Rigid Inflatable Boats. Four medium sized Jon boats.

And small engines with safety props for the boats. For what takes up a surprising amount of space in a typical garage, all the boats and engines were so precisely stacked that they took up little room in the cargo area. Near the boats was a stack of boxes of what appeared to be about twenty large inflatable tow behind rafts. The flat topped kind swimmers would lay on to rest and catch some rays during a day at the lake. Even with all that, the plane seemed less than full.

The flight included a stop at Dobbins Air Force Base in Georgia. A few more items were loaded. It looked like tents and more boxes of the inflatable rafts. A few new people joined us in the jump seats. Now the plane felt full. The weather near Dobbins was still bad as Katrina was heading inland and some bands still reached back south well into Georgia. It was a rough take off. And the flight to Mobile was not smooth as promised. Or maybe this was normal for sitting in a jump seat in a cargo cabin. I really had no good comparison other than the brief flight on a cargo plane I had in the Middle East a few years back. That one was smaller. And a very short trip.

"Any idea what all the inflatable rafts are for?" I asked Bob beside me. "I mean I get the boats. But why so many rafts?"

"It's hard to get people into boats." Bob said "It's awkward at best. They struggle. Can tip the boat or hurt themselves. It's even worse when people are dazed or injured. Some call it rescue freak-out. People have been waiting to be rescued so long, they bounce around and can't seem to follow directions. They do things they think will get them safer faster. Often those things are not good. So the boats will tow one or more of these rafts behind them. Often with someone wading in the water alongside. Psychologically the flat-topped raft feels safer to them. For some reason they stay calmer and follow directions better."

“I guess that makes sense.” I said, feeling like there was more Bob wasn’t saying.

“And of course once the rescues are done…” Bob continued, “The flat-topped rafts are easier to get recovered bodies onto and make a good flat surface for getting the bodies into body-bags. Especially when there’s no dry ground around you and the bodies are heavily waterlogged.”

There it is. I knew there would be something.

“Most of the urgent rescues are done by now. There may be some stragglers, but from here on the rescue teams will mainly be shuffling the rescued people from the lily-pads to a more official shelter area.”

“Lily-pads?” I asked.

“During the first wave of rescues the helicopters are just trying to get people above water as fast as they can.” Bob explained, “They grab people off roofs and drop them off at any higher, dry ground available. Sometimes that’s a little island of grassy high ground, a highway overpass, or the deck of a barge. Those places are referred to generally as lily-pads.”

“And most of that is done?” I asked.

“Probably. We’ll find out when we get there.” Bob said. “They also use larger places like the Superdome and the convention center as lily-pads because they’re on high ground. But they’re still inaccessible due to flooding all around them. So, no power, food or water. That makes things dangerous. Lots of scared angry people that feel trapped. Someone much higher up than us will need to figure out if they want to move the people or get supplies in for the people. Likely the former.”

“And we probably won’t be a part of that.” I said.

"Probably not. Our part is probably going to be related more to the recovery. Going to the hardest hit areas. Helping the responders who find and recover the bodies. Or helping with the occasional survivor who stayed somewhere surrounded by loved ones that were killed. That's where our trauma training kicks in. We'll need to be out in the skiffs with the recovery teams."

That's not the news I wanted to hear. But I think somewhere deep inside I kind of knew that would be the case.

"The helicopter pilots and rescue swimmers have a max amount of time that they're allowed to be on a shift. So they'll be coming and going from the Mobile ATC. We'll probably get to most of them before the guys from the 505th get there. I expect a full day at the ATC and then out in the boats with the 505th after that. The latter could take several days in boats until the water recedes. Then it will be by truck and on foot."

I leaned back, stretched my legs out in front of me and took several deep breaths. No window to stare out to distract myself. It didn't matter anyway because it was still dark. So for the rest of the flight I was stuck with my own thoughts, and the horrible mental images Bob just painted for me.

We arrived in Mobile about 8am. The Coast Guard's Aviation Training Center there consists of a building, a couple small hangers, and a large concrete surface, all adjacent to, and about the same size as, the smallish Mobile Regional Airport. Both shared the two available runways laid out like a backward checkmark. One for larger planes and jets. A shorter one for smaller planes.

The concrete surface near the larger hanger building on the Coast Guard site was where the training planes would generally park. But this morning it had nothing but helicopters. As our C-130 taxied in from the runway I couldn't imagine where we would be parking. There was no large plane sized space that I could see. Orange helicopters were everywhere. On the concrete. Off on nearby flat grasslands. Even scattered in a large area that looked like it was being graded for development, maybe a new Coast Guard hanger building going up soon. Some of the helicopters were even coming and going as we taxied in. It was like a bright orange beehive. No doubt an air traffic control nightmare.

To my surprise, we taxied past the Coast Guard complex and made our way to the small plane runway and some concrete space where private planes were probably parked before they were all flown out of the area to safety ahead of the hurricane. There were a number of forklifts organizing a few pallets covered in color coded plastic wrap. Some forklifts were driving pallets over to various helicopter pads for the larger helicopters that could load them inside. Other pallets, that looked more sturdily wrapped, were taken to nearby fields where they would be carried by sling cables.

The rear loading ramp began to open before we had come to a complete stop. And there was a lot of activity in and around the cargo area. Bob, Kevin and I grabbed our packs and gear and moved quickly off the plane to get out of everyone's way.

"With this many forklifts, it won't take them long to unload." Bob yelled over the engine noise "They probably won't shut down the engines. They'll just turn around and take off to their next destination."

We walked in a direction away from the deadly rotor blades of the plane and tried to stay out of the most likely forklift paths to avoid getting run over. Unfortunately, that seemed to take us in the opposite direction we needed to go to get back to the Coast Guard buildings. Just then a bright orange extended cab heavy duty pickup truck pulled around from the back side of the pallets.

“You guys need a lift?” the driver said.

“That would be great.” We all answered after looking at each other. None of us wanting to walk too far with these large packs of gear.

“Sorry I’m late. I needed a bathroom break. Been non-stop around here for the last two days.” The driver said. “The Incident Commander asked that I bring you straight to him as soon as you got here. I hope you didn’t have other plans.”

“Nope.” I said.

“Take. Us. To. Your. Leader.” Kevin said in a mechanical alien voice.

The driver helped us drop our gear in a tent with a grid of cordoned off squares. We dropped our gear, the large backpack and sling bag we each brought fit snugly within a square. On our way out of the tent we wrote our square number, name and contact info on the large whiteboard. The driver then walked us to the main building of the aviation training center.

“Good morning gentlemen, welcome to Aviation Training Center Mobile.” A man, not much older than us said as we shook hands.

He smiled. "I'm Rear Admiral David Wyatt. Edwin's told me a great deal about you. Not that he needed to. I knew you were good people when you showed up with the very first plane-load of supplies, and brought all your own gear."

"So you know Dr Ellison?" I asked as Wyatt led us to a chart table and offered us coffee.

"I think everyone knows Edwin." He said. "But Edwin and I go way back. Maybe twenty years now. We were both part of a Joint Task Force on a classified incident. I think we both quickly realized how we could help each other. There's a lot of psychology needed to serve on a ship long term. And also keeping our pilots and swimmers on point. Swimmers especially. They have to deal with fatigue along with their own psychological baggage. But adding to that, being able to adjust on the fly to the unpredictable conditions and behaviors of people they're rescuing, it's one of the most stressful jobs in the military."

"I completely agree." I said "I was on the Kennedy during Floyd. I saw what those pilots and swimmers were able to do making open water rescues in hurricane force wind and waves. They were truly amazing. And that was just a relatively small rescue of a few people. What's happening here has been going on non-stop for a couple days now. Considerably scaled up. Both in what they have to do and what they have to see."

"I don't think anyone's stopped to think about it yet." Wyatt offered.

"And that's why we're here." I transitioned the conversation "Not thinking about it and not talking about it can allow it to get buried in the present. Then it's easier to avoid talking about it in the future. But it does take a toll. Research shows that just gathering for a few minutes after each mission to debrief with some specific questions massively reduces occurrence of PTSD, alcoholism, drug use, and other behavior problems. It greatly extends the operational life of your team members."

"You don't need to convince me. I know if Edwin sent you guys to me that you're the real deal." Wyatt said "So let's get you situated so you can get started."

Commander Wyatt broke into a description of how the Coast Guard command structure operates in his area and how they are interacting with the Coast Guard Air Station in New Orleans. He described that the air assets, all the different types of helicopters they use, were relocated to Mobile or Houston before the storm for safety, and so they would be close enough to respond quickly afterward. The Commander moved his coffee cup and pointed to a location on the map as he continued.

"The maritime Coast Guard base is located right here on the Industrial Canal near the lock that gets ships and barges through the different water levels between the higher canals by Lake Pontchartrain down to the Mississippi River to the south. The main route of the Industrial Canal makes a bend and heads east over by the massive Michoud NASA Assembly Facility and then out through various bays into the Gulf. There's a smaller canal, called the Inner Harbor Canal that runs from that bend up to Lake Pontchartrain. South of the maritime base and lock you hit the Mississippi which heads east and then south down to the Gulf. To the west the Mississippi heads back up to New Orleans proper, downtown, the French Quarter and all that."

"Unfortunately, the maritime Coast Guard base was destroyed and everyone there had to evacuate outside the city." Wyatt continued, "We have some early satellite images. Not great images, but they show us enough."

Wyatt spread the enlarged photos out on the table next to areas of the map so we could see the points of reference.

"If you're not aware, there's a very complex levee system built around the city and surrounding area to control the massive volume of water moving between Pontchartrain and the other lakes, the Mississippi and the Gulf. Without that levee system, most of the city would flood regularly since it's at, or in some cases, below sea level."

"Here," he pointed "on the east side of the Industrial Canal the levee broke in two places dumping massive amounts of water into this neighborhood. If you look closely, you can see how the houses, mostly older wood-frame homes, were swept off their lots and piled up in several areas, or were simply knocked down and destroyed by the floodwaters."

"What's this?" Kevin asked pointing to an elongated shape in the image sitting at an angle at the edge of the neighborhood against or on top of what looked like remains of houses.

"That," Wyatt said "is a barge."

"A barge?" I asked incredulously.

"Yep. A Barge. It was waiting to go through the lock. It broke free from its tender and went over, or through, the levee into the neighborhood."

"These other photos show that most of the city got flooded. But most of the city was a little higher ground, or were newer homes. So they were flooded with a few feet of water inside. But not the rapid 10-12 feet of water in a matter of minutes that these homes got hit with." He explained pointing to an area labeled Lower Ninth Ward. Those newer and higher houses to the northwest in Lakeview are still standing for the most part. But this area here, east of the Industrial Canal. The Lower Ninth Ward. This place is devastated. Like someone dropped a massive bomb on it."

"Luckily," he continued pointing again, "The Coast Guard Air Station had some damage but is still operational. It's on the southern outskirts of the city, in Belle Chasse, right on the Mississippi."

"That close and it's not destroyed like the others?" I asked.

"I guess I need to explain a bit more." Wyatt went on, "Katrina was a Cat 3 hurricane at landfall and there was a pretty good 125mph wind and storm surge. That did its typical damage along the coast like you'd expect. But that's not what flooded most of the city. What flooded most of the city appears to be a whole bunch of levee breaks. The floodwater came down into the city from Lake Pontchartrain at the north, not the storm surge of the hurricane from the south. The further you were away from Lake Pontchartrain, even toward the southern coast, you were generally better off in terms of flood waters."

"As for the Air Station," he continued, "it's operational with two big exceptions. First, there is no power in the area. Their only power source is an old generator that's on the fritz. All the power lines, telephone lines and cell towers are either down, damaged or otherwise out of commission. So, the second operational exception is that they have no air traffic control. Every pilot flying in, out, and around the city is flying solely by sight."

"Don't they have radios to communicate?" Kevin asked.

"The aircraft have radios. But the channels are too busy for any effective communication. The Commander there at the Air Station has a satellite phone. But he has to use that for communication with various command centers coordinating getting troops and other assets into the area. That satellite phone is busy twenty-four-seven.

We set up a protocol early on and have just been doing it without any communication since then."

"What's the protocol" Bob asked, very engaged now that we were getting to the structural part of the incident where he thrives.

"The mission objective is simple. Rescue people and don't crash." Wyatt said. "Here in Mobile, we're the key staging area. The helicopters fly from Mobile to Air Station New Orleans. About a fifty-minute flight. Land. Refuel. And head up in the air over the city rescuing people off rooftops. A few at a time since most of the helos are HH-65's that can only hold about three rescued adults. The helos drop the rescued off at a lily-pad nearby and head back to the neighborhoods for more. When fuel gets low, they head back to the Air Station and refuel and go back out. When the pilots reach the max flight time they head back to Mobile. They get rest and our mechanics check the aircraft and make any fixes needed. Then a different flight crew will take that helo back to the city for more."

"Sounds simple enough." Kevin said.

"Yes and no." Wyatt corrected. "The mission is simple. Carrying it out has been extremely difficult. It was easier the first day. Just look for anyone on a roof waving at you and drop your swimmer and a hoist basket. But at night it got very dicey. Power lines, telephone lines, various cell and other towers, none of them had lights. That made it dangerous to fly low enough to get people off the roofs safely."

"And then people happened." He continued.

"People happened?" Bob asked.

"Human nature." He said, "after the first few hours of rescues, people left on rooftops got anxious. Got impatient. Or felt slighted. The pilots were legitimately just grabbing whoever they could find first. A rooftop with more than three or four people on it at times led to fights, sometimes among family members, trying to get into that rescue basket. Our single swimmer on the roof with the basket was often outnumbered and in danger of attack. A few were attacked. Eventually they stopped using the baskets and just used strap harnesses to move people one at a time. Even then there are a couple of reports of people on rooftops firing guns at helicopters that go to other roofs instead of theirs. I'm sure you'll get to hear those stories when you talk with the crews."

"Now as we're reaching the end of operational day two since landfall, pilots are telling us that the rescued people are still on the lily-pads. They have no water. No food. And are starting to attack the helicopters when they come to drop more people off." He said.

"Problem is there's no power and in many cases no shelter from the sun in a lot of those places." He continued, expressing real concern, "It's nearly a hundred degrees outside with high humidity and these folks are just baking out there. They're going down to the edge of the floodwaters and swimming to cool off. Or even worse drinking the floodwater. That water is all highly contaminated."

"Has anyone tried to tell them not to get in the water?" I asked.

"They aren't listening. Everyone's dehydrated or hungry to the point of animalistic psychosis." He explained, "Our pilots are trying to get some supplies out where they can, but what little we had on hand has gone quickly. We bought everything left in our area we could find. You may have seen some of the last of it staged for delivery. It will go to the Air Station where we're putting some on every helicopter. At least a tiny bit of food and water to be given out to the rescued people as they get into the helo. But they're on their own once they're dropped at the lily-pads. At least for right now. We're trying to coordinate some larger supply drop-offs to hold them over until the National Guard can get to them. But until now, we haven't had enough supplies to do that."

"We're thankful for you guys." Wyatt went on, "You were the first supply plane to arrive. And we heard you and the coast guard guys pretty much bought the supplies yourselves. You should get medals for that. Even though it's pretty much their job, it's taken days for the National Guard to get supplies here through their channels. The first big group of National Guard troops will be getting here today. They are supposed to be deployed to those locations with food and water. And to keep the peace until there's a plan to get the people off the lily-pads and to a proper shelter. But their logistics teams haven't gotten any food or water here for them to distribute yet."

"What a clusterfuck." Kevin said "Excuse my language sir."

"No apology necessary. A clusterfuck is exactly what it is." Wyatt said, "our Coast Guard teams are out doing miraculous things in terrible conditions. That's our job. We just do it. But I can't for the life of me figure out why the National Guard isn't here yet, and why their supply chain is so delayed. The plans are usually to have boots on the ground within twelve hours and food and water shortly after that. Needless to say, I'm sure there will be a lot of high-level discussions when this incident is debriefed at the command level in a few weeks. Speaking of debriefing, I hear one of the helicopters coming in. They'll come to me to give me an update on the situation during their shift. You guys can sit in on that and then spend some time with them afterward to do your thing."

As luck would have it, that first debriefing was a doozey. A few of the helos had just returned and a few other crews joined the debriefing before they headed out on their next mission. That made for a larger than expected group. Many had been operating since the first day. Lots of stories to be told.

"Good morning everyone." I began "I know you're all either just finishing or just starting a long shift. So we'll keep this brief. We may move faster than you like through some of the discussion. So, if there's anything additional you want to talk with me about feel free to grab me and pull me aside after we're done, or whenever you see me over the coming days."

The tent we were using was sitting on a grassy area. The grass was dry and many of the crew members stretched out on the grass rather than the metal folding chairs that had been provided. From the looks of it, those that just returned from a shift were the majority of the ones stretched out, those getting ready to head out were mostly in the chairs.

"We want to talk about things that have been upsetting to you. Things you've seen. Things you heard. Even things you smelled. Just a short statement or brief description for now." I added. "Is there anyone that would like to start?"

A young man with an Aviation Survival Technician (AST) emblem on his uniform raised a hand. I pointed for him to begin.

"We were riding out the storm in Lake Charles and were just on our way back to Air Station New Orleans to get set up for rescue missions. Before we got there, we got word that there was a radio signal from a small aluminum skiff that was stuck in a tree. So we went to check it out. It was three women and their dogs that all climbed into the boat when their house got swept away in the surge. They floated on the surge and ended up in the middle of a tree. When we got there the surge was going down and the skiff was unstable. But there was water all around below them. The only way to get to them was to drop down through the tree."

"You did what?!" one of the pilots said.

"I know. The last thing anyone wants to do is be dangling from a rope in a tree, with downwash from the rotors tangling you up in the branches. But there was no other way. What made things worse, our rescue equipment isn't designed for dogs. I was terrified I was going to drop one of these dogs to its death on my way up."

"I have a similar story." Another AST offered. "It was a balcony, not a tree. But it was several women and children. One of the women hands me a baby. No gear fits a baby. So I had it in both my arms trying to hold it tight without crushing it. I had no hands to signal for the lift. So I blindly just kicked myself out, away from the balcony, with my feet. Luckily our AMT up top was paying close attention and started the hoist fast enough so I didn't swing back and slam into the edge of the roof. I held that baby with everything I had. I was terrified of dropping it."

"I had a baby too." A different AMT added, "We were doing a basket hoist. It was an older guy, a dad, or maybe grandfather, and a newborn, had to be less than a month old. As the basket's getting near the helo, the guy starts trying to stand up. I keep pushing him back down. But then he hands me the baby. So I'm holding this tiny baby and trying to keep the man in the basket with my foot. I just knew one or both of them were gonna fall. We were about a hundred-fifty feet up. They would have definitely died from a fall like that."

"But you got them all up safe." Another man said slapping him on the shoulder supportively.

"I have something a little different." Another AST said. "I don't know if it's the same as those, but…"

"It can be anything." I said "Anything that was upsetting during your shift out there."

"There was a woman on a roof." He began, "she was older but not really old. We saw her waving and I went down to get her. When I got to the roof, she said her husband was still in the attic. She crawled through a small window in the attic to get to the roof, but he couldn't fit through. I could hear him. He said he was ok. But there was water in the attic up to his waist. I grabbed the small hatchet that we carry and tried to chop a hole in the roof. But the hatchet was too small. I had to take the woman with me alone up to the helicopter, leaving her husband in the attic. Our pilot said the GPS coordinates weren't gonna be good enough to find the exact house when we come back. So I went back down and tied a big bright ribbon to a board on the house so we could pick it out from the others. We had to leave to refuel and get her to safety. I needed to find something that could break through into the attic. I found someone and borrowed a fireman's axe while we were refueling. But the lady refused to stay behind. She wanted to come back with us to make sure we got her husband out."

"You let her?" one of the others asked. "That's not our procedure."

"Normally it would be a hard no." He said. "But in a way I needed it. I felt the heartbreak when she had to leave him behind. I needed to see them reunited."

"He could have been dead when you got back." One person said. "Then you would have had to deal with her losing her husband."

"Or you could come across a more urgent rescue and she could have been in the way. You can only get a few people in these HH-65's."

"I know. I know. In hindsight maybe it wasn't the right call. But at that moment…at that moment it was for me. I needed the win."

"I think…" I said choosing my words carefully "once this is all over you'll find that it's those decisions, those times where you're faced with a situation and you have to make a call, that more often than not, the call you make will be the right call."

"That's probably right." another person that hadn't spoken yet said, "If you think about it, the worst that could have happened would have been a delay in a rescue. If one of our team members mentally crashes and burns, that's six hours of rescue time and dozens of rescues that are lost."

"During massive events like this," I added, "you have to think of it like a marathon rather than a sprint. And it can be those little things that keep you going and get you to the finish line. Mentally and physically. You know about the importance of nutrition, hydration and rest…the physical things you've been taught. Those are nearly the same for everyone. But the stuff we need to keep our mental health on target is a different story. It's different for everyone. And most people have no idea what it is until they're faced with it. Like he was. That's a win for him. And believe it or not, it's a win for all of you too. Every win helps."

"So I encourage you guys to meet up after your flights and talk like this." I continued, "If there are twenty of you in a room, and nineteen of you had your worst day ever, but one of you had a win, and shares it, it might be that little bit that can keep everyone going."

"I appreciate all of you taking the time to do this today." I said beginning to close it out, "But I know you have to deal with that physical stuff too. Go get food and rest for your next shift. I'll be around if you want to talk about anything or have any questions I might be able to help with. And in case you haven't heard it today…thank you for everything you do."

The group acknowledged the end of the session mostly with nods. Some jumped up quickly and went on to other things. Some lingered to talk to the other teams. Some just took some time to sit, or lay, quietly. One of the AST's was sitting alone. I made my way over to him.

"Did you by chance talk to anyone about the axe situation?" I asked.

"What do you mean?"

"That your axes are too small?" I clarified "Getting that fire axe was a brilliant idea. I'm kind of surprised you guys don't have those on the helos."

"They strip the helos down to keep them as light as possible, for lift and fuel reasons. And those axes are super heavy."

"I think, as we're heading into day three, most of those on the rooftops have been rescued." I thought out loud, "The search will likely turn to finding those in attics or trapped in other spaces. With the water still not receding, I'm guessing you guys will remain the key players for search and rescue. If every helo had an axe, I bet it would help a lot."

"You're probably right. I'll see if I can get a message up the chain." he said. "By the way. Thanks for doing this. And for what you said. It helps."

The group debriefings seemed to be a success, or at least were accepted without push-back. I did three groups that first morning as other returning helos arrived. They all had similar stories of heartbreak and success. Several had made tough on-the-spot decisions that may not have lined up with traditional protocols. They all liked the axe idea and offered to push it up their chains as well. But one of the teams in particular had a slightly more dangerous situation arise.

An AST and his HH-65 flight team saw a group of over a hundred people on the roof of a hotel. He lowered himself down and was trying to organize the people for rescue by urgency of need, serious injuries first, and things like that. But three men armed with knives approached him and threatened him if he didn't take them first. The HH-65 could only hold three rescued people at a time and there were others on the roof in clear medical distress. He was somehow able to de-escalate the situation, got the group organized and evacuated them based on medical need. When I asked about where he learned to do that, he explained that crowd management was part of their search and rescue training. But it's taught to address struggling swimmers scratching and clawing trying not to drown. They train on how to keep themselves safe by calming the chaos of those frantic drowning attackers. He said the psychology is similar even though this was on a sturdy dry rooftop. Luckily the psychology worked because he was alone and would have been easily overpowered by the mob. The story he told made me decide to add that type of crowd control psychology to my training sessions in the future.

As I tried to digest everything the teams were going through, I heard the Commander's voice calling out to me from a nearby doorway.

"The 505 landed about an hour ago. Two of their search and rescue teams are staging from the Coast Guard Air Station. Time for you guys to grab your gear. We've got an HH-60 heading that way in about ten minutes."

I felt like I was moving too slow. Or maybe everything around me just looked like it was moving too fast. There was a surreal bustling at the Air Station. No one was still. Even those that were sitting down were energetically shifting in their seats, looking over maps, communicating with other pilots, making plans. It was a very different feeling from the exhausted undertones of the staging area at Mobile.

"Sirs, if you'll follow me, I'll take you to the command tent where you can coordinate with the 505 commander." One of our HH-60 pilots said. "We're just dropping you off. Once we're refueled, we need to get this big bird back up in the air."

"The HH-60s are bigger than the HH-65s. They can hold about ten people, sometimes more." Bob clarified for me "So they need them to make the larger rescues. And they only have a few of them in service."

"Why don't they use more 60s? If they're so much bigger…" I started to ask.

"A bunch of reasons. Mainly because they're so big. They're hard to maneuver in tight spaces. They're gas hogs. And they're much older tech. The 65s are newer, smaller, better on fuel, can get into tight spaces and have all the latest tech, they even have an autopilot system for conducting a search grid which means more eyes on the water and less staring at the gauges."

"Like what happened with cars, always getting smaller." I said.

"Basically." He added "But the 65's have their problems too. I heard a couple pilots talking about it back in Mobile."

"Oh? What's their issue?"

"They're way underpowered in certain conditions. Unfortunately, the power issue is mainly in the conditions we're experiencing right now. Hot and high humidity. To compensate they have to lighten their load by not filling the fuel tanks all the way. They go out half full. Which means they have to come back to refuel twice as often."

"Seems like that's a pretty big design flaw."

"It's being corrected. Some of the 65's are being upgraded. They're called the 65c variant. It fixes the problem. But they just started the upgrades last year and only a few have had the upgrade installed so far. Good news is the main search areas, the lily-pads, and the fueling station are all fairly close."

The pilot opened the field-house door and followed us inside.

"This is Captain John Roberts, Commanding Officer for Air Station New Orleans." The pilot said. "Sir, these are the men Rear Admiral Wyatt mentioned. They'll be working on the ground with the 505 teams."

"Ah, yes. Thank you gentlemen for coming and helping out." Captain Roberts said. "Sorry about the heat. Our generator's on the fritz."

"Petty Officer Geoffrey's been doing an amazing job keeping that hunk of junk running." Roberts continued, "But he's over at the

Navy fuel yard at the moment. Seems their generator crapped out too, and they need it to fuel the aircraft. They get priority over our comfort."

"No worries sir, we're from Florida and used to the heat." Bob said.

"That's good. Lots of complaints from some of the teams from up north. And speaking of lost comforts," Roberts added "Sewer system is out of commission. And we only have one porta-let for everyone to share. So we're asking that it only be used when you gotta drop a deuce."

"What about…" I started.

"There's a ditch right over there." Roberts said "That's the pee ditch."

"Just like when we were kids." Kevin said with a smile as a group of the 505s from the 82nd Airborne walked in.

"Good. I'm glad everyone is here. You'll be split into three teams and one of these guys will go with each team" Roberts said addressing the whole group and pointing to Bob, Kevin and I before he continued.

"The main maritime Coast Guard base was destroyed. It's in one of the hardest hit areas. But we have a makeshift launch direct to the Mississippi just off the air station here. It's right across from the main entrance off Highway 23. We have a light utility boat that will take you over to the affected area where you can launch a RIB, a rigid inflatable boat, to go through the neighborhood streets."

Several of the 505's looked at each other after hearing that.

"Yes, the streets and homes are still flooded. Waters haven't receded much if at all yet. Ten feet in some areas, most are six to eight feet. Those of you going to the Lakeview area, the houses there are newer, most made of block and are still sturdy. Those of you heading to the Ninth Ward area, those are much older homes, mostly wood on slab. The ones that are still standing should be considered dangerously unstable. Use extreme caution as you enter them. If they appear too dangerous just note it and move on to the next one."

"Excuse me sir, with communication systems down, how are we noting what we find?" one of the 505's asked.

"You'll have a notebook. Someone from your team will be assigned to keep track of things. We'll be using the X system. Is everyone familiar with that?" Roberts asked to an audience with a lot of shaking heads.

"Each team will have spray paint. On a prominent part of the structure seen from the street, you'll spray a large X. In the left quadrant of the X you'll note your team identification, 3-505, etc. In the top quadrant you'll note the date and time you left the structure, in the right quadrant you'll note any hazards you find. Hazards can be anything from an alligator or a vicious dog, to structural things like damaged staircases, anything that can help the next team that may come through. Then the bottom quadrant. That's where you'll note how many living or dead persons you find. You can also note pets there too. If you note living pets, note whether you left them there or, if you take them somewhere, note where. All of this information should be spraypainted on the structure. As teams come through after you, they'll add any new information. In the notebooks you'll draw the same X info and describe the location as best you can. If you're in the Ninth Ward you likely won't have any addresses so you'll need to use some form of description related to intersections. Third house north of such and such intersection. Something like that. There will be some structures that were completely floated off their lots and dropped a block or more away. Try to describe that as best you can."

"Now for the hard part." Roberts said, "You will be the first teams going into the homes. So far, we've only been doing rooftop rescues and a few attics or balconies. You absolutely will come across dead bodies. You're being directly ordered to leave the dead bodies in place at this time. You will be searching for living persons to rescue. Is that understood?"

Everyone looked at each other and nodded back to the Commander.

"Good." He acknowledged. "You will be approaching from the Industrial Canal. There will be space for the light utility boats to tie up at the dock area of the flooded maritime base just north of the canal locks. It's right across from the Lower Ninth Ward. Those going to Lakeview will go past the old base and up to Lake Pontchartrain. You'll tie up off the south bank by Lakeview. The utility boats will be your local command stations. There will also be some larger boats or barges in the area. Some of them are identified as drop off points for survivors. Grab a couple cases of water and a box of MREs for each RIB so you have something for any survivors you find. Any questions?"

Heads shook and no one spoke out.

"One last thing before you head out." Roberts said "I assume you know this, but it bears repeating. The water is absolutely contaminated. Chemicals, gas, oil, sewage, you name it. Stay dry. Keep your water gear on and if it gets torn then you need to stay out of the water. Nothing is where it should be. Cars, bikes, mailboxes, scrap wood and metal. There are a lot of things that can rip a suit or your skin. If you get a cut of any kind, get back to your

RIB and use the med kit to clean it out and get it covered. If you have any open wounds do not get in the water. People can lose limbs and even die from contaminated water infections. Don't end up dead because you thought you were tough."

A bunch of 505's looked at each other and smiled at that comment.

"Ok, start gathering what you need and head over to the launch area. Your utility boat command ships will be heading out in about a half hour."

The Mississippi River was crowded with boats of all sizes and types. Most were anchored, tied up or otherwise sitting motionless. But there were a few of the medium to large ships trying to navigate through the bends of the river even though the typical visual cues were either underwater, damaged or obstructed. I assumed those trying to move through had more modern navigation systems that weren't dependent on local pilot knowledge or visual cues. Smaller boats were moving at various speeds around the larger obstacle boats.

"Those barges can probably get by, but I don't know where those tankers and cargo carriers think they're going." The utility boat captain said as we moved slowly through the waters. "With the water this high, they won't be able to clear the bottom of the bridges."

"They'll find out soon enough." One of the others said.

I didn't catch any of the names of my team during the rush and the normal name plates on uniforms were covered up by the high water gear. They all knew each other. I was the outsider. It was easy for them to remember my name. But I eventually nicknamed them to keep it straight in my head. There was Tall Kid, a tall, skinny, dark haired kid that looked about twenty years old. Another was Squat Man, a shorter thirty-something guy that clearly did a lot of extra leg days at the gym. And rounding out the team was Beast Girl. She was blond. But that was the only traditionally feminine thing about her. Above average height, broad shouldered, thick waisted and muscular, she looked like she could rip any of the rest of us in half without breaking a sweat. She was friendly when spoken to, but otherwise seemed to keep to herself. She didn't offer unsolicited comments like Tall Kid and Squat Man. She just attended to tasks and did what needed to be done without complaint.

As we slowed to tie up at the maritime base, you could see water flowing back and forth through the levee breaches on the eastern bank of the canal. But your attention was quickly drawn away from the breaches toward the top of something out of place in the nearby neighborhood just over the levee bank.

"Holy shit." Tall Kid slowly let out as he took in the sight.

"Is that a barge on top of those houses?" Beast Girl asked.

"Yep." Squat Man said as everyone stared quietly now realizing how fast moving and high that water level must have been to get a barge that big over the earthen levee.

We watched as the Lakeview bound utility boat passed by with all aboard staring at the same unbelievable sight. That's when reality set in. This may not be much of a rescue mission.

The rigid inflatable boat, RIB for short, was quite durable. It didn't feel too much different than the light utility boat when it was moving slow. And slow is what we were. The main breach looked to be about two blocks wide. As we came over the levee and into the Ninth Ward, the scene was apocalyptic. Houses and parts of houses were strewn all over, most having been floated further east from where the levee must have been pouring water into the neighborhood.

Jordan Avenue runs along the western edge of the Lower Ninth Ward. There are eleven blocks of Jordan Avenue between the Claiborne Bridge to the south and the Florida Avenue Bridge to the north. Before the storm, along that stretch there were about sixty homes fronting Jordan Avenue. What we saw was the partial remains of about five homes on their actual lots. About twenty or thirty roof structures were floating and clumping in a few areas, the lower portion of their houses nowhere to be found. Wood debris was strewn everywhere. The water was brown and sludgy with a deep film across the top. It was clear that water was still flowing from the breaches into the neighborhood and piling up all the loose, floating debris further to the south and a few more blocks inland.

From where we came in at the main breach there was nothing for two blocks in every direction. The power of the flowing water destroyed or otherwise moved everything. The few remaining partial structures further north and south along Jordan Avenue looked too dangerous to enter. We decided to head to the north and go around to the next street over, Deslonde Street, where we could make our way back to the south and where there appeared to be more potentially accessible structures.

The boat was mostly just drifting, Squat Man using a hint of engine power to try and keep us over what should be the road, but it was impossible to tell. Power lines had been overhead but most of the lines were missing now and many of the wooden poles fallen. But you could use the remaining poles to try and judge where the road might be below.

The prop on the motor had a safety guard, essentially a solid open-ended tube around the prop itself to deflect underwater debris so the prop wouldn't chop into it. Even moving as slowly and cautiously as we were, you could feel the jerking of the RIB as the lower part of the motor came into contact with things not seen underneath, probably roofs of submerged cars parked along the street, maybe mailboxes when we drifted a bit too far off the street's edge.

About a block and a half down we came to our first structure that appeared to still be in its original place. Water was high, about a foot below the roofline. Squat Man carefully eased the RIB up into the yard to get as close as possible to the structure. We called out for survivors and heard no response. Tall Kid grabbed a hand ax and chopped through a weak attic vent cover. He shined a flashlight inside.

"I don't see anything." He said, "Also, it looks like the water line inside was about a foot deep in the attic. Which means it was floor to ceiling flooded below in the house. I don't think we're gonna find any survivors in this area if the water was that high."

"Okay. Let's make our way further south. It looks like the water isn't as deep that way." Squat Man said.

We moved a few blocks inland to Reynes Street and decided to work the block grids toward the south. We stopped at about four structures on each block that had water up to the base of the attic. We called out and knocked on the attic wall. But there were no responses. Even though we were going slow and relatively silent, we shut down the motor intermittently and called out to see if we could hear anything. It was quiet. Dead quiet. No sounds of bugs or birds. Nothing you would normally hear in a place like this.

We finished searching the northwestern grid, about fifteen blocks. No signs of life. Most structures still intact had clear waterlines well above the bottom of the roof. So we decided to head even further south. It was starting to get dark when we crossed what we called the barrens, that several blocks wide, several blocks deep area where the rushing water swept everything away. It looked like a lake in the middle of the surrounding chaos.

The first couple blocks on the south side of the barrens were similar to what we saw on the north. Water up to the attic. We did our simple checks there. No sounds. No signs of movement. But then we got down to Prieur St, just a few blocks north of the Claiborne main thoroughfare. The first thing we noticed was the street sign. The signs at Prieur and Reynes were the first we saw. They weren't on their own metal pole in the ground like most street signs in other cities. They were fastened to the power pole that was at the northwest corner of the intersection. We figured they had to be about eight feet off the ground. And they were about two feet above the water level. Doing the simple math, water at the street was about six feet deep. The lots were getting higher in this area and with the homes more settled on their higher slabs, the water was only about three to four feet deep at the front doors. There could be survivors here.

We pulled the RIB over closer to the porch of the nearest home and killed the motor. Tall Kid and Beast Girl slid out into the water. Both were in full waterproof suits, which was good because the water came up almost to Beast Girl's armpits. Tall Kid had quite a bit more clearance. He called out. And then knocked on the door, making tiny ripples rolling away toward the porch roof support columns.

"You really think you need to knock?" Beast Girl said.

"I don't know. It just feels wrong not to. I mean to just push through someone's door and go into their house. Seems like we should knock first." Tall Kid rationalized.

Beast Girl subtly smiled and shook her head as they wedged open the door and stepped cautiously into the house. They left the door open as they entered, which is standard procedure for safety. A few minutes after they disappeared inside, something orange, wet and moppy looking floated out the front door towards us. Squat Man probably had the same terrible thought as I did when he reached down and grabbed the extendable pole we brought, using the hook end to pull the orange ball closer. To our relief it was just a horrible, waterlogged orange shag throw pillow. We looked at each other and smiled then he pushed it floating on its way southward down the street with the other flotsam.

Tall Kid and Beast Girl came out of the house a bit faster than they entered.

"No survivors. We checked all the rooms. One body floating in the kitchen. Looks to be a heavyset middle aged man." Beast Girl said solemnly.

"I'll mark it up." Tall Kid said quietly, grabbing the spray paint can and making the X and its notations on the now closed door.

I think until that point we were holding out hope that we would be finding survivors. The reality that we would also be finding bodies was buried deep in the back of our mind. Not anymore. It was already dark when we entered the last twelve or so structures in that quadrant that looked safely accessible. Most were empty. Two were not.

In a heavily damaged house near the intersection of Tennessee and Derbigny streets, we found four bodies. What appeared to be an elderly man floating in a closed bedroom, and what appeared to be a young adult woman and two pre-teen kids in the kitchen. The woman and kids were still huddled together with their arms intertwined. Beast Girl made the decision not to disturb them and left them floating, huddled in place.

In the last house we went into in that southwest quadrant, near Jordan and Derbigny, we found a mess. This house had been hit hard and fast by the floodwaters. But worse than that, the occupant was clearly a hoarder. There was random debris floating everywhere in the house. The whole surface of the water inside was covered with plastic items, paper and all sorts of other things. Tall Kid described it as feeling like one of those ball pits at a Chuck-e-Cheese. He was walking through feeling his legs hit things that moved but had no idea what they may have been. There were loads of throw pillows and clothes floating around among the plastic. Hard to tell exactly in the darker rooms. Eventually Tall Kid grabbed one of the awkward looking pillows and held it up to his flashlight to see it better. He saw a distorted face looking back at him.

"Is everything ok in there" Squat Man yelled after we heard a startled screech.

"It's fine." Tall Kid replied, catching his breath. "This place if full of dead cats."

"That sounds fun." Squat Man said to me sarcastically "Glad I'm not in there."

"And one human body. Middle aged female." Beast Girl said as they walked out, pushing some floating cats back inside. "I hate when stereotypes are true."

Tall Kid grabbed the spray paint can and made the X. He noted one body. And many dead cats.

"That's a hard one to see right at the end. I really don't want that to stick with me." Tall Kid said as they jumped back into the RIB.

We made the turn back up Jordan Avenue toward where the levee breached. But before we got there, we saw one more thing to check out.

On the east side of the street there was something bobbing up and down in the now deeper water as we were getting closer to the breach. We slowly worked our way over to it. Tall Kid shined his flashlight from the side of the boat. It took a while for us to figure out what it was. But eventually we did. It was feet. Well, shoes. The bottom of bright red Air Jordan high top shoes.

Our mission wasn't to recover any bodies. But we were done for the night and thought we could make it easier for the crew that would be doing recovery later once the water receded. So we got some of our extendable poles and poked and prodded to try and figure out what was going on. Beast Girl's pole got snagged on something and she gave a hard tug with all that Beast Girl strength. Something popped and floated to the surface. It was a plastic mailbox. She had ripped it off its post. Beside the mailbox, the body popped up to lie face down in the water. We rolled it over to see what looked like a teenage boy. His arm appeared to be held down by something. Maybe tied down even. Tall Kid used his pole to try and pull the arm free. Eventually, after much effort something holding the arm popped free and floated to the surface. It was a dog. A big dog. Like a German shepherd mix. And the kid's arm had a leash wrapped around his wrist several times, the way you do when walking a big strong dog. What we deduced from the scene was that the boy must have been walking the dog when the levee breached. The rushing water knocked them down and wrapped them by the leash around the mailbox pole. Neither the boy nor the dog could get free from the leash tangling them to the mailbox. Both drowning together.

"How do we note that?" Tall Kid asked as the body and dog floated in the current down to the south with the other debris.

When we got back to the utility boat, Bob's 505 team was already there stashing their RIB for the trip back to the Air Station. About an hour later, Kevin's 505 team and their utility boat made it back to us from Lakeview. Bob, Kevin and I decided to wait until we got back to the Air Station where we could do the debriefing as one group. But that was a lot of alone-time to quietly reflect, or dwell, on the day.

Or sleep. As it turns out, mental and physical exhaustion, the sound of a boat engine and the rhythm of the waves at night will put you straight to sleep. All of us. We all had to be awakened when we got back to the launch area. We were stiff. And hungry. Seems my team and I forgot to eat our MREs while we were out. Which is a problem. We drank a few waters. But not eating any food took its toll. And MREs aren't good to binge on to catch up on calories.

Thankfully there was a truck to give us a ride from the launch area back to the main air station building complex where they dropped us off. We grabbed our gear out of the back, and stiffly, if not painfully, hoisted it for the walk to the command center. Captain Roberts was still there running operations as the helicopters were coming and going.

“You made it.” Roberts said to us, “How was day one for you?”

“Not productive. All bodies. No survivors.” Bob responded.

“That’s probably gonna be the case from here on out.” Roberts noted “We may come across the occasional pocket of people. But even though it’s not official yet, we’re pretty much in the recovery phase at this point. Actual body collections won’t start until after the water recedes more and everything is accessible by truck or at least small pull behind skiff.”

“How long until the water recedes?” I asked.

“It’s already receding in a lot of areas. The problem is the levee breaches. The storm’s rainwater eventually makes its way to Pontchartrain. Normally it would stay there and flow out through the canals in a controlled manner. But now Pontchartrain and the canals are acting more like a river. Depending on the timing of it cresting, more water might come into those areas where the breaches were especially bad.”

“Like the Ninth Ward.” I said.

“Definitely there. That more southern breach in the west quadrant was massively wide and the water came through so fast it eroded it pretty deep. Quite a gouge. You can still get skiffs and RIBs through it without grounding them.”

“The water by the northwest breach was the deepest we saw” I said.

“Yep. Even though that was a much narrower and shallower breach, it’s going to be the bigger problem.”

“Why’s that?” Bob asked.

“There’s a railroad line that runs east-west across the north side of the ward. Its elevation tails upward a bit on a bridge to get over the Industrial Canal. There’s a control facility there that helps move the water back out to the large main outfall canal, more like a large open marshy bay really, that leads out to the gulf. With the low point of the Ninth Ward in that northwest corner, that’s where we would want to pump the water from. Pumping the water back into Pontchartrain would just bring it right back down the canal to those breach areas, and back into the ward. So it needs to go out to the outfall canal at least until the water in Pontchartrain levels off.”

“It felt like the current at the big breach was moving out of the neighborhood.” I said “But most things floating in the water were still moving south away from the breach. And not toward that low spot to the north.”

“The main currents in the Industrial canal may have been pulling some of the water outward at the edge of the neighborhood. But the rest inside was probably still flowing inland away from that breach area.” One of the officers said. “The latest report I got was that the actual floodwaters are beginning to recede as of late today.”

“This is one of our civil engineers.” Roberts said by way of introduction, “He’ll be working with the Army Corp of Engineers to try and get all this fixed.”

“Some of these neighborhoods are gonna be hard to drain out.” The officer said, “the ground is fully saturated and the way they are designed to move their stormwater out of the area is going to be working against them for a while. The water level will go down over the next day or so. Maybe as low as a foot deep in some of the higher areas. Which will make access to the structures much easier."

"And the other areas. The lower ones?" Bob asked.

"They could stay under a few feet of water for a while. Could be a week or more."

"And the levee breaches? Will they keep re-flooding them?" I asked.

"We think the water level in the canal will be low enough to begin repairing the breaches in a couple days. We don't expect much more water to pour in. We just don't have a way to get what's already inside pumped out of the neighborhood. The rail tracks are the issue there."

"Commander Roberts mentioned that railroad before. Why is it an issue?" I asked.

"Railroad tracks are very delicate and the space around them is highly regulated. We aren't allowed to lay a makeshift pipe over the top of the tracks, and we aren't allowed to drill under them to run a pipe. Both are considered dangerous and would create delays for rail cars getting back online, with all the economic impacts that would bring. Most of this region's oil, gas and other goods come up those rail lines for the rest of the surrounding states."

"If you can't pump it north to the outfall canal system, what about pumping it south?" Bob asked.

"Same problem. To get the water where we need it to go, the pipes would need to cross two major thoroughfares. Blocking tanker trucks and semi-trucks. There's also not enough pipe available for a pipe run that long, and the pumps would have trouble moving that much water that far." The officer explained "And before you ask, no, we wouldn't be able to spread the water by dumping some into drier areas on the outskirts of the Ninth Ward. That was done before, about twenty years ago, and led to massive lawsuits from residents and insurance companies in those drier areas."

"Gentlemen." Roberts said getting our attention "I'd love for you to stay here and help us solve our problems. But your ride back to Mobile is getting set to take off. You'll be on a bigger HH-60 again for the ride back. So you can stretch out a bit."

Back in Mobile, Bob, Kevin and I dropped our gear on our assigned squares and were starting to discuss how to gather everyone up for a debriefing since it was so late already. We were exhausted and we knew the other crews were more exhausted. We walked toward the command building and veered past to the adjacent tent where we held the first debriefings earlier today. It was hard to believe that was earlier today. It seemed like weeks ago. As we walked up, we heard voices. And as we turned the corner, we saw a small crowd of about twenty people standing outside the tent.

"What's happening?" Kevin asked.

"We're waiting for the guys inside to finish their debriefing so we can start ours." He said.

"They started on their own?" I asked.

"I think so." He said "they've been going on all day. Whenever teams get back from a shift. A couple swimmers had some overlapping shifts early today and were talking about this morning's debriefing and that it was a good thing. Said they got to say what they were thinking. Not like the old meetings where people just flung data back and forth trying to be more efficient. News of that traveled fast."

Just then the tent door opened and people started walking out, mostly in small groups. Most were having pleasant conversations or just smiling and joking. No one looked exhausted. No one looked angry or irritable. Bob, Kevin and I just looked at each other as we let them pass and then made our way into the tent.

At the front of the tent was a familiar face. Well, sort of a familiar face. It was someone from our first debriefing this morning. He didn't speak at that debriefing. But he was speaking now. Several people were walking up to him and thanking him. Some telling their stories while he listened. He looked up to see us staring from the back of the tent and excused himself to come greet us.

"Thank God you guys are back!" he said. "I don't know how you do this stuff. Hearing all these stories. It's so hard to mentally process it."

"Did you start doing these on your own?" I asked.

"I did. I hope that's ok." He said

"It's definitely ok." I said.

"This morning helped me so much you'll never even know. I didn't even speak and felt a weight lifted off of me." He continued "So I went to the Commander and asked if I could do it until you came back. He said it was ok. So here I am. I wasn't expecting too many people to come talk to me. But the first group was about fifteen people. The next about thirty. And they stayed about that big."

"How many group sessions have you done?" Bob asked.

"Five so far."

"What things did you talk about?" Kevin asked.

"Same things you asked us this morning. What did you see, hear, smell that bothered you."

"That's the gist of it." I said. "Thank you for that. Sounds like you did a great job."

"Not sure if it was great. But I feel better after doing it."

"I'm not sure what your regular duties entail, but you're welcome to help us do these whenever you want." I offered.

"That's the thing." He said "I have an old back injury. It started acting up after my last flight. This morning at your meeting I was upset because the doc told me I wouldn't be able to get back out there doing search and rescue for at least a week."

"We'd love to have you help us. And with four of us doing these we should be able to get them down to a more manageable three apiece per day."

"That would be better!" he said "five was a lot."

"Tell me. Do you think there's anyone else on injured reserve that might want to help?" I asked.

"I'm sure of it. I've had a couple people that are flying active shifts offer to do it in their limited rest time. We could easily pick up a few others." He said.

"We're just getting into day four of this. And from everything I'm hearing it's going to go on for several more weeks. We can use all the help we can get." I said. "Would you be willing to take charge of that recruitment and training?"

"Definitely!" he said, a smile beaming.

"I'll talk with Commander Wyatt in the morning and see if we can make that official." I said. "But right now I need to get this next debriefing started so these guys can get some sleep."

The number of helicopter rescues waned significantly over the next twenty-four hours and helicopter work leaned more toward delivery of supplies to areas still cut off by floodwaters. Some of the smaller HH-65s were used to reach particularly difficult spaces. But most of them sat idle. A few of the un-used HH-65 pilots helped by doing pilot and copilot shifts on the larger HH-60s and the massive Chinook helicopters the Airborne team brought with them. But that still left several pilots that wanted to remain engaged but had no official duty. Many joined the debriefing team at Mobile. By the end of the week there were at least ten group leaders doing the debriefings. With the Mobile station now pretty much organized and operating smoothly in terms of the debriefings, we decided that Kevin would stay in Mobile and Bob and I would go into New Orleans proper to assist the National Guard to set up a similar debriefing process.

"Absolutely not." Dr Ellison said.

"What do you mean? It's why we're here." I argued.

"It *was* why you were there." he rebutted "You did exactly what you were there for, with the Coast Guard and the Airborne 505's. The National Guard is a whole different situation."

"Why is that?"

“The National Guard is only doing a little rescue and recovery work these days. Their time is mostly spent in a war with a bunch of makeshift gangs. The city proper is experiencing complete lawlessness. Killing, robbing, looting, raping, it’s all happening every day on every block. And there are larger uprisings at the Superdome and the Civic Center where thousands of people have been sheltered with vastly insufficient supplies. The National Guard there are fighting back daily riots and trying to manage the food and water supplies airlifted to them. It’s the wrong kind of danger for you to be a part of.”

“But…”

“My decision on that is final. You’ve trained most of the National Guard units over the years. They have the tools they need. It’s not worth the danger of sending you in there just to give them a quick refresher.”

“So what do you want us to do?”

“You can stay where you are. Keep working with the Coast Guard or the 505 on the recovery.” he said, voice softening some as he continued “the recovery of the bodies at this point is probably some of the hardest work to be done. The Army Corp made the temporary fix to the levee breaches by the Ninth Ward. And they’re actively pumping water out. It will take a while to get it all out. But I hear about fifty percent of the area outside of those deeper spots only has water in the roads now. So trucks and pull behind skiffs can get in for recovery. A few blocks a day. And it should give those deeper areas time to clear out before you get to them.”

“We can do that. Will the 505 be expecting us?”

“I’ll make a call.” He said “Your original search and rescue teams are still there. They moved down further south for a couple days looking for stranded survivors but now they’ll be going back into the area you were in before. To begin the body recovery. It will be horrible. But it's important work."

"I'll let Bob and Kevin know the options. How long do we have before we'll need leave the area?"

"This was an all-hands-on-deck event. So I think you will be able to stay as long as you need. But I don't want you guys to over-stay. It's helpful for you to be there now. But soon it will be better organized and the other groups trained to handle it should be the ones doing everything. At that point you guys should politely bow out and head back home for some much-needed rest. And I'm sure you've got a lot of new ideas you'll want to get integrated into your training program."

We hitched a ride from Mobile in one of the HH-65's the next day. With most of the water receded along the Mississippi coastline the devastation was clearly visible in the light of day. Most structures along the coast were destroyed. Trees knocked down. Those left standing had few leaves remaining. The wind damage was the worst just east of the point of mainland landfall at the Louisiana-Mississippi border. But then we got to the Louisiana peninsula.

Very wet. Way more wet than it should be this long after the storm. The coastal areas were better here. Still lots of wind damage, but the water had receded, and work crews were busily making repairs to get their main roads and power grid back up and running. Looking out the left side windows you could see the various industrial buildings along the only road from the Coast Guard Air

Station south to Venice where the Mississippi hits the gulf. Most had cleanup activity going on. Some even had smoke coming out of smokestacks. Getting closer you could see ships docked at some of the berths. Definitely not business as usual. But things were starting to get moving. Then you looked out the right side windows.

The sun's light reflected off the water looming in most of the neighborhoods. There was little visible movement. At least not meaningful movement. There were small groups of people gathered in some places. Larger groups gathered in others. A few better equipped trucks were seen in some of the less flooded neighborhood yards trying to begin what clean-up activity they could.

We flew past the new staging area because two other helicopters were in the only available landing spaces. We took a brief flight over the Ninth Ward, most of which was still under water, except for the southernmost area near the Mississippi. We flew over Algiers which fared surprisingly well. Almost completely dry. And then over the Garden District, Superdome and the French Quarter. These spaces were a mixed bag. There were intermittent blocks that looked mostly dry. But they were surrounded by other blocks that were still flooded, at least in the streets, making those few dry blocks look like islands.

The Superdome itself was dry but also an island among the flooded roads surrounding it. There were helicopters in the parking lot but not much movement. One of the helicopters was a big Chinook. The giant twin rotor system helicopters for troop and supply transport. It had likely been used to bring National Guard troops in and not supplies since the main National Guard supply convoy hadn't made it to the area yet. It wasn't clear if they couldn't, or just hadn't, gotten there yet with supplies. Which was odd since the Coast Guard C-130's out of St Petersburg had been flying supplies in non-stop to Mobile for several days now. A portion of the Coast Guard's Mobile supply stash was taken to Coast Guard Air Station New Orleans where the smaller HH-65's could drop off the small amounts they could carry near the forward staging areas they could get to. Which is what the two helicopters were doing when we first arrived.

After our brief tour over the area, we circled back to our staging location, a rail yard with a shipping berth on the Mississippi just east of the Ninth Ward in St Bernard Parrish. There was a less obstructed road from that location through the southern portion of the Ninth Ward. And trucks were able to get down closer to the affected areas. You still needed skiffs to go more than a block or so north of that road.

"We've got nine people and three skiffs." One of the 505 leaders said, "so let's split into three teams. One team per street on these three westernmost streets. We'll check the houses heading north until the water gets more than waist deep. Then, depending on time, we'll move east and do the next three streets. And so on. Until dark."

"There's rafts and bags in the lockers on the skiffs." Another 505 said for Bob, Kevin and my benefit. "We also have a cooler with water and MREs for us. And a stash in case any residents approach us. But we've only had residents come up to us when we're in a foot of water or less. They'll likely go toward the trucks as long as they can see them."

"We're using color coded spray paint now when we can." Tall Kid leaned over and said to me "We're designated as 3-505 for the X Codes."

"Hopefully we won't need too much paint." I said.

"Well, we were working search and recovery on the south side of St Claude Avenue, between the canal and Fats Domino Avenue. It's maybe about forty square blocks." Beast Girl said, "And the flooding there was lower. From no flooding at all down on the edge of the Mississippi, to maybe four or five feet up here closer to St Claude. We found seven bodies. One of them was in a home with no evidence of flooding."

"Must have been a medical thing. Maybe a heart attack during the storm." Tall Kid added.

"These houses we're going through today, north of St Claude, water was up to the roof on almost all of them." Beast Girl said, "I expect we'll find a lot more bodies. We already know where a few of them are from last time we were up here."

"I don't know if we'll make it up to Claiborne Avenue or not." I said "We flew over earlier and the water looked like it was still pretty deep up that way. So we may not even get to that area we were in before."

"We may not have time to get there anyway." Tall Kid said "each of these streets has about fifty or sixty houses between here and there."

"Then we'd better get started." Bob said. "Let's get the skiffs unloaded off the trailer."

It was hot. The sun was up. The air was still. The high-water gear was thick and bulky, allowing little air circulation below the armpits. Long sleeve shirts covered our upper torso and arms. Rescue gloves, a modified version of a scuba diver's glove, to protect our hands from scratches and subsequent infection by the many contaminants in the water. Helmets, in case something inside were to fall on us. And half mask respirators. The respirators were only to be on when we were inside the houses. But it seemed even that would feel like too long in this heat.

The skiffs were unloaded and set up with our gear, waiting for us at the edge of the floodwaters. Bob, Kevin and I bid each other farewell for the day and headed to our separate skiffs where the rest of our teams were waiting.

The three streets didn't technically connect to St Claude Avenue. They connected to St Claude Service Road that ran parallel. Bob and Team One were starting on the westernmost end. Sister Street. A short distance away from the canal and the St Claude drawbridge that was stuck in the upright position. That portion of Sister Street was only a two-block run. When they finished, they were going to merge back with Kevin and Team Two along Jordan Avenue. There were a lot of houses on this end of Jordan, and a few dead-end streets going toward the canal. So they decided it would be best to have one team on each side of the street. That left my Team Three on Deslonde Street. We decided it would be most efficient to just go up the west side first. And then back down the east side toward the truck. It didn't take long for our first gruesome discovery.

Between Jordan and Deslonde, in what would have been the backyards of the homes, there were large piles of debris. It was hard to tell if it was localized debris, like pieces of wood fences around the homes that came down, or if it was debris that floated to this area from the push of the initial flood currents. Two of the lots on the Jordan side had no structures on them. So the debris may well have been the remains of the former homes, shattered by the raging waters and floated into a pile in the back yard. The piles were offset somewhat and created a makeshift meandering creek of shallow floodwater. Like an arthritis mangled finger of water desperately trying to maintain a grasp on the higher ground as the bulk water behind it was trying to recede.

I could see from my vantage point that Team Two was not looking in the backyards at all. And didn't look near that rubble or near that makeshift creek. They stayed within the front yards and in the structures of the homes that were still standing. When Tall Kid and Beast Girl came back to the skiff from the second structure on our street, they agreed to let me walk that rear perimeter while they made some notes about the two structures they just searched in our log. Not willing to give them time to rethink their decision, I quickly stepped away from the skiff making my way through the knee-deep water gradually walking up to the drier land between the first two houses.

From my prior vantage point standing in the water next to the skiff I was looking mainly at the larger piles of debris. But now, from ground level, I noticed that there was barely anywhere on the ground that didn't have some kind of debris. Paper of all kinds, cardboard, wood scraps, plastic containers. In some spots you could tell it was wet toilet paper, paper towels or newspaper that had soaked itself into some kind of wet paper machete holding other items of trash at odd angles on the ground. Some of it would have made interesting art. Much of it had to be kicked to the side to get by. This was the area where the rush of water flushed all the garbage from all the yards and homes, collecting and depositing it at this last basin before the edge of the higher built St Claude Avenue that acted like a dam.

After making my way to the creek and piles of debris it was clear that not much would be found without some serious moving of the boards and other clutter. That was beyond the scope of today's mission. Today was to do walk throughs, mark what we find, and recover the bodies in plain sight. I moved to the far side of one of the piles to begin my walk back toward Deslonde Street. A few steps around the pile and I saw something out of the corner of my eye up against the back of the third house. I'm not sure what made me look. There was odd debris everywhere. But I turned my head to try and focus. And there it was. A bright red Air Jordan high top. One shoe. No foot or body attached.

A wave of nausea hit me hard. I don't know exactly what I was feeling. I wasn't going to throw up. It wasn't that kind of nausea if that makes any sense. It was more like anger? Maybe sadness? I looked around briefly and didn't see anything resembling the former owner of the shoe. At this point it had been days since we first found him floating upside down. And the reality that he is probably still out here somewhere was a gut punch. I slowly walked back between the houses and across the front yard of house three to where the team had relocated our skiff, preparing to enter that third house.

"What's got you so spooked" Beast Girl asked, clearly seeing the distressed look on my face. "Is there a body back there we need to get?"

"No body. Just a shoe." I said.

"A shoe? There are hundreds of random shoes all around here. It's worse than my closet." Beast Girl said, trying to make light of things to uplift my mood a bit.

"A bright red Air Jordan shoe." I said quietly as they both immediately stopped chuckling about Beast Girl's closet comment.

"Oh…wow…" Tall Kid said thinking through the math and coming to his own realizations. "That's far. Like nine or ten blocks away from where we cut him loose."

"I guess we need to be sure and look in the yards too." Beast Girl said softly. "Are you okay doing that while we do our write-ups every couple houses?"

"I'll do it. I'm not sure I'm really okay with anything right now though." I said. Both nodded in understanding but had knowing looks on their faces that the worst was yet to come.

House three was the first body of the day for our team. Tall Kid came out to the skiff to get a body bag and set up the tow behind raft.

"I think we'll need you to come in and help us with this one." Tall Kid said as he was getting ready to head back into the house. "It's pretty big."

"It?" I asked.

"Some of the bodies we find, especially the larger ones, are hard to tell if they're male or female. It's worse with the bloating. If the clothes don't make it clear, we don't know until we can get them out to the raft to investigate further." He explained.

It was big. Probably around four hundred pounds before the waterlogging. A black person. Short hair. Wearing a sweatshirt and sweatpants. No shoes. Laying in a space between the living room and a hallway. Probably between a couch and a dining table.

Except that the couch and dining table had been floated around the room. The table on its side against a nearby wall next to an angled couch that was not flipped but clearly out of place.

"Is this where you found them?" I asked, preferring to say *them* instead of *it* when referring to the body. "Not in the kitchen?"

"Found right here. We wouldn't have been able to move 'em alone." Beast Girl said, choosing not to use the term *it* as well.

"It is different." Tall Kid said, referring to the location, not the person, "Almost everyone we've found so far has been in the kitchen or the bathroom. Except a couple times in the bedroom. But they looked elderly and may have been bedridden anyway."

Beast Girl talked me through the process of opening the bag, where to lay it and how to roll the body, and then roll it back into the bag. She called out the cadence. And the task was done. Once the bag was zipped up, she told me to grab the foot side while she and Tall Kid grabbed the heavier head side. They would be walking forward holding the handles behind their back and using their legs to bear the weight. I would be walking forward too, with a lighter, but more awkward stride.

"We need to lift them fully off the ground and carry until we get outside." She said, "Once we get to where the water's a foot or so deep, we may want to lower the bag and let it partially float the rest of the way to the skiff's raft."

It was a heavy and awkward lift. And as soon as we got to the water's edge, just off the porch at this particular house, we sat the bag down gently. After removing our respirators and taking several deep breaths from the exertion, we slowly dragged the bag to the raft. I saw first-hand why the flat top rafts are used. We never would have been able to get the bag up into a skiff.

Beast Girl unbuckled a sturdy strap I didn't even know was there.

"Grab the end of this strap, put it through that loop on the side of the raft and then wrap it underneath the bag." She said.

Tall Kid flipped the bag upside down in the water and then did as told, bringing the long strap back over the top of the bag and tossing the end back to Beast Girl on the other side of the raft.

She asked Tall Kid to lift the body bag in the water so it floated slightly higher. Then she asked me to try and pull the edge of the raft down under the bag as much as possible. While Tall Kid and I were struggling with our tasks, Beast Girl pulled the strap tight through what appeared to be a ratcheting buckle. As she shifted the lever back and forth, the strap got tighter and tighter, pulling the bag slowly up onto the edge of the raft and rolling it over right side up.

Once the bag was right side up and steadied on the raft, Beast Girl unzipped it. First, she checked for a bra strap. No bra. Then she checked around the hip for the side of any underwear, to determine a more masculine or more feminine style. No underwear.

"Not it!" Tall Kid said immediately.

"Not it what?" I asked.

"He doesn't want to do the next check." Beast Girl said.

"What's that?" I asked.

"To see if there's an in-ee or an out-ee." Tall Kid said pointing at the crotch area of the bag.

Beast Girl first pulled open the sweatpants to see if anything was visible. Nothing was visible due to the belly flab that hung down past the hips. So she took the next dreaded step and pulled the belly flab up out of the way to make the genitals visible. She quickly let everything fall back in place and zipped the bag shut."

"This guy has something seriously wrong with his junk." She described "blistered and discolored way beyond the effects of waterlogging."

"I read that some opportunistic infections take advantage of other infection sites. It's been several days. Maybe something in the water is latching onto some herpes blister or something." Tall Kid said.

"I don't think it matters to him now." Beast Girl said, "but we'll need to put a red tag on the bag and make a note of it on the bag insert."

Beast Girl walked me through the paperwork part of the process since I hadn't seen it yet. There's a form that gets put into a clear outer pocket on each bag with as much information as possible about the body, where it was found, etc. so teams can help make identifications. It's easier if there's only one body and there's a purse or wallet nearby. Neither was seen here. So a description of the house location and where in the house he was found, what position he was found in, that he was alone in the house, etc., was described on the form.

While Beast Girl was explaining it to me, Tall Kid was spray-painting the X Codes on the wall beside the front door of the home. *3-505* on the left side of the X, the date and time at the top, the words *infection on body* to the right, and the words *One Dead Body to Rail Yard* at the bottom.

I waited with the body while the team went through house four. Nothing found there. Tall Kid painted the X code noting nothing found. And we moved on toward the fifth house.

While Beast girl and Tall kid were writing in the log about nothing found in the fourth and fifth house, I backtracked to do my yard search for houses three, four and five.

House Five had more standing water in the side yard, and floodwater in the back yard came up to within a few feet of the house. There wasn't much large debris here. It was mostly just smaller trash that got beached or that was floating back and forth with the tide, or maybe with the small ripples of wake from the skiffs on the other streets to the west. But one thing I noticed here was definitely different. There were dead fish floating at the water's edge, and a few beached along the back of the house. It was hard to tell fish from bottles and pieces of plastic floating around. At least until you got close to them. And it wasn't so much the sight of the fish. You knew there were there when you could smell them.

I didn't notice the smell as much the first day. But now there was a definite underlying odor everywhere you went. A soggy, dank, spoiled milk, cesspool type of odor. Not at all like the beach, even though it was basically salt water from the gulf that got pushed into the neighborhood. In reality it was a combination of stagnant salt water, sewage that seeped out of the sewer system either backflowing up through the toilets or out of the de-powered sewage lift stations, along with rotting food, gasoline and oil from cars that were submerged, paint, pesticides and other chemicals from garage storage shelves and solvents and cleaners from under sinks. All mixed together into a soup that still sat several feet deep throughout most of the neighborhood. But fish…for some reason the smell of dead fish stood out.

Thinking my thoughts about that, I stood about knee deep in the backyard water, swirling the end of my extendable poking stick across the surface, moving the trash around. The rescue prongs on the end of my stick caught on a branch of a tree limb, or a shrub or something. I gave it a good tug, and the branch came toward me. I pulled the stick but couldn't fully untangle the prongs from the vine laden limbs. So I pulled the nearest part of the limb up onto the drier part of the yard near the house and walked back out into the water to get closer to where the prongs were tangled near the other end of the limb. It took quite a bit of effort to pull. It looked like there was some kind of thin metal wire, maybe heavy test fishing line tangled in the branches of the limb and vines, and my prongs were tangled in the mix. I gave a massive tug upward and most of the waterlogged limb came up out of the water. The wave moved the surface-water trash off to the side for a moment. Among the tangles of the smaller branches on the bottom of the limb was a face looking up at me.

Thank God it wasn't human. But startling nonetheless. It was a dog. A large dog. Maybe a German shepherd but it was hard to tell with the bloat mis-shaping the face and body. I remembered the red shoe and to ease my own mind decided to pull it fully up to the water's edge to see if this was the same dog. There was only one way to really tell. So I pulled the branch further and it lifted the dog part-way out of the water by its collar. The collar had been caught on a branch. Attached to the collar was a leash. Or part of a leash. The upper part of the leash with the handle was missing. Good chance this was red shoe's dog. The leash looked like a match. I didn't think we cut the leash when we pulled them up. But I didn't really check. They were tangled pretty good around something, a jagged edge of a rusty metal mailbox pole maybe. The pop we heard could have been the leash snapping.

At that point I wanted to leave. To go back to the front and sit in the skiff. But I felt obligated to continue searching the area for red shoe's body. Really hoping I wouldn't find it.

I didn't find him. Which was good. But my aimless swirling of my stick did expose some dead fish and a dead squirrel. Or a squirrel hat, or squirrel stuffed toy. Too hard to tell. Soggy fur strip that resembled a squirrel. Feeling a little defeated but mostly relieved, I made my way back to the skiff.

"Find anything?" Tall Kid asked, while laying back in the skiff pouring bottled water into his mouth.

"You've been gone a while. We were about to send out a search party." Beast Girl said sipping water and leaning against a power pole. "Oh wait, we are the search party."

Everyone seemed to force a smile for that quip.

"I think I found the dog from that first day. The one with the red shoe guy." I said "So I did a little extra wading around to make sure red shoe guy wasn't back there in the yard."

"I'll add that about the dog to my log entry." She said.

"And I'll update my X Code," Tall Kid said, "That was behind house five right?"

The updates were made, and we moved on. It seemed odd to just be moving on after these finds. A body. Now a dog. In any other situation you would instinctually stop and do things about it. But here, we just bagged a body, left the dog and moved on up the street. We searched almost twenty more houses before coming across the next body. A middle aged man. Then two more bodies as we came back down the east side of the street. Then another in a house right across from the one at the corner where we started. Five bodies. It felt very strange parading them back to the truck on the rafts. Like we were the garbage men. Just picking them up and moving on. Which was disturbing for me since these were people.

***

At our debriefing back in Mobile that night, everyone could tell I was struggling. I wasn't leading this one. Just attending. I told my stories. But I still felt off. Numb. I didn't get that sense of release, or relief, like the others seemed to get from it. After the last person volunteered their story, the leader asked a question.

"Did anybody notice any smells that bothered you?"

Smells? I think that was it. My issue was with smells. Well, not really smells, but the lack of smells.

"I smelled a lot of things" I began describing, "I could smell the sewage. The chemicals in the water. The stagnant swampy smell in some of the homes and yards. Even the dead fish smell when they were around."

Several people were nodding.

"But I never smelled the bodies." I said. Hesitating to go further.

"Can you describe what you mean" the leader said, perfectly prompting me to continue.

"It's hard to explain. And I don't want to offend anyone. But…you know how when you're around old people, there's that old person smell?" I said, some people smiled and nodded.

"There was no old person smell. There was no cat lady smell. No sweaty fat guy smell. None of the bodies had those smells my brain thought I should have smelled. Everyone just smelled like whatever around them smelled like. And more than that, we're a week into this now, and everything in my soul was telling me I should have smelled dead rotting human. But I didn't. I smelled dead fish. But I couldn't have stood in the doorway of a home and said, yep, there's a body in there, I can smell it. Maybe that's just too much TV. I don't know."

"Same here." Someone said. "I had that same thought. It made things very surreal."

"Surreal's a good way to put it." A third person chimed in "I thought it was just my respirator, maybe a filter clearing those smells away. But now that you mention it, I did smell everything else. Lots of dead fish. Even a weird smell in one house where a perfume bottle was broken open. Strong flowers. But no flowers anywhere."

The discussion of smells continued for several minutes. One person tried to give a technical reason. That the bodies wouldn't really be rotting yet, that it would take longer because of the salt in the water they were soaked in. But he clearly missed the point. Our brains thought it should have been there, and it wasn't. And that was hard for some of us to come to terms with.

I did a few more shifts with my 3-505 team recovering bodies in that same area making it a few blocks further to the east and a block or two north of Claiborne Avenue. At that first block of Tennessee Street north of Claiborne, in the first two houses we entered we found families. Four bodies in each house. Even though we'd found numerous individual bodies by that time, I felt something switched off in my brain when we found those families. That was it. I was done.

"I need a ride home. I'm done." I said on a call to Dr Ellison the next morning.

"Seems like you're a little past done." He replied, "The C-130's are making loops between Mobile and St Pete with supply runs. You can hop on any one of them to get home."

I sat quietly on the line.

"But before you do," he said "Get with Bob and Kevin and sit though one more debriefing. Describe when it clicked. When you felt you were done. And maybe some thoughts about why you kept going a little longer after you were done. I think that's a good lesson for all first responders in situations like this. The whole *know when to say when* thing."

I talked with Bob and Kevin that evening as we were sorting and freshening up our gear.

"I know exactly when you were done." Bob said.

"When was that?" I asked "I don't even know exactly."

"It was the day my team found red shoe guy. The day after you found his dog." Bob said, "We were all tired. But you went absolutely flat when I mentioned it back at the truck while we were loading up the body bags."

I remembered that now. Red shoes was the first actual body I saw that first day, upside down feet up in the water. Such tragic circumstances. A kid just trying to walk his dog. Wrong place, wrong time. Then, we found his shoe so far away several days later. Then I found his dog. When I heard Bob's team found his body the next day it created a storyline in my head. Almost like he was haunting me. I remembered thinking I wanted to open his body bag and actually take a moment to look at him. I hadn't seen much of him before and probably wouldn't recognize him if you showed me a photo. Other than the shoes. And it was eating at me. Instead of saying anything, I just shut it off in my brain. Went on auto-pilot. And apparently everyone but me noticed I wasn't ok.

After a C-130 ride that next morning, I was back home in Tampa, mid-September. I'd spent about two weeks total working with the Katrina effort. Bob and Kevin were still going strong in New Orleans. And I felt weak. Like a failure. Like I should have been with them to the end. But there was no way. I could feel the mental and physical darkness coming over me. It was everything I could do to remember to eat during that first week back. Zero energy. I finally worked up the strength and ordered a pizza.

I sat on the couch and turned on a football game to watch mindlessly while I forced myself to eat a slice straight from the greasy pizza box on the coffee table in front of me. Two bites into my slice, the game cut away to a breaking news story.

"The latest information is in from the hurricane hunter team, Hurricane Rita entered the Gulf and is now a Category Five hurricane with winds over 180mph. The current track has it making landfall in Louisiana in two days just west of New Orleans who is still reeling from Hurricane Katrina that made landfall there just a few weeks ago."

The pizza slice fell out of my hand onto the floor. I leaned back into the couch with my hands limp at my sides staring up at the ceiling. Suddenly there was a swell of empathetic anguish, and I felt a single tear roll down my face.

Epilogue
Here I Stand, At the Crossroads Edge…Again

Tampa, Florida
2025

“You work too much. Every day I see you’re already here when I come in. And still here when I leave. You’ve gotta get out. Live your life. It can’t be all about work.” A random coworker from another department said, “You don’t want to be on your deathbed with regrets that you didn’t spend more time doing things with your family, seeing nature, traveling or helping others.”

“Really. I’m good.” I said, hopefully snippy enough to end that line of discussion, and glancing at my display of about fifty challenge coins I’d received for various helpful accomplishments over the last thirty years. “I’ve had a very fulfilling life.”

“Well. I hope so.” He said, taking the folder he came for and walking out of my office.

For the life of me I don’t know where some people get the idea that they know a person’s whole history after interacting with them just a few times. Even more, I don’t understand why anyone would think they have any right to openly confront someone and pass judgement about something they know so little about. It’s infuriating. But that’s probably just who he is as a person. I could imagine his bookshelf full of self-help books written by everyone with an opinion on how other people should live. I shook my head at the thought.

"You know, there's a name for people like him." One of my nearby coworkers said, watching to make sure he was out of earshot.

"What's that?" I asked.

"Self-Righteous Asshat" she said. "I find that when I refer to him as Mr. Self-Righteous Asshat in my head while he's speaking to me, I can tolerate his bullshit much better."

"One day I'm gonna say that to his face." I said, signing the paper she brought me and handing it back to her.

"You know we all have your back if you do. Just sayin." She said, smiling as she walked away.

I too smiled at the thought of that. I was pretty confident that everyone in my division would indeed go to bat for me. They wouldn't give up their job over it. But I wouldn't want anyone to do that.

I looked over at my multi-tiered rack of challenge coins again. I don't often focus on it. Most of the time I forget it's there. But I have new coins for hurricanes Helene and Milton sitting on my desk that need a home. The rack is full. So which ones should I replace?

Every coin has a story. There's a coin from the counter-terrorist team of DISIP, the Venezuelan intelligence service. A coin from USAMRI, engraved from Edwin Ellison. Several US Army Civil Affairs Psychological Operations Command coins. There's a coin from the Command Chief Master Sergeant of the Oklahoma City Air Logistics Center. A coin from the John F Kennedy Aircraft Carrier (CV-67), and one from the Tridents Helicopter Squadron. A coin from the Expeditionary Medical Support Group at Incirlik Air Base in Turkey. There are coins from the Florida Department of Law Enforcement's Chemical, Biological, Radioactive, Nuclear and Explosives (CBRNE) team and the Coast Guard's Port Security Unit out of St Petersburg. A coin from the FBI and NTSB's Civil Aviation Security Program. A coin from the FBI San Antonio Joint Terrorism Task Force. And many other coins, each a part of the history that shaped me.

But most prominent in the display rack were my coins from Katrina, taking up nearly the whole top row. One coin was from the Commander of the Coast Guard's New Orleans Station. Another from the Department of Defense Joint Task Force that responded to Katrina. And a third, an Award for Excellence coin from the Command Sergeant Major of the US Northern Command for efforts with the Civil Support Team during Katrina. I even had an 82nd Airborne Division coin, parent division of the 505th Parachute Infantry Regiment with whom so much time was spent in the trenches during Katrina. But there was one coin on that row that bothered me to see. I kept it there for a reason. It was a small coin. About the size of a nickel. It looked worn, but really was just a low cost, low relief metal coin. It was a coin from the Masons.

The Mason's coins are very rare, the real ones anyway. This one was real. In their society they used the coins to recognize people they felt lived up to the reputation and ideals of the Masons. This coin in particular was specially made for Katrina, and was only presented to certain people, the people who helped through the hardest times without seeking recognition or compensation. The coin was intended to be a source of inspiration. Something to keep in your pocket, to feel or rub whenever doubt arises. To help give you the strength to power through obstacles and keep going. But that's not really what it meant to me. At least not why I kept it nestled among the other coins on my display rack. To me, that coin is a reminder of the first time I truly gave up. The time I left when others stayed to finish.

Saying I left may be an understatement. After my experience with Katrina, I never quite recovered. I stepped aside from the team I helped form. That great team with the worthy goal of reducing PTSD for first responders. Over a decade of my life was spent with them. Awesome adventures in hindsight. But by the end of that time, during and after Katrina, the struggle was too hard. The damage began to bleed into other parts of my life. And that wasn't okay. A difficult choice had to be made. Hard to believe that was more than twenty years ago now.

I turned the small coin over and over between my fingers, looking deeply at the worn lines. On the front were a pair of helping hands lifting a house up out of the floodwaters. On the back, even more worn down, was the masonic symbol. It was now time to make another decision in my life. To give up or to push through.

I've spent my life so far, on three different career paths, all dedicated to helping people somehow. My first career, working with trauma victims, ended after a decade, in the wake of Katrina's impact. My second career spent a decade revisiting trauma in a different role, working to help kids recover from abuse. That ended when funding was abruptly and unexpectedly eliminated. That career ending choice was made for me. For my third career I stepped away from traditional psychology and into the applied psychology realm, managing teams in the government sector.

My instinct has always been to help people. To give them the tools they need to develop strong functional relationships so they can get through difficult times and perform to the best of their ability. That concept spanned all three decades of my work life so far. But now, at the end of this third decade, everything seems to be changing.

The most recent changes were radical and hard to digest. Many of the changes I strongly disagreed with. And even though I voiced my concerns, and in many cases more reasonable options, my thoughts were dismissed, and I was expected to toe the line. But over time, good people were being pushed out for arbitrary reasons, often simply for the sake of change. People that dedicated decades of their lives to low pay, high pressure, thankless public service, gone in an instant without a second thought. In most cases there was no consideration of the actual situation. And never was there any concern shown for the people being pushed out, or for the remaining team members that had to pick up the pieces.

My work world is very different now. Gone are the lofty goals of helping others help themselves. Now it's all triage. Constant bandaging of wounds after the arbitrary excisions by the new leadership.

I can't help but see parallels with my time in New Orleans during hurricane Katrina. Back then I waited too long before walking away, and it permanently broke parts of me, both mentally and physically. So where am I now. Drilling into it, I think there may be some level of burnout. That's apparent from how hard it's getting to hold my tongue, to not speak my mind about the stupid shit I see every day. I'm still protecting the team any way I can. And the team is still excelling under tremendous external stress. But maybe now the best way to protect them is to step aside. Maybe they would be better off with a leader who is more in synch with the new administration. Someone that could remove those external stressors altogether rather than just reducing them to a tolerable level. It's been ten years after all. Ten years seems to have been the magic number for my two prior careers.

This core team stayed together, committed to each other, and thrived through economic downfalls, through COVID and all the anxiety, illnesses and deaths associated with it, and through massive, rapid technological and organizational changes. Most recently the team survived the dual impact of two back-to-back direct hit hurricanes, Helene and Milton. Team members whose homes were destroyed showed up at work and somehow managed to excel at their jobs amidst the destruction. The team always comes together to help each other get through difficult times. Would this be any different?

I took a deep breath…And with the masonic coin held tightly in my left hand, I moused over the email with my resignation letter attached…and clicked send.

Writer's Notes

This is a work of fiction. Names, characters, places, agencies, incidents and events are either a product of the author's imagination or are used fictitiously. Any resemblance to actual persons, living or dead, businesses, companies, organizations, agencies, or to actual events, incidents or locales is entirely coincidental.

The writer's notes below are based on publicly available information, and research that played a role in the themes found in this book. It is provided for reference only and has not been fact checked. It should not be considered factual and, at most, be considered opinion.

Chapter One

The Venezuelan economy was historically based heavily on oil production and export which kept the economy stable under a democratic government for many decades until the 1980's. In the 1980's the middle eastern oil producing nations, led by Saudi Arabia, began manipulating world oil prices, which destabilized the Venezuelan economy and drove the majority of Venezuelan citizens into poverty. The economic instability and poverty resulted in a number of grass roots organizations forming, many wishing to seek political power. One of the movements was led by Hugo Chavez.

A January 1992 coup attempt led by Hugo Chavez against President Carlos Andrés Pérez failed and Chavez was imprisoned.

A second coup attempt in November 1992, led by military leaders loyal to Chavez, while Chavez was in prison, also failed.

In 1993 President Carlos Andrés Pérez was impeached and removed from office for allegedly embezzling money and using that money to assist with the protection and election of a leader in Nicaragua. Following the impeachment, Ramón José Velásquez was appointed to complete the Presidential term. President Velasquez was sympathetic to Chavez and his movement, eventually pardoning Chavez in 1994.

Chavez was ultimately elected president in 1998 and served as President until 2012. Chavez's original political party was reformed in 2007 to become the United Socialist Party. The United Socialist Party has been in power in Venezuela since Chavez. President Nicolas Maduro, also part of the United Socialist Party, was elected in 2012 and remains in power at this time (2025). However, the elections in 2018 and 2024 were disputed, with opposition claiming their independent, non-socialist party candidates had won those respective elections. The Venezuelan supreme court agreed that Maduro was not legally elected and declared the elections invalid. Maduro's government has ignored that supreme court ruling and remains in power today. In 2024 Florida Senators Rick Scott and Marco Rubio introduced a bill to declare Maduro an unlawful regime official (dictator), offering a $100 million reward for information leading to his arrest and conviction.

Chapter Two

The Friendly Cab Company was a real cab company in Virginia. It was founded in 1947 by Ralph Collins who died in 1951. Doug Collins took over the company after his brother's death in 1951. William Collins Sr inherited the company from Doug and ran it until the 1990's. After William Sr gave up control, there were many offers to purchase it. But the company was kept in the family until recently when it went out of business due to the emergence and impact of popular ride sharing services.

The US Army Research Institute (USARI) for Behavioral and Social Sciences (USARI BSS) is described to have a core role to create the best soldier possible both on and off the battlefield, what they refer to as "the ultimate smart weapon." They did immense research on traits and characteristics that could predict the success of a soldier. And are a leading research institute on post combat psychology and reintegration of solders into civilian life. They were also a primary research entity for development of tools and training programs of all kinds to improve performance on the battlefield. Foremost for this chapter were rumors of their work related to using psychology and parapsychology principles to improve intelligence gathering.

Lucid dreaming, also called astral projection, is a fascinating concept in which the sleeping dreamer appears to have some control over aspects of their dreams. Despite widespread reports of the existence of this phenomenon, available scientific research on it remains limited, at least for the public. There are a growing number of books on the subject. Some of the best known include *The Llewellyn Practical Guide to Astral Projection: The Out-of-Body Experience*, and the *Llewellyn Practical Guide to Creative Visualization.* In 1997 a Spanish film called Open Your Eyes brought the concept of lucid dreaming to the public audience. An English language remake of that film, called Vanilla Sky, was released in 2001 starring Tom Cruise, Penélope Cruz, Cameron Diaz, Jason Lee, and Kurt Russell. Cameron Diaz received Screen Actors Guild (SAG) and Golden Globe nominations for her role. To date it is still one of the best on-film examples of the lucid dreaming concept.

Captain Michael Zarbo (US Army) authored a research paper *Remote Viewing: Parapsychological Potential for Intelligence Collection* in 1992 as part of his Master's Degree program. The paper was not distributed and remained classified until it was redacted and made publicly available in 2001. The paper contains reproductions of drawings and other scientifically documented evidence of the remote viewing phenomenon from past researchers around the world. It also contains a number of excerpts from interviews with Dr. Edgar Johnson, Director of USARI-BSS. Mike

Zarbo was eventually promoted to Colonel in 2009 and was assigned as Director, Forward Operations in Kuwait, and then as Deputy Commander (Forward) for the 401st Army Field Support Brigade (AFSB) and Chief of the Logistics Support Element for Iraq until his retirement in 2018.

Colonel John Shannon was Undersecretary of the Army from 1989-1993, appointed by President George H.W. Bush. From January of 1993 to August 1993 Col Shannon was also in the higher role as Acting Secretary of the Army. However, in August 1993 Col Shannon was arrested outside the post exchange in Arlington for allegedly leaving the store with $30 worth of items in a bag he did not pay for. Although details of the alleged theft were highly controversial and disputed, and the charges were ultimately dismissed, the incident likely ended his formal military career when incoming President Bill Clinton appointed someone new to the position.

Joseph Westphal was head of the department of Political Science at Oklahoma State University from 1975-1987. He continued to do guest lectures at Georgetown University while working for the prestigious and well connected law firm of Patton Boggs in Washington from 1987 to 1998. In 1998 he was appointed by Bill Clinton to be the Assistant Secretary of the Army for Civil Works and served in that role until January 2001 when he was briefly promoted by George W Bush to the higher role of Acting Secretary of the Army. That role ended in May 2001. Westphal served as part of Barach Obama's transition team and Barach Obama ultimately appointed him to Under Secretary of the Army in 2009 where he served until 2014. He then served as Ambassador to Saudi Arabia from 2014-2017 focusing on stabilizing the oil trade and Middle East relations.

Pat the Horse's story is believed to be accurately described based on commonly available information. The Grave of Pat the Horse still exists at Joint Base San Antonio today, just inside the Cunningham post entrance on Wilson Street. The grave also has a number of informational markers that tell his story. In 1953, Pat died at the old age of 45. He was honored with a military funeral attended by more than 100 mourners and dignitaries who joined in a service that included a eulogy and the playing of Taps. Four horseshoes are embedded in concrete over the wide burial site, and a portrait of Pat is etched on the headstone.

In 1992 there were very few publications on quantum psychology, and they were generally self-published as most of the popular scientific journals avoided the topic. However, in 2022, Psychology Today magazine published an article called *Consciousness and the Quantum Mind.* This article summarizes the now mainstream acceptance of the concept in the scientific community and quotes the latest research and thinking of Karl Pribram, published in 2012, as the foundation of further studies. The concept is now taught in undergraduate and graduate college courses at most universities that offer psychology degrees.

Chapter Three

The *Bio-Terror Trauma Intervention Specialist* certification was a specialized extension of a program developed by Jeffrey Mitchell called *Critical Incident Stress Management* (CISM). The program was the first widespread comprehensive, integrated, systematic, and multi-component crisis intervention program for treating trauma response in first responders. He has lectured in 28 countries and authored 19 books and over 275 articles on the subject. CISM is now used by most civilian and military emergency responders as well as many businesses and corporations.

Sami Al-Arian founded a Muslim school and co-founded the World and Islam Studies Enterprise, a think tank on Middle Eastern topics at the University of South Florida (USF). He was invited to the White House by Presidents Clinton and Bush, and actively campaigned for President Bush. Political sentiment turned following the September 11, 2001 terrorist attacks and Al-Arian lost his standing at USF despite a number of USF professors lobbying on his behalf. In 2003 he was indicted on 17 counts under the Patriot Act, a very broad document allowing arrest, imprisonment and deportation for many seemingly innocuous acts, including the open exchange of information, which Al-Arian always did freely as an educator. At trial he was acquitted on 8 of the counts and the other counts were left as a hung jury. Rather than a new trial, a plea agreement was reached where all but one of the charges were dropped in exchange for a short jail sentence and his deportation. However, prior to his deportation, a different federal judge demanded he stay and testify on a separate case. Al-Arian refused on the basis that it would violate his plea agreement. But in 2006 the federal judge incarcerated him for contempt of court over his refusal to testify. During his thirteen months in jail, Al-Arain held several hunger strikes and became an icon for those opposing such political incarcerations. In 2008 he was placed on house arrest. He remained under house arrest until 2014 when all remaining charges against him were ultimately dismissed in exchange for his voluntary deportation to Turkey, which occurred in 2015.

Dr Barbara Bunch was an admired, long-time professor at the University of North Florida, now retired. She was a part of the UNF graduate psychology department in the 1990's. Among her works was a prolific study of violent offenders called The Psychology of Violent Female Offenders: A Sex-Role Perspective, published in the Prison Journal.

John Douglas is often described as the founder of the FBI Behavior Analysis Unit. His history is depicted in a number of books he authored as well as biographies and crime texts authored by others. Characters in the Hannibal Lecter books and movies are based off John Douglas' work. The bio-pic tv series Mindhunter is based on his early work with the FBI and the beginnings of the BAU. John Douglas retired in 1995 but continues to travel the world offering lectures and consultations on unsolved crimes.

Danny Rolling confessed to committing 8 murders between 1989 and 1990. The first three in Shreveport, Louisiana, the last five in Gainesville, Florida. He was captured in September 1990 less than two weeks after his last murder. In November 1991 Rolling pled guilty to all five Gainesville murders. Though he also confessed to the three Shreveport murders, those never went to trial. In 1994 he was sentenced to death. He was executed by lethal injection in Florida in 2006.

Bobby Joe Long is believed to have abducted, sexually assaulted and murdered at least ten women in the Tampa Bay Area in 1984 and has numerous potential links to other unsolved rapes, assaults and other crimes. On November 4, 1984, Long released his last abducted victim, seventeen-year-old Lisa McVey. McVey provided ample information to law enforcement who then captured Long less than two weeks later. The legal process was complicated and included confessions that were thrown out. He was ultimately convicted of eight murders and other crimes, for which he received 33 life sentences and one sentence of death. He repeatedly appealed his death sentence but was ultimately executed by lethal injection in Florida in May 2019 under the first death warrant signed by newly elected Governor Ron Desantis. What was perceived as mishandling of his original confession led to extensive legal issues delaying his execution and allowing him to live on Florida's death row for over thirty-four years. At the estimated cost to care for a death row inmate, Florida Taxpayers paid well over two million dollars for Bobby Joe Long's thirty-four year incarceration. The related criminal cases are taught in law schools around the Country as examples of both successes and failures of our legal system.

In 1995, Lisa McVey began working for the Hillsborough County Parks and Recreation department. In 1999 she became a dispatcher and reserve Deputy. She put herself through the police academy and was officially deputized as a Hillsborough County Sheriff's Deputy in 2004. She now works in the same department that captured her former captor, combatting sex crimes and protecting children. She also works as a middle school resource officer and uses her story to teach students how to handle potentially dangerous situations.

The Oklahoma City Bombing occurred on Wednesday April 19, 1995, at 9:02am local time (10:02am EST). It is believed that 167-168 people were directly killed in the attack and another responder died from falling debris during a rescue attempt. The final death toll was not confirmed as a leg was found that allegedly could not be matched to a body or any known individual at the scene. 684 people were injured. To date it remains the largest domestic terror attack on US soil. It was perpetrated by Timothy McVeigh and an accomplice Terry Nichols, using a Ryder rental truck filled with ammonium nitrate fuel oil (an ANFO fertilizer bomb) that he parked near the front of the building. On August 10, 1995, McVeigh was indited on eleven counts related to eight federal agents that died on duty in the building at the time of the explosion. He was convicted in 1996 and executed by lethal injection at a federal prison in Indiana in 2001. Terry Nichols was sentenced to 161 consecutive life sentences without possibility of parole, the longest sentence ever issued in the United States. He is currently incarcerated in ADX Florence, a maximum-security federal prison in Colorado that also housed bombers Eric Rudolph and Ted Kaczynski.

OKC Firefighter Chris Fields was photographed carrying the nearly lifeless body of one year old Baylee Almon from the rubble of the OKC bombing. Baylee died on the scene a short time after the photo was taken. The photo became symbolic and won numerous awards. Fields participated in a number of interviews throughout the remainder of his nearly 32-year career. He retired in 2017. When discussing trauma, Fields described that he had no symptoms of PTSD from the event until ten years later, but that when they hit him, the symptoms hit him hard, impacting every facet of his life. Fields eventually became an advocate for treatment of PTSD and, at least unofficially, the CISM treatment model. He now travels the world giving lectures and hosts a webinar series called Trauma Behind the Badge where he facilitates discussions related to trauma experienced by first responders.

Chapter Four

The USS John F. Kenndy (CV-67) aircraft carrier was launched in 1967 as the last of the Kitty Hawk class of conventionally powered aircraft carriers. It was a transitional variant from the older Kitty Hawks with some of the more modern tech upgrades and underwent a large refit in 1984. In the early 1990's CV-67's home port was transferred to Mayport Naval Station in Jacksonville, Florida. In 1999, CV-67 and its rescue helicopter teams participated in multiple rescues during Hurricane Floyd. CV-67 was ultimately decommissioned in 2007. The original CV-67 made one last sail to Brownsville, Texas in February 2025 where it is set to be scrapped. The new nuclear powered USS John F. Kennedy (CVN-79) aircraft carrier was christened on Pearl Harbor Day in 2019 and is scheduled to enter service in 2025.

In 1999, Hurricane Floyd prompted the fourth largest evacuation in history as a Category Four hurricane with 155mph winds that skirted just off the Florida, Georgia and South Carolina coasts, ultimately making landfall near Cape Fear, North Carolina. The storm produced hurricane force winds as far north as the New England states. The storm's devastation in North Carolina overshadowed news of the offshore rescue of the Gulf Majesty's crew by the Kennedy and her helicopter squadron, the Dragonslayers (then HS-11, now HSC-11). Articles were published on the rescue by the Associated Press, Tampa Tribune and Los Angeles Times, as well as a brief article in Time Magazine. Two of the Dragonslayers SH-60 Seahawk helicopters rescued eight persons in two different areas, in thirty-five foot seas and hurricane force winds, after the Gulf Majesty sank. Over thirteen hours were spent flying in hurricane conditions during the rescue operations. The pilots and rescue divers were awarded for their efforts and bravery by the Navy, but the situation otherwise went largely unrecognized by the general public.

The Tridents helicopter squadron, then designated HS-3, later re-designated as HSC-9, participated in numerous activities during their 1999 deployment including extensive support in Serbia and Kosovo. During the deployment, HS-3 lifted over 1.8 million pounds of cargo, completed over 2,000 small deck landings, and numerous other missions. For their efforts in 1999, HS-3 received the Navy's coveted Battle Effectiveness Award given when a combat team proves to be superior in handling their ship (in this case their helicopters), weapons, tactics and ability to fulfill mission objectives.

The Adana-Ceyhan Earthquake in 1998, magnitude 6.3, killed 145 people, wounded over 1,500 and left thousands more homeless in the Adana and Ceyhan provinces of Turkey. Two additional earthquakes hit in nearby Istanbul, Turkey in August 1999 and November 1999. Personnel at Incirlik Air Base provided extensive relief efforts to the Turkish community for several years following those devastating earthquakes.

Depleted Uranium (U-238) is a very strong, very heavy, radioactive metal used to encase military grade explosive devices meant to penetrate bunkers or armor plating. It is also used as an armor coating on vehicles and equipment needing the highest level of protection. Over 30,000 depleted Uranium shells were used by NATO forces during an eleven-week period of the conflict in Kosovo. It is believed many attacks by the Slobodan Milošević led Serbian and Yugoslav forces used similar depleted Uranium weapons obtained on the black market. Approximately ten tons of depleted uranium tainted airborne particulate debris was spread over Kosovo during that eleven week period. Depleted Uranium is one of the most abundant naturally occurring heavy metals on Earth. Though technically radioactive, the radioactivity is not considered a significant danger as it is relatively stable in its solid form and has a long half-life of 4.7 billion years. However, the radioactivity does compound the danger of the chemical toxicity of the heavy metal if it is ingested or inhaled. Along with the typical symptoms and effects of heavy meatal toxicity such as lead, exposure to ingested or inhaled depleted uranium allegedly results in changes at the cellular level. One such alleged cellular change is the impact to the body's biological repair systems, making them unable to effectively repair or replace damaged cells. Advanced deterioration of lung tissue, rapid loss of tooth enamel and tooth deterioration are allegedly frequently seen in those with inhalation or ingestion exposures to depleted Uranium.

The Simulation Technology Integration division of Simulation, Training and Instrumentation Command (aka STRICOM) develops technology to train soldiers in realistic battlefield situations in a controlled environment. Their initial training simulators evolved over the years and are now used for both training and combat purposes.

Reeves Decontamination Systems, including their Deployable Rapid Assembly Shelters (DRASH), have been used by the military for many decades and more recently by local community emergency first responders when responding to events that could involve exposure to chemical, biological or radiological hazards. Individual local firefighter agencies are beginning to see the importance of rapid decontamination, and many have incorporated decontamination systems into mobile vehicles to be used at the scenes of local fires. It is believed that doing so will substantially reduce cancer and other illnesses for firefighters later in life.

Chapter Five

Several weeks after the September 11th attacks, unspecified government agencies allegedly received intelligence reports of a credible threat to the Port of Tampa. That threat was related to a cargo ship allegedly carrying a nuclear weapon intended for detonation in the port. Although the threat had little to no official media coverage at the time, rumors of the threat spread quickly. However, at the time, just after September 11th, there were constant unfounded rumors of looming attacks, so the public quickly dismissed the threat to Tampa. The Tampa Mayor at the time, Dick Greco, did not dismiss the threat. After September 11th, the city team dug deep into security of the city infrastructure assets and identified a massive security weakness for the Port. Mayor Greco worked with the Coast Guard's Captain of the Port, Allen Thomas, to address the water-based threat. The mayor also worked with then Governor Jeb Bush to get Florida National Guard troops assigned to the Port to assist with land-based security. As it turned out, the threat never transpired. The mayor's work in regard to securing the Port was lost among his many other accomplishments while in office.

In 2019, the Coast Guard's Captain of the Port for the Tampa Bay area, Allen Thomas, was presented the Captain James McKay Port Achievement Award for his "long-time service and commitment to the maritime industry of the Ports of Tampa Bay." Over his 30 year career with the Coast Guard, Captain Thomas received a number of awards including, the Legion of Merit, the Defense Meritorious Service Medal, the Coast Guard Meritorious Service Medal, the Coast Guard Commendation Medal with two gold stars and the Coast Guard Achievement Medal.

On January 5, 2002, a single engine Cessna was stolen by a 15-year-old student pilot, Charles Bishop, during a pre-flight check for a training session. According to NTSB documentation, the plane took off from St Pete/Clearwater International Airport shortly before 5pm and began heading straight for Macdill AFB. The tower reported that it reached an altitude of over 3,000 feet before getting to the base. Later reports also identified that as the Cessna flew across Tampa it flew less than 1000 feet above a Southwest Airline jet that had taken off from nearby Tampa International Airport. Once over Macdill AFB, the plane decreased altitude and flew at about 75-100 feet above two KC-135 Tankers in ready position on the runway. The plane then flew in front of and just below the Macdill control tower before heading northeast toward downtown Tampa. According to the NTSB documentation, Coast Guard pilots attempted to get the Cessna to land at Peter O'Knight Airport at Davis Islands. However, the Cessna flew "steadily and directly" into the 28th floor of the 41 story Bank of America Center building.

At the time of the incident, the 28th floor housed the law offices of Shumaker, Loop and Kendrick. It was reported that two people were in the office at the time of the incident but were not injured. They stated that another person, working at a desk impacted by the crash, left the office about an hour earlier.

According to the NTSB, a two-page suicide letter was found in the student pilot's pocket when his body was recovered from the aircraft. A transcription of the suicide note is below. Images of the handwritten note are available from several sources online.

> *"I have prepared this statement in regards to the acts I am about to commit. First of all, Osama bin Laden is absolutely justified in the terror he has caused on 9-11. He has brought a mighty nation to its knees! God blesses him and the others who helped make September 11th happen.*
>
> *The U.S. will have to face the consequences for its horrific actions against the Palestinian people and Iraqis by its allegiance with the monstrous Israelis--who want nothing short of world domination!*
>
> *You will pay--God help you--and I will make you pay!*
>
> *There will be more coming!*
>
> *Al Qaeda and other organizations have met with me several times to discuss the option of me joining. I didn't.*
>
> *This is an operation done by me only. I had no other help, although, I am acting on their behalf.*
>
> *Osama bin Laden is planning on blowing up the Super Bowl with an antiquated nuclear bomb left over from the 1967 Israeli-Syrian war."*

According to several news articles, Bishop's mother filed a $70 Million lawsuit against Roche Laboratories claiming Bishop's use of the acne medication Accutane was a cause of his suicide. That lawsuit was ultimately dropped.

The NTSB documentation noted a finding by the medical examiner that there were no indications of alcohol or drugs in specimens taken from Bishop.

On January 5, 2002, then President George Bush, and Thomas Ridge, the Director of the newly formed Department of Homeland Security, were informed of the incident in Tampa. According to the NTSB, there were a total of six small plane crashes reported on January 5, 2002, in the United States. Two were concluded to be suicides and a third could not rule out suicide as the cause. The three suicidal crashes were deemed to not be directly related or coordinated by any terrorist groups, and the letter from Bishop is the only one referencing a terrorist group. Although not connected to terrorism directly, the three suicide-by-plane incidents led to a number of changes in how the FAA handles training of new pilots.

The long-time director of the Tampa Water Department, David Tippin, retired in 2003 after 29 years of service to the City. In 2003, the City of Tampa passed an Ordinance (Ordinance 2003-67) to rename the historic Hillsborough River Water Treatment Plant as the *David L. Tippin Water Treatment Facility*. A local artist, Candice Knapp, was selected by the City to create a meaningful water fountain for the front of the facility. Ms. Knapp used a sculpture called *The Waterbearers*, by David Tippin's wife, Nancy Tippin, as inspiration for the fountain. In 2003 David Tippin also received a Key to the City, presented by then Mayor Dick Greco.

Chapter Six

In his September 20, 2001, testimony before the Committee on Governmental Affairs of the US Senate, Henry L. Hinton, Jr., Managing Director of Defense Capabilities and Management, offered the following:

> "U.S. intelligence agencies had reported an increased possibility that terrorists would use chemical or biological weapons in the next decade. However, terrorists would have to overcome significant technical and operational challenges to successfully produce and release chemical or biological agents of sufficient quality and quantity to kill or injure large numbers of people without substantial assistance from a foreign government sponsor."

This thinking, whether intended or not, appeared to fuel the shift of focus of anti-terrorism activities almost solely toward foreign sponsored terrorism. Prior to September 11th, federal funding for antiterrorism defense related activities was approximately $13 billion with a large portion dedicated to domestic terrorism. In 2002, federal antiterrorism related program funding went up to over $50 billion. However, the portion dedicated to fighting domestic terror activities actually decreased from the previous year. By focusing on foreign sponsored terrorism, federal funding was diverted to large defense contractors who had international networks with large workforces, and away from domestic law enforcement agencies, state and local governments. During this time period, defense contractors received the largest single portion of the federal budget and were the largest contributors to presidential campaigns.

The Tyler cyanide gas bomb plot would easily have been the largest terrorist attack in world history. It's estimated 30,000 fatalities would far surpass the total deaths of all terror attacks on

US soil, foreign or domestic, combined. The plot is not believed to have included any assistance from foreign governments, and it is believed to have utilized an intricate web of locally coordinated covert communication and activities, contrary to Mr. Hinton's testimony to the US Senate in 2001. Only two years after that testimony, this potential major domestic terror event was only uncovered and thwarted due to an accidental delivery error by UPS and an unrelated traffic stop.

Despite the possible seriousness of the threat, the Tyler cyanide gas bomb plot received very limited media coverage. There is a great deal of speculation as to why. At least one source interviewed by the Southern Poverty Law Center believes that the incident was hushed for, or directly by, then President George Bush. That source suggested it was determined at the highest level that any news shifting attention away from foreign sponsored terrorism, toward domestic terrorism, would be detrimental to support for the war in Iraq that began at the same time. That source also speculated that "...it might be embarrassing to the US government if weapons of mass destruction were found in America [in the home state of then President George Bush] before they were found in Iraq." Others went a step further to suggest that it was hushed to ensure continued funding for government sponsored anti-terrorism programs, keeping the federal budget money flowing to the large defense contractors, and subsequently to keep presidential campaign contributions flowing to the Bush administration.

William Krar allegedly never identified a target for this alleged terrorist attack, repeatedly denied that he had any intent to use the weapons, and never admitted to any covert network or communications.

According to available information, Federal authorities had allegedly been aware of Krar and had investigated some of his activities as far back as 1995 when his name came up related to a plot to bomb an unspecified government building. Krar had been mostly off the radar until June 2001 when a storage facility he leased in Goffstown, New Hampshire caught fire and responding authorities found a stockpile of guns and ammunition. Authorities allegedly dismissed the incident because his attorney convinced them the guns and ammunition were part of his legitimate business.

On January 24, 2002, a resident of Staten Island, New York informed the local FBI office that he had received a package errantly delivered by UPS to his address. According to available court records, the package contained a North Dakota birth certificate, a Social Security card, a birth certificate from the State of Vermont, a birth certificate from West Virginia, and other photo identifications including a United Nations Multinational Force Observer identification card and a Defense Intelligence Agency (DIA) identification card. The package also allegedly included a letter from William Krar to the intended recipient of the package, Edward Feltus. The letter stated:

> "HOPE THIS PACKAGE GETS TO YOU O.K., WE WOULD HATE TO HAVE THIS FALL INTO THE WRONG HANDS."

According to court documents, in August of 2002, Edward Feltus was interviewed by the FBI about the package of false documents. Feltus allegedly stated that he was a member of the "New Jersey Militia" and had coordinated with Krar to get the false documents for himself. Feltus allegedly told the FBI "…the false identification documents were for him to have as an 'ace in the hole' because he could not predict future events and they would give him peace of mind knowing he could use the documents to travel freely in the United States."

According to court documents, in January 2003, A Special Agent from the Memphis FBI Office informed the Dallas FBI Office that Krar had been stopped while driving a rental car in Shelby County by a Tennessee State Trooper, and subsequently arrested due to contents of his vehicle. Items found in the car included, one bag containing what is believed to be seven marijuana cigarettes, one syringe of an unknown substance, one white bottle with an unknown white substance (later determined to be military grade pure sodium cyanide), forty wine like bottles of unknown liquid (later determined to be acids, including hydrochloric acid), a 9mm handgun, a .22 caliber handgun, sixteen knives, a stun gun, a smoke grenade, three military style atropine injectors (a known antidote for several types of nerve gases), over two hundred 9mm rounds, two 9mm magazines, fifty .22 rounds, one set of handcuffs and keys, thumb cuffs, one pack of five fuse ropes, one pair of binoculars, an expandable baton and other various hand to hand combat items.

The searches of the storage facility and Krar's Tyler residence allegedly occurred on April 10, 2003. According to a Wikipedia summary, "…investigators found weapons, pure sodium cyanide and white supremacist material in a storage facility in Noonday, Texas rented by Krar and Bruey…The weapons included at least 100 other conventional bombs (including briefcase bombs and pipe bombs), machine guns, an assault rifle, an unregistered silencer, and 500,000 rounds of ammunition. The chemical stockpile seized included sodium cyanide, hydrochloric acid, nitric acid and acetic acid…The cyanide was in a device with acid that would trigger its release as a gas bomb."

In November of 2003, Krar plead guilty to building and possessing chemical weapons. In May 2004, Krar was formally sentenced to 135 months in prison (a little over eleven years). According to the Bureau of Prisons database, Krar died in prison in May 2009.

In November of 2003, Judith Bruey plead guilty to the charge of "conspiracy to possess illegal weapons." Bruey was sentenced to 57 months in prison (a little under five years) and was released in May 2008.

No information appears to be available on the whereabouts of Edward Feltus, the intended recipient of the errant package of falsified documents in 2002. There is speculation that he may have been placed in the witness protection program, but this has never been confirmed.

The fabricators of what would have been the most deadly terrorist attack in history were only sentenced to a combined total of 16 years in prison. By comparison, according to Bureau of Prisons data, the average sentence imposed for a single non-premeditated murder is 17.5 years.

Krystal restaurants tend to be predominantly in the south and White Castle predominantly in the north. However, a Krystal and a White Castle in close proximity to each other were actually observed in Nashville. The two fast-food chains did co-exist in Nashville for several decades until recent hardships resulted in closure.

Chapter Seven

There's a great deal of information and speculation on the preparation and response for Hurricane Katrina that made landfall as a Category Three hurricane just east of New Orleans the morning of August 29, 2005. The hurricane itself would have caused some wind and rain damage for sure. But the most significant damage allegedly came from numerous failures of the levee system protecting New Orleans from the waters of Lake Pontchartrain. Those levee failures allegedly resulted in over eighty percent of the city flooding, with many areas seeing ten to fifteen feet of water in their neighborhoods.

The initial federal response to Katrina by FEMA in general was allegedly considered disjointed and delayed. The coordination effort was alleged to have improved significantly when leadership of the response effort was shifted away from FEMA to US Northern Command (USNORTHCOM). The Coast Guard was the earliest and most proficient responder during the early days of the search and rescue phase. Their training and standard procedures allowed them to effectively function independently despite the weather and other response coordination problems. Coast Guard helicopters were on the scene a few hours after landfall making rescues before the winds even fully died down. And Coast Guard C-130's out of St Petersburg/Clearwater were the first cargo planes to arrive with supplies, including water and other supplies purchased by the local Coast Guard units in St Petersburg and Mobile.

In some areas where the National Guard was operating, basic supplies like water took more than a week to arrive and survivors were left to fend for themselves. With most local responders cut off by lingering floodwaters, the city, mainly the downtown area, quickly fell into lawlessness and riots. Much of the National Guard response during those first weeks was directed toward peacekeeping. Later, the National Guard played a key role in recovering bodies from the flooded areas. But there were still alleged concerns about the timeliness of their actions.

Delays in the removal of bodies was highly publicized. In one instance, often referred to in the media, bodies of a family of three allegedly washed up on a city street and laid in place for several weeks before being collected by one of the mortuary recovery teams.

The Lower Ninth Ward received by far the most media attention, likely due to the strikingly visible structural damage in that area. However, more deaths occurred in the similarly sized and much more modern Lakeview area, and far more deaths occurred in the Mid-Town area near the Superdome.

Even with pumping, some areas of New Orleans still had standing water in early October. Luckily, the massive Category Five Hurricane Rita developed a rare dual eye wall that collapsed quickly, dropping it to a weaker Category Three storm before it made landfall near Johnson Bayou on September 24th, about 200 miles west of New Orleans. Comparatively speaking it was a non-event for New Orleans. But it did draw away a number of rescue and recovery responders which delayed the ongoing efforts in New Orleans.

What actually happened during Katrina is difficult to imagine and impossible to describe. But there are a number of documentary films and books written on the subject that can help bring some of the issues to light. One article published by Steve Sternberg in 2015, ten years after Katrina, contained interviews with many of the responders, including the person holding the Director of Emergency Management Services position in New Orleans in 2005, who happened to live in Lakeview, one of the harder hit areas in terms of deaths. The article emphasized that many of the responders felt it was too painful and refused to talk about what they'd experienced until that interview some ten years later. The article alluded to the long-term effects of the stress they experienced. In one case an interviewee alleged there were cancer clusters related to the event, suggesting physical manifestations of the trauma previously thought to be only a mental health issue. Although it's nearly impossible to draw cause-effect relationships for such things, ongoing research with first responders is showing clear correlations between trauma experiences like Katrina and early emergence of physical health problems in addition to the mental health problems that were expected.

We should never forget, amongst all the concerns, finger pointing, and lawsuits, there were countless acts of heroism that occurred throughout the months-long response to Katrina. Countless individuals went far above and beyond their own exhaustion to fearlessly save lives and help those in need get reconnected with resources. Many of them are still doing that thankless job today. So, to all our first responders and local heroes, THANK YOU for everything you do!